Ron,

DEAD AIR

To a fellow storyteller!
Enjoy.
Scott Overton

To a fellow storyteller!

Enjoy.

With Care
Carr

DEAD AIR

BY

SCOTT
OVERTON

ScrivenerPress

Library and Archives Canada Cataloguing in Publication

Overton, Scott, 1956-
  Dead air / Scott Overton.

ISBN 978-1-896350-51-6

  I. Title.

PS8629.V475D42 2012   C813'.6   C2012-904771-6

Book design: Laurence Steven
Cover design: Chris Evans
Photo of author: Shaun K. Overton

Published by Scrivener Press
465 Loach's Road,
Sudbury, Ontario, Canada, P3E 2R2
info@yourscrivenerpress.com
www.scrivenerpress.com

We acknowledge the financial support of the Canada Council for the Arts, the Ontario Arts Council, and the Government of Canada through the Canada Book Fund for our publishing activities.

Dedication

For Terry-Lynne, the foundation of everything I do and everything I am. This novel wouldn't exist without your faith.

Acknowledgements

A novel is not the creation of one person alone. At the very least it is the sum of the author's life experiences, and that life is touched by many others. As a writer, I've been helped by so many friends, acquaintances, and strangers. But for their direct assistance I'd like to thank: Sean Costello, both mentor and friend; my publisher Laurence Steven for believing in the novel and in me; Staff Sergeant Richard Waugh and Brian McMillan for valuable information; Scott Broderick and Steve Jones for their support; and the devoted listeners of AM790 CIGM and Rewind 103.9, because your love of radio kept me doing what I do, and sometimes even writing about it.

1

THE BEE GEES SANG ABOUT STARTING A JOKE, but the lyric made no impression on his mind. His fragile early morning contentment had been pierced by childish block letters from a fat, felt-tipped marker. Red ink. A square of paper torn from a brown grocery bag. A message of hate.

He fingered the paper and read the words again, then a third time, one by one, as if reading them together he had somehow misunderstood their meaning. Most were unnecessary; one conveyed the meaning of all: *death*. Like the most feared tarot card or the pirates' black spot, the scrap of paper in his hands had suddenly brought a breath of the grave into his private sanctuary.

Shit. He'd been in a good mood until then.

It had to be some kind of a joke. He shook his head to clear it, and looked up at the digital clock above the control board. 5:27 a.m. The computer had one more song scheduled before he had to take over, and he still hadn't finished mapping out his breaks. He looked down at the music log, where the top of the page read "Lee Garrett Show", and flipped to the 7:00 hour. There were a couple of songs scheduled that had played on the CTBX "Five O'clock Flashback" Friday afternoon and he ought to mention that. The song logged at 7:26 was "One Of These Nights" by The Eagles—a thirty-four-second intro before the vocals, easily long enough to mention the Block Party contest coming up. He pencilled it in.

Who would make a death threat for a joke? Damon Allen, the evening guy on Z104, slipped out for a toke in the back parking lot every now and then—maybe it was stoner humour. On the other hand, the security system had been down for more than a week, and the building was empty all night. They were on the ground floor. How hard could it be for a stranger to get into the place?

Would some wacko go to the trouble of breaking into a radio station just to leave a death threat on the control board? Without stealing anything? The equipment wasn't the kind of thing an average thief could sell on the street, but the control room had shelves of CDs stored along two walls. There didn't look to be any missing. It didn't make sense.

Lee's gaze wandered back to the brown scrap of paper on the desk beside him. He crumpled it into a ball and tossed it into the trash can. He couldn't think about it now. He had a show to do.

"25 Or 6 To 4" by Chicago went into its last, long chord. A station ID fired, with a ballsy voice over a musical 'stinger': *620 CTBX "The Box": Favourites of the 60's, 70's, and 80's.* George Harrison's "What Is Life?" followed, and Lee tapped the screen of the music computer to kick it out of Auto Play. Then he cranked up the volume on his studio monitor and let the juicy riff settle his nerves.

The Lee Garrett Morning Show was on the air.

At three minutes to 6:00 David Berg pushed open the soundproof door, muttered a greeting and continued through into the news booth. Jerry 'J.J.' Jamieson was just behind him but stood against the wall to wait his turn to do sports.

"Rough night last night, man?" J.J. flashed brilliant white teeth against black skin. "I heard you stomp on two song vocals already and you only been on the air a half-hour."

Lee gave him an irritated look. "Just distracted. But if I'd known you were listening I'd have stomped on three, just to show you who's boss." He stabbed a button on the control board and leaned into the talkback microphone that connected him to the news booth. "Midas Muffler for news, Tim Horton's for sports, and the Weather sponsor is Clambaker's."

"You'll be happy as a clam at Clambaker's," Berg muttered over the talkback.

The news stinger came on. "Good Morning, I'm David Berg with CTBX News. At 6:00 o'clock it's minus five degrees…" Lee cranked the monitor volume down.

"They didn't change their slogan, did they?" J.J. asked.

"Hell, no. Dave's just getting punchy, thinking about leaving this place for the new job in Windsor. Or maybe he got laid last night."

"Well you didn't, I can tell that much."

"No need to rub it in." Lee grinned. His gaze swept over the trash can and the ball of brown paper inside. His mind could no more leave it alone than a tongue could ignore a sore tooth. But he didn't want J.J. to see it. He picked up a couple of old printouts from the counter and tossed them into the can. "Ratings will be in tomorrow. You nervous?"

J.J. shrugged. "C'mon man, it's a crap shoot half the time, right? Isn't that what you always say?"

"Since when did you start paying attention to what I say? Besides, it's all we've got." Lee ran his fingers through his hair. "Arnott says the Favourite Hits format has run its course. Guess we'll find out."

"Asshole wouldn't know where his dick was if he hadn't read it in a research study somewhere."

Lee laughed. It was good to know he wasn't the only one who felt that way about their Program Director. And he liked J.J.'s straight talk. The kid had fallen for the same lies that drew everyone else into radio: the show-biz glamour, the big money, the easy hours. He'd wised up sooner than most.

Lee had spent twenty years learning the truth: all the evenings and weekends away from home; the anorexic bank account, even before his divorce. And most of the time the people loved you. But sometimes they hated you.

It was just before the 8:30 news that he remembered the joke.

Was it Wednesday? No, Tuesday. There'd been a news story about gangs moving into the north from the Toronto area. The local cops had rounded up some members of a neo-Nazi gang called The Skins. Trashed the Jewish cemetery once. Lee had decided to get a laugh at their expense. What was it he'd said?

"Three reasons Skins don't make good friends: Number one: They keep swiping your bowling ball cover when their head gets cold. Number Two: They never buy you anything but *vanilla* ice cream. Number Three: They draw Hitler moustaches on all your Bono posters."

Juvenile stuff—some would think it was funny. Someone had thought it wasn't. Someone with a red felt-tipped pen who couldn't spell.

As he lifted his head he realized the song had ended and Dave Berg was sitting on the other side of the double glass with a look like a thundercloud, waiting for the news stinger. Lee flicked the computer screen too quickly. A McDonald's jingle came on instead.

"*Shit!*" He stabbed the screen again to trigger the news intro, then slapped the volume fader on the board to kill the commercial. He spun around and glared at the trash can.

Will Peters took over at 9:00.

"Where's Rob?" Lee asked. It was a couple of weeks too early for the regular midday announcer to be taking his Christmas vacation.

"Uh…Dan Arnott wants to have the midday show voice-tracked from now on," Peters said, sidestepping the question. "I'm going to record the tracks today and see how it goes."

Lee shook his head and slumped back onto the desk. As far as he was concerned, voice tracks were bad for radio. When he'd started in the business he'd played songs from vinyl records, for God's sake. The control room console still included a couple of boxlike wooden mountings where turntables had once been installed. Now, nearly every sound that went out over the air—every song, every ID, jingle, or commercial—was recorded on a massive array of computer hard-drives and played by software. The words of the announcers could be recorded, too, letting the system operate endlessly without ever running a 'live' break. In practice, morning shows were too complex and immediate to be automated that way, but more and more stations used pre-recorded voice tracks for the rest of their broadcast day. It freed up announcers to perform other duties, or voice track shows for affiliated radio stations in other cities. To Lee, it destroyed the real-time connection between performer and audience, the 'live' element that made radio special. He'd argued that one before, and lost. Radio was a business, and money was the bottom line.

"So why isn't Rob recording the voice tracks for his own show?" he asked. "Is he sick?"

"I just do what Dan tells me to do." Peters nervously brushed back a stray lock of sandy hair and straightened his glasses as he dropped into the chair. He pulled the heavy Electro-Vox microphone forward on its multi-jointed arm. Stalling—that was obvious. Whatever the reason he was filling in for Rob Weller, he wasn't going to say. Lee would have to find out from Arnott himself.

A couple of large Tim Horton's with double cream were enough to get him through most mornings, but this time he wandered down the wide hall toward the lunch room, dredging change from his pocket for the coffee machine. Maybe it was pre-ratings jitters. Or maybe it was that damned threat. Why was it getting to him? He'd had hate mail before. Lots of crank calls—some loudmouth would spit insults and invective, then hang up before Lee could say anything. Or they'd rake him over the coals for his occasional sexual innuendo, quoting Bible verses at him. The ones who trashed him by email didn't seem to realize their addresses could be traced. He never bothered. His life had never been threatened before.

An involuntary squeeze crumpled the paper cup and spilled hot coffee over his fingers. He swore and tossed the cup into the lunch room garbage pail, angry at the bite of the hot liquid and his own thoughts.

He decided to check his voice mail on the phone in the announcers' lounge. He didn't have a desk—didn't need one. There was a cupboard with his name on it where he kept assorted papers and paraphernalia he rarely touched, but he did most of the preparation work for his show at home where there were fewer distractions.

The first message was from a charity that wanted him to DJ a fundraising dance. He'd call them back later and offer to help some other way. Public appearances were part of the job but he wasn't a *disc jockey*, and hated the term.

As the second message began to play, the breath went out of him in a long sigh. Michaela. The woman he still thought of as his wife. Except the divorce court judge hadn't seen it that way. Her memory could make his best days bad and his bad days worse.

The message just said to call her back. What could she want? His payments were on time…the kids weren't due to visit for weeks.

At Christmas. He forced his fingers to the phone and punched her number at the dental clinic, but when he was shuffled to her voicemail he killed the connection without saying anything. He'd try again later. After he talked to Arnott.

In the doorway of the Program Director's office a tang of garlic and anchovies made Lee's nose twitch. Caesar salad was Arnott's favourite menu item from Clambaker's, next door to the radio station. Which meant he'd probably worked through the dinner hour the night before. The aroma oozed from his pores for twenty-four hours afterward.

The office was a cube of clutter. Where the walls of the announcers' lounge were decorated with music posters, Arnott's were adorned with mounted plaques and framed certificates above shelves full of binders. The top of his filing cabinet was home to a half-dozen coffee mugs that hadn't made it back to the cafeteria.

"Let me guess," Lee said, leaning against the door frame. "You got some new research from Owens yesterday."

Arnott looked up, his mouth slightly open, and waved Lee to a chair. He acknowledged the guess with a nod.

"As a matter of fact, I think you'll find it interesting." He tossed papers across the desk. "More or less what I've said before. A lot of twenty-five to thirty-four-year-olds are really getting into the music of the seventies and eighties. Not the disco shit—no matter what the TV commercials say. They don't get off on The Turtles and Simon and Garfunkel either. Just the rock music."

"What about The Beatles?"

"Sure. But the funkier stuff like "Come Together," not "Eight Days A Week." I've decided to weed out a lot of the pop music and heavy up on the Aerosmith and Foreigner."

"I thought company strategy was for The Wiz to go after the younger demos while we stick with the thirty-five to forty-nine-year-olds. Make our two stations the perfect advertising combo."

"Good theory." The corners of Arnott's mouth twitched. "Except you and I know that The Box's best numbers are over forty-five. Even with CMOR pumping out their elevator music and gabfest down the street. If we're going to take over from Z104 at thirty-five, then we've got to *have* the thirty-five-year-olds…lots of 'em. The advertisers go where the money is, and forty is getting to be just too damned old."

Lee looked at the floor. His fortieth birthday had hit like an express train a month earlier. He'd emceed a beauty pageant at the Greek Festival the night before, and the teen contestants had treated him like a creepy uncle. So his milestone day had been celebrated with a long, solitary drunk and a handful of Clint Eastwood movies.

He felt like changing the subject. "Is Rob Weller sick today?"

"We…uh, we let Rob go."

"What?"

"We'll be voice-tracking the mid-day show from now on. One guy can do that plus the Music Director's job for both stations. Will Peters has a lot more experience with MusicMaster software."

"He's also young and cheap," Lee said quietly.

Arnott sighed, spun his chair away. "Welcome to the real world."

The words were a dismissal. Lee walked away, feeling he should have said something. He and Rob Weller hadn't been close friends, but the man had a wife and a year-old baby. He was good at the job, but not exceptional, so if he found any radio work it would almost certainly be in another city. His wife was a hometown girl. Somebody's heart would be broken. Or maybe Weller would be smart enough to get out of radio and find a real job.

Lee headed toward the production studio by way of the reception area. His mail slot near the front desk rarely held anything but memos. Management was addicted to those. Hard copies, as if no-one trusted email. Lee picked up a handful of papers and began to cross the lobby. Two women were standing with their backs to him, looking over the life-sized Lee Garrett cardboard cut-out that stood near one wall. The picture was a couple of years old and the suit made him look like a used car salesman, but it was still a good likeness. The women were probably fans. He drifted over, drawn like a bee to nectar.

"Is there anything I can help you with?" he asked.

The women turned around, startled. The taller of the two, late thirties, said "We're here to pick up a prize my friend won on the radio."

"On Z104," the second one added. Neither showed any sign of recognition, even with the cardboard version of him only inches from their fur-draped fannies.

"Sure. Karen can get that for you. Here she is now."

The receptionist switched on a smile as she returned to her chair. Lee switched his off, escaping toward the door in the far wall. He should have known the women were Wiz fans from their garish coats and accessories. CTBX fans, *his* fans, were salt-of-the-earth types, with better taste.

In Prod Studio #1 a crown of white hair bent over a pile of scripts.

"You're late." The words were followed by the squeak of a felt-tipped marker pen on a Production Request Form. Black ink, not red, Lee noticed. Mel Smythe was the manager of the CTBX/Z104 Production department, and its only full-time employee.

"What are you giving me a hard time for?" Lee countered. "You haven't even picked all the music, yet."

Smythe's white head slowly lifted, overhead track lighting glinting off thick glasses.

"You just worry about *your* job, Son, and I'll worry about mine."

The face didn't crack a smile, but Lee gave a loud laugh. Their banter sometimes fooled people into thinking the two men didn't like each other, but that was far from the truth. More than just affection, there was respect. Smythe knew exactly how to get the sound he wanted from his equipment, and accomplished feats that would've been tough with an extra pair of hands. Lee didn't have the best voice in the business, but he could use it like a fine instrument. Both men made their jobs look easy. And they both recognized the kind of skill it took to do that.

"Mel, you ever hear of The Skins?"

"If you're talking about the kind of books and magazines you like, you should keep it to yourself."

Lee laughed again and went through a soundproof door to sit in the adjoining voice booth.

Smythe grinned, punched the talkback button. "You serious?"

"Yeah. I got a love note from one of them over a joke I made last week. Seems they weren't amused."

"There was an article about 'em in the paper the other day. A gang moving in from Toronto, right? Sound like violent bastards. What'd you want to piss them off for?"

"I didn't think about it. Who'd figure a bunch of neo-Nazi punks from Toronto would be listening to The Box?"

"Maybe one of them was visiting his mother. Think punks like that only grow in Toronto? They're all over. Nobody's got a monopoly on being a goddamned bigoted prick, you know. It's universal."

"As you can testify firsthand." Lee laughed, while Smythe acknowledged the scored point with a finger stroke in the air. "But I haven't noticed any bald-headed punks around town. A swastika painted on a chrome dome would kind of stand out."

Smythe waggled his head from side to side. "Nah, that stuff's just for show, when a few of 'em get cocky and want to grab some media attention. Most of the time you can't tell a Nazi from anybody else."

It wasn't what Lee wanted to hear. Could one of the staff be mixed up with these assholes? That was an ugly thought.

Smythe gave a shrug, but there was concern on his face. "Maybe if you leave it alone, they'll forget about you. Maybe." Then he rasped,

"Now can we get some friggin' work done? If you *stars* keep holdin' me up I'm gonna be sleepin' here tonight."

Afterward Lee went to see Maddy Ellis. There was a chance that somebody had broken into the building to leave the note, and if the Station Manager learned about that secondhand there'd be hell to pay.

She was on the phone but motioned him into the office. She was always on the phone. Her hairstyle had begun to form a permanent curve where it was pushed back by the handset. While she finished the call, Lee mentally compared her to the Maddy Ellis who'd come across as a dragon lady at his job interview, and then the Maddy of a couple of years later, after a fundraising dinner, when they'd both had too much to drink. She was still attractive, with a reddish tint to her short, permed hair, and clear blue eyes that made her look younger than she was. Well-chosen suits disguised the few extra pounds she'd gained.

What would she see looking at him through the same lens of memory? Six feet tall in the right pair of shoes, he had a couple of love handles that loose shirts usually hid, but no paunch yet. Eyebrows and nose too prominent for Hollywood, but strong cheekbones and full lips. He got his share of second looks from women. Or used to. Maybe he gave off the aura of the badly divorced these days: a patina of defeat. Did Ellis see that too?

She dropped the phone into its cradle and blew air through pursed lips. "Roger Simpson threatening to pull his account. For the fourth time this month. He approves the scripts, we produce them, and once they're on the air he says it's absolutely not what he asked for." She shrugged. "What's up, Lee? Michaela want me to give you a raise?"

He gave a pained smile. "Only if her hairdresser has raised the rates. Nah, Maddy, this is a weird one." He explained about the note.

"Have you mentioned it to anybody else?"

"Just Mel Smythe."

"So you haven't asked any of the other guys if it's just a sick joke? I wouldn't put it past Mr. Rhodes."

"Doug wouldn't do that." Lee shook his head. "I don't think he would. I'll ask around. I just thought I should tell you because maybe somebody broke into the building. The security system..."

"I know. We're waiting for a bloody part." She frowned. "Ask the announcers and if none of them confesses, we'll decide what to do next. If it was somebody in the building, they'll mention it sooner or later. A practical joke is no fun if you don't know whether it worked or not."

Lee began to leave, then turned back. "Tell me it wasn't your idea to dump Rob Weller."

"You know me better than that. Are you asking if Corporate gave me a choice? Yeah, the same choice they always give: keep my job or find something else to occupy my time."

There was a warble from her desk. She gave him a look of regret and reached for the phone.

He went to the announcers' lounge and tried calling Michaela's cell, with no luck—she almost never remembered to turn it on and never checked its voice mail. Then he called her dental clinic again and left a message so she'd know he wasn't ignoring her.

Lee's mobile phone account had been cancelled at the beginning of the month after two many missed payments, but he found he liked it that way. It meant he wasn't accessible every minute of the day. If he needed a cell phone for a radio event the station supplied one. Michaela occasionally nagged him about getting one again, but that only made him more determined not to.

In the dull December light of the back parking lot his fifteen-year-old Volvo was the closest car to the door, one of the few advantages of arriving at 4:30 in the morning. He'd bought it new, in the days before alimony and child support. On the car radio Jethro Tull sang about the allure of living in the past.

≈

The smell of damp rubber would survive any renovations he could afford to make to his basement apartment. It was the ghost of carpets past, as much a part of the building as the two-prong electrical outlets, and the crack-and-stain images in the ceiling plaster.

Lunch was a can of soup that boiled over and added to the crust on his microwave tray. After another attempt to reach Michaela he turned the phone's ringer off and lay down to sleep. Even a daily nap couldn't make up for a 4:00 a.m. awakening. Morning announcers were the chronically sleep-deprived, their mental functions as badly impaired as a drunkard's. Yet the success of multi-million-dollar media properties depended on these groggy misfits. The madness of it always brought a smile to his face.

The smile faded as he thought about Michaela.

His world had changed so much since they'd met, during his first radio gig at a small dawn-to-midnight operation in Tillsonburg, Ontario. Tobacco country. He hosted the evening show until 8:30 and then played taped religious programs that were an important source of the station's income. That year, when the annual Tillsonburg Fair came around, Lee did his show from the fairgrounds Thursday and Friday evening, and Saturday and Sunday afternoon. It was a blast. Kids who hung around the booth thought he was a star. Even the old-timers treated him with respect. And the girls—he appreciated the view of long, tanned legs they thoughtfully provided. Some passed by again and again, usually in groups of three or four, trying not to let him catch them looking. It made him smile, but it also stirred a hunger.

The first night, as he was packing up the equipment, he saw a small group of girls beside the refreshment stand to his right. Only one of them had a cup in her hand. The other three had been eyeing him all night, but Michaela looked bored. He shuffled over to buy a drink, fumbling for change and a clever line. But as his eyes met hers he lost the words. He forced a smile and returned to his equipment. One of the other girls got up the courage to say, "Are you coming back tomorrow? On the air?"

"I'll be here."

Another piped up, "Good!" And three girls giggled. Not Michaela. She was looking toward the midway as if to disassociate herself from the rest.

He had to get back to the radio station to finish his shift that night, but on Friday a summer student handled the control room duties to let Lee stay at the fair and set up interviews for his weekend shows. He got that done early, hoping to have something better to do in the warm hours of darkness.

Michaela didn't appear. Her three friends waved shyly as they walked past a few times, but he wasn't interested in them. Trying to deny his disappointment, he decided to wander around a few of the displays and then go home to an empty boarding room.

He found her at a booth run by some local churchwomen, showing a crocheted tablecloth to a customer. She looked wryly at the appliquéd tea cozy in his hand.

"Drink a lot of tea at the radio station?" Their eyes met, and they laughed.

She was staying for a few days with a friend who had a farm in the Tillsonburg area. Lee couldn't remember her friend's name, but he could never forget hers: Michaela. So unusual, before it was popularized by a '90's TV show. A name that spoke of flowers ruffled by a summer wind in a century gone by. It suited her.

The rest of the weekend was a succession of fleeting smiles, the accidental electric touch of bare arms, a furtive goodnight kiss that almost didn't happen then turned into a hungry embrace in the sheltering darkness of the farm driveway. They were inseparable on Sunday and he was invited to dinner.

Evening shadows had just begun to lengthen as he and Michaela stole away for a walk across the fields, hand-in-hand. Sunset was created for hair like hers: auburn, with strands of flame and highlights of gold that floated above her blue eyes. The sun-warmed bales of hay gave the air a sharp, earthy scent. He pulled her down behind one of them and kissed her hard, then lingeringly.

Below cut-off denims, the skin of her legs was tanned ruddy gold. Her blue and white gingham blouse had started life as an elasticized tube top, but some less daring soul had added a pair of thin security straps which kept slipping toward her shoulders, exposing lines of un-tanned skin, bordered by a light sunburn. Lee brushed the straps farther to the side, kissed the smooth skin of her shoulders and inhaled the tang of her hair and neck. Almost without thinking, he began to roll the tube top downward. The world stood still.

Her breasts were damp with perspiration, dimpled with goose-flesh, and when she shivered in spite of the warm breeze, he realized that it was the first time she'd allowed herself to be seen in that way. He felt privileged.

She waited for him to say something, but the words felt thick and dull in his mouth. Instead he laid his head gently against her breasts, listening to the fevered beating of her heart while she brushed her fingers through his hair. After a time, he stripped off his T-shirt and pressed against her warm flesh, finding her lips. They kissed as if to swallow each other's souls.

Finally she breathed, "Let's not go any farther, right now." He didn't mind at all. He wanted to make it last. He even thought about forever.

Twenty years later, forever had come and gone. But he fell asleep remembering sunset hair and satin skin.

≈

The warm glow of the memory was gone when he awoke, replaced by evil words. Red words. Red as blood. The light on his answering machine flashed, but he was afraid. What if it unleashed words like that into his home, his sanctuary?

No. His number was unlisted, always had been. He looked at the caller ID.

Michaela.

He flopped back on the couch. No need to listen to the message— he could already hear the accusatory tone in his head.

Had he really failed her so badly as a husband?

The answer to that question was always the same: Yes. And No. He'd never meant to hurt her. Neglect was the husbands' crime he hadn't recognized in himself. His morning show took his heart and soul, energy and intellect; it stole his evenings and weekends. Yet he'd willingly let it swallow him, shutting his eyes to what it robbed from the ones he loved. He spent so many nights working at public events of every kind, there was nothing left of him for private pleasure. He stopped taking Michaela to movies or restaurants or theatre shows. Somehow he never saw that the walls he built to keep the world out were also locking her in.

Then the fights started—silly quarrels about decorating schemes and missed parties. She sneered that his radio job was like a life-long adolescence, never growing up. As if nine-to-five drudgery in an approved suit was the standard of success.

He often wondered when the point of no return had been, and whether it would have made a difference if he'd seen it coming. The divorce was a wrenching dismemberment. He'd never accept that it was the only solution to their problems.

He should return her call, but his groggy brain rebelled. Instead he worked up a sweat on his exercise bike, feasted on reheated Hamburger Helper, and spent the evening doing show prep on the computer. When he finally looked up it was ten-thirty. He stood to get ready for bed, then dropped back onto the cushion with a muttered curse, and reached out his hand.

The phone at the other end rang three times … four … then picked up with a sharp click and a pause long enough for him to remember she'd never had an answering machine.

It was a man's voice.

"… Michaela and I can't take your call, right now…."

Michaela and I.

He didn't hear the rest of the message, dropping the phone like a hot poker.

Sure, they'd been divorced for a year … separated before that, but … *Michaela and I*?

A moan escaped from his throat. He drew up his knees and dropped his head onto them, ashamed to feel his eyes burn.

A moment or an hour later, he reached for a pen and a pad of paper, and scribbled the words: *Michaela and I.* He underlined them once … twice. Then beneath them he wrote the other words that had defiled his world that day, robbed of some of their power now.

3 REASONS SKINS MAKE BAD ENIMIES:

PAIN   SUFFERING   DEATH

2

LEE AWOKE SPRAWLED ACROSS HIS COUCH. Adrenaline shot through him as he realised he wouldn't have heard the alarm clock in the bedroom. *What time was it?* His eyes found the blue numbers of the DVD recorder above the TV and he released the breath he was holding. 4:07 a.m. Late, but not too much.

He shaved a few minutes off his morning routine, snapping from one task to the next with total focus. His mind had settled during the night, and when images of the previous day tried to intrude, he pushed them aside. There were specks of red in the sink—he'd made his gums bleed a little.

He shouldn't have let things get to him. He was forty years old, goddammit—he ought to know who he was, not let other people define him. Not Michaela, not some crackpot with a radio and a red pen.

As he wheeled onto Notre Dame, a bread truck pulled in front of him. The streets were empty, but the driver hadn't waited for Lee to go by. The truck accelerated to just over the speed limit, but Lee stamped the gas pedal to the floor, swung into the left lane, and roared past. He didn't slow down until he reached the radio station driveway.

Unlocking the door of the building put his new confidence to the test. Another break-in wasn't likely, but he listened with his full attention as he walked through the halls. The control room garbage can was empty. The cleaners must have done their rounds during the night, and the crumpled wad of brown paper had gone with them. Good. He felt his shoulders relax. He had work to do. People counted on him to help them start their day. He wasn't going to let a few morons sabotage that.

He went on the air at 5:30, and with each word he felt the old Lee Garrett return.

After eight o'clock he told J.J. about the hate note. The young man nodded. "I knew there was something going on. You shouldn't oughtta let a chickenshit like that get to you, man. What is it you always say? If they don't have the guts to sign their name they ain't got the balls of a ballerina. Fuck 'em, if they can't take a joke."

Lee laughed. He turned on his microphone to talk over the intro of the next song. "620 The Box, Favourites of the 60's, 70's, and 80's. Here's Eric Clapton saying 'Lay Down Sally'. These days Eric'd have to get her permission in writing." He smiled to see J.J.'s eyebrows rise. Then the flashing of the phone line indicator caught his attention.

"You gonna answer that call?" J.J. asked.

"Nah. Probably a feminist with no sense of humour." Lee shuffled some papers and made a show of checking the computer screen for the next song.

"You want me to answer it?"

"Be my guest."

J.J.'s face and voice revealed nothing as he muttered "Yes, ma'am" and "No ma'am". At last he hung up the phone and shook his head with a sober expression.

"She wasn't happy. Wanted to know why we never play anything from the Partridge Family!" He gave a howl of laughter.

"No doubt. I just played a promo for the Request Show, too."

J.J. brushed his eyes with a finger. "At least it wasn't a femi-Nazi. Bein' a man these days—it's like you should have the words *I'm Sorry* tattooed on your forehead."

"Try being a white man."

Their laughter brought the receptionist into the room to investigate the noise.

Most of the on-air staff had gathered in the announcers' lounge; the Bureau of Broadcast Measurement report was due in that morning. As Lee walked in, Doug Rhodes was talking about the Country Music station that had just signed on in town: CWLF "The Wolf".

"C-Bitch, the *dog* of the ratings. Tune in for a great piece of *tail*!" He rubbed his hip suggestively against his counterpart on Z104's afternoon drive show, Rick Johns. Johns reacted as if he'd been stung.

Lee laughed with the rest, then said "So which one of you jokers likes to have fun with a red pen?"

Their faces went blank. Z104's evening host Damon Allen looked at him. His mouth twitched, and he asked, "Is it a big, long pen … ?"

Rhodes took over. "Yeah, with a vibrator function? Tracy, you've got one of those, don't you?"

Tracy Banderjee was used to jokes about the long evenings she spent in the CTBX control room. She curled her lip. "Not since you borrowed it and wore out the battery."

Lee waited to get their attention again and explained about the note. "Not your handiwork, Rhodesy?"

Rhodes shrugged, then shook his head.

"No hard feelings, guys. A joke's a joke. But if we don't know who did it, Ellis might have to assume somebody broke into the building, and get the police involved." He wanted to make sure they didn't hold anything back.

"It wasn't me," Rhodes said to the floor. The faces of the others were sour. None of them liked to think an outsider could have invaded their inner sanctum. Lee forced a smile. "No sweat. Maybe Mayor Warden has decided to reveal his true skinhead self." The mayor's bad toupee was legendary. The laughter cleared the air, but Lee shuffled away toward the Production studio.

His mood wasn't improved by twenty minutes of recording hard-sell commercials. He could never understand why business owners thought their customers wanted to be yelled at.

He should call Michaela—find out what she wanted. Instead he went to find Dan Arnott. The ratings report would be in by now.

Arnott was with Rene Charette, the PD for Z104, in Charette's office. The two men were taking turns calling up graphs on a computer screen. Z104's morning man Barry Wright stood leaning over Charette's shoulder and looked up as Lee entered.

"Looks good so far, buddy."

"You picked up women," Arnott said to Charette, running his finger along the screen that compared The Wiz's performance figures to the previous book. "Softened the sound just enough without pissing off too many guys. Nice job." He looked up. "Lee. I printed off some preliminary stuff. Uh…better come to my office and we'll look at it." He didn't want to talk about it in front of the others. Not a good sign.

Arnott dropped into his chair and spread a handful of printouts on the desk. "Close the door," he said as he searched for the pages he wanted, then handed two of them to Lee. One was from the most recent ratings period, the other from the previous survey. Both showed the average number of listeners during each quarter-hour of the day in the 25 to 49 age bracket within the city itself. The so-called *core* numbers. CTBX usually had better results with the *full coverage* rankings that included listeners everywhere the station's signal reached. But most advertising dollars came from the central core.

Lee looked for the morning show, especially between 7:00 and 9:00, comparing the pages.

"We're down. A few small gains…mostly drops. 8:00 o'clock, 8:15…." He glanced farther down the page. "Not just mornings, though. Looks like a decline all through the day."

Arnott nodded. "Yeah. We especially lost women." He handed over two more pages labelled "Time Blocks". They showed the results organized according to blocks of time: morning show, midday, afternoon drive. The trend was downward and obvious.

"What about thirty-five to fifty-four-year-olds?" The older audience was traditionally more loyal to The Box because of its older music.

"Better. Down a little. I haven't had a chance to get into too much detailed stuff yet. From this, I'd guess we're down about five per cent in the twenty-five to forty-nine-year-olds, basically flat in thirty-five and older…down a shade in the mornings. And most of the loss seems to be women. Maybe they went to The Wiz—Barry and Sandy have had better chemistry lately."

Lee shifted in the chair. "And the company pours a ton of money into The Wiz—look at all the stuff they were giving away this time. And the TV ads."

"Sure, but our vacation packages were hot. We were counting on them to draw more women. Ellis isn't going to be happy, and I'll have to eat crow. No bonuses for us this time, my friend."

"Shit!" Lee slapped the desk. "Street talk was good, too. You think it's an accurate book? For the money BBM pays, kids are the only ones who bother to fill out the ballots anymore. You can't get the straight goods from a sample of a few hundred people when most of 'em are under twenty, with iPods glued to their hips."

Arnott waved the suggestion away. "We can't cry 'bad book' every time it doesn't go the way we want. Sometimes we have to accept that the listeners are trying to tell us something."

"How did CMOR do? Did they pick up the older women we lost?"

"They took a tumble, too. But they've been struggling for a while now. Ron Wayne was the King of the Hill for years until you came to town. You kicked his butt off and he's been getting grass stains ever since."

Lee started to say something, but stopped. Then he said, "No one stays on top forever."

Arnott was staring at the pages. "Let's face it, this BBM is just more proof of the slide of AM radio. We're in the same boat with CMOR and Talk 960, and there may not be a damn thing we can do about it."

Government regulators could have levelled the playing field by allowing AM stations the choice to move to the higher quality FM band, but year after year they refused.

The room was quiet for too long. Arnott must have more to say.

"This isn't all the bad news, is it? What aren't you telling me?"

The program director opened his mouth, then cleared his throat.

"I've talked it over with Maddy Ellis. We're...we're going to go with a team morning show on The Box."

Lee felt cold sweep over his body.

"Meaning what?"

"Don't worry, you're not out of a job. We're going to hire some-one...a new partner for you. With Dave Berg going to Windsor, we'll bring in a replacement news anchor in January—one with more personality—and we'll get J.J. more involved. I think he can...spark something. Bring a young element to the show, too."

His words were like a slap in the face.

"How long have you been cooking this up?"

"Ellis said to wait and see what this book was like. I think we've seen. We've got to do something."

"You know I've always worked solo. I do a hell of a good job all by myself."

Arnott's embarrassed flush developed thin white patches on his cheeks and lips.

"Do you know how many morning guys work solo in markets this size anymore? The Lee Garrett Show is a dinosaur! Everybody has a team morning show these days. Don't you read the trades? For shit's sake, Lee…." His voice softened. "It's not a criticism of you, it's just the way things are. She won't be calling the shots. You'll still…."

"She…?"

"I…what I have in mind is a younger woman. Someone who'll be a good counterpoint for you. Present the female point of view." He searched for words. "We need a woman. It's what everybody else is doing."

"Well that makes it right then," Lee hissed, dismayed that he hadn't suspected anything. Then, like a burst of light in his brain, he realized that the plan had gone even farther than Arnott was admitting. He was instantly sure of it.

"You already have somebody in mind, don't you? You've already got somebody interviewed and ready to start!" He read the truth on the other's face and slammed the desk with his fist. His voice was probably carrying through half the building, but he didn't care. "*Christ!* You never even considered that I should be a part of hiring my own goddamned partner, you little shit!" He stormed out of the office, the slam of the door like a cannon shot, leaving Arnott staring at the doorknob.

Maddy Ellis was out of the building, but Lee vowed to give her an earful the next chance he got. On the station corkboard near the back door a short memo from Ellis offered the usual bullshit congratulations. Most of the staff never saw the actual ratings numbers, and with statistics like the BBM's there was always a way to find some obscure result that made you look like a winner. The company would spring for a couple of rounds of drinks after 5:00 at Clambaker's.

Lee decided not to go. He'd never missed a ratings party, but he was in no mood to listen to Charette gloat or Arnott fabricate.

And he didn't need a reminder that the glory days of the Lee Garrett Show were a thing of the past.

He was halfway home before he remembered his lunch appointment with Tom Gowan. *Shit.* Could he cancel? Gowan was an old friend—the morning newscaster at CTBX when Lee was hired. He'd understand Lee's frustration better than most. On the other hand, it might be good to have someone to talk to. Someone who'd been through all the bullshit and survived. Gowan had turned to selling cars and now computers—not glamorous stuff, but at least it was honest.

Lee turned the car around.

Waiting at a red light he found himself looking at a woman in a light-coloured Ford Fiesta beside him on the right. Their eyes met, and he saw wavy dark hair framing a face with fine features and well-defined cheekbones. She had the peaches-and-cream skin of an English girl. Her full lips curled into a rueful smile under his scrutiny. Then the cars in the line began to move. He let her merge into the lane ahead of him and make the turn, and she raised a hand in acknowledgement. A couple of blocks later she turned left again and was gone. Lee felt a brief lift of his heart vanish with her. What was *that* about? A man entering the second half of his life wasn't supposed to get a schoolboy's rush at the sight of a pretty face.

Gowan was waiting for him in the entrance of the King's Buffet. After hanging up their coats they followed a server to a table and ordered drinks. Gowan wrapped his sports jacket over the back of his chair. "Shall we hit the buffet right away?"

"Sure." Lee's stomach twisted at the thought of the deep-fried chicken balls and shrimp. It was already on acid overdrive. He loaded his plate with rice and some of the dishes with lighter sauces. Gowan stocked up on fried food, confirming Lee's impression that the man had put on twenty pounds since they'd last met.

There wasn't much for the two divorced men to say about their families, so the conversation inevitably turned to the radio business.

"I caught some shit from a listener the other day," Lee said. "Sent me a nasty note. Very nasty. That happen to you much?"

"All the time. Even convicted criminals tear a strip off you for reporting their names. And remember when Mayor Warden was so pissed at me? The other candidates kept catching him in lies and he claimed I was harping on it." Gowan took a gulp of his rye and coke. "He was right, though. I was playing it up. Son of a bitch had been a fat cat too long and was letting too much of the cream show on his whiskers."

"He got re-elected anyway."

Gowan sighed, "Yeah, and that's why he dropped his complaint. Anyway, I remember you taking heat when you got on the bad side of that police sergeant. What was his name?"

"Dieter. Fred Dieter. He just wasn't a fan of poetry, I guess."

"'Ode To The Incompetent', right?" Gowan rubbed at his smile.

"The man screwed the pooch on his investigation and the drug dealers walked. Didn't take a genius to see that. Besides, I never mentioned any names. And 'The Ode' generated a lot of water cooler talk. That's my job."

"Sure, but don't expect him to see it that way as he watches promotions pass him by."

The observation had already come true; Lee had heard through the grapevine that Dieter even blamed him for a failed marriage. He shook his head. "Were you ever threatened by a listener?"

Gowan finished his drink and ordered another. "You wanna go for dessert? Nah, I guess I shouldn't, either." He fidgeted with his empty glass. "I haven't told too many people this story—I don't know why. It was about five years before you came to town. My kids were all young. Annie had just started kindergarten."

Lee had a memory of a sandy-haired girl with bright blue eyes. He knew Gowan didn't see her very often since his ex-wife had moved the family two provinces away.

Gowan cleared his throat. "That was back when we still did editorials on the radio, remember? 'Comment'. No. 'Speaking Out'—that was it. Anyway, I'd done one about immigrants. Nothing bigoted. I just said that too many of them were coming into the country, working the minimum, and then winding up on welfare. Or using student loans from our government to get an education here, then refusing to pay the money back." He looked up at Lee. "I had a neighbour once who bragged about doing that. To *me*, a Canadian taxpayer. I should have turned the bastard in."

Gowan's drink arrived, and he took a deep pull.

"One day, while Annie was walking home from kindergarten this big white car with a lot of rust on it pulls up beside her. Driver rolls down his window and calls her over. Thank God he didn't know her name, or she might have gone to him. Annie was such a sweet little kid, she could never believe anybody'd want to hurt her. She stays on the sidewalk, and the guy starts talking about how he knows her daddy's on the radio, and maybe her daddy thinks he's a big shot, but he'd better watch his mouth or somebody might get hurt.

"Annie starts walking faster and faster to get away from him, but he keeps up with her in the car, repeating that somebody could get hurt…like maybe Daddy's little girl, walking home from school all by herself every day. Maybe one day she wouldn't be coming home to Daddy."

Gowan's voice had dropped to a near whisper as he stared into space. "Annie started crying, and began to run—she was only a few houses away from ours. The guy sped up and pulled into the next driveway to cut her off. Fortunately Gloria was watching for Annie from the front window, like she always did. She ran out of the house and the guy chickened out. Backed up, and squealed off down the street."

"Did they ever catch him?"

"Nah. Gloria was too scared to think of looking at the license plate. White car with rust…the driver was a black guy with a moustache. That's all Ann could remember. The police kept an eye on her for a while. But the guy never showed up again. And her big, strong daddy couldn't do a thing. You know what that feels like?" His dark eyes hardened. "We decided to move. We put Ann in a new school, but she had nightmares for months after. Maybe she still does." He grabbed his glass and shook a few drops from the melted ice cube into his mouth. "I know I still do."

The two men were silent for a moment. Gowan reached for the cheque the waitress had just left.

"No, my treat," Lee insisted. He couldn't really afford it. But the meal had already cost Gowan enough.

They were both quiet as they put on their coats and left the restaurant. When they'd said their goodbyes and Lee turned toward his car, Gowan spoke once more.

"I guess my point was…never *ever* underestimate what a listener can do. It only takes one whacko. God knows there are plenty of them around. And they listen to the radio just like everybody else."

≈

Gotta love Neil Diamond, he thought as he turned up the song playing on the old fridge-top radio and slung his coat over the nearest chair. As Neil was giving it all away for the sake of a dream in a penny arcade, Lee saw the flashing light on his answering machine and pressed the playback button. The message was like sulphur in the air.

"Lee, *for God's sake* call me back! I need to talk to you about Christmas. I'll be out this afternoon, but call me tonight at home." The clang of the phone in the cradle came through clearly on the recording.

He wondered if a man's voice would answer when he called. Then he scolded himself for thinking like an adolescent, afraid to call a girl in case her father picked up the phone.

He scribbled "Call Michaela!!!" on a piece of scratch paper, stuck it to the fridge with a magnet shaped like a bowl of fruit, and replaced the pen in a pencil holder made from a tin can. His daughter Sarah had covered it with crayon-decorated paper in the shape of a clown. In kindergarten or grade one, he thought. He smiled at the memory, then shuddered as he imagined Sarah being stalked like Gowan's daughter.

The sloppy block letters of the note he'd just written caught his eye. They were in *red ink*. Was his mind playing some kind of game? A hate message from his subconscious?

Nonsense. He didn't hate himself, and he didn't hate Michaela. He never had, even through the worst of the divorce. It might have made things easier, in a way.

He rolled into bed for a nap and pulled up the blankets.

A man wasn't supposed to be in love with his ex-wife. They'd been apart for two years. Christmas was coming around again. Not his favourite time of year—not anymore. The first Christmas after their separation was when he'd truly come to understand that their marriage was broken beyond repair.

They'd always spent Christmas with her side of the family in London, and Boxing Day with his parents on their small farm near Gravenhurst. Even after his father was killed by a falling tree branch in a November windstorm the holiday routine had remained.

After the separation, as they faced the prospect of their first Christmas apart since falling in love, Michaela suggested Lee drop in to her parents' place around lunch time Christmas day and stay for dinner. She said the children would want him there.

From the moment he came in the door they were all walking on eggshells. Sarah and Jason were young teenagers—they couldn't pretend nothing had changed. Michaela's parents tried so hard not to say the wrong thing. And Michaela's nearly-theatrical efforts to act normal only made things worse.

Lee ached for her. He wanted so badly to hold her, comfort her …to make her smile a real smile. But there was no opportunity to be alone. The harder Michaela tried to recreate the old trappings of Christmas, from the carol sing to the mulled cider, the more her efforts failed, and she escaped to the kitchen. Lee finally became convinced it would be better to bring the ordeal to an early end, and prepared to leave.

Michaela screamed at him, accusing him of selfishly spoiling other people's plans whenever the mood struck him. The ugly exchange ended when they heard sobs and running footsteps from the other room. He stammered an apology to his embarrassed hosts and left without saying goodbye to his children. On Christmas Day.

By mid-February the divorce had begun.

No, he thought, as he drifted into sleep. *Please, God, not another Christmas like that one.*

Dinner was a can of microwaved Cordon Bleu stew. He had some bread that was a few days old but it'd be all right toasted. As he pushed down the toaster handle he heard the snap of a spark and a tendril of ozone-scented smoke drifted like a finger into the air. The elements stayed black. He wiggled the power cord, but all it produced was a fizzing noise.

With a guttural sound deep in his throat he grabbed the toaster and threw it across the room.

The ounce and a half of Beefeaters Gin that had sat in his cupboard for three months tempted him, but he'd need it more *after* he called Michaela. Instead he stretched his after dinner tea as long as he could. When it was gone, he reached for the phone and pulled it far enough to let him perch on the edge of the couch.

Michaela answered.

"It's about bloody time, Lee. You may not have much use for me, but a little consideration for Sarah and Jason..."

"Knock it off, Michaela." He lowered his voice with an effort. "Do we have to start a fight in the first five seconds, or did you actually have a two-way conversation in mind?" When she said nothing, he continued on. "I called back three or four times. I didn't always leave a message because I'm hardly ever home—you know that."

"Better than anyone else, I expect."

Lee sighed. "What do you want?"

"It's about Christmas." She hesitated. "I...*we*...Robert and I... we're going to take the kids to Florida over the Christmas holidays. Robert's partner at the clinic has a condo near Fort Lauderdale that he's offered to us. I thought you should know. So you could make plans to see the kids before we go. ...Lee? Are you there?"

A weight pressed against his chest. From the moment she was hired by the dental clinic, it had been obvious to him that Robert Farrell had more than a business interest in Michaela. Lee had all but accused them of having an affair a few years later. What hadn't been true then, had now become a reality. Maybe he'd even helped to fulfil his own prophecy.

He tried to speak, but had to clear his throat.

"How kind of you to tell me your plans for my children. Or is it because Farrell's hoping I'll demand to take the kids myself, so the two of you can go off alone for a week between the sheets?" The jab had been a sudden intuition, and as he said it he heard a gasp from Michaela that was more than outrage. He pictured her glancing at Farrell, as she weighed the truth of the slur.

"*God... damn... you!*" she hissed, injecting each word with more venom than he'd ever heard in her voice. She slammed the phone with enough force to make the line crackle.

He let his hand drop into his lap, still holding the receiver, and whispered, "I love you, too."

3

HE WAS AT THE DOOR OF MADDY ELLIS'S OFFICE moments after the 9:00 o'clock news ended.

"There was one conspicuous absence at last night's ratings get-together," Maddy said, looking up. She frowned as he closed the door. "Let me guess—you're pissed off at me."

"When were you planning to tell me about the team morning show?" Lee ignored the gestured invitation to sit. "When I saw the new chick's name on the music sheets?"

"Chick? I assume you mean Dale Lawson. So they've hired her?"

"You didn't know that?"

"It's Larry Wise's decision—he's the News Director."

"Except Arnott says it's going to be a team morning show—this woman, J.J., and me. That's a change in programming strategy—don't tell me you weren't involved. And nobody thought to ask my opinion about the person who's supposed to be my partner?"

"Since when do you have a say in news department hires?"

"That's a goddamn cop-out, Maddy, and you know it." He could feel his temper slipping from his control.

"Jesus, I give you ten years and that's all the respect I've earned?"

"Dan worked with Lawson at his last station. He thinks she'll be a great fit. As for telling you, that was his job. I didn't know how he planned to do it, and I didn't ask."

"Sure. Easier just to pass the buck."

"Listen, Lee." Her eyes sparked. "I've got a business to run. It involves a lot more than one morning man who doesn't want to share his sandbox. Your ego's bruised? Suck it up. 'Cause you'd better find a way to get along with this woman. Want more advice? *Don't rock the boat when you're on a sinking ship.*"

The meeting was over. Lee stalked to the back parking lot and stood in a slushy snowfall to let his head cool. He thought about climbing in his car and driving home, but when melted snow began to drip into his eyes he turned back toward the office and his work.

~

For someone with a taste for people watching the Christmas Craft Fair was a human smorgasbord. From his vantage point on a raised platform Lee watched the milling crowd. He got shy looks from the kids, but a lot of the adults pretended not to see him. He'd pick up his microphone, and they'd veer like a school of fish from the passing shadow of a gull, as if the mic were a TV camera and they might accidentally get on the radio.

He was hard to miss: a wide banner overhead declared "CTBX 620 The Box, Favourites of the 60's, 70's, and 80's" and a smaller banner in front of the table identified "CTBX Morning Personality Lee Garrett". It amused him to think how long the banner would be if it used his real name: *Leeman Ryan Grettenwald.* His parents had been hurt when he changed it. He had no brothers, so the family name died with his father. But Leeman Grettenwald was too clumsy for the radio rock jock he'd wanted to be—for that you needed a name people could easily get their tongues around, and remember. That was why so many announcers used two *first* names, like "Keith David" or "Peter Michaels". Easy to say, easy to recall.

He remembered the bull sessions about it in his broadcasting course.

"You gotta have a name with familiarity. Like Edgar Allen."

"Poe? A little obvious, isn't it?"

"But you don't use the last name. You just want something that twigs people's memories. Look at the magician David Copperfield. An obvious steal, but people never forget it."

"What about a career reference? Your business is talking, so you call yourself *Oral* Roberts."

"Even more memorable: *Oral Secks.*"

"Right. The shortest radio career ever—five minutes, and then he gave his *name.*"

At Lee's first job he'd actually used a second made-up name and a slight change of voice when he had to do weekend newscasts. No one ever made the connection between his two aliases.

His craft fair cut-ins back to the radio station were going well. With dozens of on-location broadcasts every year—*remotes*, as insiders called them—it was second nature for him to ad lib sixty seconds worth of fluff about Christmas decorations and embroidery kits. The fair's promoter had even kept the exhibitors off Lee's back, knowing that a few would always try to get more than their share of mentions on the radio.

He'd just finished a 'live' cut when an elderly Asian man stepped out of the crowd, a woman at his side.

"You're Lee Garrett, aren't you? From 'The Box'?" Lee's name tag and banners were superfluous—people always wanted verbal confirmation.

"That's right. How do you do?" He extended a hand and the man shook it, but didn't introduce himself or his wife. Bright eyes sparkled in a friendly face, and the accented voice was unaffected by age.

"Your ex-wife make any good investments lately?" The man waited expectantly.

Lee used a non-committal smile like a mask until he could place the reference. Then he got it: a couple of weeks earlier he'd mentioned an article about investment counselling, and ended by saying, "I have somebody who looks after all my money, too... my ex-wife." It was a worn old bit, but the old man wanted to show he remembered it. Lee's real smile took over.

"Well if she has, she hasn't told *me* about them!"

The couple chuckled, pleased to make a connection. Emboldened by the exchange, the woman turned to her husband. "You'd better watch out, or he might make you sing for your breakfast!" She laughed while the man shook his head and said, "Not the way I sing."

Lee suppressed a groan. The "Sing For Your Breakfast" contest had ended more than a year before he arrived at the station.

God's way of making sure his head didn't get too big.

He smiled and thanked them for dropping by. CTBX listeners were the best: friendly, salt-of-the-earth people.

Of course, there were always a few who wore out their welcome— the radio groupies. Lee's smile vanished when Dennis showed up. Dennis had been known to scare paying customers away from a store.

In his early twenties and unnaturally skinny, his oily sand-coloured hair pushed out from under a dark blue Toronto Blue Jays baseball cap wherever it could find an opening. Dennis always had two-days growth of beard and eyebrows so blond they were all but invisible. Indoors his eyes picked up some blue from the ever-present ball cap, but in sunlight his irises blended into the surrounding whites with an effect that was spooky.

"Hi, Lee Garrett."

"Hey, Dennis. What's up?"

"Not much. I came to see you, Lee Garrett. You going on the radio soon?"

"In a few minutes, yeah." Any real conversation would encourage the man to hang around. Doug Rhodes sometimes pretended not to see Dennis at all.

"I'm making deliveries for the drug store, Lee Garrett. Somebody at the Ukrainian Federation booth needs cold medicine."

Lee nodded and smiled at a vaguely familiar face in the crowd.

"You got any free pop?"

"Nope. The Exhibition Centre's refreshment stand wouldn't be happy with us if we did that."

"You got a contest?" Pale eyes lingered over the cardboard ballot box near the end of the table.

Lee sighed. "Yeah, Dennis. Fill out a ballot—just one. You could win an artificial Christmas tree." He watched the man peel off a ballot slip from a pad and laboriously print his name. "You know, Dennis, there must be at least twenty booths here with free draws. You could win all kinds of good stuff."

"Yeah?" The corner of his mouth lifted into a smile that showed a crooked tooth. "Where?"

A booth nearby was selling Christmas tablecloths. It featured a draw for a quilted runner for the top of a buffet. Lee pointed. "You could win a kind of tablecloth for your Mom."

Dennis's face darkened, then he said, "Grandma would like it. Thanks, Lee Garrett." He meticulously folded his ballot three times and poked it into the top of the box. "See you later."

Lee nodded. The ploy might have bought him a half hour of peace.

The song on the radio caught his ear—Jonathan Edwards singing about a man trying to run his life. Everybody felt that way sometimes.

Lee looked at the faces passing by. If he could see beneath the skin of pink and tan and brown, beneath the brows thick and thin propped up by assorted eyewear, past the tentative smiles and non-committal frowns… would he see someone who had threatened his life?

"Excuse me."

A woman and a boy stood near the table. There was something familiar about her: dark hair framing a pale complexion, delicate features and long lashes. She was memorably pretty, but he couldn't place her. The boy just stood staring into space.

"Hi. What can I do for you?"

At the sound of his voice, the boy looked at him. But it was the woman who spoke again.

"You're Lee Garrett, aren't you?"

"That's right."

"My name is Candace Ross. This is Paul Schwartz. He's a very big fan of yours."

There was an appealing innocence to the boy's smile and tousled blond hair, but something unusual about the eyes. Perhaps he was mentally challenged. "Hi, Paul," Lee said, and the boy raised his right hand with a copy of the craft fair program in it.

"Can I have your autograph?" Quiet, a little uncertain.

"Sure. My pleasure. But can you wait just a second? I have to go on the air right now." From a small portable boom box on the end of the table he could hear Doug Rhodes finish a Public Service Announcement and go into an introduction about the craft fair. Lee straightened and brought the microphone to his mouth.

"Thanks, Doug. And I have to say that this year's fair really has something for everyone …" His words trailed off as his mind registered the sound of a jingle coming from the radio. Something was wrong. Rhodes had gone to commercials instead of to him. The Promotions department provided a cell phone for remotes. He snatched it up.

"What's wrong, Doug? Everything was working fine."

"I don't know," Rhodes said. "The signal's gone. It was there a minute ago—I could hear background noise. Now it's dead. Did you lose power?"

Lee checked his cordless microphone. The mic was on and the battery was good.

"I don't know," Lee answered. "I'll check the transmitter in a minute. But first, is this phone signal good enough to put on the air? You don't have room to do a make-good if we miss this cut-in."

"You're right about that. The cell signal's shitty with all that metal around you, but it's not breaking up. I'll introduce you again. Hang on." While Rhodes punched buttons to put the telephone on the air, Lee gathered his thoughts and launched into his report as if nothing had happened. When he was done he scanned the crowd, but there was no sign of Pete, the station's remote set-up technician. With a muttered curse, he jumped down from the platform and began to push his way through the crowd, like swimming against a current. Pete had put their equipment just outside the Exhibition Centre's doors: a receiver for the wireless microphone and a portable transmitter unit that sent a signal back to the radio station. Lee squatted to check the gauges.

They registered normal—the equipment was still getting electrical power. He spoke into the microphone and the needles of the volume meters on the mic receiver bounced the way they should. He began to check the cable connections on both pieces of gear.

As he shifted position, he glanced up and caught the face of the dark-haired woman, about thirty feet away. Candace…something, with that boy. He'd completely forgotten about them! And she clearly wasn't pleased. She snapped her head around, and walked quickly away, with the blond boy and a light-haired man at her side.

Lee rocked back on his heels and sighed. If they'd been fans before, they weren't anymore.

He looked back down at his hands just as his fingers found the end of the antenna cable where it connected to the transmitter—where it *should* have connected.

The wire had been cut.

He slowly stood, the end of the severed cable in his hand, and peered into the faces of the people flowing past. Did one of them have a pair of wire snips in his pocket?

There should be a spare antenna cable in the station van parked nearby. Pete could make the swap within a few minutes. Lee examined the cable and a muscle in his jaw twitched.

~

As he stood beside the rink boards that evening, Lee closed his eyes and savoured a sound distinctive to hockey arenas and nowhere else: a rustle of sibilants created by voices, bass notes lost in distance while higher-register sounds took on a life of their own, bouncing between hard ice, steel girders and corrugated roof. The boom and echo of a frozen puck rocketing off the boards, and the harsh scrape of a skate blade making a quick stop brought back memories of his school days. He'd never been a great skater, but he appreciated the skill of players who made the game look effortless.

The traditional red carpet was rolled out to center ice and he adjusted his tie of the same colour. He wasn't the only one in a suit. The sport of hockey involved massive protective padding, and often bandages and stitches, but it still maintained a firm tradition that officials, coaches, and off-duty players should be seen in the attire of gentlemen.

His first words boomed too loudly out of the speakers, turning into the ringing whine of feedback until a technician brought the volume down. This was his fifth time as master of ceremonies for the tournament's opening and it always began the same way.

"Thanks for coming tonight. Glad you could be here. Leave it to Canadians to complain for half the year about slush and snow, and then gather around sheets of ice *indoors.*" There were polite chuckles. The opening ceremonies never drew a large audience to the Countryside Sports Complex, mainly the families and friends of out-of-town players who had nothing better to do between games. He offered a few more quips, made the requisite introductions of dignitaries and listened to their speeches.

Afterward he climbed the stands. His old friend Matt Miller was ready to begin the cable TV broadcast of the next game with a single camera and a desk just big enough for two chairs. Miller was a sports writer for the *Sudbury Star,* but calling hockey play-by-play for the Eastlink cable community channel was a sideline he enjoyed. Lee thought he was good enough for network TV, but Miller had chosen the small city life for the sake of his family. Lynn Miller worked as an accountant for CTBX/Z104.

Miller had a big, friendly smile, and he used it a lot.

"Thanks for coming out, Lee. Having somebody to do the colour commentary gives me a bit of a break."

"No problem. I get a kick out of it. Is Gary playing this weekend?"

"Not in this tournament," Miller replied. "He and my other son Jeff are both playing in a tourney in Quebec. Wish I could be there, but I've got another commitment tomorrow."

The cameraman gave them a one-minute-to-air warning, and they quickly discussed a few points. It didn't take long for Lee to get comfortable, analysing some of the standout shots, and offering a verbal instant replay the cable company couldn't provide on video. The game was a close victory for the home team, thanks to a goal in the final minute of play.

"If that one's any indication, we're in for an exciting weekend," Lee said in their post-game summary.

"Better believe it," Miller replied, and gave a closing wrap-up, thanking the sponsors and volunteers, and urging his audience to buy tickets for the rest of the games.

"Coming for a beer in the VIP lounge?" he asked as he hoisted himself out of the plastic seat and massaged a sore butt.

Lee didn't really feel like socializing. But it was a Friday night and no one waited for him at home.

"Sure. I'll even let you buy."

Miller laughed, and turned to invite the cameraman, insisting that Lee had a generous expense account.

The small banquet room high between the two ice surfaces had been set aside for VIP's and media people. Lee's smile slipped away as he spotted a man across the room in crisp grey slacks and a sparkling white golf shirt with a beer company logo embroidered on the left breast. Of course he'd be there. His company was a major sponsor of the tournament.

Ken Cousins looked like a Ken doll with his sculpted good looks, impossibly perfect hair, and Polo Ralph Lauren wardrobe. His presence always made Lee feel like a slob.

Lee turned quickly toward the bar, but he knew Cousins had seen him. Sooner or later they'd have to put on an act and exchange small talk.

It turned out to be sooner. With drinks in hand, Miller steered him over to a group of minor hockey officials and sponsors. Lee congratulated the tournament organizers and accepted their praise for his handling of the opening ceremonies, but when Miller was asked for his coaching opinion on some of the young players, the circle tightened and Lee found himself on the fringe.

"Lee, how the hell are you?"

"Good, Ken. You?

"Keepin' out of trouble. Damn it." The smile was pasted on. "Besides, Rita keeps a tight rein on me these days. How's Michaela?"

Cousins certainly knew about the divorce.

"She's fine. How's Barbara?"

The man's jaw tightened and a light flush rose under the perfect blond hair. Cousins turned to the man beside him and offered to get him another beer.

Miller had caught the exchange. "Who's Barbara? I thought Rita was his girl, for years now."

"She is. Barbara was his assistant last year."

"The one with the long blond hair and the big…?"

"That's the one. And before Barbara there was Liz. His assistants don't last too long."

"So how do you know all this?"

Lee hesitated, then decided the young woman wouldn't care.

"From Lisa. She was on Cousin's string once, for a few weeks. She caught on sooner than most and confronted him. I think he actually bragged about his conquests."

"Lisa? Lisa Moore?" Miller seemed surprised that the Z104 midday announcer with the sweet face knew what sex was.

Lee shrugged. "The guy looks like a male model, and I'd bet he spends every spare hour at the gym. I've seen Tracy Banderjee practically throw herself at him, but he wasn't interested. For once."

A roar of laughter behind them proved that Cousins could also entertain an audience with a well-stocked repertoire of jokes, and beer for those he liked. There were a few guilty looks in the circle of faces, as if the joke had been particularly tasteless.

"I'm going to head home, Matt. It's been a long week."

"Sure. Ok. Thanks for helping out."

Lee gave the table of appetizers a look of regret and pushed through the heavy glass door. He nearly ran into a paunchy man in a blue suit.

God, the evening was turning into a nightmare.

He gave a nod and received an icy glare in return. The man moved on, and Lee ran a hand over his face.

André Menard had been the first person to invite Lee for a beer when he started at CTBX. He was hard not to like: loud and garrulous, able to say the most scandalous things without causing offence. He had the perfect salesman's personality and the station's best client list. They'd discovered a shared interest in old cars and hockey, and the friendship had become a close one. Until one day at a remote broadcast when one of Menard's clients had asked Lee about the off-the-record premiums he paid for special placement of his radio commercials.

Lee's curiosity had led him to the truth, but he wished it hadn't. With subtle favours and little gifts Menard had charmed station staff into giving his clients preferential scheduling on the air. The extra fees he charged for it didn't end up in company coffers.

Lee lost sleep trying to decide what to do. He probably would have let the whole thing drop if it hadn't been for one bad day.

Feeling as poor as he'd ever been—late in his alimony and behind on half a dozen bills, he approached Arnott and Ellis for a raise, only to learn the corporate bosses had declared a salary freeze. As he stormed out of the building in a fog of anger, Menard rolled into the lot at the wheel of a brand new BMW, grinning like the Cheshire cat.

It was more than Lee could take. He invited the salesman for a drink and ambushed him. There was an ugly scene that ended with Menard pounding on the trunk of Lee's car while it drove away. The phone rang all evening, and Lee reached a new low as his former friend pleaded, raged, and even offered to cut him in on the scam.

Menard resigned and Lee kept his mouth shut. Everyone was utterly dumbfounded that the station's top account executive would leave it all behind. Everyone except Lee Garrett.

What a night. Could he make his escape from the arena without running into anyone else who hated his guts?

"Hi, Lee Garrett!" Dennis's off-kilter smile gave him an eight-year-old's face on a man's body.

Good God. Not now.

"When I heard you were coming here, I volunteered. I'm giving out programs."

Lee's practiced smile failed to ignite. "It's good that you're helping out, Dennis. But I'm afraid I've got to get going. See you later." He pushed through the doors before Dennis could think of a response. The bite of the fresh air was sweet relief, but it lasted no more than a few steps.

His mind recoiled at the scene exposed by the dull lights of the parking lot. Someone had run a key down both sides of his car, making deep gouges in the paint. All four tires were slashed flat. And on the hood was scratched a stylized "S".

4

LEE'S CHILDHOOD MEMORIES INCLUDED A FEW PETS: a cat, a couple of dogs, a goldfish. And he'd once rescued a baby squirrel that had been pushed out of its nest. A red squirrel—small and hyperactive. Just the right size for a borrowed hamster cage, though the squirrel only used the exercise wheel as a shortcut from one impenetrable wall of the cage to the other. Lee kept the cage near a window, close to sunshine and fresh air.

One day he'd come upon a disturbing tableau. A neighbourhood cat was perched on the window ledge, greedily eyeing the cage. The squirrel was madly racing inside the wheel, desperate to escape. Lee chased the cat away and made sure never to leave the window open, but the cat returned time after time, calmly watching through the glass. Lee would pull the window blinds down, but his mother would forget and leave them up.

The squirrel stopped eating. Within a week it was dead.

≈

"You think the cable was deliberately cut at the craft show?

Lee shrugged at Maddy Ellis. "Yeah. A heavy object wouldn't leave that clean a cut. And it wasn't any place it would be pinched or flexed. Wire cutters are my guess. But why not just disconnect the cable? It's easy enough to do."

"Whoever did it wanted to cause us more inconvenience than that. Maybe take you off the air for the rest of the night." Ellis's face was tight. "Are you thinking it may have been the same person who sent you the hate letter and vandalised your car?"

"Doesn't take a genius to put two and two together."

"It's time you told the police about this. Station property has been damaged, and there's a chance someone broke into the building to leave that note."

He nodded and stood to go.

"Lee. If there's a *nut* out there, he could be just toying with you so far. Be careful, ok?"

The station's secondary production studio was unoccupied. A few minutes of hunting produced a beat up telephone book. He punched in the number for the police general information line and sat down in a ratty office chair with some of its foam showing through a seam.

There were a few instructions to follow from the automated system, then the voice that came on the line was younger than he'd expected, the "How can I help you?" straight out of an operations manual.

"I'd like to speak to someone about a harassment situation," Lee began, then realized his explanation was going to be complicated. "Not a sexual harassment or anything, I…"

"Relax, sir, and just give the details. Your call will be recorded."

Lee identified himself and began to recount the past few days. Put into words, it sounded trivial, but the police officer was earnestly helpful.

"Let me check with the duty sergeant on this, Mr. Garrett." He put Lee on hold, and some soft music played down the line. A moment later a carefully-modulated voice began to deliver a message about road safety.

Four such recordings played before the original voice came back on the line.

"Mr. Garrett?"

"Yes."

"From CTBX, right?"

"I told you that. Yes."

There was a hesitation before the man continued. Was that another voice in the background? "Are you sure the letter wasn't a prank from one of your co-workers?"

"As I told you, I asked them. They denied it."

"Did you ask *everyone* who works there? All of the staff?"

"No, but..."

"Then it could still be a prank?"

"I don't think so. What about the cut cable at the craft show?"

"A cable that could have been cut by a cart or equipment dolly running over it? There are lots of those around a place like the Exhibition Centre, Mr. Garrett. We can send someone to take a look at the damage to your car, but you say it was at a hockey tournament... with lots of kids from out of town?"

"Officer, are you saying none of these things is worth pursuing?"

"The thing is, Mr. Garrett, in the first two cases there doesn't appear to be any evidence that a crime was committed. As for scratched paint and flat tires... I'm afraid that kind of thing happens all the time where kids gather. There's not that much we can do except open a file on it." When Lee didn't respond, the man said, "I'm sorry."

Lee slowly dropped the phone into the cradle. The cop had sure lost interest in a hurry. But he was right—Lee had no proof that any of the incidents were related. Even if he had, what did he really expect the police to do? Assign him a bodyguard?

He shook his head, and tried to push the whole thing from his mind. There was still work he could do at the station. Or he could just go home. But when he thought about his empty apartment, the image that came to his mind was a broken toaster.

~

A couple of hours later, as he was packing his gear away in his locker he heard his name over the paging system, summoned to the front lobby. He stepped into the hallway and almost collided with Chuck Norwood.

"Did you hear the page?" the station's Promotions Director asked.

"On my way now."

"Well if you're lucky, I won't see you again today." Norwood grinned and moved off down the hall.

It was the dark-haired woman from the craft show, looking even more attractive in a businesslike plum-coloured jacket and skirt, set off by a white blouse with just enough frill at the collar to make the outfit appealingly feminine. She was examining the Lee Garrett cardboard cut-out. His mind hunted for words that would start them off on a friendly note.

"Hi. It's a pleasure to see you again, if a bit of a surprise..."

"I didn't think you'd remember me," she said through tight lips. "You're obviously a man with many more important things on your mind." His offer of a handshake was ignored.

"Look, Ms. ...?"

"Ross. Candace Ross. The boy who *was* such a big fan of yours is Paul Schwartz."

"Yes, I remember, Ms. Ross. And I'm very sorry..."

"You'd have been sorrier if you'd seen his face," she interrupted, her cheeks colouring. "You were a hero to him, and you acted like he didn't exist. He didn't even cry. I wish he had." She noticed her fingers twisting together at her belt, and consciously moved her hands to her sides.

"I'm very sorry, Ms. Ross. I had a sudden, serious technical problem. I lost contact with the radio station just as I was supposed to go on the air. Paul must've seen what happened."

Her head snapped up. "Paul didn't see anything," she said. "Paul is *blind*."

The shock on Lee's face seemed to mollify her. "You really didn't know that?"

He gave a slow shake of his head. "I really didn't know that. I noticed something…different about the way he looked at things. Didn't look at things, I suppose." He cleared his throat. "The technical problem was urgent, and there's more to it than I feel like explaining right now. Just please believe that I didn't mean to snub him."

The woman's face was a study in contrast. She wasn't yet ready to forgive, but she wanted to believe the apology was sincere.

"Do you want to make it up to him?" she asked.

"Uh…what did you have in mind?"

"Visit him. Come to see him personally."

Lee blinked. "Ms Ross…"

"That's what I thought. Goodbye, Mr. Garrett."

"Wait. I didn't say I wouldn't do it. When…when would you want to schedule this visit?"

"It would be best if you came with me the next time I go to his house. I'm his Orientation and Mobility instructor. From CNIB—do you know it?"

He nodded.

"O & M means I help him learn how to get around on his own. Paul only lost his sight three months ago—he was accidentally hit in the side of the head by a bat while playing baseball. At first it was only his right eye that was blinded, but his left soon followed. They do that sometimes." She stiffened her neck. "I wasn't going to visit again for a few weeks, but sooner might be better. A surprise, I think. That way he won't…" She gave Lee a furtive glance, as if embarrassed.

"He won't get his hopes up, in case I don't show," he said it for her. "I'll be there, Ms. Ross. Let's set a time right now."

They agreed on the following Monday at 4:00 p.m. when Paul would arrive home from school. Then Candace Ross gave a quick nod and marched out of the building. He watched her with a stab of regret. Her frosty attitude would take a lot to thaw, but it might be worth a try. The visit would be a major pain in the neck, but to refuse it wasn't worth the risk that she'd badmouth him to her circle of friends.

He couldn't afford to lose any listeners.

≈

Wednesday was Dave Berg's last day. He'd accepted a job at a station in Windsor, with its huge Detroit market across the river. Lee spent a few minutes reminiscing with him on the air after each of the newscasts, and paid him some sincere compliments, along with a few that were exaggerated. He offered to put listeners on if they wanted to call in a tribute. No one called.

Although Lee had worked with Berg for four years, he couldn't really say he knew the man. On any given subject they disagreed more often than not, but it was important to get along in the insular world of a radio station, and they had, most of the time.

After his last newscast Berg suggested they go for a beer later, and Lee agreed. Both men knew it probably wouldn't happen, and it didn't. The next day Berg was gone.

The morning show routine carried on without a hiccup. Larry Wise, the News Director, recorded the CTBX newscasts in between his live 'casts on Z104. That would get them through until Dale Lawson came on board in the new year. Once Christmas week arrived the stations ran on a skeleton staff anyway.

As Lee passed the reception desk after his production shift, Karen handed him a package. He opened it to find a box of Kellogg's Corn Flakes and a handful of leaflets that fluttered to the floor.

"Oh, good. Breakfast and some reading material to go with it," he said, as Karen helped him pick up the papers.

"Eyes off the cleavage," she muttered.

"You cut me to the quick. Nice bra, though. I like black."

She slapped his chest with the gathered sheets, trying to suppress a grin.

"They're about Breast Cancer," she said. "Barry and Sandy got the same thing for Z104."

"Bras, breasts...they've got my attention." She cuffed him again as he turned away and began to read the introductory letter. It was a *special edition* box of cereal, with tips for healthy eating on the packaging. Kellogg's hoped Lee would mention it on his radio program, maybe even air a full interview about the promotion. He remembered something similar from a few years earlier, and approved of companies that attached their brand power to social issues once in a while, instead of some over-hyped Hollywood movie. He wasn't naive; he knew it was an exercise in public relations. Mentioning it would make him look good, too. But it didn't merit a full-fledged interview.

He'd racked up lots of brownie points lately anyway, giving plenty of coverage to the United Way campaign. At the wrap-up luncheon in half an hour he'd be accepting a small plaque for CTBX and Z104. It should have had his name on it, but an award to the radio stations was politically wiser. He stopped at his locker to grab his jacket and tie and shrugged into them on his way to his car.

United Way functions provided some of the community's most fertile ground for networking. The cavernous upstairs hall of the Caruso Club was packed. Lee was seated between one of the most powerful union leaders in town and the deputy fire chief.

"You still wake me up every morning, Lee," Dave Richards said with a rock-solid handshake. "Half our union membership, too, I think. Doubt if you get many favourable write-ups in the press these days, though." Richards nodded toward a table against the far wall.

It took a moment for Lee to recognize Elliott Dean; the man had lost weight and let his hair grow. Recently reinstated as city editor at the *Star* after a failed attempt at politics, Dean would never be president of the Lee Garrett fan club.

"You were right, though," Richards continued. "That extension to the highway bypass was a white elephant. Dean should never have hitched his political star to it. Too expensive, and it wouldn't have created enough local jobs."

Especially not public sector jobs, Lee thought. He'd trashed the bypass project on the air for all of those reasons, but also because it generated terrific buzz on the CTBX Facebook page.

Deputy Al Truman leaned over. "A lot of big investments went up in smoke when the bypass plan was sunk."

Richards nodded. "One of my guys told me there was even mob money in there. Sure, Dean resigned from Council for health reasons. He knew what was good for him."

And he blames me, Lee thought. He shrugged it off. He knew more than half the people in the room. They couldn't all like him.

Even so, they all applauded when he collected his plaque for Media Partner of the Year. He allowed himself to bask in the brief glow.

As the gathering began to break up he sensed someone beside him.

"Lee Garrett. How are you? You don't remember me, do you?"

Lee stifled a groan and looked at the young man with the outthrust hand. Closely-cropped blond hair with a reddish tint capped a face that bore a hint of old freckles on young skin. The teeth were as perfect as an orthodontist could make them, and blue eyes hid behind a pair of fashionable wire-framed glasses. His clothes spoke of money too.

"I'm Eric Van Horne. I shadowed you once, my grade eight Shadow Day. We've met since then, too, but you didn't remember me that time either. I guess I have a forgettable face."

Lee vaguely recalled a shy boy who sat in the back of the control room most of the show and had to be coaxed to say anything, none of it into the microphone. This college boy with the confident manner didn't match those memories.

"Eric. Sure. I'm sorry I didn't recognize you. Did you change your hair or something?"

"I guess I've grown a few inches, too. Anyway, I just wanted to say hi. Maybe you'll remember me next time we meet." The kid was determined to rub it in.

"It's nothing personal, Eric. I'm not good with names. Take it easy. Better bundle up, too. I can see the wind's picked up out there."

Van Horne turned in the doorway. "Don't worry—I've got my bowling ball cover to keep my head warm." He disappeared around the corner.

Lee didn't get it right away, walking slowly to the coat check room. Then he cursed and ran out to scan the parking lot. There was no sign of Eric Van Horne's blond hair. He jogged a few steps and looked up and down the street, but the kid was gone.

"Bowling ball cover. *Goddamn it!*"

The choice of words couldn't be an accident. Van Horne had nearly quoted his Skin's joke verbatim. Was it just another case of a listener trotting out something they'd heard on the show to prove they'd been listening?

Van Horne had said, "to keep *my* head warm", tossing out the tidbit of information like a table scrap to a dog. He was calling himself a Skin, and thought he was untouchable.

He was goddamn right. The cops wouldn't do a thing.

Lee swore a cloud of steam at the car windshield and bullied the cold engine to life. He'd parked in a far corner of the lot to hide his vandalised car, only hastily touched up until he could talk his insurance company into a new paint job. Had Van Horne enjoyed a good laugh over that?

By the time he reached home his anger had settled into nausea. He couldn't be certain Van Horne had anything to do with the death threat. The cocky young prick might identify himself with bigots, but it didn't mean he'd left the hate note. There were plenty of other suspects. Apparently in over twenty years of broadcasting he'd gathered enemies like a dog gathered fleas. He felt a chill in the pit of his stomach.

They couldn't really want him dead, though. Surely not. Embarrass him, hurt him, yes. But dead was forever.

He glanced down at the Corn Flakes box on the counter. Breast cancer. That was how his mother had died. For most of her struggle he'd been halfway across the country—he wasn't even there when she finally lost the fight. The memory was a taste of gall.

He scanned the Kellogg's letter for the telephone number and made a note to himself for the next day. Maybe he'd give them a full interview after all.

5

THE ANSWERING MACHINE WAS FLASHING WHEN HE AWOKE from his nap. He punched the call-back button.

"What's up, J.J.? You never call me at home."

"Hey, man, no emergency. Just calling to see if you wanna share a cab tonight."

"Tonight? Oh shit, I forgot all about it. What time does it start?"

"Hell, I guess you go to big parties all the time, but to us *peons* it's a big deal." The sportscaster laughed. "Cocktails at six, dinner at seven. And you know the company only springs for the drinks *before* dinner."

"So you intend to be there the moment the doors open—I get it. Sure, call a cab. I'll be ready." Lee hung up, trying to remember the last time he'd looked forward to the staff Christmas party. Junior announcers were paid peanuts; for them nothing was more attractive than an open bar.

In the cab J.J. gleefully speculated about which of the guys would be first to become falling-down-drunk, and which woman would show the most flesh. Lee laughed and confidently chose Doug Rhodes and Tracy Banderjee. He knew J.J. had a thing for Tracy, and hoped the kid wouldn't get his heart broken.

When they arrived, the bar already looked like the surface of a fish tank at feeding time. Rhodes was just abandoning his first empty beer bottle and reaching for a fresh one. Tracy Banderjee appeared in a tight red sheath of shiny material, ending well above the knee, that contrasted perfectly with her chocolate-milkshake skin. When she contrived to pick an imaginary piece of lint from her nylon-covered shin, the low neckline left little to the imagination. She had the body for it, and Lee couldn't deny a stirring in his belly.

"Nice dress, Tracy," he said. "Must be that spray-on material I've been reading about."

She smirked at him.

He craved a scotch, so he took a beer—the carbonation might slow him down and keep him from getting blasted. He was too old to court a hangover.

The rest of the partygoers gradually straggled in, most dragging spouses who looked as comfortable as vegetarians at a barbecue. Lee ended up sitting with the senior staff for dinner, as usual. Ellis liked it that way, and he didn't mind too much—he had a lot more in common with them than with the young crowd. But it bothered him to see Barry Wright ushering Shelly Henderson over to their table. Shelly was Lee's favourite of the station's remote hostesses—a great sense of humour, and mature for her age. Which was half the age of the Z104 morning man. What was Wright thinking? She was too young to drink, too, but Lee doubted that the Coke in her glass was pure; she was smiling too much.

He shrugged it away—watching for stuff like that was Maddy's job.

"Roast beef buffet again, Maddy?" he asked.

"What else?" The corner of her mouth pulled up. "Don't you remember the time we tried to do something different and went with a Thai menu? Everybody bitched for a month!"

"Pay for the drinks after dinner and they'll never remember enough to complain."

"Dream on. Paying for the cab rides home is a much better idea."

The worst part of the seating arrangement was that it encouraged shop talk, and Arnott wasted little time getting onto the subject of some recent research he'd read. When the meal was over, Lee ordered a glass of scotch instead of the second beer he'd meant to have.

The lights dimmed and the hired D.J. began cranking out noise with a painful bass thump. As Lee tried to escape the worst of it he bumped into Matt Miller. He hadn't seen Miller since the hockey tournament, and his friend wanted to know why André Menard and Ken Cousins had taken such pleasure in trashing Lee that night.

"Yeah, well, it's tough when everybody loves you," Lee said with a straight face. He looked at Miller and they both burst out laughing.

Lynn Miller appeared out of the crowd, looking beautiful in a blue satin gown, and firmly took her husband's arm. "I don't know what you two are giggling about, but Matt has a husbandly duty to perform."

"Right here? On the dance floor?" Miller got a cuff on the shoulder.

"I gave up on *that* years ago," Lynn said with a wink at Lee as she pulled her man into the jostle of bodies.

Soon afterward Mel Smythe and his wife began to make their farewells. Staff parties could be divided into three groups: the young party animals whose aim was to get drunk as quickly as possible, the older shoptalkers who drifted from table to table, repeating the same old stories, and a third group who always left early, seemingly embarrassed by it all. Lee ruefully acknowledged that he'd soon be relegated to the middle category, as he stood on the fringe of a group listening to Larry Wise. Wise even made his voice sound like a newscaster at parties, for God's sake.

"He was gay, you know. I worked with him in Swift Current."

"*Hobart?* He was a fucking Dan Rather, for shit's sake." A half-dozen beers hadn't helped Chuck Norwood's language.

"Oh, yeah. Had a boy-toy in Regina. A room at a hotel every Friday, too. Station contra'd it for him, for Christ's sake—it was in his contract."

The newsman shook his head. "He was cool, though. You couldn't break his concentration."

"Like lighting his news copy on fire?" Norwood asked. "I've heard that bullshit story about at least five people."

"No." Wise smiled. "We never tried that one on him. Although somebody did pull that on me at my first station in Smith's Falls. Burned all the hair off my goddamned fingers before I could empty the trash can and drop the papers in. Only about ten seconds of dead air, too, but I did have to cut straight to the weather." His audience chuckled on cue. "One thing I remember we did to Hobart… Lanny Smith was leaving to go to Lethbridge, I think… Hobart was taking his place. Anyway, Hobie had grown this little beard 'cause he thought it made him look older, and on his last day Smithy walks into the booth during the noon 'cast, pulls out a can of Foamy, and starts shaving Hobart right on the air, while Hobart's trying to read the obituaries! He went ballistic in the newsroom after, throwing stuff around and threatening to punch Smith out. But he never broke up on the air." Wise hoisted his beer in tribute.

One of the young reporters said "Wasn't it Smith they got with the stripper in Windsor?"

Wise nodded and swallowed a mouthful of brew. "Yeah, heh, Bud Borland and I got him with that one." He looked around at the uninitiated. "Borland and I hired this stripper for Smithy's birthday and sent her into the booth during the 8:00 o'clock 'cast. Big knockers, and before the days of silicone, too. She starts peeling and his eyes keep getting wider and wider but, God love him, Smith keeps on going. The sweat's breaking out on his face, and she's so close you can hear the mic bracket ring as she tosses her blouse onto it. Then just as he's going into Sports, off comes the bra and she waves these big beauties right in his face." Wise laughed and gulped more beer, pausing for effect. Norwood took the bait.

"So, what happened?"

"Well…" Wise looked thoughtful. "He probably would've made it, if he hadn't been doing the football scores: 'Houston over *Tits*burgh 38 to 24 to…38.'" The group roared. Even Lee joined in, although he'd heard the story a couple of times before. He knew it was mostly true, but Wise had picked it up second-hand and given it a better punch line.

"Try a stunt like that now and they'd can your ass," somebody said.

"Too fuckin' right," Wise nodded. Lee took that as a cue to drift away.

A scuffle in the corner of the room caught his attention, and he was surprised to see J.J. angrily shove his way through the crowd while Dan Arnott stood against the wall, looking sheepish.

"What was *that* about?" Lee asked him.

Arnott looked confused. "I was just trying to warn J.J. about Tracy. About the way she…strings guys along."

"Shit, Dan. How did you think he was gonna react? With her nearly falling out of that dress his balls are putting out hormones like Florida puts out orange juice. You want to talk to him, talk to him on Monday. Come to think of it, he's never gonna listen to that anyway, so save your breath."

"Little slut's like an animal in heat." Doug Rhodes slouched nearby with half of his shirt hanging out.

Lee glared at the man in disgust, then turned and walked away. He needed some air. In fact, he needed to go home. It was nearly midnight—later than he'd planned to stay. He'd call a cab then grab his coat.

As he stepped into the doorway of the dim cloakroom, a sound made him stop. A moan. Somebody was among the coats: a man with a beard—Barry Wright. Then the light glinted off strawberry-blond hair and green fabric. *Shelly Henderson*. Lee watched in dismay as a black bra strap slipped off a milky shoulder.

Goddammit. What now? Was he supposed to rush in and rescue the girl's virtue? It didn't look like she wanted rescuing, though she was probably too drunk to know what she was doing. He cursed again under his breath and began to back away. Then his mind formed a picture of the scene with his daughter Sarah instead of Shelley. In sudden inspiration, he thumped his fist against the wall, clattered some metal hangers together and bellowed thickly, "Where the fuck's my coat? Goddamn hotels oughta put some fucking lights in here!" He tugged his coat noisily off its hanger and stomped down the hallway. When he paused beyond a corner, he heard the girl run from the room. He slumped against the wall for a moment, then pulled his collar high and stepped out into the cold.

The light on his answering machine was flashing when he entered his apartment. He thought about ignoring it—the call of his bed was strong. But he gave a sigh and pushed the button.

It was Sarah.

"Daddy? I hope you hear this soon. A friend from school decided to visit her folks in the Soo for the weekend, so I tagged along. But we stopped for a break at a restaurant here in town, so if you call my cell before eleven, I'll stay with you instead and catch a ride back on Sunday. But she has to get going again by eleven. Are you home, Daddy? Call me."

Numbness gripped him as he looked at his watch. He called the number anyway, but all he got was her bored voice on the recording, asking him to leave a message. When the beep sounded his voice caught in his throat. There was nothing he could say—no way for words to fix what had happened. The phone tumbled free as he slumped to the floor.

He hadn't seen her since the summer, wouldn't see her again for God only knew how long. She'd be gone at Christmas and back at school right after.

He was too late. *Too goddamned late!*

He held his head in his hands and cried.

6

WHEN HE HEARD THE VOICE OF CANDACE ROSS on his voicemail Lee hoped she was calling to cancel their visit to Paul Schwartz. No such luck. She suggested he meet her at the CNIB office so they could travel to Paul's together. That would give her a chance to prepare him a little more. Lee suspected she was more interested in keeping control of the situation.

He had a vague memory of the yellow brick building on York Street. He knew it had once been a residence for blind people and a workshop too, but both of those had been closed down years ago. Now it offered a range of modern services for the visually impaired.

Candace Ross was waiting, buttoning up an expensive overcoat that had seen too many long winters. She gave a puzzled look at the briefcase he was carrying, then dismissed it.

"I'm out for the rest of the day, Clarisse," she said, tugging her thick collar straight, and pulling her hair free of it. The receptionist nodded, and Lee thought he caught a trace of a smile on her face. Probably wondering whether his appointment with Candace was business or pleasure. The question had crossed his mind too.

They took the CNIB van, decorated with logos of the national organization and the local Lions club. She drove with easy movements, but her face stayed stiff.

"Paul isn't just blind," she said, skipping the pleasantries. "He's an orphan. His parents were killed by a drunk driver...about two years ago now."

"I think I remember the story."

"Such a senseless tragedy. So he had some tough issues to deal with even before his accident with the baseball bat. Try to remember that. This is a kid who's suffered. He's good at hiding it, but nowhere close to being healed. I'm not sure he ever will be."

"Who does he live with?"

"An uncle. He's...well, with luck he won't be home." She left the remark unexplained. "Paul had everything going for him: a good student, a good athlete, lots of friends, a loving home...then so much was taken away from him within two years." She pressed a knuckle to the bottom of her nose for a moment. "I shouldn't say it like that. He's still got a lot of potential."

"You said he was injured by a baseball bat?"

She nodded. "Another inch lower and it might have killed him. There wasn't any actual damage to either eye, but within a few days he was totally blind. And I mean totally. Most people you would call blind actually have some vision...they might see movement out of the corners of their eyes, or blurred shapes. But Paul is in a world of total darkness."

"Could it reverse itself?"

"Spontaneously? It has happened, but you'd have better odds of winning the lottery. It's good to keep some hope, but not false hope. And people can compensate in ways that would amaze you. Paul's come a long way in the past few months. But I'm sure he could double his progress if I could just get him interested in something again.

Anything. That's why I brought him to you. He wondered if he could have a career in radio." She looked the question at Lee. "What do you think?"

"Seriously? I mean… it's been done." His shoulders lifted. "I remember there was a sportscaster who did colour commentary for one of the American baseball teams. But if you mean the kind of show I do… it'd be one hell of an uphill climb. So much of the job is reading. I know there are technical aids that can help with that, but frankly private companies wouldn't be willing to spend the money. Even the CBC probably wouldn't."

"That's what I thought. Let's keep that to ourselves for now, ok?"

"But these days he doesn't have to be a broadcaster. What about podcasts and audio blogs on the internet? Some of them are incredibly popular. I don't know if anyone makes a living at it yet, but by the time Paul enters the job market…"

"D'you really think so? Or is that just a way to let him down easy?"

"Didn't someone just tell me it's good to have hope?"

She pulled over in front of a semi-detached home of dull red brick and wood siding that showed at least twenty years of wear.

"Hi, Paul. It's Candace," she said as the door began to open.

"I know, I heard you come up the sidewalk. High heels." The boy looked pleased with himself. Now that he was aware of it, Lee could see that Paul's eyes didn't focus, but they still aimed at Candace's face. "Who's with you? A man, right? Those are a man's shoes."

"Hello, Paul."

"Lee Garrett!" A smile burst into view, but quickly dimmed. "What are you doing here?"

"I'm really sorry about what happened at the craft fair. I had a serious problem with the equipment and had to fix it right away. I should have… well anyway, I wanted to make it up to you."

The boy gave a knowing nod.

"Candace asked you, didn't she? It's ok. She thinks she's my mother." He hesitated, then abruptly stuck out his right hand, as if remembering the correct adult behaviour. Lee grasped the hand firmly and gave it one polite tug. The boy said, "Come on in."

A smell of breakfast and ashtrays hung in the air, as if vaporized bacon grease had permeated the carpets and upholstery. A secondary odour of unwashed laundry revived Lee's memories of college dorms.

The hallway's faded carpet might once have been blue, but was now a dirty grey shading to brown in the centre. Off-white walls bore the residue of cigarette smoke, darker near the ceiling. Even if Lee hadn't been told, he would have known that no woman lived here. The few shelves around the living room held only a sparse collection of sports or automotive magazines, some ashtrays, and an empty beer bottle.

"I hope the place isn't too much of a mess," Paul said. "Uncle Lenny leaves stuff lying around. Sometimes I trip over it. He's getting better, though. I asked him once about getting a housekeeper. He got pretty pissed at me." He hesitated. "Sorry. I shouldn't've said *pissed*."

Lee stifled a laugh and opened his briefcase on the lone bare patch of arborite on a nearby coffee table.

"I brought something for you. I hope you're a Blue Jays fan."

"Oh, yeah. What is it?"

With a nod from Candace, Lee took the boy's left hand and placed a CD in it.

"This is a CD called 'That Championship Season'. Heard of it?"

"Yeah! The Jays' 1993 season, right? Cool! Thanks!"

"Right. Tom Cheek and Gerry Howarth. It's got some great clips. A lot of the World Series, especially. I, uh, had an extra at the house. I hope you like it."

"Maybe we can listen to it together."

Lee laughed, and said, "*Maybe*." Candace's eyebrows looked to be telling him, 'Don't make promises you're not prepared to keep.' Lee just shrugged. He put his briefcase near the front door and laid his gloves on top. "What other things are you interested in, Paul?"

"Come on. I'll show you a new model I just finished."

Paul's room was like a Hollywood version of a boy's bedroom, with carefully placed sports equipment and plastic models of spaceships, but far too neat. In Lee's experience, a young boy dropped things wherever they lost his attention. Obviously piles of clothes or toys would be hazards to Paul Schwartz. But it took a moment for Lee to identify what was really wrong. The walls were a flat blue, with no posters or pictures, no *Star Wars* wallpaper. Even the comforter on the bed was a solid blue, not a picture of Adeiny Hechavarria diving for a hard line drive toward second base. The room felt incomplete. Even a boy without sight himself would want such things to show off to his friends.

"Look at this." Paul went straight to a shelf near the head of his bed and returned with a large model of the starship *Enterprise* from the 2009 *Star Trek* movie and its sequels. "I just finished this one. Cool, huh? Uncle Lenny only helped a little, when I couldn't tell what the part was supposed to be." He waited expectantly.

"Great job," Lee said sincerely. "When I was your age I would've smeared glue all over the place. You're a pro."

"I *love Star Trek*," Paul said. "You?"

Lee nodded, then realized with embarrassment that the gesture wouldn't be seen. "Yeah, since I was a kid. I had *Enterprise* blueprints all over my room."

"Cool."

The model was impressive, but it was like the room itself: barren. No paint, no decals. What was the *Enterprise* without NCC 1701 sweeping proudly across the saucer section? The rest of the models were the same: fighter jets without the Canadian Forces maple leaf; sports figures with unbranded uniforms; a racing car in the dull grey of the original plastic.

Paul wouldn't see the extra touches himself, but that was no reason to skip them. Lee felt it was another mark against the unseen uncle, but then he had a mental flash of the models in his son Jason's room. Some were painted but most were not. The required father-son time had been sacrificed to an increasingly hectic schedule. Maybe he wasn't in a position to throw stones.

"Mr. Garrett…?"

"Sorry. I was…somewhere else for a second, uh, remembering that I shouldn't really stay too long. I have things I have to do. Actually some Christmas shopping I haven't quite finished." *Hadn't started* was closer to the truth.

Candace's face closed like a fist. He looked quickly to Paul and saw the *Enterprise* model dangling from slack arms.

"That's ok, you can go. I know you're a busy guy. Why would you be interested in a kid's toy models?"

Lee took a deep breath and rubbed his temples. Hadn't he learned anything? "No, Paul. I am interested. My shopping's waited this long, it can wait a little longer." The change was abrupt, but the boy seemed willing to accept it. "Is there anything you want to know about radio? Do you listen a lot?"

"Yeah, sure. I listen all the time. Do you guys get to pick all the music you play?"

With a smile of relief the morning man fell into explanations he'd given dozens, maybe hundreds of times before. The strangeness of the surroundings faded, and there was just a man and a woman and a boy. The next time he checked his watch it was after five o'clock.

"I think Mr. Garrett and I will have to get going, Paul," Candace said for him.

"Aw, we didn't get to listen to the CD. Could you…?"

"Sure," Lee said. "I'll see you again. Maybe you can come and meet some of the people at the radio station."

The boy's normally expressionless eyes lit up. "Yeah. That would be *great!*"

Candace had begun to lead the way out of the room when they heard the sound of the front door closing, and a few scuffled steps. The noises stopped for a moment, and then there was a loud thump as if from a heavy object flung to the floor.

"Who's here? *Who the hell's here?*"

Paul's uncle appeared at the corner of the hallway. He was a few inches taller than Lee, with shoulders that would have been broad even without the quilted jacket he wore, but the arms and legs under the blue work clothes showed a wiriness rather than bulk. A heavy steel lunchbox had been thrown to the floor, and Lee's overcoat was clutched in a large hand. Crooked bottom teeth showed through thin lips as the man spoke again.

"*What the hell!* What are *you* doing here?"

Surprise flashed in the blue-grey eyes, but also something more: not just anger—a naked hostility. He turned on Candace Ross.

"Why did you bring *him* here? I never said you could bring people. What the hell were you thinking?"

She could only stare, shocked speechless.

"I invited him, Uncle Lenny. Don't be mad. I didn't think you'd mind." Paul pushed between the adults as if to offer his protection. A gutsy move. Hopefully it meant that Lenny Schwartz wasn't given to beating his nephew.

As if to confirm that, the man's fury began to cool. He looked down at the boy for several seconds, then pulled a faded baseball cap from his own head and flung it across the room.

"*Dammit*, Pauly. You gotta ask me first. It's my house, too, you know." The cold eyes shifted to Lee's face. "So you do notice the little people every once in a while, huh, Mr. Radio Star? Or was it a short *skirt* that changed your mind?"

Candace's mouth fell open and her hands went to the hem of her dress. Lee reached to take his coat from the man's hand, their eyes locked. "I had a nice visit, Paul. See you again soon." He had the satisfaction of seeing a smile on the boy's face as Candace led the way outside.

In the van they rode in silence. A few blocks away, he snapped straight and said, "*Shit!* We have to go back."

"*What? Go back there? Now?*"

"My briefcase. I left it there."

"Well, couldn't we…?"

"No. I need it for work. I can't do without it." His voice softened. "I'll go up to the door myself. You can stay in the van."

Lenny Schwartz had not used the time to comb his dishevelled hair. Nor had his voice gained any warmth.

"What do you want?" he asked, blocking the doorway with arms folded across his chest.

"My briefcase. It's right there, against the wall."

The man reluctantly gave a nod. Lee took a step inside and grabbed the handle of the case. His gloves had fallen behind it. He picked them up and went out the door. Neither man spoke, but Lee felt eyes on the back of his neck all the way to the van.

Candace stepped on the gas. Blocks away she turned her head to Lee and said "I'm sorry. I've never seen Mr. Schwartz like that before. So angry."

"Not your fault." He paused for a moment. "Obviously it was because of me. Working in radio…most people treat us like celebrities. Others figure we work five hours a day with our feet on the control board, a cup of coffee in one hand and counting all our money with the other. Of course they resent it."

"You mean it isn't like that?"

He snapped his head toward her, opening his mouth for a reply, before the grin on her face stopped him. They laughed.

"Paul really appreciated your visit. And so did I. Maybe I owe you a favour." The van pulled into the CNIB parking lot. "Who do you have to buy Christmas presents for? Or was that just an excuse?"

"My kids. Son and daughter. Teenagers."

"Not your wife?"

"*Ex*-wife. No, we don't exchange gifts anymore; insults only."

"Maybe I could help... if you want? I have a few more things I should pick up myself," she added quickly. "And it is almost time to eat."

"Great. That'd be... that'd be great." He bit his lip before he could say anything more feeble. The awkwardness forced them to laugh again.

They took separate cars to the Southridge Mall. Lee had invited her for a sit-down meal at a restaurant first, but she'd declined. She probably felt it would make the evening too much like a date. They ended up at moulded plastic tables in the food court eating Chinese food. The owner of the stand knew him and threw in extra egg rolls.

"There are some perks to the radio biz," Candace observed.

"Some."

As they were about to eat a woman in a loose dress appeared at Lee's shoulder. He smelled ketchup and alcohol when she leaned in, her neckline hanging indiscreetly open.

"Lee Garrett, remember me? At the Rotary dance last month. You had some pretty smooth moves." She gave Candace a smug smile then turned back to Lee, put a hand on his shoulder. The motion pushed her dress fabric out still farther; he could have read the brand of her bra.

"Sure. It's nice to see you...?"

"Marjorie. I knew you'd remember." Lee nodded but said nothing. After an expectant silence she said, "If you ever want to pick up where we left off, I work at the Stallion's Head pub. See you. Soon." She lazily dragged her hand free and sidled away with an exaggerated swing of her hips.

"Another *perk* of the job?"

"If you imagine I enjoyed that, yeah." Lee scowled. "We didn't even dance. I was the MC. The woman has a fertile imagination."

"None of my business."

"Speaking of business, how did you get into yours? Was there someone close to you who was blind?" When she didn't answer right away he raised a hand. "Sorry. It's personal, right? Forget I asked."

"No, it's ok. It's a natural question. It's just … well, my father lost his job when I was about nine. He was a proud man—he looked hard for work. But when he couldn't find any he began to spend more and more time in the bars. My mother tried to fight the loneliness with rye and ginger." She tried to pour some tea from the metal teapot and half of it spilled. With an apologetic look, she fumbled with some napkins to wipe it up. "Anyway, my family was self-destructing. I was a kid—I didn't understand, didn't know what to do.

"The day before Christmas Eve a couple from the Salvation Army came to our door with a Christmas basket of food and a few treats. Mother cried, but she didn't drink. Some people from the neighbourhood church came by and gave her something—it had to be money, because Christmas morning there were dolls for my sister and me under the tree. Daddy stayed home with us all that day, and the next. The first week of the new year someone from one of the service clubs in town found a job for Daddy, driving a delivery truck. It didn't pay much, but he came home to us at night. Tired, but smiling, and no beer on his breath."

She stopped speaking, and random noises rushed in to fill the gap: a frustrated toddler squawking at his parents, a bored cleaning boy scraping paper plates and cups off a table into a plastic tub on wheels. When Lee was sure there would be no more to the story, she raised her head.

"They gave me my family back, those people. We could never repay them. But I thought there might be … another way to give back."

Her eyes looked into his and what he read there was a revelation. Then the moment was gone and she laughed self-consciously. "Got more than you bargained for, huh?"

"No, no. Thanks for telling me."

"So how about you? How did you get into radio?"

He told her about being a class clown because his parents had to give their attention to his sister with cystic fibrosis; about thinking a radio career would make him a star, and still leave time for golf. About moving to six different cities within a dozen years. About filling in for a vacationing morning man and realizing he might have what it took to do a morning show after all.

"Except, I should have looked before I leapt."

"What does that mean?"

He tried for a casual smile. "It took over my life."

After an awkward moment he pushed back from the table and said, "Ready to do some shopping?"

She looked thoughtful as she grabbed her purse from the floor and carried her tray back to the Chinese food place. Lee had started to walk away from his, but went back for it.

On their way out of the food court a burly man in a poor-fitting suit caught Lee's eye and broke into a grin. The man's hands were full of parcels, but he stopped to introduce his wife, who was clearly uncomfortable meeting a celebrity while only dressed for shopping. After a bit of small talk Candace stepped forward and introduced herself. There was a quick exchange of Christmas wishes and Lee managed to pull away.

"How do you know them?"

"He's a listener. Runs a carpet business." He smiled. "I could tell you don't listen to CTBX. Listeners act like they've known us for years."

"Well, you're right. I usually listen to…what is it? The new one. The Wolf?"

"*Country* music? But I thought you were English."

She laughed. "What's that supposed to mean? My parents are English. I was born here. Anyway country music is big in Europe. Here too, actually. You shouldn't sneer at what you don't know."

Lee held up his hand as if to ward off a blow. "Ok, ok. I've run into big country fans before. I should've known what to expect."

"Where are we going, anyway?" she said, slowing her steps. "How old did you say your kids are?"

"Jason's thirteen, Sarah's fifteen."

"Did you have any ideas about what to get for them?"

"Not a clue." He gave an embarrassed shrug. "I never was any good at this." They were close to Zellers so he stepped toward the entrance.

"Hang on. What are you going to get them in there?"

"I don't know. Clothes, maybe? CDs? A baseball glove for Jase, or something like that."

"Do you know what sizes your daughter wears? Does *she* buy her clothes at Zellers?" His blank look gave her the answers. She asked what he knew about his children's interests and tastes. It embarrassed him to realize how little that was. Finally a mental picture of his daughter at the piano led him to find a book of show tunes from Broadway and the movies. Candace gave him an approving smile.

"So what about your son? What would he most like to do?"

The expression that came over his face caught her by surprise.

"Spend some time with me," he said quietly.

"Oh...Ok. Then give it."

"How do you gift wrap something like that?"

"Well, what kind of things did you like to do together? Camping? Fishing? Going to a hockey game?"

"Fishing. Jase always wanted us to take a fishing trip together."

"Then surprise him with some fishing gear and a gift certificate redeemable for one father/son fishing weekend. Make the date his choice, and *make sure you follow through*."

"Yes, ma'am. Whatever you say, ma'am." But his face removed the offence from the remark. The suggestion was a great idea.

While he'd been struggling to find two presents, she'd quietly picked up odds and ends for a half-a-dozen people or more. Standing in the checkout line, she found a small Toronto Blue Jays wall clock with the logo, hands, and numbers raised from the face. "For Paul," she explained needlessly.

Back in the mall concourse he said simply, "Thank you. I think Sarah and Jason will like this year's gifts. For a change."

She hesitated a moment, then asked, "What about...what about your ex-wife? You're not getting her *anything*? Not even for Christmas?"

Lee's expression hardened. "I play Santa Claus for her in a big way, once a month."

"Well, she does have to look after the children doesn't she?"

"So, naturally, since the man is always to blame in a divorce he should make it up to the woman somehow."

"Now wait a minute!" she snapped back, drawing looks from other shoppers. "You think men are the victims in a divorce?"

A victim was exactly how he felt. Especially now that the woman who'd promised herself to him forever had found someone else.

"Of course not. Everyone knows that women are the victims of the world. I'd beg for forgiveness, but I forgot my knee pads."

Her face turned livid, the lips pressed white.

"I was right about you the first time. You're the hollow centre of a shallow little world. I'd feel sorry for you but you already feel sorry enough for yourself." She spun around and began to walk away.

"It must be wonderful to be so perfect."

He thought her next step faltered but she kept going.

His eyes turned to the bags in his hands, then to the people nearby, conspicuously looking everywhere but at him. He willed his legs to move, and slowly they obeyed.

How had the night gone so wrong? He'd been enjoying the company of a woman, with no expectations or pressure. That hadn't happened in a long time. Now it was a shambles, sweet pleasure turned to poison. He searched his feelings for anger, resentment, indignation, but found none of them. There was only a numbness that swallowed him whole.

7

CHRISTMAS EVE THE SNOW BEGAN ON CUE, first with small flakes drifting lazily down and then thick clouds that clogged the air, defeating streetlamps and pushing garishly-primped houses into the hazy distance to transform the mundane street into a picture postcard. Lee let the curtain fall back into place and turned to face the empty apartment.

He didn't feel like washing the bowl from his festive dinner of canned stew, but there were still fifteen minutes until *A Christmas Carol* started on TV. He cranked the hot water tap and squirted a few drops of Palmolive into the sink. *The Muppet Christmas Carol* was on another channel, but he didn't want to watch that without Sarah and Jason. The grim black-and-white of the Alistair Sim version was a better fit for his mood. Complemented by a modest single malt and no-name potato chips.

He was looking for distraction. Instead the movie made him uncomfortable. He nearly got up to turn it off, but closed his eyes and just listened to the disembodied voices. Sleep claimed him before Scrooge could find redemption.

He awoke with daylight filtered through his favourite scotch glass, prisming bands of colour across his stained sweatshirt.

Fragments of a dream floated in his mind like dust motes in the air: a party scene, a lonely street, a graveyard, or maybe just an empty field, he couldn't be sure. He saw Michaela in a radio station, but not any of the places he'd worked, and then on the front porch of the home he'd lived in as a teenager, a house she'd never visited in reality. She was pulling at his sleeve, trying to explain something to him, pleading with him. He felt himself distracted for a moment, and then it wasn't Michaela but Candace Ross reaching her hands toward him in a dark field, with a wind whipping the branches of a willow around her head like wild strands of hair. She was looking at him, but couldn't see him, and his throat wouldn't work when he tried to call out to her.

Michaela and Candace? Ghostly Christmas Past and Christmas Present? No, the *Future*, he decided—the vision of Candace had no root in the here and now. He tried to remember any part of the dream that related to the present, but couldn't. It had no form. No *meaning*, was that it? His eyes came to focus on the wall clock, watching ten full jumps of the second hand before he pulled his gaze away. Ticking, marking nothing. He groaned, and swung himself upright, his left foot coming down to crush the potato chip bag.

He had no plans for the day. Christmas Day. He'd almost asked Arnott to schedule him for work, but to admit he had no one with whom to share the holiday was a confession of failure he couldn't bring himself to make.

A lot of snow had fallen during the night, maybe eight or nine inches. Normally the landlady's son came to shovel the driveway after a storm, but he'd taken her to a relative's place out of town for Christmas. Lee put on his parka and boots. He knew where she kept the snow shovel. The exercise would do him good.

The simple exertion swept his mind clean of other thoughts for a time. The snow had stopped but it was cold—a light breeze made his face tingle. The muted echo of someone else shovelling out of sight down the street reassured him that he wasn't the only one not opening presents around a glittering tree. When the job was done, he walked over to the older couple's driveway next door and shovelled that too. Afterward he stood for a few minutes blowing clouds of steam into the air while he admired his handiwork: the neat lines of the new snowbanks, the sparkle of sun off tiny crystal surfaces whose sharpness would soon melt and reflect no more. And the very particular pale blue of the sky near the horizon that meant winter and no other time. He seldom stopped to notice such things anymore.

When he went inside, the TV was about twenty minutes into *White Christmas* with Bing Crosby and Danny Kaye. Together with Rosemary Clooney and (what was her name? He'd used it as a trivia question once) Vera Ellen, they'd just finished singing about "Snow" on the train to Vermont, and then disembarked to find there wasn't any snow. He'd always told Michaela it was a sappy movie, and wondered if she'd noticed that it was always Lee who tuned it in every year.

He microwaved some soup for lunch. Dozed a little after that. It was a way to slip out of the stream of meaningful time, without having to acknowledge the emptiness of his waking hours.

He was idly flipping TV channels, looking for another movie, when Michaela called from Florida.

"The kids and I thought we...I mean, we wanted to wish you a Merry Christmas." Her voice sounded unsure. "I'm glad we caught you at home."

Instead of *Where the hell else would I be?* he said, "Merry Christmas to you, too. Uh...how's the weather? We've got some new snow."

"No snow here." She gave a weak laugh. "It's not quite warm enough to swim today, but sunny. It doesn't feel like Christmas without snow. But Disney World goes all out—the kids have been enjoying that. Today…well, actually I was just watching *White Christmas*. Nobody else wanted to. Sappy movie, but…you know."

His throat tightened and he had to hold the phone away from his face. When he brought it back Michaela was saying, "Lee? Are you there?"

"I'm still here."

She paused at the sound of his voice, then pressed on. "Are you going anywhere for Christmas?"

"Um…actually Matt and Lynn Miller asked me to come over. I'm going to start getting ready soon."

"Oh, good." She didn't call him on the lie—a gift in itself. "Say hi to them for me. Would you like to talk to Sarah?"

"You bet." He took advantage of the pause to cover the phone and clear his throat.

"Daddy…?"

"Hi, Sweetheart. Merry Christmas."

"Merry Christmas to you, too. I…I guess Mom told you how warm it is here…." Her voice trailed off as if she'd already run out of things to say.

"Listen, Sarah. The night you came into town…I'm really sorry I missed you, Sweetheart. Our staff Christmas party was that night and I just got home too late. I tried calling your cell, but…"

"That's ok, Daddy. You don't have to explain."

"I *do* have to explain. I would…a hundred times rather have been with you that night. It drives me crazy to have you guys so far away. But your mother… Well, anyway…."

"I know, Daddy. I miss you, too. We'll…we'll get together sometime soon. But I better let you talk to Jase." She passed the phone without waiting for a reply.

"Hi, Dad." His son's voice sounded older than he remembered.

"Hi, Jase. Merry Christmas."

"Yeah, Merry Christmas. Uh…one of these days you're going to have to try this place over Christmas, Dad. It's pretty cool."

"I'm glad." And he was. "I've got presents for you and Sarah but I'd rather not mail them."

"Yeah, well, Mom says she's going to bring us over when we get back. She's waving that she wants to talk to you again. Anyway, have a good Christmas, Dad."

"You, too." The silence was like a hole. Then Michaela came back on the line.

"Lee? I was thinking I'd bring Jason over to stay with you on Tuesday, if that's all right. Sarah's got a ski trip with some friends that they've planned for months. Is that ok?"

"Sure, Tuesday would be fine. Tell…tell Sarah to have a good time. I guess we'll see each other one of these days."

"Yeah, we'll figure something out." Silence returned—there was nothing to say and too much to say. "I guess I'd better let you go."

"Michaela?"

"Yes."

"Have a good Christmas."

"You, too."

"No, Michaela. I *mean* it."

Her voice softened. "I do, too, Lee. See you soon."

He sat there listening to the dial tone for twenty seconds, then slowly returned the phone to its cradle.

Whether it was from optimism or masochism, he couldn't be sure, but that night he communed with the spirits of Christmas Past. The Garrett household of years gone by, in grainy VHS images transferred to DVD so Michaela could keep the original tapes: frenetic figures swimming through a sea of discarded wrapping paper; a flash of Jason's face filling the lens, the camera pulling back to reveal a pewter set of

"Dragonquest" figurines; Sarah holding a white smocked dress to her chest, then waving a plastic-covered tray of multicoloured patches— her first makeup kit, purchased over Lee's objections because he couldn't bear for his little girl to grow up.

Michaela made a face of pretended annoyance and held up a hand to block the camera. Her hair was dishevelled—she wore no makeup. A close-up even revealed faint lines where the pillow had creased her skin overnight. His heart ached for her.

He pressed the stop button and sent the machine into fast forward, then randomly punched play to see what would be revealed.

Fathers' Day the next year. Not for the first time—but ultimately the last—Sarah and Jason had hidden his present and concocted a treasure hunt with a trail of clues on scraps of paper. "Time Flies" meant the next clue was hidden under an old wooden duck with a clock in its belly. "For The Record" sent him looking under the cover of the dusty turntable still taking up space in the entertainment unit. Then, just as the Lee on the TV screen was about to discover the first part of his present, he remembered it vividly: a bulky white sweatshirt that boldly proclaimed, "World's Greatest Dad".

The room closed in on him, the edges of his vision turning grey. He stumbled to the door and pitched to his knees in the snow, sucking lungfuls of icy air.

He couldn't fall asleep that night. Hell, he hadn't done anything all day. His eyes drifted slowly around the room and came to rest on a flash of gilded lettering on the spine of a small book. He stepped to the shelf. It was *The Princess Bride* by William Goldman, Michaela's favourite book—how could she have overlooked that? He'd have to give it back to her on Tuesday.

He lay the book on the dinner table, so he wouldn't forget, but the front cover flipped open and he found himself reading in spite of himself.

Sometime during the night he drifted off to sleep with visions of princesses, swordplay, and right and wrong as clear as black and white.

⁓

He was glad to be back at work on Boxing Day. He made a lot of wordplay involving the station's call letters CTBX "The Box". You didn't pass up an opportunity like that.

After 8:00 o'clock he asked listeners to call in with their favourite Christmas memories. Software let him record the calls and edit them before playing them back as if they were 'live'. The phones were slow—most people had better things to do—but each call triggered more, and many of the stories were heart-warming. People were often broke at Christmastime, but cash windfalls would arrive in surprising ways. Loved ones would unexpectedly return from war to show up on a doorstep Christmas morning. Romance would blossom, old friendships would be rekindled. They were stories that propagated the mythology of Christmastime, but you wanted to believe them.

He didn't air a call from a woman in a nursing home.

"My first Christmas here everyone came," she said. "My son, my daughters... their families. They said I needed the nurses to watch me, so they couldn't take me home. But at least they came." Her voice quavered. "Last year my children came, but none of their children, and not for long. I know I haven't looked so good lately. I lost weight here." She paused again—Lee simply waited. "This was my third year... my third Christmas, and... *nobody came.*" He heard her break into tears. "No one at all. I suppose they thought I didn't know what day it was. Maybe they'll come today. Do you think so?"

He hesitated. "That's probably it. I'm sure they will."

He let her talk until she ran down and her tears stopped. Then she softly thanked him for his kindness and hung up.

He felt like a coward for not playing the call. Instead he just reminded listeners to think of shut-ins and others who might be lonely at Christmas. It was a cop-out, but only the latest in a long line.

Unbidden, a line from a Gilbert O'Sullivan song came to his mind, about all the broken hearts in the world that could never be mended, left unattended.

He fielded another couple of calls that were barely worth airing, then the phone lines went quiet for a while and he was content to leave it that way. He played more songs and talked less, pacing himself to last the extended holiday shift until noon.

After 9:00 o'clock he got a call from Doug Rhodes on location at a Boxing Day sale in Espanola. The nearby town was too far to use the remote transmitter, so Rhodes did the report by phone line.

Some time later the phone flashed again.

"G'morning. Is that you, Lee?"

"It's me."

"Oh, good. Merry Christmas, Lee. Did you have a great Christmas?" The woman's voice was fuzzy. Maybe she'd just woken up, or had some kind of speech impediment.

"Sure. How about you?"

"Could've been better. Didn't do many Christmassy things. Don't have anybody to do them with this year. How about you? You're not married anymore are you?"

"Uh…. No. Not anymore." *Why the hell would she ask that?*

"Nobody should be alone at Christmas. Hey, maybe we should get together. What do you think?"

He'd identified the sound of her sloppy sibilants. The woman was drunk. At 9:30 in the morning. "I've seen you lots of places," she said. "You're cute. People say I look a lot like Elizabeth Taylor…lots of womanly curves in the right places. Maybe you could play Santa Claus and stuff a big *present* up my *chimney*." She broke into a wicked laugh.

Lee felt a shudder, but tried to keep his tone light.

"That's very flattering," he began, "but I've got plans..."

"Oh, come on," she interrupted. "I'll bet a healthy man like you could use a long ride in a good saddle. And I am good. When do you get off work?"

God, no. She might wait outside the building.

"Today, not 'till one o'clock. Maybe later."

"What about tonight? A hot woman sure beats a cold bed." The husky whisper was full of yearning. Pathetic. *But also attractive? Was his body really responding to it?*

"I've got to go. I hope you find someone. Have a good holiday."

He broke the line before she could say anything more, then leaned back and wiped a hand slowly down his face.

Mother of God, was that was his life had come to? Was it just an alcoholic fantasy, or was the woman responding to some need she'd heard in his voice? Which of them was the pathetic one then?

He slowly sat forward and something on the control board nagged for his attention. The volume slider for the phone. *It was a quarter of the way up and switched on.* He slapped it hard, like swatting a wasp. His throat went dry. He must have left it there after Rhodes' cut-in. Ice water ran down his spine. *Could the drunk woman's call have got on the air?*

The phone line was flashing again. Rhodes? Or her calling back?

"Good morning, CTBX."

He was relieved to hear a man's voice on the other end. "Yeah... uh, what I was wondering was... if you guys might have another radio station breaking in on you?"

Alarm bells.

"Why would you think that?"

"Well, I was just listening to that last song, and I heard something in the background. Voices. I'm not sure but I thought I made out the name 'Santa Claus' and... I don't know. One of the voices sounded kinda like you, though." A hint of accusation. He'd heard more than he was letting on. Lee felt a prickling under his arms.

"Huh. I didn't hear anything here," he said. "But I was out of the room for a minute. Sometimes a two-way radio from a taxi or something else close by can get picked up by a radio receiver. That happens to our monitor system all the time." That part was true, but the fragments of speech rarely lasted more than seconds. "Probably something your radio picked up."

"Well…it sounded more like a phone conversation." There it was: he knew what he'd heard and was trying to draw Lee into a confession.

"I'll keep an ear out, just in case. But thanks for calling. Have a Happy New Year."

"Sure. Ok. You, too." The man gave in and hung up. Lee let out a long sigh of relief and realized he had a case of the jitters. Not from caffeine. A phone call like that, unintentionally put on the air, could be the end of a career.

～

Noon finally came, and he carefully scanned the parking lot through a window. No sign of the drunk woman, or anyone else. He was about to leave when he heard someone call his name.

"How's it hanging, my friend?" Vernon Anishwabek hosted an alternative jazz show on Z104 Sunday nights. His deep voice matched a slow smile that creased the edges of dark brown eyes.

"It's hangin' kind of dejectedly, Vern. Not enough action lately."

"I thought you white guys' peckers just always looked like that." The two men burst into laughter.

Anishwabek appeared to be in his fifties, but it was hard to be sure. His shiny hair was at least half-grey, pulled neatly back into a ponytail, and his face was deeply-lined in places. He was a professor of Native Studies at Laurentian University, but Lee had never seen him in anything but blue jeans and loose-fitting shirts with hand-woven vests. Yet his almost-new pair of Nike Airs didn't seem out of place either.

"You got time to shoot the shit? I was just heading for the Prod studio to get my show together."

"Sure, yeah." It wasn't as if Lee had anywhere to go. They sauntered down the hall.

"You have a good Christmas?"

Lee hesitated. He'd never been less than honest with Vern. There was something about the man—you could tell him things. But bullshit would make him walk away without another word. Lee had seen it happen.

"Pretty shitty, actually. Michaela went to Florida with the kids—and her boyfriend."

"That sucks. If I'd known, you could've had dinner with us."

"You have a big turkey dinner and all that?"

"No, actually I go out and shoot a bear. Then after I've dragged it back to our lodge and Sheila has given the hide a good chew…"

Lee held up a hand and laughed. "Ok, ok. The truth is, I thought you were *Jewish*."

Anishwabek roared. "Hey, you're a funny guy. I just might start listening to your show one of these years."

The laughter was like a tonic. Before he knew it, Lee had spilled his guts about Michaela, the loneliness, and even about the hate letter and the incidents since then. Anishwabek listened as if the studio had become a shrink's office. His manner somehow massaged the quiet into a zone of comfort instead of a barrier.

"Have you ever talked to Michaela about the break-up of your marriage? Ever told her you're still in love with her?"

"It wouldn't bring her back to me."

"That's not really my point. You've got separate lives, now. But you used to say she was the best thing that ever happened to you. Is that no longer true, because you're divorced?"

Lee slowly shook his head. "No, it's still true."

"Then you don't toss away one of the best things that ever happened in your life, my friend. Tell her how you feel. Find a way. Bring each other some joy instead of pain."

Lee didn't say anything and Anishwabek was content to let the silence stretch, shuffling some papers and tapping at the computer keyboard. Finally he said, "What did you do about the hate letter?"

"Told the cops about it. They weren't interested."

"Most of 'em are good heads. A few are pricks. But even the good ones are overworked."

"Might have been that. I don't know what else I can do, though. I've never been threatened before."

"Yeah, it's a bitch. Maybe you'll believe that I know a bit about racists." He gave a sad smile and paused to choose his words. "Imagine you've got a hole in your gut—an ulcer that sucks the pleasure out of life. Could be from a bad upbringing, abuse…could be just that you want what others have and you can't get it. Then one day it occurs to you that all of your problems are caused by someone *else*. Suddenly, all the regret you ever felt can be blamed on that one group. Those people have what you want, therefore they must have taken your share. You become obsessed with that thought—it becomes a fire in your belly, and every bad thing you draw to yourself is fuel." He let the image hang in the air. Then his voice became still softer. "No logic to it. And no cure either."

Lee looked into his friend's eyes. "No cure. So once they start, they don't stop. Sounds like you're saying I should make up with Michaela and get the kids back into my life before something happens to me."

The other man hesitated, and then rumbled, "Life's too short, my friend. Life's too short."

8

"Now there's Florida the way I remember it." Lee tossed a photograph back across the table to land in front of Michaela.

It was a bus window view of a flat and featureless landscape flanking one of the highways in the Orlando area. Lee had been to Orlando once, on his way to Cape Canaveral. The airport was scenic, with aircraft taxiways that circled around ponds and marshes and over highway lanes, but the highways from there to the coast offered little but scrub growth and swampland.

The crease in Michaela's face didn't quite make it into a smile.

"The area around Disney World is gorgeous, and you know it."

The Disney World photos looked like every picture he'd ever seen of the place, except the tourists posing beside the costumed characters and famous attractions wore faces he knew. No shots of Robert Farrell, though. Michaela would have removed those. There was no hiding the man's presence—someone had to have taken the pictures. Michaela hadn't wanted to show them to Lee at all; Jason had insisted. Then the boy quickly lost interest, as if sharing the experiences wasn't what he cared about, only seeing Lee's reaction to them.

Some kind of punishment? Lee wondered. He made a point of showing more enthusiasm about the pictures than he really felt, to please Michaela.

"Damn. I almost forgot the Christmas presents."

Jason had a bemused look as he opened the individually-wrapped bits of fishing tackle and read the home-printed gift certificate.

"That's great, Dad. D'you mean it?"

"Of course I mean it. Let's make it a canoe fishing trip—kill two fish with one stone."

Michaela insisted that whatever dates they chose, she'd work around it. She was also impressed with the music book for Sarah—Lee could see it in her eyes, though she was careful not to imply criticism of his past gifts.

Maybe the kids weren't the only ones growing up.

The cold cuts and fresh bakery buns he'd picked up for lunch went uneaten—Michaela and Jase had stopped at McDonald's on the way. His morning spent trying to make the apartment as presentable as possible was probably a waste too. Michaela's mere presence made the ancient rooms look shabby.

He couldn't persuade her to stay for a dinner of Kentucky Fried Chicken—one of Jason's favourites. She needed to help Sarah get ready for her ski trip.

Once, when Jason was in the bathroom, Lee almost told her about the hate letter and the vandalism. She would have given him sympathy, but that was a poor substitute for what he really needed from her, and could never have again.

He walked her out to the car through a light snowfall.

"Thanks for coming, Michaela. It's been…nice. Just because I screwed up doesn't mean we have to be at each others throats the rest of our lives. That would make all of our time together a mistake, and it wasn't that. Was it?"

"No, Lee, it wasn't." She gave a tentative smile. "I don't know what's different this time, but I'm glad I came. Take care of yourself." She leaned forward and brushed his cheek with her lips.

"You, too. Drive carefully."

As the car rolled down the street he caught a flicker of movement in the window of the apartment. Had Jason seen the goodbye kiss? It would be best if he didn't get his hopes up.

≈

Jason was a zombie in the studio the next morning, endangering his jaw muscles with the force of his yawns, even overcoming his dislike of coffee. When 9:00 o'clock came Lee teased, "You look like you could use a little nap."

"Yeah, well I've heard that you don't need as much sleep when you get *old*."

"I heard that, too. I'm still hoping it comes true."

The station's sales and copy departments were closed over the holidays so there weren't any commercials for Lee to record. While he was packing his show materials away in his locker, Jason reached into Lee's briefcase and picked up a small spray bottle of concentrated breath freshener.

"Gee, Dad. You in the habit of sneaking babes into the booth with you, or what?" He tossed the bottle in his palm. "Morning men got to fight *morning breath*?" He shot a few squirts in Lee's direction as if to ward off an offending bug.

"Listen, smart ass." Lee took a grinning step toward him with palm outstretched. "I have to go to a lot of special…" He choked off in mid-sentence as his nostrils recoiled in shock. His throat suddenly felt on fire and his eyes streamed tears.

"Dad, what's wrong? Dad *what is it?*"

The boy's frightened hands grabbed his shoulders, but Lee tugged away, sliding along the counter, coughing convulsively. He stumbled to a chair and hung over the back of it, then fumbled in his pocket for a Kleenex to wipe the fluid from his nose and lips.

Jason's voice began to penetrate the fog of shock, and through a watery blur Lee saw the panic in his son's face.

"Dad! You all right? Do you need an ambulance?"

"Ok..." He waved a hand through the air, his voice a harsh croak, "I'll be ok...in a minute."

He blew his nose again and leaned weakly on his knees. Then he slowly straightened, blinking hard and dabbing at his eyes with a fresh tissue. The acrid odour spoke of scrubbed floors, hospital stair wells...

Someone had filled his breath spray bottle with bleach.

Numbed, he leaned on the edge of the desk, not trusting his legs.

Poison. Corrosive poison.

If Jason hadn't discovered it by mistake, Lee would have sprayed the stuff right into his mouth. The thought made him gag again, and he hung his head over the trash can for a couple of minutes.

"What'd I do, Dad? Was it the bottle? I thought it was breath spray. God, Dad. *I just thought it was breath spray!*"

"It's ok, Jase. It's ok. Not your fault. I...I used one of these bottles at home for some bleach. To spray mildew and stuff. Guess I must've accidentally switched them." It hurt like hell to talk, and it hurt to lie, but the truth...he couldn't burden the boy with that. "Stupid of me. I'll get rid of it when we get home." He fished a discarded plastic bag out of the trash and wrapped the bottle in it, then put it in his briefcase. Maybe there'd be fingerprints. Something.

Jason was too relieved to see the holes in the story.

"Man, if only I hadn't sprayed it at you..."

"No way. No way you could've known. Anyway, you might have saved me from something even worse."

"You should see a doctor."

"No, I'm ok now. I'm fine." But when he saw the look on his son's face, he said, "All right. Just give me a minute in the bathroom."

He flushed his eyes with running water and rinsed his mouth and throat the best he could, then got a drink from the water cooler. He was half afraid that it would make him vomit, but he was spared the pain of that.

The hospital ER doctor cleared him of any serious damage, but warned him to come back if the cough didn't go away.

Lee left most of their pizza dinner untouched, and found it hard to concentrate on the Batman movie they watched afterward. The irony of the choice wasn't lost on him. Hollywood loved the myth of the vigilante: the crime victim who turned into an avenging demon, exacting violent justice upon his persecutors. Life wasn't like that— victims felt fear, shame, helplessness. Were forced to face the fragility of their small lives. Knew themselves for cowards.

Vengeance delivered at the point of a gun was the stuff of adolescent fantasy. An adult knew better. It was a sign of maturity to know your limits—to accept reality. At least that's what you told yourself in the dark silence of the night.

~

His throat was still so raw the next morning that it hurt to talk. His hand shook as he reached for his small bottle of Chloraseptic, hoping it would numb the pain. He tested it three times into the air before he could bring himself to spray it into his mouth.

After the show he dropped Jason off at the bus station. That brought him a different pain.

"Give Sarah my love, ok? I guess she's really busy."

"Yeah. Especially now she's got a boyfriend."

"*What?* She never mentioned that."

"Well, he really likes her, but she's mostly too busy for him."

God, Lee thought, that story was painfully familiar. Should he say something to his daughter? Would she even welcome fatherly advice? Or was it already too late?

"There's no need to tell your mom about the breath spray. I'll be all right. She doesn't need any more reasons to think I'm a klutz."

"She doesn't think you're stupid, Dad," Jason replied. "She just says you've never really known what you wanted." The boy went up the stairs and disappeared down the aisle.

Lee stood there long after the bus had gone.

⁓

"You might have *died* if you'd sprayed that stuff down your throat."

Maddy Ellis's eyes were white circles. She brushed a hand slowly through her hair. "Jesus. Harassment is one thing. We're talking about attempted murder here."

"They might still have been trying to scare me ... figured I'd notice the smell before I actually sprayed it into my mouth."

"Bullshit. You're calling the police and you're not taking No for an answer. I'll call a staff meeting. Get everyone watching for strangers in the building. I can't believe any of our people could be involved."

"I don't know what to believe anymore."

He left her staring into space and went to find a phone, hoping he'd reach a more helpful cop.

"You say you called before, Mr. Garrett?" The woman repeated the date he'd mentioned, and he heard the tapping of a keyboard. "There's no record of that call."

"Well, would there be? I mean, he took down a few details at first, but it didn't go any further. Would he have kept a record of that?"

"We're supposed to keep a record of all incoming calls from the public. Certainly any calls that might involve a crime. Are you sure...?"

"Of course, I'm sure. Look. Can you patch me to the Chief's line?"

"I'm certain there's no need to bother the Chief, Mr. Gar..."

"I'm not looking to get you into trouble, officer. You've been helpful. I know the Chief personally. I'd like to speak to him, please."

There was a long hesitation, then a click...

"Good morning, Chief Gavin's office."

"Morning, Janie. It's Lee Garrett. Has your hand recovered from the Big Brothers bowling night? You mashed it pretty hard, as I recall."

"Lee, hi. Oh it's fine. Bowling balls and my skinny fingers don't make a good combination. Were you looking to speak to the Chief? He's on another line.... Oh, he's just hung up. I'll put you through."

The booming voice of Art Gavin came on the line.

"Lee, how the hell are you? Haven't drained any bars dry since the Big Brothers thing, I hope. You know I can't arrange bail."

Lee laughed. After shooting the breeze a bit, he told his story.

"Jesus, Lee. That's assault causing bodily harm—and maybe even attempted murder." The Chief's chummy tone vanished and he was all business. "And you say there's no record of your first call? Just a minute. I'll have Janie get me the shift schedule." He came back on the line after little more than a minute. "Yeah, I thought it might have been a trainee," he said. "But one of my sergeants was supervising. A man named Fred Dieter. He should have caught that."

Fred Dieter. That explained a lot. A helluva lot.

"I don't know what to say, Chief. Dieter and I aren't exactly the best of friends."

"What do you mean? You and Dieter? Oh, shit, yeah. Now I remember." His voice took on a harder edge. "You made the man look like quite an asshole. He probably deserved it, but I don't like any of my men..."

"I know, Chief, and I'm sorry. I'm sure Dieter is still pissed at me. Can't even say I blame him."

"That's no excuse for him to stonewall you. I'll have to bring him into the office."

"Please don't do that. Maybe he was right when I called the first time. It was only a threat, and I didn't even have the note anymore. The other things...well, they could have been coincidences." If the cop got another reprimand, he might really want to cause Lee some grief.

"I appreciate that, Lee, but he not only acted on a grudge, he involved one of my younger officers. I can't let that go. In the meantime I'll send one of my detectives over to see you. Tomorrow ok?"

"Thanks, Chief. I really appreciate the help."

"Call me Art. And if you have any more problems with the department, call me directly. But Lee? Be careful. Sudbury isn't the sleepy town it used to be."

~

He'd just finished reading the last commercial script of the morning when Mel Smythe told him he'd been paged to the lobby. Probably the detective, he thought, and realized that his hands were sweaty, his mouth dry. He felt like a schoolboy called to the Principal's office.

There was a blond-haired woman in a severe suit studying the Lee Garrett cardboard cut-out, but no cop that he could see. He leaned over the reception desk to get Karen's attention. She finished transferring a call and said, "Detective Davis is here to see you." She pointed behind him.

"Mr. Garrett?" the blond woman asked, extending her hand. "I'm Detective Sergeant Davis."

Lee finally reacted and shook her hand. "Uh...thanks for coming, Detective. Sergeant."

"Yes, I am a woman, Mr. Garrett." Her mouth turned slightly upward but it transmitted no warmth to the eyes. "Is that a problem for you?"

He sighed. "No, Detective Davis, that is not a problem. Yes, I was expecting a man, but I think we've got more important things to discuss, don't you?"

She didn't answer right away. "Where can we speak privately?"

"This way."

The boardroom wasn't being used, so they chose one end of the long table. As Lee closed the door Davis opened her briefcase to pull out some forms and a small digital sound recorder.

"Normally a uniform officer would be doing this with a video camera. You're getting special treatment," she said.

"Consider me flattered. Is that the Chief's doing?"

"I'd prefer to think that the case was bumped up to CID because of the combination of serious vandalism *and* a threat against your life." She must have seen the blank look on his face. "Criminal Investigations Department. The detective division."

He nodded, she switched on the recorder, and he went through the whole ordeal one more time. It was uncomfortable, but her approach was thoroughly professional, and he felt his confidence rise.

His first impression had placed her as ten years younger than himself, but a closer inspection revealed the lines traced by life. Straw-blond hair, cropped short, framed a face that was slightly too square to be really pretty, but then she wore no makeup. The drab suit didn't hide the fact that she was in excellent shape, with a well-proportioned figure. Her best feature was a pair of clear blue eyes crested by long, pale lashes and set off by eyebrows that were a shade or two darker than her hair. It was a striking combination. There was a plain gold band on her left hand, the only jewellery he could see.

He realized that he'd gone from resentment to an appraisal of this police officer as a potential bedmate. She would not be amused.

"Was anyone's job affected when you started the morning show?"

"Doug Rhodes filled in for a month or so after the last morning host moved away, and I know he wanted to keep that time slot. They hired me instead. But he wouldn't pull something like this."

"I'm not pointing a finger at anyone, but obviously the people who work in this building had the greatest opportunity to leave the note and tamper with your things. What about your competitors? Could they want you out of the way that badly?"

"Enough to kill me?" Lee's laugh had a bitter edge. "Not anymore."

"What do you mean by that?"

"I mean, when I came to town I knocked Ron Wayne at CMOR off his throne and they've never been the same. Now? Let's just say I'm not the king of the hill either."

"Maybe they still blame you."

"Look somewhere else, Detective. When people say radio is a cut-throat business, they don't mean it literally. Why aren't you asking more about the Skins? It seems obvious that the note was from them."

"Does it? I don't think there's any established connection at all, except that whoever did write the note had heard your joke on the air. This young man at the United Way luncheon. Van Horne. Did he strike you as a gang member?"

"I don't really hang with enough gang members to know."

"Do you have a problem with me, Mr. Garrett? Would you prefer to deal with someone else?"

"I … no, Detective. Sorry. This whole thing is getting on my nerves, and I guess I just don't see where all of your questions are leading."

"They're leading in the direction of whoever tried to hurt you. By eliminating the wrong directions."

He looked into her eyes for a moment, then nodded. "All right. What else do you want to know?"

"Do you owe anyone any money?"

"Only the bank. I don't think I actually own anything anymore—they just let me use it."

"No large gambling debts?"

"No one would let me near a game. Don't buy into the myth that radio pays big bucks. Not here, it doesn't."

"Not in this company?"

"Not in a city this size. It's the myth that everybody believes: we work five hours a day and get paid like movie stars."

"Not true?"

"Not even close. Sure, in cities like Toronto a difference of a few share points in the ratings can mean thousands, even millions of dollars in revenue. So they pay big money to their stars. For everybody else, it's supply and demand. Everybody thinks they can be a radio jock. Some people take college courses for it, only to find out there are hardly any jobs. So they either give up on the dream or they swallow their pride and accept a pathetic paycheque. Even with years of experience you don't have a lot of bargaining power when there are dozens of people begging to take your job for less money. Veteran miners and teachers make more than I do."

"You're not serious."

"I don't find it funny enough to joke about." His face spoke as clearly as his words. "Anyway, if I owed money, wouldn't a little note with a picture of a baseball bat be a simpler means of persuasion?"

"Are you married?"

"Speaking of bats? No. Divorced."

"Difficulties with any women recently? Or one night stands?"

"You mean something like *Fatal Attraction*?"

"You'd be surprised how often broken relationships turn into harassment, or stalking. It's certainly a whole lot more common than individual problems with street gangs."

"But most people don't call gang members morons on air."

"I'll ask our Intelligence Unit about the Skins." She checked her notes. "The Forensics Identification Unit would have gone over your car, but since it's been repainted ..."

"I couldn't keep driving it that way."

She nodded. "The FIU will check this spray bottle for fingerprints, too. I need to take your prints now, so they can be eliminated from the findings. And do you have anything with your son's prints on them?"

"The coffee mug he was using should still be in the control room. I'll get it. Don't worry, I'll only touch the inside."

When he returned with the mug Davis put it in a plastic baggie and set it in her case beside the breath spray.

"Not much to go on," Lee said.

"We'll send the bottle to the Centre for Forensic Science in Toronto to be analysed. Maybe it's more than bleach. We might get lucky."

He sensed the interview was at an end, and as he stood to open the door he said, "The answer to your question is 'No.'"

"Pardon me?"

"No relationships. No one night stands. Nothing." Then he realized how pathetic it sounded. She was already walking up the hallway.

He held the outside door for her and said, "Do you have a first name, Detective?"

"Cheryl."

"Well, thanks for coming. And for your thoroughness. I'm grateful."

She nodded. "Maybe we're not all *incompetent*, Mr. Garrett." Then she turned and walked to her car.

She'd wanted him to know she remembered Fred Dieter's humiliation at his hands. Was she also saying she was on Dieter's side—that the badge made them kin? That he shouldn't expect any real help? He hoped that wasn't true. He'd sensed an integrity and intelligence in her, even as she'd sparred with him. If she gave him the runaround too, he didn't know where else to turn.

She'd also stirred up some unwelcome thoughts about his relationships with women over the past couple of years. There weren't many, and only two had lasted longer than one date. One of those was a lawyer, the other a director of a local charity.

Then there was Maddy Ellis.

A one night stand in a sexual sense. What if her husband Ray had found out about them? No, that was ludicrous. If he could suspect Maddy or Ray, then anyone was a suspect.

But then, maybe that was the problem.

9

THE LAST DAY OF A SHITTY YEAR.

He'd spent the morning show doing the traditional look back at the city's big news stories of the year and taking a few listener calls about the highlights in their personal lives, but in the back of his mind was the story he didn't mention: threats to the life of a local radio personality named Lee Garrett. Would that qualify as a big item? Or just another media tidbit to ignore over a bowl of Cheerios? His own news department didn't even know the whole story—Maddy had warned the staff to watch for strangers, but she'd left out any mention of the bleach in the spray bottle for the sake of Detective Davis's investigation.

The news staff was preoccupied anyway. The new employee, Dale Lawson, showed up at 7:00 o'clock and spent the rest of the morning leaning over shoulders. Larry Wise brought her into CTBX Control after the 7:30 newscast to introduce her to Lee.

"I'm surprised to see you here today," Lee said.

"Well, I don't start on the air until Monday, but I thought it was a good idea to sit in on things for a day or two first. Get a feel for the newscast formats and everything."

"It's New Year's Eve. You don't have any better place to be?"

"Apparently not." Her pale blue eyes acquired a layer of frost.

"Well, you two can get acquainted later," Wise said. "We've got work to do."

Lee turned back to the music computer. He didn't even look to see if she had a nice ass. Part of his mind filed an impression of mediocrity: a mid-brown pantsuit over a white top on a slim figure, light brown hair cut mid-length, average features. Thin lips. Or maybe that was because of the impression he'd made on her. Too bad. He didn't want her there, hadn't asked for a partner, and he damn well wasn't going to pretend otherwise.

After 9:00 o'clock he should have spent some time telling Lawson what she needed to know about the morning show. He went to do his production shift. Then he drifted over to Chuck Norwood's office.

"New Year's Eve in Whitefish tonight," Norwood said. "Are you sure you're up to it, Lee?"

"What do you mean 'up to it'? I'm not sick, Chuck."

"I know, it's just that…you must get nervous in crowds of strangers, not knowing…"

"It's a charity casino night. A crowd of rich business people. I'll be emceeing from a stage half the time. You think someone's going to, what? Cap me, in the middle of all that?"

"What if something did happen? Right in the middle of a big crowd of people?"

"Jesus, Chuck. You're not worried about me. You're afraid of the *bad publicity*. Good God."

Norwood blinked. "No! Of course I'm worried about you, Lee. But who knows what kind of psychos we're dealing with here? I only meant that…other innocent people could be hurt, too. Maybe we have a responsibility."

"To keep me locked away, where I can't be a danger to anybody."
Lee bristled. "I don't believe this." He stormed out and started toward
Ellis's office, but realized it wasn't a smart move. If she shared Norwood's paranoia she might just order him to stay home. Instead, he
packed up his gear for the day and left the building.

The air was bitter. A cold snap had moved in overnight, dropping
the temperature to minus twenty-five Celsius. When he got into his
car and keyed the ignition the engine turned over twice and no more.
He turned the key again, got one reluctant crank, and then let off on
the switch. *Shit!* Unbelievable!

He could ask one of his co-workers to give him a boost, but
the thought of going back into the building didn't appeal to him.
Sometimes a cold car battery could be brought back to life by using
it. He flicked the headlights on, and decided to give it five minutes. It
was a bitch sitting in the silent cold.

When the time was up he crossed his fingers and turned the key.
The starter lasted longer, and on the fourth turn the engine kicked and
caught. He blew a noisy stream of air at the windshield. It had fogged up,
but he wiped a patch clear with a gloved hand. He kept the engine at high
revs for another few minutes, then put the car into gear. With a buck of
protest, it rolled ahead, stiff tires jolting over frozen ridges of snow.

The car had been due for a tune-up months ago. In the driveway
of his apartment he popped the hood. The battery connections
had a lot of oxidized crap on them. He dug through the bottom of
the hallway closet for his toolbox and a rusty battery charger, then
cleaned up the battery posts and leads with a wire brush. There were
eight hours before he had to leave. The half-hour drive out of town to
the casino night would provide some charge too, if he didn't run too
many accessories. The Volvo had seat warmers, but he wouldn't be
able to spare the juice for that.

≈

The cold had deepened by evening. The car springs creaked; even the foam of the cloth seats was stiff. Steam rose ramrod straight from chimneys and storm sewers. There'd been a brief snowfall mid-afternoon, just enough to dust the existing snowbanks with a coating that sparkled in the headlights, and Lee actually enjoyed the drive through the silent darkness.

Loud music leaked from the doors of the clubhouse as he hurried in from the car. Diamond-bright stars told him the night was going to get colder still. Just outside the hall entrance, he walked through a wall of cigarette smoke. By law, smokers were supposed to keep well away from the door, but these addicts had decided to risk a fine rather than frostbite. As he emerged into clearer air he bumped into Bob Laframboise, one of the casino night's organizers.

"Lee! Good to see ya buddy." The man's smile made his bald scalp wrinkle. "Thanks for coming. Can I get you a drink?" It was the only question to which Laframboise allowed room for an answer.

"Later." Lee smiled back. A quick look around the room showed a few dark suits but the small town dress code included a lot of sweaters.

"Great, sure. Anytime. Just ask. So what we're gonna do…" Laframboise turned and started to walk. Lee kept up, but it wasn't easy through the crush of bodies. The gaming tables took more space than the room could afford to lose. "We're gonna just have you get on the stage for a minute and we'll thank you folks for helping us out. We'll get started in just a second. Hold on, I gotta ask Max something." The big man was swallowed up by a mass of shoulders, bobbing heads, and swaying beer glasses.

Lee gave up the pursuit and made his way to the side of the stage. Overhead the blue-on-white of the CTBX logo clashed with the orange banner of the brewery sponsoring the event. Ken Cousins' beer company, unfortunately. Lee scanned the oscillating sea of heads. Most were turned away from the stage, but he frowned to see Elliot Dean talking to a short blond woman. A few other faces were familiar, though he couldn't place them. Next to the stage he nodded at a young man in a black T-shirt who looked to be putting the final touches on the P.A. equipment, and smiled at the tech guy's requisite earring.

Bob Laframboise appeared out of nowhere and took his arm.

"Sure you don't want a drink? Ok, we're just about to start. I have to check with a few more people, that's all." Then he was gone again.

At 9:50—only twenty minutes behind schedule—the speeches got underway. Lee wasn't happy to share the stage with Ken Cousins. As always, Cousins looked like a fashion star, modelling a light cream-coloured sports jacket over a blue turtleneck that set off his eyes to perfection. The warmth in his voice and smile vanished when he passed the microphone to Lee. The blond eyelashes didn't blink.

Lee's best suit suddenly felt like a cheap rag as he watched Cousins strut away, but he knew that he had the advantage when it came to using his face and voice to good effect. He drew more laughs and more applause than Cousins, and stepped off the stage feeling pleased with himself. The beer company rep had vanished into the crowd. Then Bob Laframboise was at Lee's elbow asking if he was ready for a brew. This time Lee laughed and nodded, while the band began to thump through some loud tune-up riffs.

He made announcements from time to time through the evening, but otherwise he spent the time trading trivialities with people who recognized him, and turning down invitations to dance, as graciously as he could. Later, he even tried his luck at blackjack at a table where the dealer was a redhead in a black sheath gown who offered views of more than just the cards.

He was sure she didn't need to lean over quite so far to retrieve the chips, but he appreciated her zeal. Her creamy skin was perfect and Lee seemed to have the prime vantage point to observe it. He wondered about that, until she mentioned offhandedly that she often won contests on his show. He recognized her name immediately. Did she think the display of her wares would improve her success? If so, it was wasted effort. Lee had no control over the way contest calls lined up, and didn't even ask names until he had a winner. He hoped her attention was less mercenary than that.

Ken Cousins' appearance at her side was a splash of cold water.

"How's it going, Wendy?" He touched her arm possessively.

"Great, Kenny. Have you met Lee Garrett?"

"We've known each other a long time," Lee answered for him, but the two men didn't look at each other.

Cousins gave a smirk and said, "You have to watch out for these radio guys, Wendy. They're smooth talkers, but what he's looking to handle isn't your cards." He leaned over to plant a light kiss on a cheek that was already turning red with embarrassment and drew a hand over his head, though it was impossible that a hair could be out of place. Then he strolled away to find a new audience.

Wendy gave an awkward smile.

"Don't pay attention to Ken when he gets like that, Mr. Garrett... Lee. He can be a pig when he drinks."

"Have you known each other long?" he asked.

"A few months. He can be very charming when he wants to be, but he doesn't have any claim on me, if that's what you mean." She flashed a smile of bright teeth and full red lips, but Lee's head had cooled. It was a bad idea to get involved with somebody who had his work number on speed-dial, unless he was prepared for the hook-up to last longer than a night or two. And he wasn't. With real regret, he told her he was going to call it a night.

Her crestfallen face said that she wasn't sure what she'd done wrong. She managed a cheerful "Good night". Then by accident or design, she leaned her folded arms on the table and gave Lee one last lingering look at what her body offered.

A shiver ran through him as he turned away. The old rutting buck was never far below the surface.

He found Bob Laframboise who gave his back a friendly slap that propelled him halfway to the door, and he nearly left without retrieving his coat from the coat check.

The cold was the kind that made nostrils recoil. The wind had picked up, and it raked like claws across his exposed skin, peppering him with sharp snow crystals off the roof of the barn-like municipal services building next door. He pulled the collar of his coat around his ears, and worried about whether his car would start. It teased him with a half-dozen lethargic cranks, but then the engine caught, chugged a little, and finally smoothed out.

He left the heater fan off—the engine would need all the help it could get to come close to running temperature. It was going to be a cold drive home. He thought he might shave a few minutes off the trip if he took the old highway instead of backtracking to the new section of the Trans Canada. The old two-lane route might be more sheltered, too—the strong wind had begun to cause whiteouts in open spaces.

The ancient pavement was rough, and strips of packed snow gleamed in the headlights. They shouldn't be a problem, as long as he stayed alert. The cold would take care of that. In the meantime he'd have to think warm thoughts. Maybe about Wendy. There was a woman who could keep a man warm.

The first sign of trouble came fifteen minutes later. The engine suddenly bucked and kicked, and when he tried to give it more gas it threatened to stall. His heart leapt into his throat as he gently coaxed the throttle back to a smoother level, though it wasn't enough to maintain speed on the slope he was climbing. There was another kick of a misfired cylinder or two, then he crested the hill. The engine settled down. He realized he'd been holding his breath.

The relief was short-lived. The engine began to buck again and abruptly quit. With an explosive curse he decided to try the starter with the clutch pushed in, while the car was still rolling down the slope. The motor turned over, coughed, turned again, kicked again. He used his lightest touch on the gas, afraid to flood the engine, but was only rewarded with a mocking chuff as a single cylinder caught a spark. Quickly losing speed, he had no choice but to pull off the highway or face pushing the car onto the shoulder by himself. The crunch of the frozen gravel and snow sounded like defeat. Without the noise of the engine, he heard a low shriek at the edges of the windows from the rising wind, and the shiver that went through him wasn't from cold alone.

He was screwed.

What could he do if the car wouldn't start? Did he dare walk for help? There'd been a couple of sideroads just before he got to the hill, but any houses on them might be a long way from the highway. McCharles Lake was far to his right by now. Looking ahead there were no lights in sight. The thick streams of snow blown across the road could have hidden a small subdivision. Unless the next houses were very close, walking would be suicide. The wind chill had to be the equivalent of the minus fifties, enough to crisp exposed skin in minutes. Suddenly he didn't feel so smug about not owning a cell phone.

He popped the inside hood release, knowing the futility of it. He was no mechanic. He wasn't going to stare the engine into life. Stretching to reach under the passenger seat, he remembered that he'd thrown out the toque he usually kept there because it had begun to stink. *Damn.* The coat he was wearing didn't have a hood—hoods were nerdy, like toques. Now he had neither. Without them, his ears would be raw meat to the wind outside. He yanked open the glove compartment and grabbed the flashlight.

It was dead.

In a rage, he nearly hurled the useless piece of junk away, but a part of him recognized the sour taint of panic. That would be the beginning of the end. He wasn't giving in to that. He'd have to hope he could see the engine by the headlights reflected from the snow.

There was still no sign of other cars. He couldn't be the only one who'd take the old highway, could he? Except it was New Year's Eve. There wasn't going to be a hell of a lot of traffic anywhere. He swallowed hard and opened the door.

Glacial air snatched at him; the meagre warmth of the car interior was gone in an instant, and he staggered back as a gust took him. Hunching his face into his shoulder he worked his way to the front of the car and raised the hood. It immediately tried to blow shut. He barely caught it in time—it could have broken his fingers.

The engine compartment was a black pit. There were no streetlights. The moon had nearly set, and was in the wrong direction. He had no choice but to tug off his gloves and feel around for anything obviously wrong—a loose spark plug wire or something. He was cautious about touching the engine block, but it didn't burn him. A bad sign—it was cooling off already. The most he could do was push the spark plug wires firmly into place. In the days when cars had carburettors he'd sometimes sprayed ether into their throats for a quick start. Not anymore.

As he hurried back to the driver's seat, the wind almost slammed the door on his foot. His hand was shaking and could barely grip the ignition key.

The engine turned over, but didn't catch. He waited a couple of minutes—it might be flooded. Should he try to drain the cylinders by cranking the engine with the gas pedal held to the floor? No. The problem had started while he was climbing a hill. Maybe there was a clog in a fuel line. He gambled, and turned the key—pumped the

pedal a couple of times. If there was no clog he'd flood the engine
for certain, but he didn't know what else to try. He keyed the starter
again…kept it cranking. Nothing.

Again.

Again.

The engine revs were slower, the battery starting to drain. It
probably hadn't picked up a full charge after being nearly flat that
morning. A dead battery would end his last chance of getting out of
this on his own. But what was the point of waiting until the engine got
too cold to start?

He tried it again. And once more—a long one. The engine was
barely turning over by then. It gave only feeble grunts, a dying animal.

Trying to keep calm, he pushed the door open again and gritted
his teeth into the wind. Maybe he hadn't tightened the battery well
enough. Maybe he could shift the clamps and get a better connection.
But they wouldn't budge, and the metal was too cold to grip for long.

He slammed the hood and pounded on it, screaming obscenities
into the night, but the tantrum lasted only seconds. With ice clutching
at his heart he climbed back into the frozen block of metal and plastic
and fabric that was no longer a moving vehicle. No longer going to
take him home.

The full weight of his predicament struck home. The temperature
was below freezing in the car—letting all the heat out, he'd let the first
taste of death in. No point trying to call it anything else. The wind
would suck every trace of warmth from the car, and then his body. He
would get sleepy. Then, if help didn't come, he would die.

Pain. Suffering. Death.

The words flashed into his brain—the warning from the Skins.
Would stupid bad luck finish the job for them?

Needing to do something, he rummaged through the glove compartment. He'd once stocked it with a candle and matches, a plastic

silver *space blanket,* and even a couple of chocolate bars. Only trash remained. The chocolate bars had satisfied a mid-morning craving, and the rest had probably shifted to his kitchen during the last hydro blackout. There was nothing there to help him. His life now depended on someone coming along a tired and patched stretch of asphalt and stopping to check on a derelict hulk off to one side.

Shit! He reached out to the dashboard and fumbled for the knob that activated the car's four-way warning flashers. He should have done that right away. The battery would still run them for a while. Without them the car would look abandoned. The shock of his oversight frightened him into another spasm of shivering. He pulled his legs under the coat, tugged the collar over his head, and pulled up the zipper.

A long time later he pressed a button on his watch. Almost midnight. Almost a new year. In another world, of bright lights and heat, people would soon be kissing.

He found himself imagining a sun-drenched beach with Wendy tucked into the briefest of bikinis. Her body kept rhythm to a song he couldn't hear. He looked into her face and it was Michaela's face beneath the long hair that was now a much lighter shade of strawberry. Michaela flirtatiously ran away from him and around the corner of a small wooden change house that jutted out of the sand. He chased after her but his feet were clumsy and slow. When he rounded the corner she had vanished. He twisted in the opposite direction, to head her off, but missed her again, and again, never catching more than a tantalising flash of skin.

Then, as he turned another corner she was there. But no, it wasn't Michaela, it was Candace Ross, with a hurt look on her face. He sensed that she was naked, but below her neck there was only blankness, like something hidden in the blind spot of his eye. She gave one more sad look and turned her back to walk away down the beach. He tried to call out but no sound came from his mouth. Instead there was the noise of a motor—someone coming in a car to pick her up, perhaps. He wanted her to stay, but he couldn't make himself heard above the sound of the car, and the wind, and the crunch of tires on gravel...

Gravel. That seemed wrong, somehow. And wind... a cold wind.

Jesus. He'd fallen asleep!

He shook off the dream and listened to the icy voice of the real wind. Had he really heard a car, or was it only part of the dream? Frantically he tried to unzip his coat, but his fingers were too numb to cooperate. It took forever to inch the zipper downward, until at last he could force his head out of the opening. As he did he heard the sound of wheels on gravel again, and motor noises that quickly faded.

He struggled to free his arms and legs. His throat was too dry to call for help. The windows were completely frosted. Was that a hint of red taillights shrinking in the distance?

No. God, no!

Someone had stopped and then gone on without helping him... without *saving his life.*

His mind struggled to comprehend it. His hands clawed half-heartedly at the windshield, but mere fingernails could barely scratch through the thickening frost. It was too much; his eyes teared from a draft of icy air—it must have been that—and his body convulsed in helpless horror. Sometime later he fumbled the coat back over his head, but he could no longer work the zipper. He hugged himself tightly and screwed his eyes shut.

His mind reached out for that car in the night—raced up the highway, caught up with it, then soared ahead through the darkness until the lights of the city appeared and he was swooping along railway tracks, straight up his own street and through a lighted doorway to the inside. He expected warmth, and the comfort of familiar things around him, but it was unexpectedly empty. There was nothing but bare walls.

In confusion he took flight again, racing through deserted streets to the radio station. There was no one there. The control room: the equipment was gone. No music playing, no talk, no papers, no posters. No welcome.

Nothing.

As his mind floated there the room began to blur, the corners flattened. Windows turned opaque and walls became translucent. Everything began to melt into one great grey sameness, and he became aware of a buzzing in his ears. No, the swell and retreat of many noises, none of them distinguishable. They swirled around him. The floor had lost its solidity and he was sinking into it, drawn downward as if in quicksand. The buzzing babble retreated; darkness closed in. He was alone in a universe without sensation.

Once, a long time later, he heard a noise...a noise from far off that sounded like the cry of a dinosaur in a Hollywood fantasy: a long screaming wail, a snort of air, and the rumble of a distant volcano.

Then there was silence.

10

THE PAIN WOKE HIM UP. HIS JOINTS FELT SQUEEZED in a vice, and other parts of his body were on fire, nerve endings dancing in torment.

Hell. It had to be Hell.

A blowtorch was playing over the sides of his head. He tried to brush at the flames with his hands, but he wasn't sure his arms had moved. An ungodly moan sent a chill through his spine. He held his breath to listen for it again. When he finally exhaled, a wheezing sob from close by made him dig in his heels and try to escape.

He couldn't. Something was holding him in place.

"Better not to move," a voice said, making him start. "That just makes it hurt more."

Hurt more? He'd already been dropped into a vat of salt water with his skin peeled off. Was he being tortured? By a female demon?

He'd have to open his eyes to find out, but his whole being rebelled at the thought. Sleep would be better. Go back to sleep. But it wasn't going to happen.

Then the eyes have it, his mind wearily punned. He had to concentrate to find the muscles that controlled them.

Light lanced into his brain, and he sneezed. Blinking tears away, he could eventually make out the blurred shape of a woman standing over him. The light was behind her, but he caught the impression of a colour: pale green.

Drab, suitable only for institutional walls and generic uniforms.

Hospital. He was in a hospital.

So he hadn't been far off when he'd thought it was Hell.

The realization wasn't a shock. He could logically accept the concept of a hospital, as he could remember his own existence, but the link between them had no reality.

The woman was speaking again. "How do you feel?"

The words were absorbed like a pearl falling through oil. Feel? He felt like shit. He said so, but he didn't hear the words. Maybe that was because his tongue was a clod of dried moss clogging his throat.

"I'll get you a drink of water," the woman said. She left his field of vision, and a flare of pain from his ears stopped him from following her with his head. She was gone a long time. Then he felt a hand against his back, lifting. He got the idea and raised himself onto his elbows, but he was curiously weak. Something dry pushed between his lips. A straw. He tried to suck on it. After a few attempts he felt drops of bliss spread over his tongue and he sucked again. Eventually he remembered he was supposed to swallow. That hurt like…like every other movement he made.

"Feel like…crap," he rasped. His mouth wouldn't make the *sh*.

"No doubt. You came in with frostbite and hypothermia. Now that you're awake I'll ask the doctor about getting you some pain killers."

Frostbite. Cold. His body had been freezing cold….

With a sudden swell of disorientation, he remembered. The car. He was in the car. *He was freezing to death.*

He writhed, trying to escape and knocked the water cup flying. Hands pressed on his shoulders, trapping him. He struggled, but the moment passed as quickly as it had come. He gave one powerful shudder and collapsed back onto the bed.

"It's all right. You're all right now. You're safe."

Understanding and memory came together. He wasn't in the car—not anymore. He was in a hospital bed. It wasn't a dream—the pain made it real. His eyes focused and found the woman looking at him with concern.

"Are you ok?" she asked.

He thought about speaking, but only risked a small nod.

"I'll try to contact the doctor. Just stay still and rest."

He watched her leave his field of vision, replaced by the dull white ceiling. He had an urge to look around, but the throb from both sides of his head told him it wouldn't be worth it. Instead he lay staring, trying to project images from his memory onto blank space.

Someone had come. Someone had taken him from the frozen car before it could become his tomb. Did he remember that?

No. But then everything before this room felt like a dream.

The memories of sensations and sounds slowly came back to him, and he wished they hadn't. Chaotic noises and waves of pain from his hands and feet; something rough and hot pressed against his ears, but the pressure elsewhere felt more...liquid, somehow: swirling surges of lava or ice against his skin. He couldn't tell which. There were sounds in the darkness like curses or screams, and he had a nauseating suspicion that they'd come from him.

How bad was it? What had they done to him? Did they have to...

Amputate?

He struggled against his restraints and thrust his head forward until the tendons in his neck felt as if they would pop. Where were his hands? He was covered by light blankets, but at least there were bulges where his hands should be, and two more at the end of the bed, sticking up like feet. He tried to wiggle them, but tears blurred his vision.

The nurse returned.

"My fingers. My toes?" he croaked.

"They're bandaged. They've got frostbite blisters and we have to keep them sterile. But they're still there. Everything's still there."

"Will I ... lose them?"

"The doctor should really answer questions like that," she said. "I'm not supposed to."

He let his head drop and swallowed painfully.

"I heard him say you got lucky, though," she offered. "It sounded like there probably wouldn't be complications. Here. Dr. Rashad said I could give you something for the pain. He'll be around tomorrow morning to see you." She put the pills in his mouth and gave him more water. "Are you hungry?"

"No." His stomach was queasy.

"Because if you are I'll try to get you some soup from the kitchen. Otherwise it's bedtime. Do you think you could sleep again?"

"What day is it?"

"Saturday. You were brought in late last night ... actually very early this morning, I guess."

"So I've been sleeping all day."

"They had to give you something during the treatments. Stuff knocks you out. You still look pretty drowsy."

"Yeah. But can I get these things off my arms and legs?"

"Sure. They were just so you wouldn't move and hurt yourself while you weren't fully conscious." She pulled the cuffs free from his upper arms and shins. Presumably those areas hadn't been frostbitten. He drew his arms from under the blankets and looked at the swaths of bandages. The nurse gave him a reassuring smile. "If you need anything, just buzz. Oh ... sorry."

"Yeah. Maybe I can reach the button with an elbow. If I get lonely."

"They say a sense of humour is a good sign." She turned to leave.

"Wait…Damn."

"What is it?"

"What if I need to use the bathroom?"

"You've got a catheter in right now, so unless you have to…?"

"No, not yet."

"Ok."

As she reached the door, he asked, "Do I have to dream?"

"With the stuff I gave you, I don't think that will be a problem."

~

He was trying to convince a nursing assistant that he didn't want another mouthful of oatmeal when Maddy Ellis came to the door.

"Sorry to interrupt," she said.

"Interrupt. Please interrupt," Lee said. The young woman holding the spoon took the hint, replaced the tray on its cart, and wheeled it out the door.

Ellis pulled a chair to the side of the bed. "How are you feeling?"

"Nothing that a half bottle of scotch and a skin transplant couldn't cure. Sit down and stay awhile. I don't get a lot of company. In fact, I'm surprised to have the room to myself. Is that your doing?"

"Not me. There was another patient when they first brought you in here, but I guess you weren't in any shape to notice. They'll probably bring another one in soon. What about you? What have the doctors told you?"

"The one who treated me should be around later with more details, but an emergency room doctor came by for a minute this morning. It sounds like I should be ok. Frostbite on my fingers and toes and ears, but I shouldn't lose them. Barring any nasty surprises." He shrugged. "I got lucky."

"No shit. What the hell happened, anyway?"

"That's what I was going to ask you," Lee said. "I don't even know how I got here. I thought I was a goner."

"Too close to the truth. Too damn close. What were you doing on the old highway on the coldest night of the year?"

"I figured I'd take a short cut, but the frigging car broke down, obviously. What I want to know is, who found me? I don't remember a thing. I guess I fell asleep."

"And almost never woke up." She sounded angry, but he realized it was only because she'd been genuinely scared for him. "It was sheer luck. A truck driver who lives out that way was coming home after a run and saw your flashers. He brought you in. You were pretty far gone."

"A trucker? Anyone I know?"

"How should I know? A guy named Tucker. Big guy. Looks just the way you'd expect him to look."

"*Tucker* the *Trucker*?"

"You mean you do know him?"

"No. It's just the name. It's ... too much."

"Well, I wouldn't suggest you tell him that to his face. Anyway, the guy hung around the whole time they were treating you, and you should have seen him light up when I got here and told him you were Lee Garrett. You'd have thought I'd made his day."

Lee felt his throat constrict. He coughed to clear it. "I guess somebody up there likes me after all."

"I wouldn't push it, if I were you."

Ellis expected him to take a week off. Lee refused. They were into ratings again—an experiment BBM had tried once before that involved ballot sampling for the first two weeks of three consecutive months, instead of the usual solid six-week stretch. He wasn't prepared to miss a week of that. He'd just need an operator to handle the equipment for him. They sparred a while over it, but the businesswoman in Ellis won out over her motherly side.

After she left, Lee wondered if he could walk well enough to get some exercise. He'd been lying in a bed for more than twenty-four hours. Then he remembered other visits to hospitals. Depressing. He'd always felt like a voyeur if he looked into the doorways he passed. The occupants of the rooms were people at their most vulnerable. They didn't need spectators.

Instead he stared out the window at the drab buildings and streets, the giant spire of the Superstack in the distance fountaining greyish white effluent from the Copper Cliff nickel refinery into the sky, as if it had produced the whole gloomy ceiling of cloud all by itself. Below him, just across Ramsay Lake Road, the metal snowflake of Science North perched beside slate-coloured water rimmed with new ice, a fitting symbol for a city that seemed locked in frozen stillness. Or maybe it was only because it was Sunday of New Year's weekend.

New Years. He'd spent New Year's Day in a drug-induced stupor. The end of the old year had nearly meant the end of Lee Garrett. It was hard for him to connect with the fact of his mortality. Was he ready to meet his maker? He still wasn't sure he believed in one of those. But the universe had given him a second chance. What would he do with it?

He found himself thinking of Candace Ross.

It had been ten days since their argument. Enough time for her to cool off? Or had he been the only one to feel a connection between them? Either way, he owed her an apology. He could call her. The CNIB number would be in the book, but there wouldn't be anyone in the office on a Sunday. Then he remembered that not everyone worked in radio and paid for an unlisted number.

The thin pages of the phone book were a bitch to turn with hands wrapped like a mummy's, but perseverance paid off. She was listed. Then he looked at the phone in dismay. Even if he could manage to hold the thing, the idea of it touching his ears was a non-starter. He was about to give up when he saw the speaker-phone button. He prodded at it and managed to get a dial-tone, but the keypad nearly defeated him. It was an achievement just to reach the hospital switchboard.

He started to explain his predicament, but the operator caught on right away and put the call through for him.

"Candace? Hi, it's Lee Garrett. I…I just called to apologize. For the other night."

"For the other night more than a week ago?"

"Yes. At the mall. I was an ass. I wanted you to know I'm sorry."

"Sorry enough to call me at home?" Her tone was guarded. "Your voice sounds hollow. We're not on the radio, are we?"

"No. No, I wouldn't do that. I'm on a speakerphone. I had…a little problem." He haltingly explained.

"My God. I don't know what to say."

"Just say you accept my apology. That's all I'm calling for."

"Of course I do. It's not a big deal. We were both… Anyway, are they going to keep you for long?"

"I don't think so. My doctor hasn't come by yet, but I'm hoping I can get out today. They probably need the bed, right?"

"I'm not far from the hospital. I can be there in a few minutes."

"You don't have to do that."

"No? How were you planning to get home?"

He felt like an idiot.

≈

Candace knocked lightly on the door and took a few tentative steps forward. A pair of nurses was helping another patient into the room's second bed. One of them pulled the curtain closed around it.

Lee was glad to see her. The strength of the feeling surprised him.

"Are they painful?" she asked, frowning at his bandaged hands.

"Only when I move them or keep them still." He enjoyed making her smile. She had a wonderful smile. "Actually, I can take things for the pain, but they're beginning to itch like a bugger."

She made a sympathetic noise. Then she moved closer and lowered her voice.

"I'm glad you called because I wanted to apologize to you, too. I was way out of line interfering with your relationships. I'm not usually that dumb." She paused. "Although I am usually that stubborn!" She blushed and they laughed.

"I'm both," he said. "And Michaela is very much a sore point."

"You still love her."

He looked into her eyes and thought about denying it, then quietly said, "I'll always love her." They sat silent for a moment before he continued. "But I wasn't right for her, and I never will be. I suppose I'm touchy about treating her badly because ... that's probably the only way I ever did treat her."

"Hang on," Candace said. "Did she meet you halfway? Try to be a part of your radio life, and share in the pleasure you got from it?"

He opened his mouth to come to his ex-wife's defence, but stopped to consider the question seriously. Candace was right. Michaela had never wanted any part of radio. He remembered the way her father had kidded about Lee someday getting a real job, and it occurred to him that Michaela had felt that way about it too, all those years.

"No," he replied softly. " I guess she didn't."

"Marriage is a two-way street. Maybe it's time you stopped blaming yourself."

He looked into her eyes for a moment. "You're very wise."

"I talk a good line."

"Have you been married?"

"Not quite." She hesitated, but decided to push on. "He was a good guy, but he had a problem with me setting out to save the world.

He hadn't bargained for a whole bunch of other people's problems when he thought he was just marrying me. He was right. I was very full of myself: God's gift to the needy.

"Not anymore."

"Let's just say I've realized I can only change the world by trying to make a difference in one person's life at a time."

In the quiet of the moment, a doctor bustled into the room, startling them. He didn't seem to notice. Flipping through the pages of a chart in his hand, he strode quickly to the bed.

"Mr...Garrett." His voice was a rich baritone. "And Mrs. Garrett?"

"No. Just a friend," Candace corrected him, with a light laugh.

"Oh. Sorry to rush things." The man smiled. "I'm Doctor Rashad. I'd offer to shake hands, but I suspect you'd rather not."

"I think we can skip that for now."

"You were lucky. Maybe you have a guardian angel."

"So I understand."

Rashad warned Lee about the risk of infection and instructed him to have his dressings changed and checked regularly by his family doctor.

"You don't have to do any heavy work with your fingers, do you?"

"Not really. I'm a radio announcer."

The doctor's eyebrows lifted as he looked back at his chart. "Of course. I should've recognized the name. Well, that's good. Your mouth got through the ordeal in fine shape." He laughed. "But your fingers and toes will be very sensitive for quite a long time. The joints will be sore—don't put too much strain on them. Do you wear earphones?"

"Headphones. Yes, usually."

"You'll have to find a way around that. I guarantee you won't want anything pressing against your ears for a few weeks."

"Yeah, I've already noticed that."

Lee thanked the doctor sincerely, then endured one more change of his dressings by a nurse. The air outside smelled like freedom, but

---

its cold sank deeply into him long before they got to Candace's car. She cranked up the heater as soon as she could.

"Where's your car?" she asked.

"It's been towed to my mechanic's. I don't know whether I want him to fix it or just blow it up."

As they pulled into the driveway of his apartment she said, "I was planning to take Paul Schwartz tobogganing sometime soon. Would you like to come?"

"When it's a little warmer. I've got this thing about the cold."

She looked alarmed. "Oh, of course! Well, maybe it's not a good idea then. Or we can put it off for a few weeks."

"A couple of weeks will be fine, I'm sure," he said, less confident than he sounded.

He thanked her for the lift too many times, then watched until her car disappeared.

Maybe he did have a guardian angel.

11

HE PROMISED HIMSELF HE'D NEVER COMPLAIN about ordinary Mondays again. This one had been an unqualified disaster. Because of Lee's bandaged hands, a college freshman named Darryl White operated the equipment for him. Cues were missed, phone calls were cut off, a microphone was left 'live' by mistake, capturing the noise of Dale Lawson moving out of the news booth and Lee moving in.

Lawson's presence made things worse. Trying to give her best for her first day on the air, she was full of questions while Lee was trying to get his own breaks organized. His replies turned into growls. By mid-morning she was only speaking to him through Darryl.

Lee could barely use a computer, so he'd printed off his material, but handling papers with mitts of gauze was a refined form of torture. At one point he threw all of his pages at the wall in a rage, then had to spend two whole songs painstakingly putting them back in order.

J.J. found the whole thing hilarious. Lee swore to cross him off his Christmas list.

It didn't help to know that ratings had begun again. He was in a richly foul mood when 9:00 o'clock finally came.

Things got no better when he called his mechanic. Emil was a big fan of The Box and Lee considered him a friend, but neither felt like small talk this time.

"You figured out what's wrong with the goddamned piece of junk?"

"Well in this case a Cadillac wouldn't have done any better."

"What do you mean?"

"I checked over all the usual things twice before I finally noticed that one of the gas lines was split."

"The *metal* gas lines?"

"Yup. There was water in the tank."

"*Water?*" Lee's brain wasn't keeping up to the conversation. "Water in the gas tank?"

"Yeah, water. The stuff you like to drink and your car doesn't. A few litres, maybe. I didn't measure it. But I had to drain the tank. You can't soak up that much with methyl hydrate or anything like that."

"I always get my gas from you guys. That tankful, for sure. Are you saying you've got water in your tanks?"

Emil raised his voice in mock outrage.

"I ain't saying that at all. You didn't get all that water from *my* tanks. No way. Maybe you went through a car wash with the filler cap open. It doesn't lock anymore, right?"

The image was so absurd in the dead of winter that Lee would have laughed, as Emil intended. But an ugly thought had come to him.

"Seriously, how do you think it got there?"

"I got no goddamn idea. Probably some asshole kids with nothing better to do. Thought it'd be a good goddamn joke to have you stuck in your driveway. Wouldn't figure on you getting stranded somewhere and freezing to death."

"No." *But someone did figure exactly that.* His stomach suddenly felt hollow. It took him a moment to realize Emil had spoken again.

"What was that?"

"I said, I can't see any other damage. Must've been just enough gas mixed in so nothing else cracked. I guess you can't drive, eh? I'll have a couple of the guys go with you to drop it off later."

"Thanks. What do I owe you?"

"I'll put it on your tab!" A friendly shot, but also a subtle reminder that Lee hadn't paid Emil's last bill.

"You're a prince." He hung up the phone and stared at the wall.

≈

"You think *what?*" Ellis's face was white marble.

Lee brushed the back of his hand across his forehead. God-damned bandages were getting on his nerves. "There's probably no way to prove it, but the water must've been put in my tank at the club-house. Any sooner and the car wouldn't have made it that far."

"To try to *kill* you?"

"I'm not ready to believe that. They would've expected me to take the main highway back, and there's always lots of traffic along there."

"Unless they knew the old highway was your shortest way home."

"You're giving them too much credit. Probably just an unexpected opportunity to cause some shit for me. Anyway, Detective Davis is sending her forensics people to my mechanic's to go over the car."

Ellis just stared at the desk. She had no idea what to say.

He drifted through the lobby on his way to the other side of the building. A figure caught his eye and he turned to ask if he could help with anything. It was the cardboard Lee Garrett. His doppelganger. Or maybe it was the real McCoy and he was the copy, both two-dimensional with painted-on faces—who could tell the difference?

On his way past the newsroom, he heard his name. He stopped just out of sight.

"Aw, Lee's a good head, once you get to know him." J.J.'s voice.

"Does he have to be such a *prick* in the meantime?" Dale Lawson.

"Cut him some slack, wouldja? He nearly froze to death the other night. That has to mess with your head. Even worse 'cause somebody's been threatening to kill him."

Lawson grunted. "I can understand why."

The conversation was over. Lee quietly slipped away.

≈

Davis and some officers from the Forensics unit were at Emil's garage when the cab dropped Lee off. One of the officers was leaning over the rear fender of the Volvo on the side of the gas filler door. Another was taking pictures.

"Your mechanic had to drain the tank and refill it?" Davis asked.

"That's what he said."

"Looks like the gas jockeys took a rag to the fender afterward. Not much chance of any prints left after that. We've gone over the rest of the car, just in case, and taken prints from each of the workers here, to know what we can ignore."

"Sorry."

"Never much hope anyway. If I were handling a container of water on a night like that I'd be wearing gloves, wouldn't you?" Lee nodded. "Did you see anybody acting suspiciously at this clubhouse? Was there anybody there who might want to hassle you like that?"

"There were a few who don't like me much," he answered with a self-conscious shrug. The smug face of Ken Cousins came into his mind. "Mostly we ignore each other."

"Well, it's a place to start. Let's have the names."

"You figure on having this wrapped up in an hour, like on TV?"

He tried to interpret her expression as a smile. "Save your humour for your radio show. It needs all it can get."

≈

Two turntables spun beside his left arm. One was slowing down, the other was playing "The Heat Is On" by Glen Frey. The song had about a minute left to run, and he realized with a shock that the next record wasn't ready. He reached a hand into the nearest of three long wooden boxes on the countertop to his right and grabbed the record at the front, a 45-rpm disk in a light-green paper sleeve with a numbered label in the top left corner.

"(I Never Promised You A) Rose Garden" by Lynn Anderson.

That wasn't a rock song. He desperately grabbed the next one. "The Green Green Grass of Home" by Tom Jones. His heart started to hammer.

He must have brought the wrong music.

There was no time left—he slapped a 45 onto the second turntable, put the needle on it, and turned the knob to put the motor in gear. Instead the platter spun lazily backward. The turntable was broken!

Frey had finished—the dead air was stretching to five seconds... six...

He stabbed the microphone button and began to blather about something, anything, while he stretched his arm to the limit and one-handedly swapped the Frey record for another. There was no chance to cue it up— he flicked the table into gear and mashed the start button. "Gotta Get A Message to You" by the Bee Gees caterwauled to life midway through the second line.

As he let out a moan, he saw the red light warning that his mic was still 'live'. He swatted the off button, and tore the headphones from his ears—he had to get to the music library.

The floor was littered with records like a minefield. He wasted precious time finding safe places to step. At last he made it to the door and bolted down a featureless hallway, turned to the left, took the next right. Or should he have taken a left again? He backtracked, spun around. Where was the library?

Where were all the doors?

He could hear his panicked breathing against a background of the Bee Gees from tinny intercom speakers. The final chorus of the song! His throat constricted. He had to get back to the Control Room... back in control...

He jackknifed into consciousness, gasping for air.

Goddamn it. He hadn't had that dream in a long time. Would it never go away? He hung loosely over his knees until his breathing slowed, then flopped back onto the bed, and massaged his forehead to rub the last vestiges of the nightmare away. Most announcers he knew were afflicted with some variation of it—a symptom of the pressure of live performance. Except it was out of date. Times had changed— the days when a few seconds of dead air would get your knuckles rapped were long gone. Once radio station owners took the route of computerized automation, glitches were commonplace. Sometimes a station went silent for most of the night because of some technical hiccup. Management shrugged it off. As long as the competition didn't do any better, and profits were good, that was all that really mattered.

The stockholders were in the driver's seat.

He rolled over to look at the alarm clock. It'd be going off within twenty minutes. He decided to get up.

~

A breath of winter came into the control room with Dale Lawson as she got ready to do the 6:00 o'clock newscast. She pointedly ignored Lee and got the temperature and sponsor information from Darryl White. Lee had considered apologizing, but if she was going to be a frost queen he'd let her stew for a while longer.

His resentment didn't last. When the newscast was over, he told Darryl to roll a couple of songs with an ID between. He pushed open the news booth door and held up a hand.

"Dale, you got a minute?" She said nothing, but sat back in the chair with her arms crossed. "The thing is … I've been going through a lot lately. But that's no excuse for being a prick. I apologize."

Her expression of surprise may have held a trace of guilt, but Lee pressed on. "Larry and Rob hired you to be a partner for me on the show—part of a three-way team show with J.J. Except they didn't tell me. Never asked me for my opinion. By the time I found out, it was a done deal. I've been doing this show for ten years as a solo. I don't have anything against you personally but, well … how would you feel?"

Her eyes were wide. "I don't know. I didn't know about this."

"You didn't know it was supposed to be a team show?"

"No, well, Larry said there'd be some ad lib stuff, like I did with the morning guy at my last station, but … no. I didn't know the rest."

"God, that's just like Arnott, too. He thinks he's working for the goddamn KGB—everything's on a need-to-know basis and he's the only one who needs to know." Was that a trace of a smile on her face? "Anyway," Lee said, "I'll try not to be a total asshole, and I guess we just … do our best to make this thing work."

"Ok."

"Let's get together with J.J. later and work out a few things."

"Sounds good to me."

He moved out of the way, and as she was about to step into the hall he said, "Hey. You sound good on the air."

She gave a bemused smile. "Thanks."

When she and J.J. joined him in the control room after 9:00 o'clock, they spent a good half-hour talking about how to involve everyone and keep the show running smoothly.

As they split up, Lee said, "Do me a favour and don't tell Arnott about this yet. I'd like to give the prick a taste of his own medicine." He got no argument.

≈

On Friday he was able to get his bandages off and he revelled in the feeling of freedom. Monday he drove himself to work and operated his own show. It was good not to have to depend on someone else.

There was no news from Detective Davis—he was becoming convinced there never would be. Whoever had spiked his gasoline had probably only meant to give him a bad scare, and had spooked themselves when their prank nearly became murder. Maybe that would be the end of his persecution. Was that too much to hope?

He was halfway home when he noticed the station wagon in his rearview mirror. Dark blue, with a dull finish. When he made a left turn the blue car followed him. He turned right. The car behind did too.

A shot of fear made him sit up straight. No. A coincidence—it had to be.

He took a short exit ramp onto a stretch of four-lane. He didn't see the other car as he merged into traffic, until a pickup truck moved to pass him. The blue car had been behind it. Jesus, what should he do? Whoever it was, he didn't want to lead them to his home. When he came to his turnoff he drove past it and accelerated. The space behind him grew, but not for long. Then he deliberately slowed to bring the trailing car close, and tried to see a face through the sloped windshield, but the angle of the sun was against him. He squinted at the front bumper. No license plate. It wasn't legally required on the front, but most people had one. It struck him as a bad sign.

What would happen if he stopped somewhere? Would the driver confront him? What if the guy wasn't alone? It was impossible to tell.

He gave the wheel a sharp turn to pull into the left lane, and then almost immediately made a left turn onto a side street. As soon as the manoeuvre was complete he risked a glance at the mirror.

The blue car had followed him around the turn!

Christ. His mind wasn't coming up with any answers. A startled pedestrian jumped back as Lee rolled through a crosswalk. His dark blue shadow stayed with him.

There was a police cruiser at the curb just ahead, its signal light on, ready to pull out into traffic. He swallowed hard and wrenched the wheel over, screeching to a stop angled across the front of the cruiser. Then he snapped his head around to watch for the blue station wagon to pass them by.

It didn't.

He finally spotted it in the parking lot of a building just across the street. The driver was climbing out. There was a flash of a white head. Then time seemed to slow as the details of the scene filled the spaces of his fogged mind.

The building was a Goodwill depot. The white-haired woman struggled with a green plastic garbage bag toward the drop-off box, lifted the lid, and dropped the bag in.

12

"Favourite Hits of the 60's, 70's and 80's, 620 C-T-B-X. That was the Walker Brothers, and the good news is we'll get lots of sunshine today. The bad news is that *it's cold*: minus twenty-five at 7:21." He tapped the computer's touch screen to start some polka music. "Hey, if you're over sixty and you're, uh, looking for a way to really warm up with your favourite dance partner…" The bit was about a study claiming seniors who drank coffee were more sexually active—a lightweight story, but a good fit with his audience. Until he blew the punch line. He stumbled over a word, and that was all it took.

He triggered the commercial break, turned his mic off and slammed the cushioned front of the control board. Shit. His concentration had been off all week. He'd start to say something, then change it around mid-sentence, leaving a mangled mess. He flubbed common words. His creative side was struggling, too. He had to resort to using humour from a web service Arnott subscribed to that wasn't Lee's style, because his evenings of prep work were coming up dry.

Was he burnt out? It happened sometimes, especially with morning men. One day it just wasn't fun anymore, and that was the end of a career. Or might as well be. Maybe his brain was telling him he needed a change. To another radio station—a new music format? It struck him that he'd spent ten of his prime years playing songs that were relevant when he was a teenager—many even older than that. They were relics.

What did that make him?

The thought left him shaken. He'd be lost without his job. An unwanted nobody with no practical skills. Worse: a *has-been*.

Dale Lawson came into the news booth. Lee straightened and made a show of checking the log screen. He got along with Dale now. He even admitted that she was a better reader than Dave Berg, though their banter still fell flat sometimes. Was that her fault or his?

After his production shift he was called to Maddy Ellis's office. His boss looked embarrassed. She asked him casually about the police investigation, but kept glancing at a piece of paper on her desk.

"What's that? A complaint letter?"

Her startled look made him realize he'd hit the mark.

"Yes, as a matter of fact. This guy's complaining that you're not *funny* anymore. Accuses me of muzzling you because of political correctness. How am I supposed to respond to that?"

"You're kidding."

"I thought he was." She handed the letter over. Lee skimmed the page—the man wrote well, seemed to be intelligent. A long-time listener, too. Maddy said, "Read the last line."

"Shit. He's got a ballot."

She nodded. "Says he's going to mark himself down as listening to CWLF every quarter hour of the week, as a protest. How much effect do you think that will have on the ratings."

Lee dropped into the chair. "Yeah, that'll make a difference. Wonder who gave him that idea."

"That's not really the point."

"What is the point? That I'm not funny anymore—because one guy said so?"

"You want to force me to say it? Ok. He's right. You're not up to scratch on the air. Your timing's off. You're sloppy. And I don't even hear that much of the show." She leaned forward. "You're an entertainer, Lee, but you're only human. Of course the stress is getting to you. How could it not be?"

"I have one bad week after ten years and suddenly I stink like yesterday's fish?"

"Come off it, I'm trying to cut you some slack. Cut me some, too. You know how it works: if one faithful listener got worked up enough to write a letter, how many hundreds of others are just deciding to try another station instead?"

"It could just be one guy with an axe to grind. Thanks for your *support*," he snapped, and launched himself out of the chair. He started toward the reception area then changed his mind and took a couple of steps in the other direction...stopped again. Where was he going? What was it he had to do now? He'd turned around a third time when he saw Ellis watching him through the glass beside her door. He couldn't read her expression. He didn't need to.

In the announcers' lounge he slammed his locker door in frustration, not sure whether his anger was directed at Ellis or himself. Why had he blown up at her? He'd been thinking the same things about his show only twenty minutes earlier. It just hurt a lot more to realize that others were thinking it too.

The sound of Karen paging him to the lobby made his shoulders slump in defeat. He sure as hell didn't feel like talking to anyone.

The man at the lobby window was an inch or two shorter than Lee, but with shoulders that strained the leather of his winter jacket.

"Hi, I'm Lee Garrett. Were you looking for me?"

His hand was engulfed in a rock hard grip.

"Yeah, I know who you are. We've met, but I didn't think you'd remember." Lee began to make excuses, but the other waved them off. "Name's Tucker. Maybe somebody told you."

"Tucker…the *Trucker?*"

The response was a huge crooked grin.

"You're the guy who…you saved my life! Damn, I was a goner and you found me. Saved me. I don't know how to thank you for that."

"It was a life worth savin'. Hell, who else would I listen to if you weren't around?" They shook hands again. It seemed inadequate.

"How about I give you a tour of the radio station and then buy you lunch? It's the least I can do."

"Sure, yeah, that'd be great. I been listening to you guys forever."

Tucker was like a big kid as they went through the building, a smile fixed to his square face, craggy from an acne-scarred adolescence. After the tour they went to a nearby steakhouse and Lee told him to order anything on the menu, and as much as he wanted to drink.

"Tucker…is there a first name to go with that?"

"Tucker's good enough." He laughed. "Even my mother calls me that nowadays." When his meal came he proclaimed it good. Ten times better than navy food.

"You were in the Canadian navy? Where did you serve?"

"All over. The hairiest was probably the Arabian Sea. On the *Fredericton*—one of our frigates—stoppin' pirates, supporting the troops at Kandahar. Mostly preventing drug runners and smugglers tryin' to get weapons to the Taliban."

"Sounds exciting."

"Maybe if I wasn't a mechanic." Tucker laughed. "Always been good with cars, so when I enlisted I figured an engine's an engine, y'know? Never spent a day in clean clothes the whole time I was in." He gave a slow shake of his head, with a trace of pain in his smile. "Never got a promotion either. Couldn't quite keep my nose clean and my mouth shut. Finally saw the writing on the wall and got out. Never fired a shot—wasn't any kinda hero or anything."

"Hey, I know somebody who thinks you're a hero," Lee said. "You're looking at him."

Tucker gave Lee a soul handshake, his sleeve sliding down to reveal part of a large tattoo.

"Get that in the navy?" Lee asked.

Tucker hesitated. "Aw, hell, no point keepin' it a secret. I was in the joint. Prison. Three years." He gave a sidelong look, wanting to see Lee's reaction, without appearing to care.

"Let me guess: couldn't get a job when you got out of the service?"

"Not a goddamned one. Anyway, I started drinkin', gamblin'... and paying' my bills with other people's credit cards. Holdin' up convenience stores, makin' like I had a gun. Then some tough guy clerk refused to hand over the money. Some mob guys I was into for heavy cash nearly took my head off, gave me a shotgun, and sent me back into the store." His voice had gone quiet. "I got the money. Then I got caught. Good thing, too. Who knows what shit I woulda got into? Did my time…. Gotta say, though, it sure as hell don't make it any easier to find a job."

"But you did. You work for Foster's, right? Foster's Interfreight? How do you like driving a big rig?"

"I do, you know. It can be lonely. But all that long, empty road clears the mind." He laughed and emptied his beer glass. Lee ordered another. Tucker drummed his fingers on the table.

"Just got bad timing, is all."

"How do you mean?"

The big shoulders shrugged. "You didn't hear about the cutbacks? Yeah, Foster's has to lay off some people and I ain't been with them very long. So I'll probably be on the chopping block. I don't blame 'em. Good company. Just the times, eh?"

They made small talk after that, and finally Tucker insisted he should let Lee get back to work.

"I'd been meaning to track you down," Lee said, "but things have been... well, anyway, I'm really glad you dropped by. Gave me a chance to say thanks."

"No problem. You keep up the good work, 'cause I'll be listening."

As Lee drove away the words of a Joe South song ran through his head. You couldn't judge a man like Tucker until you'd walked a mile in his shoes.

When he got back to the station he called Foster's Interfreight. Harry Foster was a good head—they weren't close friends but sometimes traded favours. Foster promised to keep Tucker on the payroll for the time being and Lee promised to let Foster win at golf. Both men knew Foster could beat Lee blindfolded. They made vague plans to see each other, and Lee hung up feeling good about something he'd done for the first time in forever.

13

HE DIDN'T EXPECT THE PHONE TO RING ON SATURDAYS and didn't want it to. It would be someone from work needing something from him. It was never personal—that would mean he had a *life*. He didn't pick it up until the third ring.

"Lee? It's Candace... Ross."

"You're the only Candace I know."

"Really? I thought you knew everybody in town."

"Not quite. There are a few mothers who wisely hide their daughters from me."

"Oops. Too late." He could hear the smile. "Anyway, I was hoping you remembered our...date to take Paul tobogganing today." She waited for a reply. "You forgot, didn't you?"

"No...well, yes I forgot. But I didn't want to forget."

She laughed. "Well, I guess that's something. Still want to go?"

Did he? It had been a lousy week—he felt drained. Excuses began to form in his mind, but he said, "Sure. Why not?"

"That took some thinking."

"Sorry. Maybe I'm still waking up. I'd love to go."

They agreed to meet at Paul's and she reminded him of the address. He found it easily enough, but as he approached the door he could hear raised voices behind it. Paul greeted him looking like his hand in the cookie jar had pulled out dog shit. Candace and Lenny Schwartz stood facing each other just inside the living room. It was clear Schwartz would have been happier to see Jehovah's Witnesses.

"Sorry, Lee." Candace barely turned her head. "We're having a little difference of opinion."

"The difference is, you talk a good line but you ain't the one who's blind. Filling him with all this shit. Pauly's the one who's gotta walk out in front of cars and get on a bus he can't even see. If it's so fucking easy, *you* do it."

"I'm not saying it's easy—it takes training. But it can be done."

"Go ahead then. No? Didn't think so." Schwartz crossed his arms. Candace turned a red face to Lee. He could tell it was taking all of her self-control to keep her professional cool. He wondered if she could gracefully back down.

She went to her coat draped over the sofa, and pulled a thick wool scarf free. She folded it into a thinner strip then pulled it over her eyes and began to tie it behind her head.

"Candace…"

"It's all right, Lee. Check it Mr. Schwartz. *Check it.* Make sure I can't see anything."

Schwartz was struck dumb. His hands twitched, uncertain. Then he stepped toward her and yanked on the scarf ends hard enough to make Lee wince. Candace didn't react. The man looked to make sure the folds of the scarf would prevent her even seeing the ground in front of her. When he stepped back, she put her coat on and snatched up the white cane leaning near it. She looked confident as she walked to the door, even making an allowance for Lee as he moved to the side and held the door for her.

"Don't say it." She tilted her head at him. "I haven't had to do this in a while. Maybe it's overdue."

She made quick progress. Lee followed closely behind, and then Schwartz walked a couple of steps ahead of Paul, letting the boy hold onto his bent right arm just above the elbow. But the man's quick tugs when Paul strayed sideways betrayed his foul temper. Candace changed her gait to adjust for the slippery sidewalk and feel it's texture with her feet as she swung the cane rhythmically in front of her. The cane told her when she reached a space where the snowbank along the side of the street had been shovelled clear for a bus stop.

She pulled her wallet from her coat, fumbling with the change pocket. Lee had to fight the urge to help her. When a bus arrived she asked the driver if it stopped at Southridge Mall. He confirmed that it did, and she stepped smoothly aboard and paid her fare. Unprepared, Lenny Schwartz took twice as long.

The passengers stared openly at the blindfold while she gently used the cane to find a seat without legs dangling from it. Lee watched her too, admiring the determined set of her jaw, disappointed that he couldn't see the fire in her eyes. Certainly this was a test she had trained for long ago, but it was like driving a car: he was glad no one made him take a driving exam anymore.

An automated system announced the names of the bus stops with plenty of warning. At the mall Lee waited for Candace to disembark and face a greater test. Even though they'd been to the same mall together only weeks earlier, she wasn't likely to remember where buses let people off. But she barely hesitated. He realized she was using sounds as much as the cane. Footsteps muffled by snow. The swish of the entrance doors. Just inside the mall she stepped to the side and stopped.

"Is everyone still with me?"

"We're here," Lee said. "Paul and … Mr. Schwartz are about four feet to my right, your left." She adjusted her head.

"Paul? So far it's been pretty straightforward. It gets a bit more complicated now. In my training we weren't allowed to ask for help, but since I'm trying to show you how *you* can get around, I'll ask people when I think you'd need to." She raised her chin. "Will that satisfy you, Mr. Schwartz? Or should I also pretend to be deaf and dumb?"

"I don't give a shit."

"No, that's pretty clear." She began to walk away. Schwartz opened his mouth to snap back but Lee put a hand on his arm.

"Easy," he said. "She knows that's not true. But why not see what she can do? What have you got to lose?"

Schwartz angrily yanked his arm free and pulled Paul forward.

"Paul," Lee continued, "you might not have got very much out of this so far, but Candace is just walking through the mall sweeping her cane from side to side and people are getting out of her way, no problem. I expect she's using the sounds of the building—the cash registers and the echoes of voices and things. You can probably tell the difference from place to place, too, right?"

The boy just nodded, still aware of his uncle's anger. From then on Lee provided occasional commentary.

Candace approached the lottery kiosk where a man was ripping open Nevada tickets. She asked the clerk for directions to the book store. The woman pointed first, even as she was staring at the blindfold, then, a little flustered, described the route in words. Lee and the Schwartzes waited outside the book store while Candace asked for help from a clerk and made a purchase that she tucked into a wide pocket inside her coat. They followed her as she made her way back to the bus stop, rarely deviating from a straight path.

Paul had begun to smile, as if witnessing a magic trick. Schwartz still wore the face of a gargoyle smarting from a fresh pigeon dropping.

No doubt he hoped Candace would fail, and he nearly got his wish on the way home. The bus let them off on the corner of the

Schwartz's block, but on the opposite side of the street from their house. Candace got off the bus facing the wrong way, and hesitated, trying to make sense of the traffic noises from the nearby intersection. Finally she made a decision, turned and listened again, then began to cross the street.

Lee heard the sound of brakes almost before he saw the car. It was making a right turn on a green light and had barely slowed down. Candace was stepping right into its path.

The scene froze into a shocking tableau: the noise of the tires, the threatening bulk of moving metal, and the woman startled into immobility, cane falling from her hand. Lee lunged forward, but there was no way he could reach her in time. The car managed to swerve just enough, lifting the hem of her coat with its passage.

The driver slowed to make sure she hadn't been hit, then gave an angry blast of his horn. Candace still hadn't moved when Lee grabbed her arm, scooped up the fallen cane, and gently pulled her back to the sidewalk. Paul's face was taut with fear.

"Is she all right?" he asked, his voice cracking.

"Stupid. I…was stupid. Paul, I hope you can learn from that mistake." Her voice didn't betray the trembling Lee could feel through her arm. "I didn't wait long enough to make sure the cars saw me and knew that I was going to cross. A lot of intersections have crosswalks with loud bird calls to tell blind people when it's safe to cross, but here…you have to pay more attention."

The light had changed, so she waited for it to change again, thrust her arm and cane forward, waited another moment, then strode across the street as if nothing had happened.

She was waiting in front of the house when they caught up. Only when they were in the living room did she reach back to untie the scarf.

"Great technique," Schwartz scoffed. "The funeral homes would love it."

"I made a mistake, yes. I was rusty... and sloppy—I didn't famil-iarize myself enough with the neighbourhood. But we'll make sure Paul is well-trained and sure of himself before he tries anything like that. What about you, Paul?" She stooped toward the boy. "Convinced?"

He thought hard. "I don't know. I guess I could do it... if you help me. It's kind of scary."

"Sure it is. But practice makes perfect. It's the only way to become your own person, and not have to depend on other people all your life." She was looking at his uncle.

"What did you buy?" Paul wanted to know. She laughed.

"Oh, it's just a CD. Somebody narrating a *Star Trek* story. Patrick Stewart, I think."

"Cool!"

Lenny Schwartz wasn't about to concede anything. "I gotta go to work for a few hours. Goddamn winter plays hell with the cables." He reached for a leather tool belt leaning against the closet door.

Lee looked a question at Candace, but she only shrugged. The situation was delicate—did she dare to ask for anything more? It was Paul who spoke up.

"Can I still go tobogganing, Uncle Lenny? They were going to take me tobogganing today." He couldn't see the look on his uncle's face, but added a quiet, "Please?"

"*I don't give...* whatever. Do what you want." Schwartz pushed roughly past Candace, drove his feet into his work boots, not bothering to lace them up, and slammed the door as he left. The sound of his truck as it drove away broke the spell, and Candace began to round up Paul's snow clothes.

Late model Toyotas weren't designed to carry full-length tobog-gans. Candace apologized for the cords that ran through the windows and across the ceiling. She'd used an old slab of mattress foam for pad-ding on the roof.

"I didn't know how else to attach it."

"I'm amazed you could even find one of these antiques," Lee said.

"Wow. It's made of wood." Paul ran his hand along an edge.

The city's Adanac ski hill had a toboggan area, but it was often crowded. The A.Y. Jackson Lookout was popular, too, but a longer drive than Candace wanted. Instead, she chose an undeveloped slope on the outskirts of the city that hadn't been travelled since the last snowfall. There weren't many smooth hills in Sudbury's landscape of soot-blackened rock, but this one was perfect: the fresh snow powdery and dry.

"I haven't done this since my kids were little. They're teenagers now." Lee ruefully looked down the long slope from the top.

"I'm sure it's like riding a bicycle."

"Absolutely. A bike with no brakes!"

He needn't have worried. It required an effort just to get down the hill the first time. The toboggan sank into the fresh snow and ploughed a bow wave. But each run after that packed and smoothed the snow until the toboggan shot along, the path stretching like an elastic band that pulled them to the top again, eager for more. Their snow-sprayed faces soon wore patches of red on cheeks creased by exuberant smiles.

"Watch for that rock!"

"You're steering too close to that little tree. Duck!"

"Here comes the bump!"

Candace deftly painted pictures for the boy, who reacted to each warning with a grunt or a squawk. Lee sat at the back of the toboggan because of his longer legs, and when Paul grumped about snow in his face he was given the middle spot, sandwiched between the grown-ups. Candace gamely bore the brunt of the crystal barrage.

At first Paul clung to Candace's coat hem to stay in the tracks they made back up the hill, but before long he was following the path of crushed snow on his own, guided by the swish of nylon from her ski suit. The sun was warm, and Lee began to sweat as he climbed. On a whim he lifted his feet and ran to the top, then leaned on his knees, looking back at the others through panted clouds of steam.

The scene was postcard perfect. For a penetrating instant this woman and child could have been his family, climbing toward him with frost-ripe smiles. A bittersweet image. When Candace asked about the look on his face, he just shook his head.

"We don't have to spend all day at this," he said. "I thought we could grab a pizza, then take Paul to a sports memorabilia shop I know. If we hurry, we could drop into Hobby Depot and check out the model kits, too."

She raised an eyebrow as she smiled. "Hurry? On a day like this? What's the rush? We can do those things some other time. Do you always live your life to a schedule?" But she didn't expect an answer. Their shoulders brushed as she turned toward the landscape spread out below. "Just soak it in. We don't get too many days like this." She drew a deep breath of fresh air.

No, he thought, *not many days like this at all.*

She gave him a grin. "Slow down, you move too fast."

Had he told her how much he loved Simon and Garfunkel? Now that song would always remind him of her.

"I wish Paul could see this," he said softly.

"Maybe he can. You're good with words. Describe it to him."

His lips automatically formed a refusal, but the look in her eyes made him change his mind. He gently took hold of Paul's shoulders, turned him toward the town, and tried to capture what he saw with inadequate phrases. The act of describing it made him aware of even more details. The craggy hills that lifted their heads throughout the city were starkly beautiful with their black shards of rock poking through a covering of white. The drab subdivision below them was

transformed by winter: houses hung from the sky by lumpy strands
of cotton; ploughed streets became the outlines of black matchstick
castles; wisps of sponge cloud wiped imagined blemishes from a vast
blue chalkboard. He was grateful that Paul hadn't been born blind, so
he knew what trees looked like, the colour of a winter sky, the sparkle
of sun-bathed snow. Even in such a simple scene, there were so many
things that would be impossible to describe without a set of common
references. It made Lee feel humble. He hadn't stopped to look—just
look—at anything for a very long time.

On their next slide down the hill the toboggan veered off the
track, spilling them into a drift. Lee rolled to his knees and watched
Paul lick the snow from under his nose, his tongue thrust out as far as
it would go. The boy still wiped his eyes clear before anything else. His
comic sour expression made Lee laugh, and Paul laughed too.

Candace raised her head, sputtering, then flopped back into the
white fluff with a mock sigh of surrender. She turned her head toward
Lee and chuckled self-consciously.

Snowflakes melted on the ends of her long, dark lashes. The barest
wisp of steam rose from full lips. He had an urge to press her down into
the snow beneath his weight, his mouth to hers. His breath stilled,
and he drank her in with his eyes.

"Thanks a lot!" Paul stood over them. "I wanted to play in the
snow, not eat it."

Lee got slowly to his feet and pulled Candace up. If she guessed
what had been in his mind, she gave no sign, only dusted off her ski
pants and reached for Paul's hand.

They made a few more runs down the hill, then went to a nearby
restaurant for some pizza and hot chocolate. Paul talked about school.
They watched him, and each other.

Lenny Schwartz's cable TV truck was in the driveway when they
got back. The man said nothing while they helped Paul remove his

snow clothes. Paul thanked them for a great time. Schwartz kept his eyes on a basketball game and sipped at a beer.

At the street Candace stopped. "I had a great time too. Thanks."

"It was your idea," Lee said. "You made it a special day for Paul. Even the first part."

"Oh, yeah. Not too eager to try that again soon. But...well, all my clients are important to me, it's just that..."

"Paul's at a point where you could save him, or lose him. Right?"

"Something like that."

Then it came to them that they were standing in full view of the picture window with Lenny Schwartz on the other side. She climbed into her car and they exchanged goodbyes. On the way home Lee realized they'd said nothing about seeing each other again.

He tried to figure out his impulse on the toboggan hill—was he falling for Candace Ross? He didn't think of her as a potential sexual conquest. He liked her too much for that. Respected her. But he didn't want a repeat of what he felt for Michaela—the highs or the hurt. He had a family, such as it was. He was too old to start over again.

If nothing else, the timing was terrible. His life was a shambles even without being under a threat of death. He couldn't inflict that burden on someone else. Better not to make any more plans. Just let it drop. If she called, he'd keep things on a professional level, or even see Paul on his own. That would be best.

He tried to ignore a hole that gnawed at his gut.

14

MONDAY HIS SHOW SPARKLED. THE PUNCH LINES popped, and spawned more, just like in the old days. He was in a groove. Even Dale Lawson was witty. They laughed when someone called asking for Dale *Awesome.*

The bubble burst when he got into an argument with Chuck Norwood and Hal Leonard in Ellis's office about the ratings promotion that had begun that week. People entered the contest by filling out ballots at Greensleeves restaurant. The winner would have the morning show broadcast from their home, along with a lavish breakfast delivered by Greensleeves. Lee insisted that it had nothing to do with improved ratings—there was no requirement to listen to the station in order to win. It was nothing more than added value to a sales package, with Lee as the icing on the cake.

Leonard was a good Sales Manager, and Lee liked him, but he was totally incapable of seeing the distinction between a ratings promotion and a sales vehicle. To him, you made the sale anyway you could—if it wasn't illegal or against your religion, he didn't understand how anyone could object.

Although this was a battle Lee had lost more than once, he still couldn't surrender without a fight.

"My job is to deliver listeners to this radio station," he seethed. "I'm not a piece of property for sale or rent. There are words for that."

"*Are you finished?*" Maddy's steel tone should have warned him off.

"Or has everybody around here spent so much time on their backs they're getting to enjoy the view?"

"That's *enough!*" Her hand cracked against the desk. "Are you saying you refuse? Do you really think you're in a position to do that lately?"

The words slapped his face and took his breath away. He struggled to his feet and stepped toward the door. As he pulled it open he rasped, "Maybe you should start thinking about a Plan B, Hal." But he was looking at Ellis. When he turned away he nearly flattened Norwood's assistant Pam as she stood stunned in the hallway.

～

He cursed his reflection in the pot lid as he heated some beans for lunch. Didn't he have enough trouble without trying to get fired? He didn't even object to doing his show from someone's house—he'd done it before, and it was usually a good time. But now he'd backed them all into a corner, including himself. Had he left Ellis any room for compromise? He didn't think so. Things said in private might be forgiven—they'd been friends a long time. Insulting her in front of an audience ensured that she'd stick to her guns. As a leader, she couldn't afford to do anything else.

He was in no position to refuse the assignment. He'd have to go ahead with the contest and keep his mouth shut. Maybe that way the whole thing would blow over.

He hated to know he was in the right, but also in the wrong. Why couldn't anything be black and white anymore?

When he lay down after lunch he thought about a ratings giveaway from a couple of years back. They'd sent five couples to Jamaica! Now, with the accountants running the circus, there was never more than one grand prize winner. Lee had even gone along as an escort. He'd had a fantastic time, until he'd come back home and learned the cost.

The colours of Jamaica were what stayed with him: sand as white as the teeth of the bar girls who brought him drinks; rainforest greens so liquid he kept expecting the leaves to drip from the trees. And the Caribbean water—when they put that blue on a postcard it always looked fake. A northern-grown brain simply refused its reality.

Snorkelling had been heaven, just offshore from Dunn's River Falls, hovering over a reef of colours in crayon box profusion only inches from his chest one moment, dropping away the next into grottoes and valleys and arches six feet deep or more. Uncountable schools of fish in extravagant costume ball finery.

He'd fallen in love with the perpetual humour of the island's people. His contest winners were a great bunch too. There'd only been one cloud over the trip, but it was a thunderhead. Michaela.

How could everyone have overlooked the fact that his wife would want to go too? Would expect to go. When Lee found out she wasn't included, only a week before the departure, it was just after one of their increasingly frequent fights: a gloves-off screaming match. Otherwise he might have insisted that the station include her, or refused to go himself, or bought her a ticket with their own money. He did none of those things, and Michaela never forgave him. She and the kids were gone when he returned home.

~

He used the last of the milk in some mushroom soup he heated for dinner, so afterward he took the car to the corner store. Coming out with the milk, some lottery tickets, and a bag of Doritos, he saw a truck with the Interfreight logo parked at the bar across the street. Could it be Tucker? He could use some friendly company.

The bar was a murky pit that made the outside dusk look bright. He finally spotted a guy with an Interfreight uniform at one of the tables, but it wasn't Tucker. As he turned to leave, someone else caught his eye. A wiry figure sitting at the bar was turning a cigarette lighter over and over in his fingers.

Lenny Schwartz.

Lee pushed the exit door, but was stopped by a thought. Schwartz was drinking alone—a man didn't do that if he had friends to drink with. Could he be an alcoholic who'd driven his friends away? Maybe the man's surly character was just loneliness. Lee knew what that was about. He sighed and stepped back inside.

"Mr. Schwartz." The bar stool creaked under him.

"*Garrett.*" The word could have been 'cockroach'.

"I know you don't like me. I think we got off on the wrong foot. How about I buy you a beer?"

The only answer was silence, so Lee waved two fingers at the bartender and bottles of Molson Canadian clinked into place in front of them. A few deep swallows of the beer weren't enough to help him find the perfect words. He'd have to wing it.

"Don't sell Candace Ross short. She really does care about Paul."

"I don't need a lecture from you."

"No. But you want what's best for Paul. So does she. I think he's pretty special, too."

"Big of you." Alcohol wasn't the only reason Lenny Schwartz didn't have friends.

"It can't be easy looking after him. His parents were killed by a drunk driver, right? You must have worked hard to get custody."

"I was married then—makes all the difference. Except the bitch never wanted kids. Said it was wrong to bring 'em into a shitty world like this. You radio stars wouldn't know about that."

"She left?"

"Not until she had her fill of whining, and figured out how to take most of my money."

"No grandparents."

"You sound like a fucking social worker. My mother's in a home. Father's dead. Good thing, 'cause if he'd laid a hand on Pauly I'd've had to kill him myself. The other grandparents are in Finland. Their English ain't good, but I used to send 'em pictures all the time. Until Pauly had his accident. Now there ain't nothin' worth sending." He drained his beer. Lee ordered another and it was claimed without comment.

"That's when your wife left you—when Paul went blind?"

"Whore wasn't gonna nursemaid no blind kid wasn't even hers. He was always good to her, too. Jesus, he's a good kid. Never thought anything that good'd come out of our family." The face softened for a moment, but then his jaw went stiff. "What the fuck do you care? Bring your Blue Jays crap around—make like you're some kinda hero and I'm an asshole."

"I've never tried to come between you and Paul. I hurt his feelings by accident and wanted to make it up to him. Turns out he's a great kid. But you must realize you need help."

Schwartz's eyes spat fire. "*I don't need any help from you.*"

"Not me. Candace Ross."

"Oh, right. Radio hero's new squeeze of the week."

Lee slid off the stool. "All right, dickhead. Have it your way. Keep thinking that Paul can't enjoy the things you used to do together. Take all that away from him. Then drive away all the other people who want to help him, and what's left will be your own goddamned fault." He pulled on his coat. "It's pretty clear which one of you is really blind."

He stalked out of the man-made darkness into the honest night.

≈

When he got back to his apartment, snow had begun to fall. There was a message on his answering machine from Dan Arnott. He groaned and called the Program Director at home.

"Lee. They say this one might be the mother of all snowstorms. The streets could be impassable by tomorrow. We've decided to put the morning crew up at the Radisson overnight; you can walk from there if the snow's deep. Dale's got an apartment just off Mackenzie Street, so she won't have a problem."

"Are you serious?"

"Sure. It's ratings. Can't have the morning team off on a weekday. Wise says you've done this before."

"Yeah, my first winter here. Most of the storm missed us."

"Just get your ass over there, all right?"

When Lee checked into the hotel he found Wise, Wright, and J.J. in the bar with beers in front of them. Larry, Barry, and Jerry—a name for a comedy team maybe. They seemed to think so, from the way they were laughing. Already on their third round. Sure, they'd make it to the station in the morning, but they wouldn't be able to read for shit.

Lee hesitated, then ordered a Heineken. The drinks would be on their hotel tab, which would be paid for in advertising.

"We'll be hearing Radisson ads for a month after this," Wise said.

"Two months, if I have anything to do with it." Wright hoisted his glass to a roar of approval. "Tell the truth, Lee. Those sore hands of yours—you really just burned 'em on a hot piece of tail, right?"

"Oooh, wonder if there's any tail on the loose around this place tonight?" Wise mused. "Why couldn't there be a convention of professional lap dancers, or something?"

J.J. almost spit out a mouthful of beer.

"Look, that one got somebody all excited." Wright started lifting the side of the table with his hand. "Down, J.J.! Down, boy! Keep that love muscle under control, would you?" Their laughter drew looks from a couple of staff members near the door.

"Careful, son," Wise drawled. "That little filly over thar got her eyes on yew. Look like her saddle's ready to plumb wear your ol' cowboy right down t'the nub. Need bandages on 'im, just like on Lee's hands las' week."

"I know why his hands needed bandages." Wright leaned forward. "New issue of Penthouse show up in the mailbox, Lee?"

"I thought I heard the sound of rabble. All the way from my room on the third floor." Sandy Schell was walking slowly to their table. Her perfect blond hair made Lee feel windblown.

"You took long enough," Wise said.

"It's Barry who has the problem with *arriving prematurely*, not me."

Her morning show partner groaned and mimed being stabbed in the heart. "See how she treats me every morning?" he said. "Like a dominatrix but without the sex."

The newswoman's presence didn't change the tone of the conversation. She was on her second beer when Lee left for the men's room. J.J. followed him in. As they returned to their table, Lee asked, "J.J., you see a lot of racism in this city?"

"Still thinkin' it's Skins after you, man? Yeah, a few rednecks here 'n' there. Not too much."

"Somebody's on my case but I don't know if it's Skins or not. I would have thought a gang of kids would have better things to do than keep coming after me. That's why I wondered if there are real hard case bigots around."

"Beats me." J.J. shook his head. "I can usually tell from the way somebody looks at me if they got a problem with my skin or not. Or maybe I just think I can."

After a second beer Lee called it quits and went to bed. No one else moved. He was grateful they'd been given separate rooms. He had no desire to spend the night listening to drunken snoring. Or vomiting.

When his travel alarm woke him he went over to the window. Even from the third floor he could tell the snow on the street was deep, and no plough had come by. The snow was still coming down, blown nearly sideways by the strongest gusts. There would be drifts. Smaller streets would be clogged. Most people wouldn't be going anywhere.

Tim Horton's was open, but the evening shift was still on duty, their replacements unable to get to work. The eyes of the girl at the cash were red-rimmed. Lee took a coffee and a toasted bagel, hoping they wouldn't be stone cold by the time he got to work.

The others gradually arrived at the station. Sandy Schell was immaculate. Wright looked like a homeless guy who needed toothpicks to prop his eyes open. Wise wasn't much better, but J.J. looked the same as he always did.

All of Lee's prepared bits were set aside—on a morning like that people didn't want to hear about anything but the weather and how it was going to affect them. The phone lit up like a movie marquee, but it was always kids or their parents wanting to know if the schools were closed and the buses cancelled, usually right after Lee had mentioned all those details on the air. Snow depth, highway closures, accidents, event cancellations—the information came in and he gave it back out again. It took more stamina than talent, but he didn't mind. These were the times people really needed radio, and nothing else could deliver the goods so quickly.

He was tired when he got off the air. Most of the office staff hadn't made it in yet so there were no ads to record. He could leave early.

The snowplough crews had begun to get the upper hand on the main routes by then. Most of the side streets bore single sets of deep tracks where drivers had followed the easiest path. A plough had just made a pass through Lee's street before he got to it, so he could reach his driveway, though the mouth of it was blocked by snow. He'd have to shovel before he could get the car in.

Roy Lester used Lee's arrival as an excuse to take a break from clearing his front step. "Some storm, eh? Closed my office. Not that I mind a day off. Streets bad all over?"

"The city's a mess. Crews probably won't get to most of it before late afternoon. I'm amazed they ploughed our street so soon."

"It's 'cause we got seniors on the street." In his late fifties, Roy clearly didn't include himself in the assessment. "At least Rich has the day off high school. Now, if he'd just get out of bed I could put a shovel in his hand." He laughed. "Wish I knew where the damn cat was, though. Didn't come home last night. Suppose she'd find shelter somewhere." He resumed his shovelling, and Lee continued up the driveway, pulling his collar high to block a gust that tossed snow at his face. The walls of the two houses on either side of a narrow driveway channelled the winter winds, producing some formidable drifts. He'd shovelled only two days earlier, and scattered lots of salt around to melt the ice, especially near the door. He grimaced as he pushed through snow that topped his boots and sieved down to his socks.

Afterward, the scene would be etched into his brain in vivid detail: drifts like dunes, especially one large one over the concrete stoop at the side door; snow patches dotted haphazardly over the brick wall; a miniature white cyclone swirling crystals back into the air. He had his keys out, hand raised to grasp the handle of the storm door, when he saw a small, mottled, tan-and-white bundle half-covered by white, lying at his feet.

Tiger, the Lesters' cat.

She was clearly dead, frozen stiff, he thought. He sighed and stooped down, setting his briefcase onto the snow. It created a small cascade down the pile, revealing a strip of black. His hand froze. He used the briefcase to brush away more of the snow.

Black cable. What the hell was black cable doing against the door?

He snapped upright and quickly backed away.

Black cable. Electrical cable!

Now he could see the bare wire in contact with the metal of the storm door. In dumb horror he swept his eyes along the bottom of the wall toward the street. He looked at the hydro pole at the end of the driveway, and the long black whip that trailed down and vanished into the snow bank beneath.

Christ Almighty.

A live hydro wire. A wire that would turn a moist metal door into a death trap.

He skittered away another few feet, and began to shake—with fear, rage—he didn't know. His eyes were locked on the innocuous door and the damning mound of fur at its foot. He backed slowly to the reassuring solidity of the Lesters' wall and slid to the ground.

Storms blew down hydro wires. A strong wind could snap one around like the tail of a kite.

But he knew it hadn't been that way. The storm wasn't the villain, only the accomplice. Someone had meant for him to touch that door.

The pretence was over.

Someone wanted him dead.

15

LEE WAS AN AUTOMATON: HIS INSTINCTS WERE SHARP, the words came out smoothly. But as soon as the mic was off he stared blankly into space.

At 7:45 he'd been answering the phone for a contest, planning to record the winning call and play it back in a few minutes.

"620 The Box, you're the sixth caller, so what's the name of the WinSong from last night?" There was no response. "Hello? You're the sixth caller, so you've got the chance to win if you know last night's WinSong."

"Is that the dead man?"

A deep gravely bass. Electronically altered to sound that way.

"What? Who is this?"

There was a click and a dial tone. It droned for twenty seconds before Lee punched the button to kill the line. Dimly he registered that the song was halfway through and the phone was flashing again. He brought up the next line and took down the caller's information, but there wasn't enough time to cue up the recording and play it on air. He'd mention their name—that was all he could do. Then he realized that he hadn't even asked them to name the WinSong. They'd have a laugh at his expense.

Minutes later the phone line flashed again. Lee started the computer recording, and took the call.

"Good morning, 620 The Box..."

"Hello *dead man*." The dial tone whined, and Lee nearly threw the handset against the wall. After that he was on autopilot, the rest of his brain trying to make sense of what he'd heard.

At nine o'clock he called Detective Davis.

"Doesn't the station have caller ID?" she asked.

"No need, usually. Just extra expense. And the control board isn't wired for it."

"Well, I'd suggest somebody cough up a little money and get it. If you can email a copy of those phone calls, we'll go over them. It's probably too much to expect an identification, but we might narrow the search a little—tell if it's a man or a woman, old or young. And since they obviously know where you live, I'm going to arrange for some video surveillance of your apartment. The radio station, too, if your boss will allow it. Meanwhile I'll get forensics out to your place and see what we can come up with. Maybe a neighbour saw somebody climbing that pole. I'm assuming the cable's been repaired."

"Yeah. Not until nearly 9:30 last night, though. I wore out my welcome at the neighbours."

"All right. I'll track down the hydro worker—see if he can remember whether the cable looked broken or was cut, though I'm almost willing to bet he won't be sure. So far, whoever's doing these things has left us with nothing."

But at least no corpse, either, Lee thought. Not yet.

≈

The call from Candace took him by surprise.

"Lee? I'm not sure how to ask this…did you send me something?"

"No. Like what?"

"Like flowers. You didn't have a bouquet of flowers delivered to me at work?"

"No." He wished he'd thought of it. Then he had to remind himself they were only going to be professional acquaintances. "You mean there's no card?"

"There is, but it's only signed with the initial L. I figured that would be you."

"Sadly, I'm not that gallant, romantic, or smart—choose your adjective. You must know other people…" He caught his breath. "Lenny. It could also stand for Lenny Schwartz."

The phone line buzzed with a harsh laugh. "You can't be serious. Although, he did send me a small bouquet once, soon after I started working with Paul. I wasn't on his hate list for the first week or so."

"You probably aren't now, either. The man just doesn't have any social skills. Maybe this is his way to apologize for being a jerk last weekend. Or maybe Paul put him up to it—kids can get strange ideas."

"Like trying to match me with Lenny Schwartz? That's…that's just creepy."

Lee laughed. "Well, sorry to say, it wasn't me."

The silence after that had begun to feel awkward when Candace spoke again.

"Uh, ok. Well, I…realized the other day that we hadn't, uh, made any plans. To see Paul again…or anything." Without her usual confidence her voice sounded like a stranger's.

"No, I guess we didn't."

"Well…what about Friday? Are you busy?"

"To go see Paul?"

"No, actually I was thinking more like dinner. You and me."

"Dinner. You mean a date?"

"I've heard it called that, yes." She gave an embarrassed laugh.

So much for keeping his distance. A niggling voice in his head insisted that it would not be a smart move. Not a good idea at all.

"If you can't make it…"

"No. No, I was just checking my daytimer. Sure, Friday's good."

She suggested a restaurant and he offered to pick her up. They traded goodbyes and he stood staring into space, oblivious to the phone that remained in his hand.

He was still standing there when he was paged to the boardroom.

Ellis closed the door behind him. Dan Arnott, Chuck Norwood, and Hal Leonard were at the table. Arnott was making a conscious effort to keep his hands still. Leonard swivelled back and forth in his chair. Their carefully blank faces told Lee he was the topic of conversation. As soon as he was seated, Ellis asked for the latest news on his 'situation'. He'd hoped to talk to her alone, but it couldn't be helped. He told her about the storm, and the call that morning.

"Jesus H. Christ," Ellis breathed. "Well that pretty much settles it."

"Settles what? What are you talking about?"

She looked around at the other faces. "The past few weeks we've all tried to believe that whoever's doing these things would get tired of the game and just let it drop. Then you were nearly killed. Now you're saying someone actually set a trap for you at your own house. *Someone is trying to kill you*—there's no way to pretend it's anything else."

"I'm not trying to pretend."

"Then you'll understand why we've decided to"—she paused— "pull you off the air."

"*What?* Maddy, no…"

"Listen to me, Lee. This may not be about who you are but *what* you are."

He looked at her in confusion.

"You're a celebrity," Arnott said. "A lot of sad people try to steal their own moment of fame by hurting someone famous—like Mark David Chapman with John Lennon. Or maybe whatever got this prick angry at you is like a festering sore. He doesn't get over it because every day he turns on his radio and there you are, and he gets pissed off all over again. He's tried to scare you off or shut you up, but every morning he hears you come on as if nothing has happened and…it's like a taunt: 'You missed me'. A red flag waved in front of a bull."

"So you remove the red flag and the bull calms down. Is that it? For how long? A month? Two months? A year? Or is that really the point?" Lee scanned their faces again. "It's the publicity, isn't it? It's not just that you're afraid he's going to kill me." He looked directly at Hal Leonard. "You're afraid he's going to kill me at someone's remote! Lee Garrett spread out on the floor between the TVs and the blu ray players. Not so good for sales!"

"*Stop it, Lee.* That's uncalled for." Ellis's face was red. "We're trying to keep you out of harm's way."

"I might give *you* the benefit of the doubt on that one, Maddy. But think about it. What if I come back after a month and whoever it is just picks up where he left off? What then? We'll only have wasted company money. And at least two hot ratings weeks." He looked at Arnott, but didn't like the expression on the man's face. "They haven't tried to hurt me in any public place—maybe that's not what they're after. Meanwhile I'd be a prisoner in my apartment with nothing to do but think of them out there, waiting for me. I can't afford to go anywhere. Is that your idea of being helpful?" He sat back. "Or is it really about the publicity. Be honest with yourself."

Norwood said softly, "You're talking about living as a target. A sitting duck."

"They know where I live," Lee said simply. "Tell me how coming to work makes it any worse. And frankly," he swallowed and turned back to Ellis, "whoever it is, they're being too careful. The police have nothing. It may be the only way to catch them is to draw them out. And catching them is the only way I'll ever get my life back."

He wasn't appealing to his boss, but his friend, and she knew it. She sat still for a long time, leaning on the table and staring into its surface, as if looking for the wisdom of Solomon.

"All right, Lee," she said at last. "You stay on the air for now." She quickly cut off the protests that began. "That's my decision. *For now.* If the situation changes, no promises. In the meantime keep on the cops' asses. Tell 'em if they catch the bastards we'll contra them the biggest batch of donuts they ever had."

It was a strained attempt to lighten the mood. The room emptied like the parlour of a funeral home. No one would look Lee in the face.

Do we all overestimate the number of real friends we have? he wondered as he watched them go.

～

He was just packing up to go home when he was called to the lobby, but his annoyance evaporated when he saw the rumpled figure standing there.

"Tucker! What brings you here? How are things?"

"Things are good, Lee, thanks to you. That's why I dropped in—to thank you for calling my boss. I really appreciate it, man." He gripped Lee's hand in a vice, and then turned it into a soul grip and a half-hug.

"Harry wasn't supposed to say anything about that."

"He didn't. Not to me. I found out through the grapevine. Anyway, uh, not too many people have done anything like that for me. Thanks."

Lee searched for a flip reply, then said simply, "You saved my life."

"You, uh, wanna go for a beer? Maybe at The Palace?" The man's craggy face split into a grin.

The thought of watching strippers in the middle of the day was both tempting and repellent, but Lee could use a drink after facing the Inquisition. Tucker agreed to a counter-proposal of a quick beer at Clambaker's, next door.

It was near the end of their second beers that Lee found himself spilling the details about the harassment and the meeting he'd just been through. He hadn't meant to. There was something about Tucker. Or maybe it was the beer.

"That's friggin' unbelievable. And the cops aren't doing squat?"

"They're trying. Whoever it is has been smart...or very lucky."

"We'll see how lucky they are if they try anything when I'm around." Tucker's face was red, his jaw like a steel wedge, and Lee realized that the man was being completely serious. Tucker wasn't someone he would want as an enemy.

There wasn't any way the man could help, but it was nice to know how much he wanted to.

When they were saying their goodbyes, the truck driver compressed Lee's hand again. "If anybody comes around hasslin' you, you let me know. I mean it. Tucker'll be there for you. An' if there's any more o' this crap about takin' you off the air, I drive by here all the time and I'll park my friggin' truck in their lobby." He gave a crooked smile and turned away.

Lee walked to his car, reflecting that he'd learned a few new things about friendship that day.

≈

At the station the next morning he felt a surge of shame as he realized the new set of habits he'd formed. Checking the back seat of his car before he got in. Circling the parking lot every morning, shining his headlights into every shadow before he parked. Listening intently before walking down the silent hallways. The empty building filled him with foreboding.

Once he was in the control room he had to push all that aside and pull out every scrap of talent in his bag of radio tricks. He threw out punch lines like firecrackers, and turned callers into comedians. No one was indispensable, but he knew he'd better come damn close. He'd been served notice.

Caller ID was installed later that morning. Part of him wondered about baiting his enemy into calling. He'd have to think about it.

Norwood's assistant, Pam Hardy, found him in the hall near the Production studio. The hesitation in her step as she drew close told Lee that she knew at least some of what had transpired the previous day.

"Lee? Can you, uh, spare a minute?"

"For you? Two minutes. Maybe even three or four."

She gave a relieved smile of bright white teeth against coffee skin. Norwood dumped all the annoying jobs on her, but she never complained, was always cheerful. Lee was sorry to cause her discomfort. He'd much rather make her smile again.

"It's the Snowarama next Saturday. A week from tomorrow. Did you remember it?"

"Easter Seals, sure. Am I just riding, or do I do some emceeing?"

"They might ask you to say something, but probably not. Otherwise just go for a ride, show the flag, and have some fun. The Track Shop will provide one of their rental machines, but do you have a snowmobile suit?"

"An old one. I won't be a fashion trendsetter."

"Well, I'd lend you mine if you weren't about six inches too tall."

"You know, I do look good in pink. But those bulges in the front might be a problem."

She laughed. "Funny, they don't bother me at all. Anyway, I'll email you the rest of the details. Any other questions?"

"Yes. What's a nice girl like you doing in a place like this?"

She frowned a mock rebuke, then flashed another warm smile and walked away with an extra sway of her hips.

Later he got a call from Matt Miller, voice heavy with concern.

"I heard about your car breaking down on New Year's. Too close for comfort, the way I heard it. Are you recovered yet—from the frostbite and everything?"

"Oh sure, yeah." He still had a lot of pain in his fingers when he moved them certain ways, and all of the frostbitten areas were very sensitive. But Matt didn't need to hear about that.

"Good, then you have no excuse." Miller went on to describe an annual charity hockey game between a media 'No Star' team and a team of high school phys-ed teachers, with proceeds going to minor hockey.

"The day before Valentine's?" Lee checked his schedule. "Sure, I guess. Except, I haven't been on the ice this year."

"And just what difference would that make, exactly?"

"Ok, ok. Every game needs a little comic relief."

"That's why I knew I could count on you. Any gear you need, just talk to Reg at SportsSwap."

Lee scribbled the information into his daytimer. Comic relief or not, he definitely needed to get some ice time in the next week or he'd get hurt in a hockey game. He wondered whether Candace knew how to skate. Maybe she could come with him. With a shock he remembered that he'd be able to ask her in just a few hours.

Their first date. In dismay, he felt sweat come out on his palms. That was ridiculous—he could stand in front of thousands of people and ad lib a speech without a flutter. How could the prospect of a simple meal with just one woman put his composure through the blender?

He couldn't remember the last time he'd gone on a first date. He usually met women at social functions and asked them out for a coffee or a drink afterward. That was very different, with no time for anticipation, good or bad. Dating was a territory he hadn't ventured into since before Michaela, and he had no idea what to expect anymore.

He wasn't even sure what to wear. Teklenburg's was normally pretty casual—a suit would be too formal. He opted for a sports jacket and slacks, no tie. He wondered what Candace would wear. It was pleasant to imagine.

Her apartment building was about twenty years old, with mustard-coloured brick above concrete foundations that showed a few small cracks. It looked clean, though, the balconies free of obvious clutter. He was surprised to find her waiting in the entranceway.

"I guess the woman is supposed to put on a show of making the guy wait," she said. "But I've never been into that. I hope that doesn't shatter the mystique."

"Mystique completely intact, and the gentleman is grateful." He swept an arm toward the parking lot, thinking that his aging Volvo was a poor substitute for a chariot. He'd vacuumed it, but when Candace got in a traitorous Snickers bar wrapper jumped out from under the passenger seat. She casually scooped it up and pushed it into the ashtray.

"Get a little too hungry to wait?"

"More like an emergency boost some day I had to skip lunch."

She walked ahead of him into the restaurant, giving him a chance to take a long look. Fashionable boots reached just above the hem of her long coat, which looked to be wool and maybe handwoven. It was muted grey and tan with periwinkle accents against an ivory background. He was grateful she hadn't changed her hair. It was loose and wavy and full, the way he liked it. Only a close look under the bright light of the vestibule confirmed that she was wearing makeup. She didn't need any.

He took her coat. Underneath was a raspberry sweater with a delicate leaf motif, and a tan skirt that reached a few inches above her knees. Against her fair complexion and dark hair, the effect was striking and elegant, and he told her so.

"Thank you, sir. Now as long as I remember to steer clear of the lobster I might just stay that way."

"Too true. A little messy for date food. No ribs, no spaghetti, nothing that squirts."

"Is that the voice of experience?"

"Not really, but I have a dim memory of some coaching my mother gave me back … oh, it was probably in the Pleistocene Era."

"In that case, you've aged remarkably well. A portrait of yourself in the attic, perhaps?"

"You should see it. Dorian Gray's was a baby compared to mine."

They laughed and ordered wine and clam chowder.

"I've listened to your show a few times lately. I like it. But you sound different in person."

"I wish I had a dollar for every time somebody told me that." He laughed. "Most people have a telephone voice, too—you just don't think about it. I suppose it has to do with overcoming the limitations of the equipment: you have to work the language harder, enunciate more clearly. Even exaggerate the cheerfulness—it takes a lot to push a smile through all those electronics."

"You always sound cheerful."

"Part of the job. Who wants to start the day with some guy who sounds worse off than they are? Anyway, what with the way we have to condense things, and all of the station ID's and imaging we have to use every time we open our mouths, it's bound to sound artificial. Then you get something like those motor mouth DJ stereotypes."

He constricted his throat to force more of the sound to his upper palate, and covered one ear with a hand. "Heeeey, folks, it's a fabulous one-of-a-kind spectacular with something for everyone that you won't want to miss! *Be there!*"

Candace's laugh of surprise turned heads around the room. Lee grinned. "We can do it better than anybody."

"Yes, I can see that." She laughed again, looking sheepish. "Let's just forget I ever said anything, shall we?"

He nodded his agreement, and then sat back to let the waitress deliver their chowder.

As the first nervousness wore off, the need to fill every silence with words disappeared. Lee asked about her work, she asked about how he got into radio. Old stories with a fresh audience. The ebb and flow of her eyes and the lift of her lips was the language that held his attention the most.

He remembered to ask her to come skating with him. She was free a week from Tuesday, clearly pleased to have a place in his future beyond one date.

"I have to ask what it is you like about country music," he said.

"Hmmm, I need to think about that. What do you like about the oldies music you play?"

"It comes from a simpler time, I guess. Every song is associated with a memory. Most good, some bad. Even those are bittersweet. Plus the lyrics counted in those days. Happy. Not about how much the world stinks. If I want that, I can watch TV." He hoped she wasn't a big TV fan. "Oh, and the harmonies, too. Fantastic vocal harmonies. The Four Tops, Mamas and Papas, Crosby, Stills, Nash & Young. Nobody seems to bother with that anymore."

"Well country music is the same."

"Cheerful? Are you kidding?"

"When was the last time you listened to it? All that cheatin' and hurtin' was ages ago. Now the songs are about family values, and appreciating life, and love, and good times. And if you want harmonies, you've got to listen to Rascal Flatts or one of the girl bands—they're fantastic."

He wasn't convinced, but the smile it brought to her face made him want to believe.

"It speaks to me," she said. "It says real things about my life."

"What does it say about first dates?" he asked.

"It says…" She stopped as if she'd been about to say something facetious, but changed her mind. "It says they often stay in your memory for a lifetime."

"Here's to one worth keeping." He raised his wine glass. They drank the toast, then she lifted her glass to be filled and he rested his hand lightly on hers to hold the glass steady. Every cell of his skin was aware of every cell of hers.

He relaxed enough to enjoy his seafood lasagna, though watching forkfuls of alfredo pasta pass between her full lips was just as enjoyable. He'd forgotten the pleasure of watching a beautiful woman eat. And adjust her hair. And savour wine in a delicate throat. And breathe.

She protested that she needed to preserve her girlish figure, so he skipped the fudge and caramel dessert he'd been considering. He had coffee. She chose tea. While they were waiting for it, Candace turned her head, bringing her full profile into view with light behind it. An image flashed into Lee's mind: a profile just like that. Sunlit through a car window.

"The stop light," he muttered.

"What did you say?"

"Sorry, I just remembered where I'd seen you. Before we met."

"You're going to tell me we were together in a past life, right?"

"No." He laughed. "Not quite that far back. A month, maybe. We were beside each other at a stop light."

"And you remembered that?"

He shrugged. "You made an impression."

"A good one, I hope."

"No doubt about that."

He was strangely pleased, as if the incident had been a sign that they would be together.

They hadn't made any plans for after dinner. He suggested a movie. She picked a new comedy with Scarlett Johansson and George Clooney. He approved of her taste in actors, but the movie got little of his attention. Soon after it started he felt her fingers intertwine with his, and he gave them a squeeze. Her glance made his heart quicken. A palm filmed with sweat and an arm that threatened to fall asleep couldn't persuade him to move. When Clooney and Johansson began a slow dance, he and Candace both shifted in their seats, bringing her warm nylon-covered leg up against his. He strained to feel the smoothness of her skin through the fabric, and lost whole sections of the movie that way.

On the way back to her apartment they were quiet. He pulled into a parking space and almost turned off the ignition, then realized it might be misinterpreted. Suddenly all the awkwardness he thought they'd left behind was back in full force. He glanced at Candace and her eyes were downcast.

"Lee, I..."

He lifted a finger to touch her lips. She raised her eyes to his.

"There's no rush," he said softly. "I had a terrific time. I'm happy to leave it at that tonight."

Her eyes were shining, and suddenly she was in his arms, the yearning of the whole evening channelled into a bruising kiss. The scent of her hair and skin suffused him like the heady rush of alcohol.

Then they were apart, her eyes liquid magnets in the lamplight.

They walked slowly to the door of the apartment building, oblivious to the cold. She fumbled with the key. With the door open, she turned back and they kissed again, sweetly, tenderly, knowing it would need to sustain them through long hours apart.

16

MONDAY MORNING HE GOT A CALL FROM DAVIS to meet her at the police station. She said she had information she wasn't willing to discuss anywhere else. A uniformed officer showed him to a small room with a desk and four chairs.

"Why, Detective Davis. I didn't know you rated your own office." He looked at the bare walls as if admiring the decor.

"Funny man. Our department shares this one when we need to interview hookers and pimps, drug addicts and such. But they let me bring you in here if I vouched for your good behaviour."

He laughed. "Just as long as you promise you won't take advantage of me while we're all alone like this."

"Mr. Garrett, I think it would be best if you'd forget that I'm a woman. If you can't do that, then remember my husband is a two-hundred-pound martial arts instructor. Can you do that for me?"

"Consider me chastised, Detective." When she turned her head he looked over her figure in the grey suit, scrupulously pressed. He realized he'd never seen her any other way, but didn't know whether the crisp look was out of respect for her position, or an obsessive tidiness.

She had a good body, and the sharply-creased clothes showed it off better than loose garments would have. Maybe that was the reason.

She motioned him to a chair but sat on the edge of the desk herself. He was surprised to see her hesitate. "There's no way to say this without the department looking bad. Or me." She looked him in the eye. "I've just found out that the Intelligence Unit has a couple of sources in the Skins gang."

"*What?*" He jerked up straight. She raised a hand like a stop sign.

"Not cops. They're paid informants. They were busted for something else about a year ago, but let off on condition that they feed us information on the gang and what it's up to. In exchange for money. Not much. They've never given us anything worthwhile, either. But I read over some of the recent reports. One of the informants does mention another gang member being pissed off at some radio guy in town. No names—they never give names. Anyway, the rest of the group wasn't interested. There's no indication that anything was done about it."

"Still sounds pretty convincing to me. Why didn't you know about this before? Don't the other detectives know you're on a case involving the Skins?"

"Yes, they do, and I've asked about this very situation. I…guess I didn't ask the right people."

Lee slouched in the chair, letting air drain from his lungs. "Don't blame yourself. I'm willing to bet someone deliberately blocked that information from getting to you."

"You're talking about Sergeant Dieter. Don't jump to conclusions —he wouldn't have the authority."

"You wouldn't know who I meant if it hadn't already crossed your mind. Besides, you don't need authority if you can call in favours. We'll get a lot farther if you're honest with me, *and* with yourself, Detective."

For a moment he thought she was going to end the meeting. Then her shoulders relaxed and she looked at the ceiling.

"What matters is that the information isn't worth much. The Skins aren't a corporation—they don't have regular strategy meetings. More like rant sessions every once in a while over drugs and booze. One or two of them get fired up over something and then a few go and trash a storefront or spray graffiti on somebody's driveway. Even then, they always pick a target of another race—blacks or Asians or native people. Always. Never someone like you."

"Until now. Maybe they think I'm a traitor to my race."

"If you were carrying out a crusade for racial rights or something, I might see it. But one comment on the radio? And even if they chose you as a target, they'd take one swift action to send you a message or make an example of you. This continuing vendetta—it just doesn't make sense based on what we know."

"You just told me how little you know about these assholes."

"And I'm not going to ignore it. In fact, I've asked the Chief to have the IU put some pressure on these informants. Have them dig around and come up with something useful for a change. But my instincts and experience are telling me it's much more likely there's one person behind these things—someone you know." She caught and held his gaze. "So, let's go through it again. Can you think of anyone who has a grudge against you and the opportunity to carry out these attacks?"

"Sure. Fred Dieter." It gave him a childish satisfaction to see the clench of her jaw. "I've already told you about any others I could think of. Ken Cousins, Elliot Dean, my former friend André Menard. He wasn't at the casino night, though."

"Yes, and some of your own colleagues could just as likely be suspects." *Touché.* "What about the incident with the hydro wire? Any enemies who work for a utility company?"

"No. Wait. Not a utility company, but there's a guy who's a cable TV repairman—he's not too fond of me. Except the death threat came before I ever met the guy."

"Name?"

"Lenny Schwartz. Looks after a blind nephew that…well, it's a long story. He's a piece of work, but I can't see him trying to kill me."

"I'll check him out." She shifted, looking uncomfortable. "Have you ever considered your ex-wife? Or maybe the man she's with now?"

"Michaela could never do anything like that. Robert Farrell? He's a denturist. Doesn't know me well enough to hate me. Besides, if I kicked, there goes the alimony, making things more expensive for him."

"Life insurance?"

"My kids are the beneficiaries now. Did you ever find that Van Horne prick from the United Way luncheon?"

"Yes. He comes from money—not a likely gang member. A friend on the force told me the kid's been questioned in connection with some hazings that got out of hand, but never charged with anything. He probably just thought he was being funny when he made that remark to you."

"Guess you had to be there."

≈

Radio contests could be a lot of fun, and they could be a pain in the ass. Some people had nothing better to do than play every contest fanatically. The rules only let them win a prize or qualify for a big giveaway once a month, but they'd call until they succeeded. A few were grateful and pleasant to talk to. Many were just mercenary and didn't even sound excited to win. A lot of those had no loyalty, and played just as often on other radio stations.

But ninety per cent of the listeners were ecstatic just to get through to him on the phone, and thrilled to have a chance to win something. Lee couldn't help but get a lift from that. It was a kick to give things away, especially to people he knew were fiercely devoted to the radio station. The latest giveaway trip to Jamaica brought squeals of delight, happy laughter, bizarre incantations for luck, and promises to take Lee along. He gently deflected those.

Pam Hardy stuck her head into the control room just before 9:00 o'clock. He waved her in.

"Valentine's Day a week from Monday. Rob says you guys decided to take callers with romance stories, right? Great idea. So each daily winner gets a voucher for dinner for two at Winston's. How would you like to go, too?"

"You mean as an escort? Three's a crowd, sweetheart."

"I mean we have some extra vouchers. Chuck thought maybe you'd like to take somebody special. On your own. Winston's is a great place."

"Chuck? Really?"

"He's not a bad guy, you know."

"I know. I guess he's just been in the wrong place at the wrong time lately. Yeah, sure. I'd love one."

"Great. Enjoy." She handed him a printed voucher with the Winston's and CTBX logos on it, flashed him a hundred-megawatt smile, and walked out.

Lee grinned at the closed door. He'd been stumped about what to do for Candace for Valentine's. Winston's would be perfect—a lot better than he could afford on his own. Although a free dinner might not send quite the right message. He'd have to pick up some flowers or candy, too—something he'd actually have to pay for.

He saw a look of surprise on Karen's face when he walked past her reception desk, and realized he was whistling.

17

THE AIR CRACKLED IN HIS NOSTRILS AS HE OPENED the car door, and he blew a cloud of steam just to watch it disperse. The sky was a crisp blue, but the winter Saturday quiet was shredded by the whines and growls of snowmachines. Dozens of every make and colour were parked around the lot, waiting for their turn to fly over the frozen lake nearby.

Lee didn't ride in the Easter Seals Snowarama every year—CTBX and Z104 partnered in a half-dozen snowmobile events each winter, but usually it was their Community Cruiser reporter who was assigned to show up for them. Lee had never owned a sled—never had the spare time to make owning one worth the cost. Especially with the warming winters some of his neighbours only used theirs once or twice a year, riding an eight-thousand dollar toy along a packed-snow track to a run-down hotel for a few quick beers, then riding back.

He enjoyed it when he did ride, but Snowarama was about raising money, and he'd done his bit for that by giving the event a lot of on air mentions and an interview. His participation in the ride itself was just a promotional opportunity for the radio station.

Tarry log walls gave the outside of the old building a rustic look, but the inside had been renovated within the past ten years. A billow of warm, humid air enveloped him. In the ground level hall dozens of riders sat around stackable wood and metal tables, devouring breakfasts of pancakes, scrambled eggs, and sausages. And coffee, lots of coffee. It was beyond Lee's understanding how some people could fill their bellies with liquid and then spend hours on a jolting snow-machine. The food was free to all riders, but he gave it a pass. Instead he strode up the stairs, flattening himself against the wall a couple of times to allow Pillsbury doughboy shapes in black and navy to pass by in the opposite direction.

The upstairs reminded Lee of a primary school gymnasium, with a modest stage and wooden floor. Cheap tables were flanked by plastic chairs, but most of those were obscured by sprawled weekend trail-warriors, their snowmobile suits spread open to reveal cotton turtlenecks and fishermen's knit sweaters. The gathering looked like a celebration of Bad Hair Day, any earlier grooming erased by helmets or toques. One exception was a good-looking blonde from the local TV station, doing an interview with a man Lee recognized as the Snowarama chairman, Reg Mahood. Beside Mahood were the Easter Seals ambassadors, a young boy in a wheelchair and a pre-teen girl standing with the help of leg braces and crutches. Lee had met the kids a number of times and was always amazed at their cheerfulness in spite of a tough lot in life. They were inspirational. He felt good about being a broadcaster when he could help people like that.

It took him a minute to spot Chuck Norwood through the crowd. Barry Wright and Doug Rhodes were with him to complete their four-member team.

"Hey, Lee. We're just registering. You get the stuff you need ok?"

"I borrowed a helmet from Phil Oates. It's tight, but it'll do."

"Nice suit, Lee. Ride much?"

"We can't all be fashion gods, Barry. Good to know you'll be wearing a helmet so oncoming riders won't be blinded." Wright was sensitive about his receding hairline. He grunted and looked away.

"You aren't gonna slow us down, are you Lee?" Rhodes asked.

"I haven't seen the machine they brought for me, Doug. But last I heard it wasn't a race."

A tall man in a smart leather outfit came up to them. Norwood did the introductions. "Lionel Rivers, this is Barry Wright, Doug Rhodes, and Lee Garrett. Lionel's the vice-chairman of this year's event."

"Yeah, the one who does all the work." The other man grinned. "Reg Mahood is too busy with the media." He nodded toward the harsh light of the TV camera, but his eyes were on the reporter.

"Well, somebody has to take a bullet for the team," Wright offered, also admiring the view. "You know, Lionel, we count as media, too."

"Yeah, sure. And hey, I really appreciate all the coverage you guys gave us. We'll just get you registered. Then can you help out when we make our presentations later?"

"Sure." Norwood nodded. "Barry will act as emcee, and I'll present the cheque on behalf of our company." His voice was casual, his face turned away from Lee. So that was how it was going to be. The offer of the restaurant vouchers the day before had just been a bribe to make Lee play nice, but Norwood still planned to treat him like a poor relative with the clap. Why have Lee come at all? How many people would recognize him on the trail with a helmet over his head?

Norwood was definitely back on his shit list. On the other hand, with no official task to perform Lee wouldn't have to stick around after the ride. That was worth something.

The crowded room was dotted with familiar faces. Most were friendly: city councillor Vic Foligno, George Brickman the car dealer, Ray Carver, the president of the local community college. He'd try to avoid André Menard, and Elliot Dean. Ken Cousins was probably around, too, in the season's newest snowmobile suit, and perfect hair in spite of his helmet.

A profile across the room caught Lee's eye. It looked like Van Horne, the cocky bastard from the United Way luncheon. Lee waited for the head to turn in his direction but it turned away instead. Short hair cuts were a dime a dozen. He was probably just being paranoid.

Norwood walked up. "OK, ready to go? Let's hit the trail."

"Doesn't Reg Mahood want all of the media teams to leave at the same time for the photo op?" Lee asked.

"Shit, that could be an hour from now," Wright complained. "That chick and her cameraman are the only people from TV so far. I don't think all the newspaper guys are here either. Let's just go."

"Hell, yeah," Rhodes agreed. "Besides, if we all leave together the trail's gonna be like Notre Dame Avenue after the Bingo lets out. I feel the need for *speed*."

Lee considered letting them leave without him, but then he'd be the main topic of conversation, and the thought pissed him off.

The Track Shop had brought a bright green Arctic Cat F570 for him: a rental unit, a few years old. Usually they had him show off one of the newest models, but maybe those were in short supply because winter had started early. Lee had ridden the older Z570 model before, so the controls were familiar. He was grateful for the electric start, and the engine was already warmed up. It revved smoothly as he squeezed the throttle a few times.

His co-workers were ready and waiting, but he took another few seconds to make sure his helmet was secure and his throat completely covered by the fabric face shield. The icy air was already hungry for his body heat. Snowmobile speeds would make it ravenous.

He pulled the visor down and gave the 'thumbs up'. His hand hadn't even dropped before his team-mates were racing down the ramp onto the lake. He goosed the throttle and felt the front skis lift off the snow. It would take a while to get the hang of the machine. He caught up with the others a few hundred metres down the lake where the trail crossed a road. A bundled-up cop was stopping traffic, stamping his feet to keep warm.

The trio shot away again, but Lee's Cat could keep up. The weak link wouldn't be the machine, but his rusty driving skills, as Norwood and company ignored the posted trail limit of fifty km/h. They were surrounded by scenery straight out of a Group of Seven painting: perfect crests of white slumping over dark evergreen slashes, black-scaled shafts of trunks, and dappled-grey rock faces. All of it wasted on them.

Lee pitched over a rise and had to squeeze the brake grip hard to avoid running into Doug Rhodes. They slowed to cross a rickety-looking log bridge over a creek bed, then sped through a stand of trees and out onto the open surface of a narrow lake, too small to have any cottages on it but long enough that Norwood, Wright, and Rhodes opened their throttles wide. Lee hit the gas on the Arctic Cat. It kicked ahead with a growling whine, and he felt the wind pull at his suit, whistling around the edges of his visor. A hundred and ten kilometres per hour—faster than the speed limit on the open highway. And his co-workers were still pulling away. He tried not to imagine what would happen to him if the machine tipped over at that speed. He should let the others go ahead without him—the route was well marked—but stubbornness wouldn't let him.

The end of the lake was a relief. He braked for the rapidly approaching tree-line, and slid up over a ridge onto the hard-packed trail again. Doug Rhodes' back was vanishing around a pair of large pines twenty yards ahead. The 570's engine responded smoothly, and the sled cornered well, the handling softer than other makes Lee'd ridden, but he'd be grateful for that after a long day's ride. Fortunately the trails had been well-groomed for Snowarama, and his green machine was forgiving on the bumps that remained.

They came to another lake. With a grimace he jammed the throttle all the way to the grip, keeping it there until the muscle in his thumb ached. Patches of deeper snow tugged at one ski and then the other, threatening to tip him. He hurtled into the white plume thrown up by Rhodes' passage, and an image leapt into his mind of Rhodes' machine suddenly appearing out of the cloud, stopped still in the trail. If it were to happen in reality, Lee would be a dead man. The others were insane to go so fast—why make himself a part of their madness? Was he afraid to lose the respect of people who deserved none from him? Or to lose respect for himself?

The next hour was a torture test. Trees, rocks, and deadfalls flew toward him. His throttle hand settled into a fierce ache, and his spine protested the pounding, forcing him to raise his body a few inches from the saddle on the bumps he saw in time. Pain and fatigue stirred in his knees and calves. He was too rigid, his muscles unfamiliar with the physics of the machine's motion, the tension aggravated by shots of adrenaline. The squeeze of the helmet was giving him a pounding headache. His concentration flagged.

As he came hard into a sharp right turn, he realized too late that it was more than ninety degrees. He squeezed hard on the brake and threw his weight to the inside of the curve. The rubber and steel track caught at the edge of the trail, but the last few feet of the turn were worn down into a negative bank, right in front of a stand of mature trees. He gave a savage wrench to the handlebars and hung off the saddle on the right side. A shot of throttle at the last moment wasn't enough. He felt the crunch as he clipped a tree trunk. The Cat bounced back onto the trail and he pulled off to the side a few feet farther on to assess the damage.

The body of the sled was untouched, but there was an ugly curl about four inches long in the outer edge of the left ski. He'd have some explaining to do.

He roared curses that frosted his visor, but he couldn't indulge his fury for long. Another rider could come around the curve at any moment. He climbed back aboard the beast and revved it forward.

Anger began to translate into speed. He'd been a fool to come. He could have been with Candace instead. He tried to picture her, but the face in his mind wore a puzzled look, her mouth turned into a frown.

He got the message and eased back on the throttle. His dream Candace was right—forty years of life should have taught him how to control his testosterone. It was time to take his head out of his ass.

He kept the sled to the speed limit. Ten minutes later he reached the halfway point of the ride.

About thirty sleds were pulled up in a clearing beside a weather-worn cabin, so he was still well ahead of the main pack. A dozen riders were standing by their machines or checking them over. Lee's co-workers were in a group of five beside a nearby row, which meant they hadn't arrived much ahead of him. He swung his machine around, killed the engine, and gratefully pulled off his helmet.

"Good to see you didn't get lost," Rhodes said.

"Too nice a day to waste it breathing in your fumes, Rhodesy. You guys do what you want on the way back. I'll find my way."

"You don't have to ride alone," Wright said. "There's a group of grandmothers almost ready to head out. They're just having a last cup of tea in the shack." The crack drew a laugh, but Lee let it slide. He walked into the cabin, feeling a blast of heat like something solid. A huge wood stove lit up the far end of the room, and the air was thick with resiny smoke. Volunteers behind a makeshift counter were serving paper cups of coffee and hot chocolate, and a few half-empty boxes of Timbits sat nearby. Lee offered some waves and greetings to familiar faces under sweat-plastered hair. He nearly laughed at an image in his mind of the immaculately-groomed models in snowmobile ads. Nothing could be further from the reality.

Scalding his tongue with the first sip of hot chocolate, he fled to the colder air outside. Sweating inside a snowmobile suit could make it frost up on a morning like that. The air was still bitter. He was grateful for the F570's heated handgrips.

He should make conversation with the other snowmobilers, press the flesh, recruit some listeners for his show. Instead he spent a few minutes going over his machine to make sure he hadn't missed any damage. He didn't relish telling Hal Leonard what had happened. The thick liquid in his cup was already starting to cool, so he swallowed the last of it and looked for a place to empty his bladder. There was only one real outhouse and unspoken tradition reserved it for the women. The men made do with a trench about thirty feet from the cabin that afforded all the privacy that a six-by-twelve-foot tarpaulin stretched between two trees could provide.

Afterward, he looked around for his radio colleagues. Their sleds hadn't moved—they must still be inside. If he started ahead of them, he'd almost certainly face the embarrassment of having them catch up. He did it anyway. His stiffening muscles just wanted to get the whole bloody ride over with and go home for a long, hot bath.

He was more than half the way back when trouble found him.

It was a change in sound that caught his attention. His first thought was that his engine had malfunctioned, then he realized the deeper pitch was coming from another snowmachine. He turned his head just enough to see it from the corner of his eye. Big and black. Not surprising that some hotshot sledder had caught up with him. He looked for a wide section of trail to let the rider past, but the man couldn't wait. With a roar and a spray of snow the black machine charged by.

He hoped the guy wasn't drunk. Snowarama didn't allow alcohol, but lots of sledders carried their own flasks.

This one wasn't weaving. He didn't even race out of sight as Lee expected. A quick glance at the speedometer confirmed that they'd slowed down. What the hell was that about? Was the other rider pissed off at him for making him wait? Without meaning to, Lee closed to within ten metres of the other's tail. He eased back on the throttle. The stranger was leaning forward, and as they came to a long straight stretch, his head and shoulders dipped a little and his hands left the handlebars. The machine slowed to a crawl. Lee had a sudden fear that the man had suffered a heart attack. But then the figure snapped straight and twisted around, one arm arcing high.

A quick glimpse of a dark object tumbling through the air. A stream of glistening droplets. A shocking thump on the green cowl of Lee's sled.

He ducked his head, snapped the steering bar hard to the right and goosed the throttle. He had a moment to register the other machine leaping forward, and the projectile vanishing over his shoulder out of his field of vision. He began to swivel on the saddle for a look when a wave of heat and noise hammered into him and tossed him like trash into the snow.

A gasp turned into a grunt of fear as he tried to push scalding air back out of his lungs, his arm reflexively shielding his eyes.

What the hell...?

A boulder only metres away was enveloped in flame that bloomed into the clear sky on a stalk of black smoke. Heat grilled his face where the visor had pulled away in his fall.

An explosion! Some kind of goddamned *explosion.*

Bewildered, he looked at the bright flames as they licked over the rock and spread to some shrubs on either side. It was a moment somehow divorced from reality.

Dimly, he lifted his head and saw the other snowmachine stopped about fifteen metres away, the rider faceless behind a black visor. Watching him. A curious tableau of fire and ice. Then a gauntleted hand moved, sending a spark of reflected light. From what? A bottle?

Time began again as Lee threw his body into motion, furious at his laggard muscles. His machine had coasted to a stop a few metres away, still idling. He leapt aboard, wrenched it sideways, and twisted the throttle savagely to slew the tail around, away from his attacker. Fingers of fire reached for him as the machine shot past the burning bushes, and he felt the heat through the plastic visor and padded suit. When he could spare a look back, he saw the black snowmobile vault through a wall of smoke. Coming after him.

It was a race he could not win. He cannoned into curves and chutes, and caromed off banks, barely maintaining control, as terrified at the prospect of an oncoming sled as he was by the death that chased him. They were heading back toward the shack, toward a place his brain associated with safety. But right into the main pack of riders.

He heard the other sled's engine. His pursuer must be only metres behind. Ready to attack again? What the hell had the bastard thrown? It had looked like a bottle, trailing something from the top.

A *Molotov cocktail*? Gasoline, a bottle, and a wick—easy to come by, easy to handle. Except for someone riding a snowmachine at high speed. He'd have to stop to light the wick. Otherwise Lee was dead.

That meant the man would try to get by and cut him off, or force him off the trail into the scrub and deeper snow. Lee would have to block him, and pray they didn't meet a machine coming the other way. He began to weave between the banks, hearing the drone of the machine behind him rise and fall as its rider tried to find a way around. He probably wouldn't ram. A bent ski or damaged cowling would invite questions.

On a short straightaway Lee risked another glance backward. The black wedge was right there, the faceless mask of its master motionless and emotionless, like a robot behind the windscreen. There was no sign of a bottle. Likely it was tucked between the rider's knees, impotent without a lit wick.

Lee turned forward again, and his heart froze.

Another machine. Coming straight for him!

Banking off a curve, the big yellow sled was steering right into his path. He barely had time to register its presence before his arms jerked the steering bar over and threw his sled up the left bank of the curve. The top ski lost purchase. His snowmobile teetered on the brink, then recovered its equilibrium by a miracle. A flash-frozen image of yellow metal and astonished faces burned into his brain: an old man and a young child whose leisurely outing threatened to come to a shattering end. He braced himself for the sound of death as the innocents collided with his nemesis behind.

But it didn't happen.

As his own sled levelled he risked a look back.

The yellow snowmobile was stopped, but safe. The black machine of his enemy *hadn't made the curve.*

It was over the bank in deeper snow. Already its implacable rider was climbing off the saddle to pull the skis around and continue the pursuit. The sled probably had the power to climb out of the drift. Lee couldn't afford to wait. He dug his foot into the trail and spun his Arctic Cat around again. He didn't dare continue toward traffic—that was tempting fate too far. Instead he shot past the stalled yellow snowmobile and its stunned riders, and willed his machine to give him everything it had.

Minutes later he began to shake. He felt nauseous, dizzy, his arms and legs drained of their strength by the aftermath of the adrenaline that had scalded every nerve in his body.

Mindless panic retreated, but with the return of reason came a sudden understanding that made him cry out in shock.

Oh, God, no! A lifeline had been thrown to him and he hadn't recognized it. Because it had looked like death.

The yellow snowmobile. Other riders. Safety in numbers.

Why hadn't he just stayed with the old man and the child? The maniac on the black machine wouldn't have been willing to kill two innocents just to get Lee Garrett. Would he?

Despair swept through him like ice water.

The moment was gone, the opportunity lost. He raised his head again as the trail dipped onto the surface of a lake.

What to do now? On a flat surface, his pursuer's more powerful machine had a deadly advantage. But if it were still a few minutes behind, Lee might be able to reach the other end of the lake and find a place to hide or double back.

His momentum made the decision for him as he slid across a patch of ice. Ignoring the protesting throb of his thumb, he squeezed the throttle until he was an arrow slicing between plates of white snow and cobalt sky. After a minute he risked a glance back, steering just enough to see around his snow plume.

The black snowmobile slid down onto the lake, and sent up a spurt of white.

He was trapped! There was still three-quarters of the lake to cross. No chance at all that he could outrun the other sled. The obsidian machine could run circles around his, and probably would, to force him to slow down until its rider could light a deadly wick. Already he thought he could hear the sound of the hunter gaining. The feeling of exposure crept up his spine.

What if he let the bastard get close, and rammed the other machine? He might catch an exposed leg. But the odds were more than even that Lee would be badly injured too. Duelling snowmobiles offered no protection.

He no sooner framed the question, than he caught sight of his antagonist right beside him, pulling quickly past. With only a second to judge the distance, he gasped a breath and pulled the handlebars hard to the right.

He missed. By inches. The changed angle of his skis slowed him too quickly and the tip of his right ski caught the other machine a few centimetres behind the rider's leg, scraped down the length of metal, and nearly caught on the slightly flared rear before it bounced off. That was all that prevented the manoeuvre from rolling him over. As it was he had to fight hard to regain control of the rocking metal frame.

Sensing Lee's move, the black rider had veered away, off the trail into deeper snow. His momentum carried him about ten metres, and his natural impulse to let off on the throttle made him bog down and slow to a stop. At least the prick wasn't immune to fear.

Lee's greatest safety still lay among the trees. He had to reach them. He mashed down on the throttle, hurtling past his surprised enemy before the killer could think of lighting a wick. There was even a chance the bottle of gasoline had been flung off into the snow. That might buy Lee a few precious seconds.

He was most of the way to the trees before his attacker caught up. This time the man knew better than to pass at close quarters. Counting on the superior power of the black sled, he pulled over into softer snow at the edge of the trail, still gaining in fits and starts. The trees inched closer with maddening slowness. The scene became a frozen horse track photo finish, two adversaries neck and neck. Sun, snow, scouring wind, howling engines, fused together into one adrenaline-charged interval: survival at the brink.

Then the dark line of forest leapt toward them. The black rider tried to force Lee over and pull onto the trail in the lead. But the desperation of his intended victim was greater. Lee held his ground. Called the bluff. The other gave in at the last possible second, a moment before he would have flattened himself against a huge pine.

Lee had the lead. Death rode behind. The battle had lasted for an eternity and nothing had changed. But it would. A voice deep in his brain knew that. He'd been dealt a losing hand.

The final play came five minutes later.

As Lee hurtled into a sharp curve, preparing to shift his weight, a large bird broke from the bushes on his left, fluttering past inches from his head. He was distracted for only an instant, but that was enough.

His machine roared off the bank into the air, and the slash of snapping branches merged with the tortured whine of the drive track, still at full power but freed of its load. The scream froze his blood. Froze time. He saw his hurtling flight as if by the flash of a strobe: right ski caroming off a thick trunk and twisting crazily, cowling dropping to the left, then bucking level as it slammed into a dried branch, pulverizing it, pieces of twig and bark whipping into his visor. The frenzied howl merged into an all-engulfing barrage of sound. His metal steed plunged into the ground, flinging him over the windshield.

A thousand thorny fingers tore at his suit and helmet, crackling like gunpowder as they cushioned his fall. A cloud of snow and pine needles began to settle. He rolled upright, and spat a mouthful of debris.

Dimly aware that he was uncomfortable, he pushed onto his hands and knees and raised his head.

Just in time to see a black figure standing on the bank above him, swinging an arm.

Time to die.

With no guidance from a conscious mind, muscles coiled and sprang, flinging his body backward into the bushes just as the tumbling bottle struck, shattered, and exploded. The spray of flame tore through twigs and needles where his body had been moments before. A wave of fire coursed over the battered Arctic Cat, swallowing it whole. Lee cart-wheeled through shrubbery, and rolled in the snow, first from momentum, then deliberately, as a blanket of orange and black licked at him. His back slammed into a thick tree. Coughing smoke, he pulled into a crawl and scrambled frantically around its trunk, desperate to hide.

The second explosion seemed to shatter the world.

A wall of flame roared past him, disintegrating branches and turning needles to ash. Shards of flying metal scissored through the naked stalks left behind, and the clamour hammered his ears. A breaking comber of heat sucked his lungs empty and tossed his body onto his face in the snow. He burrowed into it, scooping handfuls to fling over his back, while small noises forced their way from his throat. A huge ball of fire roiled into the air just as he flipped onto his back to slap at patches of flame on his sleeves. Then his fingers clawed at the fasteners of his helmet and flung it off, shovelling snow into his hair because it felt as if it were on fire, too.

Rasp of air, crackle of cinders, squeal of melting plastic, chuff of burning fuel.

He lay in a waking coma as his coffin was wheeled into a crematorium oven. A misguided acolyte on a bed of coals. Meat on a spit.

Slowly, slowly, slowly the heat eased. Flames retreated. Static was penetrated by forest sounds. Incredibly, the world still existed.

With painful slowness he lifted himself to peer around the trunk of the tree. Wisps of smoke obscured the view beyond the burning bush just ahead.

Some of the smoke cleared. Behind the curtain of flame a black shape shimmering in the superheated air. Looking for something.

Looking for a body.

Moving forward, toward the embankment.

Lee pummelled his numbed brain cells—they had to find him a place to hide. Find a way to live. But suddenly the black figure stood straight, raising its head. The visor of the helmet reflected a tall pillar of smoke rising into the clear sky. The man hesitated, then slowly turned away. Lee heard the roar of an engine, the whine of tracks on snow, and then the sound began to fade.

He lay back, breath rasping in and out of overtaxed lungs. Eons later he staggered to his feet and surveyed the wreckage. The pyre was unrecognizable as a machine of any kind; twisted black bones reached grotesquely for the sky, and flapping shreds of charred fabric stirred in the oily smoke.

He looked over his own body. A patch of nylon above his knee was still smouldering. He stooped over, as if in a dream, and rubbed some snow into the shrivelled cloth. Then the pain came.

His left arm hung limp. Dislocated, maybe. As he took a step forward his right knee almost collapsed under him, and bright agony shot up his body, making him shudder. He leaned his weight against the tree for a moment, to gather his courage, then sank to his knees and began to crawl slowly up the bank.

There was a sound, an engine sound. But he couldn't tell whether it was coming or going. He didn't know which way to go when he reached the trail. He simply started to walk, limping painfully, trudging on a treadmill while forest slid past like the painted scenery of a diorama.

The sound grew louder. Some dim part of his brain noted that he was in the middle of the trail, that he should probably do something about that, but he didn't know what. Before he could decide, a snow-mobile came into view around a bend and braked hard.

There was a logo on the cowl. It fascinated him. He'd seen it lots of times. Police—that was it. Ontario Provincial Police. For some reason that made him happy. He raised an arm and took another step forward.

And collapsed face down in the snow.

18

"At least this time they didn't keep you in the hospital."

Davis looked up from her notes to see if the remark had sparked any humour in Lee's eyes. They stayed coldly blank. He finished packing his microphone into the case they used for location broadcasts.

"A mental hospital soon, if this keeps up. The doctors said my knee's just bruised and the shoulder is a bad sprain." He was supposed to be wearing a sling, but that would've prompted far too many questions from co-workers and listeners.

He shifted on his stool and winced at a shot of pain. "I don't think I'm cut out for this shit. In the movies, the hero just gets a gun and goes after the bad guys. Me? I wouldn't even have a clue who to go after. But I'll tell you one thing," he said in a lowered voice, husky with anger. "If you were to tell me right now who that bastard riding the snowmobile was, and handed me your gun, I'd blow the fucker away without a qualm."

Then a made for TV smile flicked onto his face as he realized one of the customers in the restaurant was looking at him. An older lady, probably a listener there to see him do his show. He raised his cup of coffee to her, and drank a sip. It was only lukewarm, but he managed to swallow without making a face.

What a day to have to do his show at McDonald's. He'd spent most of Saturday night at the hospital, and even a Sunday in bed hadn't restored his energy. It had taken every ounce of willpower to focus on his job, greet people, play the clown, badger customers into joining him on the air. All things considered, the show had gone well. It had to.

Ellis had hit the roof and insisted he was off the air until the case was solved. He'd reminded her that Monday's show was committed to the biggest McDonald's in town, one of the station's best accounts.

She'd still balked. He'd had to beg.

"I don't think you should watch any Charles Bronson movies for a while," Davis said. "And don't even *think* about touching this gun. It's never been fired outside a range, and I intend to keep it that way."

"Are you good with it?"

"Good enough. My big brother and I sometimes have friendly competitions. He's a cop too. RCMP drug unit."

"Two in the same family? What, was your father a cop?"

"A fireman. Scared my mother half to death, knowing he was the first to charge into a burning building and the last to come out."

"Is there a family gene that urges you to help people, or just flirt with danger?"

She gave him a sour look, and looked as if she might change the subject, but went on. "It caught up with my father. A burning ceiling came down on him. His buddies got him out, but his lungs were never right after that. He had to take a disability pension. That came closer to killing him than fire ever had. Then he got an idea that turned him around…opened a store to sell home fire safety equipment." She smiled at the memory. "Anyway, he tried to make us promise, my brother and me, that we wouldn't go into any line of work as dangerous as that."

"I don't get it. You did it to spite him?"

"No, not at all," she said. "We just couldn't help it. I guess it was his example when we were growing up. I think he finally understood. I'm not so sure my mother ever has."

"Can't say that I blame her." Lee nodded his thanks to Shelly, the station hostess, as she set two fresh cups of coffee in front of them. After a few tentative sips, the detective looked up at him.

"So how is the station going to handle Saturday's…incident?"

"The press release from the OPP had almost nothing in it—a snowmobile explosion, no one seriously injured. No mention of any attack. I suppose they only have my word for that. For once their tendency to be tight-lipped worked in our favour. I'd appreciate it if your department would keep things to themselves, too."

"I'll try, but we can't cover up the facts."

"Not asking you to. It'll come out eventually, but hopefully by then it'll be old news."

"Your attacker will know by now that you survived."

"Couldn't be helped. They would've found out anyway." He sipped slowly at the coffee and watched to make sure no customers were close enough to overhear. "You think the investigators will get anywhere with this?"

"No witnesses except the man and his grandchild who saw you racing. Black snowmobile—hundreds of those around. If this guy is part of a group he'll have no trouble establishing an alibi—probably didn't register with the Snowarama either. And he picked a weapon that's virtually impossible to trace."

"Yeah, why a Molotov cocktail, for God's sake? The only thing that saved me was that he needed to stop to light the wick. If he'd had a hunting rifle I would've been meat."

"That has to mean they're still trying to make these attacks look like accidents. Create some doubt, at least. A number of things can make a snowmobile catch fire—especially if you run off the trail into trees. The downed power cable at your place could have been taken for storm damage. By the way, all of the people we identified as possible suspects had alibis for that night."

"Even Lenny Schwartz?"

"According to his son."

"Nephew. Paul's his nephew."

"Ok. Paul says he heard his uncle listening to a Leafs game all evening. Made microwave popcorn just before the third period."

"That still gives him the first two periods to go out and come back. Or he could have done it when Paul was asleep."

Davis shook her head. "Turns out a lady across the street from you did see somebody climbing the pole sometime in the middle of the evening. Thought it was a repairman because of the storm."

"I can't figure it out." Lee looked deflated. "It's like you said before. They should be trying to wipe me out in a way that makes them look like hot shit. And then crowing about it. Why aren't they?"

"Count your blessings," Davis shrugged. "Two reasons I can think of. Maybe they think as long as there's some doubt about these incidents, we won't throw police protection around you and make their job harder."

"Which you're now going to do."

"The Chief insisted. Just two guys. I don't get why you never asked for it yourself."

"I don't want these bastards to just lie low for a while. I need you to *catch* them."

"So you stay in the line of fire without letting us protect you, but count on us to catch them the moment they slip up? You really have been watching too many movies. And I don't want that responsibility. Come to think of it, why haven't you taken a leave of absence 'till this thing blows over? Clear out and let me do my job."

"Now you sound like my boss. Frankly, I don't have anywhere else to go. And…what if my listeners realize they can live without me?" He tried to keep his tone light, but he couldn't bring himself to look into her eyes. After a while he cleared his throat. "So tell me the other reason these guys haven't gone public. You said there were two."

"The other reason is that, so far, they've failed. If they'd gone off about your imminent death in media communiqués or some such crap, they'd look like a pretty sad bunch of bunglers by now." She looked uncomfortable. "If they ever do succeed, *then* they'll go to the media." She swirled the last of the coffee in her cup, and drank it down.

Lee nodded slowly. "I guess I'll never know if you're right."

≈

By unspoken agreement the three dozen skaters at the Tuesday night Family Skate went around the arena ice surface in the same direction. So the mental comparisons to merging into rush hour traffic were only because of Lee's rusty legs. He moved onto the ice like an octogenarian, his genetic memory rebelling at the concept of a frictionless surface.

That was part of the reason he'd taken so long to lace his skates. The other was the opportunity it gave him to watch Candace. She no longer had the figure-skating costume she'd retired at fifteen, but she'd found a comparable ensemble, with a pleated white skirt still well above the knee. There was no sport like figure skating to mould a woman's legs and gluteals into their most attractive shape, and Lee thought it was too bad she wasn't the short skirt and spike heels type.

As he watched her glide over the ice he could see her confidence returning. The first tentative rotations to skate backward became short spins and prolonged S-curves; hands that dangled limply began to float and swoop, like birds circling a sapling in search of a place to rest:

the functionality of counterbalance transformed into artful motion. He'd much rather watch her than embarrass himself by joining her on the rink surface.

By the end of the first circuit he'd managed to stiffen his ankles. When his back began to straighten soon after, he felt a little less envy for the three-year-old who was holding on to her mother's hand for support. He'd played a lot of hockey when he was younger, but the old habits came back slowly. He made a wobbly pivot and glided backward, his forty-year-old muscles struggling to remember the moves. Glancing up, he saw Candace, nodding with encouragement. He felt like the three-year-old, and turned to hide a blush. Candace glided up beside him.

"I always forget how enjoyable this is."

"How often is 'always'?"

"Maybe once a year. Sometimes one or two of us at CNIB take clients for a skate. We hold their hands."

"Maybe that's what I need."

She smiled and gave his hand a squeeze, then glided away into a gentle pirouette while he stepped through the end zone curve and back onto the straightaway. Her face was a study in release, maybe even transcendence. He wasn't feeling anything so pleasant. Since Monday morning his throat had been scratchy, and by Tuesday afternoon his nose had begun to burn with the onset of a cold. Cold FX usually worked for him, but it was too soon to tell if it would this time. The damp, chilled air of the arena was harsh in the back of his throat. Before long his shoulder began to ache, too, and it wouldn't let him hold his hands together behind his back. When he turned his skates for a quick stop, a dart of pain shot up from his knee. He was pushing too hard, too soon. No way he was going to be able to play in Matt's hockey game. After a couple of dozen circuits he skated to the boards, waving at Candace to keep going.

He climbed to one of the benches and sat watching her, but shadows drifted like clouds into his mind.

The first few days after he'd nearly frozen to death, he'd had a new appreciation for life, at least for a while. Now he looked inward and sifted through fragments of emotion that lay like scattered shards. Turning them over, one by one, he found them dulled. He tried to define his feelings but they were muted. Limp. Slippery. He couldn't get any of them in a firm grasp. That part of his mind was a watercolour palette, left out in the rain.

Dulled by fear?

When he was a teenager he'd connected fear with death and dismemberment. Which was strange because teenagers—especially teenaged boys—thought they were invincible, and drove like maniacs to prove it. They lived in dread of an unwitting social misstep or an undisguisable pimple, but they didn't acknowledge that as fear. They yearned for the day when they would be fully confident adults, blissfully unaware that there was no such thing.

Lee knew that someone was trying to kill him, but that knowledge hadn't brought fear into his heart, because fear already had a permanent home there. He knew the fear of a bank calling to cancel his credit. The fear of a cancer diagnosis. The fear of losing his job—not only the loss of income that it would bring but, even worse, the loss of self-worth.

Adulthood had brought his greatest joy: his children. And also his greatest fear: the chance of losing them. He knew that he'd foolishly squandered countless hours that he could have spent in their company, but at least they were still alive, still making him proud with every venture they undertook. If anything happened to one of them, he didn't know how he would survive it.

There was another fear. Love. New love at his stage of life was as frightening as it had ever been, with its demand to lay the soul bare.

The threat of death was a terrible fear, yes. But only one of many.

He reached into his pocket for a Kleenex—his cold symptoms seemed to be getting worse by the minute. He'd feel like a jerk if he gave the bug to Candace. He should've stayed home, but then, his head wasn't calling the shots.

Two pre-teen boys played a clumsy game of tag, dark in their winter jackets; a young girl in a bright aquamarine turtleneck used a wooden chair as a prop to supplement her wobbly legs; a twenty-something couple holding hands wore matching sweaters, probably wedding gifts, with brightly-coloured leaves that contrasted badly with the gaudy inks of the rink board ads.

He tried to smile at Candace as she went by, but he wasn't sure his face obeyed. She looked to be enjoying herself, even attempting a small jump that was only a little shaky on the landing. The pleated skirt barely hid the lovely curves beneath; the cold air made her complexion glow, and with her graceful movements he tried to remember the last time he'd seen anything so beautiful.

He felt a touch of regret when she finally came off the ice.

"What happened? Didn't feel like skating after all?" she asked.

"It's my knee. Uh, an old problem that acts up once in a while." He winced as she bumped his bad arm. He'd have to tell her about the attacks sooner or later, and the longer he left it, the harder it would be—he knew that. But he was afraid. Afraid it would scare her away.

He surveyed her long legs as she bent to untie her skates.

"Enjoy the view?" She didn't even look up.

He thought about a denial, but laughed instead. "I guess I'm not a subtle guy."

"You're a guy. What else needs to be said?" Her smile said she didn't mind. "Want some hot chocolate? I spotted a coffee shop just down the street."

"Sure."

With his growing sinus headache, the light was beginning to hurt his eyes. It was a struggle to make conversation. Candace bravely tested topic after topic, but his replies were little more than grunts.

A waitress brushed back a stray lock of long brown hair as she asked whether they'd like anything else. A hint that their table would soon be needed. It was almost 9:30. Time for the after-movie crowd to start arriving. Lee looked at Candace, who shook her head.

"No thanks." He watched the young woman turn, and noticed a stain at the back of her right hip, where she'd never see it until she took the apron off. Pasta sauce, or some reddish donut filling. She'd be embarrassed later, wondering how long it had been there and how many people had seen it. The thought saddened him.

They didn't talk much in the car. When they pulled up to her apartment building Candace put a hand on his arm.

"Lee … is there something wrong? Something you want to say?"

"What do you mean?"

"Something about us."

"Why … ?"

"You've been distant. Uncomfortable." She bit at her lip and took a measured breath. "Are you having second thoughts about this. About you and me? I know neither of us was sure … "

He suddenly understood what she was saying, and an icy hand clutched at his chest. "Why would you think that?"

Her voice was like a little girl's. "You didn't want to be close to me. You didn't even try to kiss me." She attempted a laugh, but it faltered, and she turned her face away.

"*God*, no. No, it's nothing like that." He reached to take her hand— gripped it hard. Why was he such an idiot? "I think I'm coming down with a cold and I don't want to give it to you. And at the rink … I guess I was just feeling a little old, that's all. Please. You're the best … you're the best thing … " The words failed him. His throat clamped shut.

She looked into his eyes and he willed her to see his naked soul.

A cool hand touched his cheek, and the fingers drew over his skin to his lips. There was a hard set to her jaw, but a tear glistened on an eyelash.

"Lee Garrett, if you ever neglect to kiss me again, I don't care what you've got, you'll wish it was fatal!"

Then her mouth was on his, hard and hungry. They kissed and laughed and squeezed together as if to burst the very molecules of air between. Fear was released in a wave of heat, and the flame that remained was strong and pure.

19

"HAVE YOU THOUGHT ABOUT HIRING A PRIVATE DETECTIVE? Have them sniff around a little?"

Lee's cold-clogged voice was too rough to record commercials, so Mel Smythe had taken the opportunity to dish out advice instead.

"And pay him with what, Mel? Michaela's alimony money? Besides, the cops have their forensics labs and databases and they've come up as empty-handed as a beggar at a Parliament Hill fundraiser."

"Well, what about the mob?"

"The mob? What do you mean?"

"What I said. If anybody's got information about criminals, it's them. You must know somebody who's connected. What about that construction guy…Martinelli?"

Lee laughed. "Right. 'Hey, Vinnie, mind puttin' me in touch with some o' your Goodfella buddies? I need some information about crime.' 'Sure, Lee. No problem. Maybe I'll give a call to the Yakuza while I'm at it.'"

"Ok, fine, if you don't want my help. But I'm telling you, you're missing a bet. The mob don't like fascists. They're bad for business."

Lee smiled, but Smythe's idea wasn't any crazier than anything else about the whole ludicrous state of affairs. He was a grown man who had two uniformed police officers for babysitters. He'd persuaded them to sit in the lunchroom rather than the front lobby while he worked, but it hadn't been easy.

He stuck his head into the newsroom. "Hey Dale Awesome."

"Hey Lee Carrot."

"Lived up to your name this morning. Good show." He meant it too. Lawson was taken aback.

"Uh, thanks, Lee. You too."

"You're a bad liar—I sounded like shit. So I'm glad you were around to pick up the slack." He backed out of the room before she could reply. The truth was, she still sounded a little stiff in some of the ad libs, but she was trying hard, and showing real improvement. He wasn't ready to admit that Arnott knew what he was doing, but he could accept that sometimes life surprised you in a good way.

~

Friday he awoke to find that his cold had been beaten. His nose was drying up and he no longer had pain in his throat. But he still had to put up with a pain in the neck. Her name was Ruby Soames. A contest perennial. He knew she'd already qualified for the Jamaica giveaway when he heard her unmistakable rasp on the phone again, claiming to be someone else. It was a dicey thing to accuse a listener of cheating, but his patience was in short supply.

"This isn't really Susan Lambeth. It's Ruby Soames, right?"

"No, no. I'm Susan Lambeth. I haven't qualified yet."

"Susan hasn't qualified. But I know it's you, Ruby. You're calling to help a friend—I understand that—but it's still against the rules." She'd probably swung a deal to split the trip if Susan won.

"*My name is Susan Lambeth.*" The anger rang false.

"Look, Ruby. My caller ID is showing your number," he lied. It was showing a number, but not a name, and he'd have to dig through the list of contest qualifiers to see if it matched Ruby's.

There was a noise of disgust that might have been an obscenity, and then the dial tone was loud in his ear. He knew he'd been right, but he got no satisfaction from it.

Fortunately, the qualifier for the Valentine's giveaway made the morning worthwhile. The young man's story was an echo of "The Gift Of The Magi" by O. Henry. After living together for a few years, the man and his girlfriend had begun to fight more and more over money. Their relationship was heading for the rocks. He had a late 90s pickup truck that he'd customized for years—it was his baby. But, afraid that he was going to lose his girl, he sold the pickup to buy an engagement ring, and used the rest of the money on a beat-up Ford Escort with too many miles on it. He didn't know she'd been scratching for odd jobs so she could buy him a gift: an expensive polishing kit for his truck. When Valentine's Day finally came that year, she accepted his proposal, and they laughed and cried as they set out to polish the Escort. They were still together. And still broke. They could never have afforded a dinner at Winston's on their own. Awarding the prize voucher to them gave Lee a good feeling.

After 9:00 he surrendered to the inevitable and called Matt Miller. His shoulder and knee were still a long way from healed—there was no way he could risk a contact sport like hockey. He offered to do announcements for the charity game instead.

"Geritol can't cure everything," Miller said.

"You should know."

"Seriously, though, it would have been good to have you on the ice, but I'd hate to have to carry you off on a stretcher. Might ruin my whole afternoon."

"Your sympathy is overwhelming. See you there. I'll be the one cheering for the other team." Miller was still laughing as he hung up. Lee realized that Matt's friendship was more important to him than ever.

He almost made it out of the building. Instead, as he was checking his mail slot one last time, Karen hurried toward him from her reception desk mouthing four-letter words. He was about to laugh until he saw the look on her face.

"What's the matter?"

"Did you give away all of those Valentine's vouchers from Winston's?" she asked in a near whisper.

"Sure, yeah. Why?"

"Because we're one short. There's somebody here to pick up the last one, and it's gone. I don't know what could have happened. What am I supposed to tell them?"

Lee looked carefully around a room divider. There was a man in the lobby wringing a battered baseball cap as he stared at the cardboard Lee Garrett cut-out. Young. A worn coverall showed underneath a hunting jacket that had seen its best days ten years earlier. It was the guy with the "Gift Of The Magi" story—Lee was certain of it. A sour taste rose into his throat.

He thought of the voucher he'd been given. A special night out would mean so much to Candace, and to him. God knew he deserved it, after all he'd been through. Sometimes life played crappy tricks and it was every man for himself.

He stared at the blank fabric of the divider. Then he opened his briefcase, pulled out the piece of paper, and handed it to Karen.

"It's a spare," he said. But her eyes said she read the truth.

The young man was pathetically grateful and kept repeating how much it would mean to his wife. He waved as he went out the door and Lee returned as much of the smile as he could. Karen hugged him and said a quiet "Thanks."

He told himself he'd come up with something else for Valentine's. Then he thought of the pile of overdue bills lying on his kitchen table like an indictment.

≈

The hockey game gave him a temporary lift. He got a kick out of announcing penalties for "too many undressed men on the ice" after a mock brawl sent jerseys and pads flying, and "unsportsmanlike use of a water bucket" to drench the players on the opposing team's bench. The turnout was better than expected, and Miller was thrilled with the proceeds but disappointed when Lee turned down an invitation to join the players for a few beers.

"Probably shouldn't push my luck, Matt. I might not be the safest guy to be around these days." He wasn't willing to risk something noxious in his drink or food, either.

"Just don't push all the fun away while you're at it. Life's too short."

"That's what I keep hearing."

≈

A family commitment had taken Candace out of town for the weekend. He missed her all day Sunday and tried to distract himself by changing the locks on his door and windows.

Monday, Valentine's Day, he made the draw for the special breakfast show to be broadcast from the winner's home. After announcing the name he broke his usual rule and placed the call 'live' on the air. It was risky—he counted on some Valentine's luck.

"Do you know why I'm calling, Mrs. Kaufman?"

"I think so. We won something, didn't we?" At least she'd been half listening.

Lee explained the prize details, and had to sound thrilled enough for both of them. "I never win anything," she mused. The tone of her voice said she was picturing how much she'd have to clean her kitchen. Mel Smythe would need to work magic to make her sound excited in the winner promo.

At least that contest was over. Now there was just the big Jamaica trip draw the next night at the New Sudbury Centre.

He couldn't reach Candace—she had appointments all day. They'd already set a time for him to pick her up that night, but he had no idea how to tell her he'd struck out on restaurant reservations.

He didn't have to. She read it in his face. And laughed.

"I had something special lined up. Honest. But it…fell through." The excuse made him sound like a teenager.

"I don't care if we do anything at all," she said, and gave him all the proof he needed with her lips. "Let's stay right here. I'll even cook. I cleaned the place up and everything." The spark in her eyes punctured the last of his bad mood and he allowed himself to be pulled toward the elevator, then cursed and went back out to the street to tell the police officers where he'd be. *Damn*, he really was a teenager again.

Her apartment was equal parts tasteful furnishings and organized clutter. A few curio shelves in the corners were full, but not with the stuff found in women's magazines. He was sure that every item had a story, and he wanted to hear each one, to learn what they had to say about her. He turned to find Candace looking at him. Waiting. Not apologizing, as he'd known so many women to do.

"I like it," he said. "Very much. You've got good taste."

"I picked you, didn't I?" She smiled, then dragged him into the small kitchen to help her cut up the vegetables for a quick oriental stir fry. She didn't seem to measure anything, but it turned out delicious. He said so, often enough that she finally laughed and finished the sentence for him. Even so, he had to concentrate to taste the food, and not lose himself in the curve of her face, the delicate lobe of an ear that dangled a simple platinum teardrop. The soft shine of her hair.

"Earth to Lee. Come in, Lee."

"Sorry?"

"I said, what would you like for dessert. I have yogurt and … yogurt." She waited in front of the open fridge. He shook his head.

"Just a minute." He went to the door and pulled a wrapped but rumpled parcel from a fat pocket of his coat. It seemed terribly inadequate.

"The store manager told me some women like these better than sex." He forced a laugh, red-faced.

"*Truffles!* Oh God, yes. To some women these *are* sex."

"In that case, I think I just blew it."

Her look of surprise made him laugh for real, then she joined in, and squeezed him hard.

"I have a present for you, too."

It was a tie, of good silk, dark grey with an exquisitely-rendered rose in the center. As he looked at it, she gestured at the box again, and he found a delicate tie pin inside with the same rose shape. He held them out at arm's length.

"They're beautiful," he said sincerely, but his look held a question.

"It's an English rose," she said.

"That's how I think of you."

"Yes. And I want you to think of me. Often, and for a long time."

Her kiss both reinforced the words, and made them unnecessary.

They talked about renting a movie, but Lee spotted a copy of *The Sound Of Music* on her shelf, hesitated a moment, and pulled it out. "How about this one. It's got Nazis. I love to hate Nazis."

She gave him a puzzled look, but said, "Sure." With an intermission pause for some modest wine and popcorn, they had everything they needed. Far more than he'd ever thought to have again.

As the Von Trapp Family climbed over the mountain to safety, Candace pressed her head against his chest.

"Do you think we could spend some time together, just the two of us? Go somewhere? I want to get to know you, and I keep feeling that... well, that life is getting in the way somehow."

It hurt him to know the secret that lay between them. How could he ever tell her? And if he couldn't, he had no right to lead her on. Yet maybe there was a way to shut out the ugliness of his life for a time.

"I know a guy..."

She laughed. "Of course you do."

"He owns a lodge—Crystal Falls Lodge—just a ways south of the city. They keep the main lodge and a few of their guest cabins open through the winter. The scenery's fantastic. Cross-country skiing." He paused. "I'm sure some of the cabins must have two bedrooms."

"I'm a big girl." She snuggled close again. "It sounds lovely. Perfect. Do we dare?"

He had no idea how he would pay for it, but that was beyond consideration for now. "I can call him tomorrow. See if he's got anything available for this weekend."

"This weekend? I promised Paul we'd do something. But maybe he wouldn't mind putting it off. Especially if we told him together."

"Are you sure you're ready for this?"

She looked up and her eyes lingered over every detail of his face.

"I'm ready," she said.

~

The centre court of the New Sudbury Centre was packed with people. In the middle were dozens of stackable chairs arranged in the rough outline of an airplane, but no one was allowed to sit in them yet. Potted palms dotted the space, and every available wall sported a CTBX banner. Steel drum music played from a portable PA system. Bodies milled around a pair of tables that held bowls of tropical punch and trays of fruits and dip. Three station hostesses in gaudy flower-print blouses and shorts directed the human traffic.

Lee had to admit that Chuck Norwood was good at his job. When the last tardy contestant was registered, the music faded. The microphone was ready. Lee grabbed it, gave a show-biz smile, and welcomed the crowd to "The Great '600 The Box' Sun and Sandals Giveaway."

"*This is your boarding call,*" he announced like a circus ringmaster. "Contest qualifiers may now board the plane and take any seat you choose. We ask friends and relatives to stay outside in the *airport lounge.*" The words drew a few chuckles but people were already buzzing among the chairs, asking each other how they thought the prize draw would be done. Some went straight to a seat they'd picked out minutes before, others slowed things up while they tried to choose. Lee drew on patience born of long experience.

When the clamour quieted, he introduced the rest of the station staff on hand, thanked the contest sponsors, and went over the prize details again to build excitement. That wasn't hard. The minus twenty temperature outside ensured these people were feverish to win. Finally Norwood gave him a nod. The PA system played a tympani roll.

"*Now … for a trip for two to the exclusive Sandals resort in Ocho Rios, Jamaica …* one of the seats on our plane has a CTBX window sticker stuck to the bottom of it. If you're in that seat *you're our winner!*"

There was pandemonium even before he'd finished his spiel. Chairs swinging through the air nearly rearranged some dental work. A few people waited until the worst of the mayhem settled and then lifted their chairs. A thirty-something woman in the middle, seven rows back, began to jump up and down.

"It's my chair! I've got it! I've got it!"

Her squeals were nearly drowned out by moans. Norwood made his way through the row to confirm the win, followed by a man who vibrated with excitement. The man and woman danced in a fierce clinch as Norwood put his fist into the air, and the crowd applauded the couple to the stage.

Angela and Tim Gordon were perfect winners: gracious and grateful, stunned but vocal, and at the young end of the CTBX demographic. With a couple of young kids, and a small convenience store to run, they'd never even had a honeymoon, let alone a vacation trip. Their answers to Lee's questions brought some sympathetic laughs. Then he thanked the rest of the contestants and announced consolation prizes for them of Tropic Tan and vouchers to a local tanning salon, available from the station hostesses on the way out.

He kept the Gordons to do a live cut-in with Tracy Banderjee, back at the station, then had Tracy record another short interview for him to run the next day on the morning show. The couple remembered to thank the station repeatedly, and even got the call letters right. Perfect sound bites that would play for weeks to come. Lee saw Norwood pump his fist in the air again, and couldn't help smiling.

Life was a bitch, but it had its moments.

~

The absence of the cable TV van was a relief as Candace pulled over to the curb in front of the Schwartzes' house. Paul answered the door with a big smile.

"I didn't think you'd be back so soon, Mr. Garrett."

"Hi Paul. Just call me Lee, ok? Ms. Ross…Candace and I wanted to talk to you about something and since she was coming by today anyway, we came together."

"Remember I was going to take you out for a little training this weekend, Paul? And to help you get something for your uncle's birthday? Do you think it would be all right with you if we put that off until Monday or Tuesday?"

"Sure. Ok. You could come too, Lee. Or are you going away with your listeners?"

It took a moment for Lee to catch the reference. "You mean the Jamaica trip? No." He laughed. "I don't get to go along. Wish I could."

"Jamaica, yeah. That's where the black guys keep coming from."

Lee looked at Candace. "Well, I guess the colour of a person's skin doesn't make any difference to you, huh Paul?"

"I can tell black guys. They talk different. They come here because there are jobs."

"Do you have any ideas about what your uncle might like for his birthday?" Candace asked quickly.

Paul thought, then smiled. "Got any friends that look like you?"

She turned away, embarrassed. The boy had never seen her, so he was parroting something he'd overheard. Lee's voice came out sharper than he intended.

"Cute, Paul. But seriously, would your uncle like tools? Or maybe sports equipment?"

"He has lots of tools. He gets 'em from work. He doesn't play any sports. Just watches them on TV. But maybe that's something. A TV remote. One of those remotes that works the TV and DVD player, too?" He turned his head. "Uncle Lenny thinks I lost his. We could get one of those, if it's not too much money."

"That's fine, Paul. Or maybe we'll think of some more ideas while we're at the mall. How about I pick you up right after school?"

"Sure. How come you have to change it anyway? What's wrong with this weekend?"

She looked at Lee but he only shrugged.

"Uh, Lee and I have…somewhere else to go this weekend. We're going on a little vacation. To a resort. They have…they have room for us this weekend," she ended lamely.

"Are you going to sleep together?"

Her mouth fell open. Lee snapped, "Separate bedrooms, Paul. But it's not appropriate for you to ask something like that."

"Sorry. I didn't mean to make anybody mad. Sorry, Ms. Ross."

"That's all right, Paul. We're hoping to do some skiing or snow-shoeing. Maybe we can take you out for something like that one of these days."

"Yeah, that'd be great."

There was a little more small talk, but it was strained, and they wanted to leave before Lenny Schwartz could arrive.

In the car Lee asked, "What was that all about?"

"I don't know. I've never seen him like that. Maybe he got it from some older kids at school. I just don't know."

Lee had his own opinion. They didn't talk much on the way back to her apartment.

⁓

Thursday morning's breakfast show from the Kaufman family kitchen was a revelation. After Dorothy's lukewarm reaction to winning the contest, Lee expected an ordeal. The whole family was petrified at the thought of being on the radio—why people like that entered radio contests, he'd never know. But Dorothy Kaufman turned out to have an infectious laugh that saved the day. Her nervousness amplified it, and as she tittered over each of Lee's jokes, he played her shamelessly, until her helpless gales of laughter swept through all of them. That made her husband Everett loosen up, and by the end of the morning Lee was playing straight man to Ev's raucous commentary.

He didn't mind at all. It was glorious, impromptu radio. Fun radio. Even the two young kids Jeffrey and Elise ended up on his lap singing nursery rhymes into the microphone.

When the show was over, it felt like leaving good friends. The shy family who'd greeted him with such anxious faces, and fussed over the state of their well-worn home, now waved goodbye from the doorway, inviting him to come back anytime.

It was the kind of good day that made up for so many bad ones.

He was in an even better mood Friday, anticipating the weekend with Candace. The weather forecast was perfect. She'd emailed pictures of a couple of new outfits she'd bought on sale.

He was blissfully off guard when the control room phone lit up. The voice chilled his blood, then brought it to a boil.

"Hey *dead man*. Are you there, *dead man?*"

"What do you want?" Lee snarled.

"I got only one thing to say to you. Have the guts to go to the grave *alone*. Don't take others with you." The phone clicked hard, and the dial tone screamed at him. He slammed the counter. The caller ID had been blocked.

"I've been in groups of people lots of times in the past couple of weeks," Lee said to Davis when she came to see him after 9:30. "That show at McDonald's. A charity hockey game. Our big vacation giveaway at the New Sudbury Centre, and yesterday the show from the Kaufmans' place. Do you think that's it? He's accusing me of trying to protect myself by making sure I'm surrounded by other people?"

"Your guess is as good as mine." She nodded, tired. Her uniform had finally lost a little of its sharp press, and so had her face. The flat winter sunlight ungraciously revealed new lines around her eyes and

224   SCOTT OVERTON

mouth. "That makes a certain sense—a coward accusing someone else of being a coward. Except your public appearances have been an advantage to him. He's known where to find you, and roughly how long you'd be there. He didn't say anything about your police protection. Maybe he still doesn't know about it."

"You keep saying 'he.'"

"I still don't see this as a gang thing. Police services in Canada use software called Powercase. It's shared—networked. So if a case in one jurisdiction has similarities to another, a flag goes up. We're alerted, and we can make comparisons. There haven't been any other cases like this with the Skins or anybody else. None. And if it is a gang, why don't they use their numbers to make sure you can't escape? Ensure their success. That's the profile I keep expecting, and that's what we haven't got."

"Aren't you the one who tells me to count my blessings? Anyway, just so you know, I asked the Chief to call off the watchdogs for the weekend. My protection detail."

"You *what*? The Chief won't do that."

"It took a *lot* of persuasion, and it's only temporary. I'm following everyone's advice and getting out of town for a weekend. With a lady friend. And she doesn't know about all this. Seeing cops on our tail isn't how I want her to find out."

The alarm in Davis's eyes and her tight-lipped silence made him uneasy.

20

Sunset painted the tops of dark pines. Through fresh snow sparkling in the headlights Lee turned the Volvo onto a narrow lane marked by a worn painted-steel sign that read "Crystal Falls Road". The road was ploughed, but not salted or sanded. It ran between high snowbanks, with a strip of pale sky for a cover. As they drove, the sky slowly turned navy blue sprinkled with stars.

Lee felt as if he were in a dream.

"This feels like a dream," Candace said, and then looked mystified when he laughed.

The lodge was a calendar painting of rustic log buildings with stalks of smoke sprouting from stone chimneys. The owner led them to their cabin, an A-frame large enough for a modest family home, with gables jutting from the upper loft bedrooms. Modern insulation was covered by weathered cedar shakes. Inside, the log walls had been left exposed, though smoothed and finished. Braided rag rugs were strategically strewn about the polished wooden floor. Under the guard-railed loft was a small tiled kitchen with a bedroom and bathroom beside it. But most of the spacious ground floor was for lounging around a wood stove with a glass front. It looked as if it could heat an auditorium.

"There are electric heaters in the bedrooms, if you need them. Only our hydro supply out here isn't always the most reliable. That's why the cook stove is propane. Here, I'll show you how it works." It took no more then a minute to explain the simple controls, then he led them toward the stairs.

"Bruno, it's absolutely gorgeous," Candace breathed. "But you must have bookings for this cabin months in advance."

"Oh, we had a last-minute cancellation." He winked at Lee. "And your young man has sent me lots of business over the years."

It was clearly the best unit the lodge had to offer, and Lee felt thoroughly indebted. He gazed in amazement at the woven art and original paintings on the walls, the antique lampwork, and the furniture dotted with homey throw cushions. A giant oval rag rug filled the space in front of the wood stove.

Candace's eyes glistened as she blew Lee a kiss, then followed Bruno upstairs.

"Of course you don't need to cook at all," the man was saying. "My wife and the girls serve up breakfast, lunch, and supper over at the main building. Even a late evening snack, if you want. Good Bavarian cooking. Not for those on a diet." He laughed and patted his ample stomach. "If you do want to cook for yourselves, we have all the basic groceries over at the store. Just ask at the front desk anytime, and someone will open up for you."

Queen-sized beds on iron frames filled most of the space in the snug upper bedrooms. The quilts looked handmade, and the simple window dressings were chosen to match. Electric lights were shaped like oil lamps. Lee brushed a curtain aside and glanced through crystal-rimmed glass at the tiny windows of distant cabins twinkling between dark boughs. It had taken Bruno and his family more than twenty years to build the resort into its present form, but the end result was a jewel. He said so.

"You're very kind." Bruno smiled. "And sometimes it's even worth it!" He gave another of his deep laughs, and led them back downstairs. He showed them where to find the fire extinguishers, flashlights, a pair of real oil lamps, and a manual that explained everything.

"There's someone at the front desk until midnight, if you need anything. Anything at all. Make yourselves at home, my friends. Enjoy your stay with us." He waved a large hand and backed out the door as they repeated their thanks.

Snow crunched under fading footsteps. Lee pulled Candace close.

"This is so beautiful," she said. "It doesn't seem real. Are you sure we're here? Are you sure it was me you wanted to invite?"

He answered her with a long kiss, then brushed his cheek against her hair, "Without you here it would just be four walls and a floor."

They spent what was left of the evening curled up on the hearth rug, with pillows to support their backs and goblets of red wine in their hands. Candace sighed as she gazed into the flames.

"God, life is good sometimes."

Lee was struck by the simple words. Life could be good. The past few weeks he'd been on a train hurtling along a dark track while the world of beauty and wonder passed beyond his reach on either side and was swept behind. Now that train was somewhere far away in the night, and he'd found refuge within a frozen perfect crystal of time.

"Thank you for bringing me here," Candace said softly. She meant anywhere close to him.

"Thank you for being here." He meant in the world, where he had been so lucky to find her.

Many long, full silences later, when the fire had burned down to lava red and they heard the crack of frost in the trees, she asked, "Are you expecting us to…share a room?"

He kissed her cheek.

"No, love. I promised Paul. Separate bedrooms."

She cuffed his shoulder, and his laugh turned into a tender smile. "I'm in no hurry. Truly. I want it when you're ready. Completely ready." He brushed a hand slowly through her hair. "And then it will be right."

She kissed his ear and neck and hair, and whispered hoarsely, "You are something very special, you know that?"

He knew that he was only what she had made him.

He led her by the hand up the stairs, and as they got ready for bed he drew as much pleasure from the sight of her in her simple nightgown, preparing to brush her teeth, as he might have felt from a display of lingerie. Different, certainly, but a reminder that love could burn as hotly as lust. She caught him watching, and gave him a puzzled look, but he only shook his head. Then she came to his room like a high school student at a co-ed camp, fearful of being caught by the chaperones. In their nightclothes they sat together in the middle of the bed and kissed sweet unspoken promises.

~

Saturday dawned dimly, and he lay awake for what seemed like an hour, listening for any signs of Candace stirring. He felt like a child on Christmas morning. At last he heard the creak of bedsprings and went to her door.

"Just a minute." He heard the rustle of a hair brush, and the light pad of her feet approaching. The door opened slowly, and the morning sunshine was in her smile.

She wanted to try every activity the lodge offered, but the food and coffee were even better than Bruno promised, and overindulgence tempered her ambitions. It didn't matter. They decided to go snowshoeing to a beaver pond Bruno described. Candace had never used snowshoes, and her choice of equipment was more romantic than practical. Instead of one of the lightweight modern designs, she picked a traditional set in varnished wood and catgut. That demanded fur mukluks rather than Thinsulate boots. Lee enjoyed watching her try everything on, then matched her choices. He liked snowshoeing but hadn't done it in years.

Bruno gave him a compass and a GPS, then pointed out a nearby cell phone tower that was visible from high ground.

Candace tramped back and forth beside the lodge to get her bush legs, laughing at her own clumsiness.

"How am I supposed to get anywhere like this? I can barely *stand* with my feet spread this far apart!"

Lee showed her how the shoes were shaped to step closely together, creating an interlocking print.

"You wouldn't get far walking as if you're on horseback," he said. She performed a clownish John Wayne impression, and fell laughing onto her side. Struggling to her feet, she scooped up a handful of powdery snow and threw it at him. He dodged, then shook the contents of a small branch onto her, making her shriek. She bent over to brush the crystals from her neck before they could melt, and he helped.

Once clear of the food smells, the scent of fir needles, balsams, and especially the cedars pricked at their nostrils. It was air like neither had breathed in a long time, free of petrochemicals and fabric softeners. The oxygen was like liquid energy in their veins.

The February sun provided light, but little heat. They pulled their hoods up and set off.

The path to the beaver pond showed as a gap between trees, but was covered with a week's worth of snow. Walking was a little more effort but also more comfortable once off the packed snow around the buildings. Lee warned her to be careful of saplings and fallen branches under the snow cover that could snag the webbing and trip her.

Dark evergreen boughs bore a thick white frosting along their surfaces, like the plastic pines of glass globe paperweights. The swish of nylon ski pants gave their march a rhythm, accented by the crackle of an occasional broken twig and the sporadic chirrup of unseen chickadees. Sunshine fell in shafts through the trees.

"Oh, Lee, it's beautiful. It's perfect."

He puffed warm breath to melt delicate frost crystals on her eyelashes, and she blinked the moisture away.

"Not too cold?" he asked.

"I'm wonderful."

"I couldn't agree more."

They reached the beaver pond nearly an hour later, an expanse of white encircled by snow-capped conifers. A copse of dead trees stood stark and ragged on the left, the trunks stripped of most of their bark. On one of them a weathered wooden box nailed about six feet from the ground was home to a pair of small birds that flew to higher branches at the approach of strangers.

As Candace took in the scene, Lee reached inside his coat and pulled out a leather wineskin. "For medicinal purposes only."

"Surely, Mr. Garrett, you don't think I'm as gullible as all that."

"Well, if you don't want any." He made to turn away, lifting it to his lips. She laughed and snatched it from him, squirted it into her mouth, and then gave a laugh as she used a mittened hand to wipe a few spilled drops from her chin.

"Why, good sir, are you sure you're not just trying to take advantage of an innocent maid?"

"I make no promises. You enter these woods at your own risk." He pulled her to him, but her foot slipped off the snowshoe and her balance went with it. Before either could react they lay on their sides in the deep snow, laughing and blowing icy flakes from their mouths. The last traces were melted away by a kiss. He could smell the tang of her skin, the perfume of her dampened hair. He kicked slightly to free his toes from the straps, and she rolled him on top of her, the weight of his body pressing her deep into the snow. They kissed again, hard, relishing the feel of cold skin and warm lips.

"I love you so much," she whispered. "If you don't love me yet, don't feel you have to say it. It's all right. Just let me be close to you." She pulled his head down beside her as if to forestall what he might say. But he pulled back and held her eyes, and in them she saw all the love she could ever ask for, and was content.

≈

The beaver lodge had been abandoned for years. They tramped through a patch of cattails, snapping the brittle stems while a pair of ravens scolded them from the top of a tall pine. Then they stamped out a heart shape in the snow, and made snow angels in the middle of it, laughing to know they were behaving like adolescents.

Their muscles finally began to protest at the unaccustomed motion, and they decided to return to the lodge.

Just before they left the pond Lee squatted low and drew a finger in a slow line above the snow, pointing to the three-toed marks of a bird—a partridge, perhaps. The tracks snaked unevenly toward the shore, as if in no hurry, then were joined by a second set, possibly a mate. Curious, the snowshoers followed the twin path. It didn't go far. Close to a fallen log near the shoreline, the snow was scuffed and dented. Candace picked up a small downy feather. In a line from the log to the trampled snow was a set of new prints: a circular pad with an arc of four toe pads, and tiny triangular points above each toe. A large fox, Lee thought, or possibly a coyote. Only one of the birds had remained to fly away.

~

Long before the lodge came in sight they knew they'd overdone it. As they wearily returned the equipment, Ilse gave a knowing look, and suggested they forestall the worst of their muscles' complaints with a soak in the main building's hot tub. Lee had completely forgotten about it, but Ilse found a pair of swim shorts for him to buy. With more foresight, Candace had packed a red Speedo. She looked incredible in it.

Easing into the frothing water was like slipping into a fantasy. The heat sank deep into their bones, and it was an electric thrill each time their skin touched. They submerged up to their noses, closed their eyes, and held hands under the water.

When they'd dressed again Candace pulled at his arm.

"Let's go into the store. I want some things. I want to cook for you tonight."

"You don't need to do that. The restaurant…"

"If I needed to do it, it wouldn't be any fun." She smiled, and dragged him along.

"I'm afraid it'll have to be spaghetti," she said, eyeing the shelves. "My other specialties take too many ingredients they don't have here."

"Spaghetti's fine. Anything would be fine."

"I need to be able to show off my domestic skills, don't I? Besides," she added in a softer voice, "I don't want to have to come out again tonight." Her look sent a shiver up his spine.

There were still some hours of daylight left, but the combination of exercise and fresh air made them drowsy. Time didn't press. They curled up together on the love seat, and fell asleep that way. When Lee awoke, the sunlight was already pink through the picture window, and soft sounds came from Candace at work in the kitchen.

"Anything I can do?" he asked, stepping close behind her.

"Yes there is." She drew his arms around her waist and pulled him close against her back. He pressed his face into her neck and she gave a giggle as she stirred the pot of sauce. She brought the stirring spoon to her mouth and tested the sauce, giving a little nod of approval.

"You taste as you cook and still keep a figure like that?"

"Flatterer." She turned her head with a grin. "I don't like being bound by a recipe. When I use them, I change them the way I like them."

"Oh, oh." Lee laughed. "And do you treat men the same way?"

She gave him a mock frown, then kissed him with conviction. "Except for the ones I like just the way they are."

Hesitantly, he said, "I have a feeling I'm not the man you think I am. I'm no saint."

She raised a finger to his lips. "I have a feeling you couldn't admit it if you were. Besides, who wants to go on a romantic getaway with a saint?" She laughed, but his face was still serious.

"I mean it. I'm not a nice guy. I've done some shitty things. Most of them I didn't even have the good grace to be ashamed of. Michaela was right to leave me. I was poison to her." He paused, then leaned back on the counter. "I've been an arrogant son of a bitch most of my life, and radio gave me a perfect outlet. Some people have hated me. They had reason to."

"Hold on, cowboy. You're a broadcaster. You talk to thousands of people for hours every day, year after year. You're not going to please all the people all of the time."

"Don't think I haven't taken that excuse out for a spin myself." He turned his face away and continued in a low voice. "There was one time, about eight years ago. Ratings were good—I was a big man in town. I figured I could push the envelope a little. Sort of Howard Stern *lite*. There'd been a small news item about gay players in college football. I asked if they'd make all their passes at the wrong team... if they were allowed to be MVP and Prom Queen at the same time. Juvenile stuff, not even very funny. But I wouldn't let go of it, kept coming back to it. A while later I got a call—a teenage boy. He sounded almost hysterical, saying I was right, and the world didn't need another worthless queer. I tried to get his name... calm him down, but he hung up." He had to swallow hard to release the next words. "The next day I read the newspaper. A kid had killed himself with his father's shotgun. High school all-star."

"Are you sure it was him?"

"There was a note. It even contained a few of the words I'd used. I heard that second hand because I knew the school principal, but he didn't make the connection. Nobody did but me. I nearly quit. Nearly got out of the damn business. But... there wasn't anything else I knew how to do."

"Did you tell your wife? You didn't, did you?"

"No," he confirmed. "I couldn't. I guess our marriage went downhill more quickly after that. Maybe everything else, too." He hung his head. "So you see, I'm no knight, or saint, or even a very good person. I don't deserve you."

She held him close. "You deserve far better than you know," she said. "Just... don't ever keep secrets like that from me, ok?"

She didn't see the clench of his jaw or the dullness of his eyes.

While she got ready to serve the food, he sliced cheese and bread and opened another bottle of wine.

The meal was delicious. There were no candles, so they lit the oil lamps, and turned off the electric lights. Their mouths said little, their eyes spoke volumes. Her face was classically beautiful in the lamplight and he could have looked at it forever. But he sensed that she had something on her mind. "What is it?" he asked.

"Nothing. Just... well, I don't have all that much experience with men, really. I've been too involved with my work. Or maybe that was just an excuse. I nearly got married when I was twenty-five—I think

I told you that before. We seemed so well suited, but when it came time to make the final decision, I realized that he wanted to change me—take the attention I gave to lost causes and keep it for himself. And there was something missing, some spark. My friends accused me of watching too many girl movies." She gave a little laugh. "For a while they even had me convinced, and I wondered if I'd made a terrible mistake. But you know," she said softly, lifting her eyes to his, "I wasn't wrong. I didn't make a mistake."

His throat constricted and he could only squeeze her fingers.

Later, as they sat on the hearth rug with refills of wine, Candace turned to him with a contented smile and saw a shadow cross his face.

"What's wrong? You still look like a man with a guilty secret." His startled look made her smile vanish, but it was too late to take back the words. They shifted apart.

"Only guilty because I should never have kept it secret from you."

He took a ragged breath. Then he told her everything, from the first hateful letter to the incident at the craft fair that had, perversely, brought them together. The vandalism, the poisoned throat spray, the brushes with death. It was a flood that, once begun, he could not stop.

When the confession finally ended she didn't seem to realize it for a minute or more. Then she slowly raised her head, the skin beneath her cheekbones dark with blood.

"When did you plan to tell me?" Her voice was hollow, broken.

"I planned to tell you hundreds of times. And never. Part of me needed so much for you to know. The other part was too afraid of scaring you away. Finally…I just didn't know how."

"You could have died. *You could have died!*" She hurled the words at him. "I just found you, and I watched you nearly slip away. God, I barely knew you, and I *prayed*.…" Her eyes filled with tears. "And now…" She choked up. "Now you're telling me that I could *still lose you*. Oh *God*."

He braced himself for her fury, but she dropped her clenched fists, struggled to her feet, and staggered toward the bathroom as if she were about to be sick.

He could see her bent shadow on the open door. The water was running, and he thought he heard a whimper. It filled him with shame.

At long last she stood in the doorway, framed against the light so he couldn't see her face.

"I have to think about this."

He nodded, and watched her mount the staircase to her room as if it were a mountain.

Snatching up the bottle of wine, he nearly spilled it on the rug. He should finish it off, find another—get seriously drunk. Why not?

If only he'd told her sooner. He'd been an idiot. But love had crept up on him so unexpectedly, and he no longer knew how to share such pain. Especially with someone he couldn't bear to hurt. He slowly put down the wine bottle. There was no point in making things worse. Instead he emptied his glass, and sat there, staring into the flames.

Long into the evening he heard a sound on the stairs.

Candace took each step as if she were treading on glass. She'd changed into a pair of light grey track pants and a soft sweater of a darker grey. Her hair was brushed, her face calm. She came to the back of the love seat and stood resting her hands on it, looking at him. When she finally spoke, her voice was strained but under control.

"Forgive me."

He leapt to his feet and crushed her in his arms.

"Please forgive me," she said again. "I was just so shocked that all I could think about was myself. *My* fear, *my* pain. God help me, I felt... betrayed by the world, not by you. I... think I can understand why you couldn't tell me."

He squeezed her again to tell her that she didn't need to say more, but she took his face in her hands.

"It's just that I couldn't bear to lose you now."

A storm had passed.

～

The fire and the wine sank lower while they nestled together, and kissed, and talked. Of dreams, of fears, of joys and tears and plans and promises. The night had shrunk to a small cocoon of amberglow when Candace took his right hand in her left and slid it slowly along her hip, then under the waistband of her sweater. Heart pounding, he continued the motion along the line of her ribs, until his palm cupped her breast, left bare for him. He reacted with a gasp, and she breathed into his ear.

"I'm ready."

The desire that carried them up the stairs to her room gave way to a moment's hesitation as they stood apart and she waited for him to make the first move. He brought her lips to his and slid his hands under the back of her sweater to delight in the smoothness of her skin. His palms slid along her shoulder blades to her sides, and then forward still more. She gave a small gasp and rose slightly on her toes at his touch, first tender then firm. He drew the sweater over her head and stepped back. Emboldened by the look in his eyes, she pulled the drawstring at her waist and let the fabric fall loosely to the floor. Then, revelling in his attention, she slid onto the bed with a whisper of skin against linen and watched him undress. He settled lightly on the edge of the mattress and reached out a hand.

"Guide me," he said, and the night dissolved into a flow of passion and discovery.

When they were finally spent, they fell asleep in each other's arms.

～

He dreamed of partridge: a pair of them, and then only one. It flapped through the forest, barely avoiding obstacles that leapt from the darkness, landing improbably on a window ledge of the cabin. It scratched at the window to get in, then knocked at the glass with a wing. For a moment Lee was the partridge. Then he woke up. The night was still except for a small branch, tapping at the window in a light breeze. He wrapped his arms more tightly around his love, then drifted into the warm dark again.

≈

The sun was well above the horizon when they awoke. He kissed her sleepy eyes and drowsy smile, and drew a lock of her hair to his face to breathe her in, as if its fragrance could prove he wasn't imagining. She really did lie at his side in the light of a new day, leaning on a pillow, drawing circles around his lips with a finger. That life could offer such a feeling of completeness was something he'd long forgotten.

They made love again, slowly, perfectly, every move in unselfconscious union. When their breathing began to slow, he offered to do it again. She laughed and swatted him with a pillow, then rolled to her feet. She dressed, and he was captivated. Faint sounds of running water, a toothbrush, a hairbrush, were music. Magic. He was reluctant to leave the bed, afraid to break the spell, even when he heard her footsteps on the stairs. But to stay behind was to be without her near. He thought he heard her call his name, so he pulled on some clothes. The mirror showed him the face of a stranger, wearing a broad smile. Surely not his face.

He started toward the stairs.

The explosion lifted him off his feet and flung him against the wall with a deafening roar. Heat seared his face. He sprawled across the boards, the breath knocked from his chest, his ears inexplicably filled with cotton. He pawed at them, but the sounds were all wrong. Animal noises. Electronic shriek.

Smoke alarm.

"*Candace!*" he screamed, flinging himself at the railing.

A rag doll lay carelessly discarded on the floor below, tiny flames dancing on its clothing and hair. Horror broke with a moan from his throat as he snatched a blanket from the bed and hurtled down the stairs. He covered her and batted at the flames, then leapt to the wall and tore a fire extinguisher from its bracket. Hungry red tongues licked at the varnished frame of the kitchen, gathering beneath the overhang. With a shout of defiance he sprayed the chemical at the base of the flames, then upward—sprayed and sprayed until the tank ran dry. In a fury he cannoned the empty cylinder off the obscene ruin of a stove, and surrendered to a wracking cough as his lungs heaved to rid themselves of poisonous smoke. Another smell made his nostrils recoil. *Propane.* He scrambled forward and found the shut-off valve a few feet away along the wall.

Dizzy and weak, he knelt beside his broken love.

Her breathing was an erratic rasp. The lustrous skin was now blackened and rough—whether from soot or burns, he couldn't tell. Lush lashes and eyebrows had been replaced by shrivelled patches of steel wool ash. Black tears streamed down her temples.

He had to get help. He'd begun to rise when she called to him.

"I'm here. I'm here." He repeated it like a mantra, as if his voice could heal her. "I'll get you to a hospital. Lie still."

Her eyes struggled open. Shuddering fingers scrabbled at his arm, flailing like a drowning child, as her throat worked and swallowed.

The sound it produced was a cry of agony.

"I'm blind, Lee. Oh God, *I'm blind!*"

21

"IT WASN'T AN ACCIDENT."

Cheryl Davis looked weary and felt worse as she watched Lee slump across the desk.

"You know that for sure? Already?"

"The Fire Marshall's office in Orillia sent somebody up. Called in a specialist on propane appliances, too. The stove was booby-trapped. Not that hard to rig, apparently. Our FIU is doing their own investigation. Looks like the intruder found a window that wasn't fully latched and managed to jimmy it open. One clear boot print on the floor under the window—a Kodiak, one of the most common boots around. The rest of the scene was pretty well trampled by the time we got there, and outside the snow had been falling for at least three hours. No usable footprints or tire tracks."

Lee had a cup of coffee in his hand, at an angle just shy of spilling. A tremor passed through his body.

"We're checking for fingerprints, but it looks like the perp used gloves again. The remains of the stove are being sent to the labs in Toronto. I'll let you know if they find anything."

"We knew it couldn't be a coincidence." He stood and drifted over to the window. It looked out over Brady Street toward the tarred flat rooftop of the arena, spotted with dirty snow, and the surrounding parking lots with their heaved asphalt. The sky was pasty and mottled. "Which means that I'm to blame. Don't take others with you, he said. But I didn't listen. God help me, I didn't listen."

"Come on, Lee. The only one to blame is the prick who's doing this. He's the one who hurt her, not you."

"I don't understand it. Why did he suddenly decide to attack me through her?"

"He didn't." Davis riffled through the papers in front of her. "The propane expert thinks the perpetrator had extinguished the pilot light, which would've shut off its gas feed automatically. Ms. Ross wouldn't have smelled anything. The stove was rigged to explode when somebody tried to relight it. And probably only on the second or third try." She looked into his face. "I don't know about your family, but if a gas appliance like that doesn't light right away, I call my husband. I could do it myself, but I'd bet most couples are the same, and a neo-Nazi would expect that. Ms. Ross just may have been too independent for... Anyway, I'm sure you were the target, if that really makes you feel better."

~

When he made a stop at his apartment he called Bruno. The man had been beside himself, fearing that Candace's injuries might have been because of something he'd neglected. It was hard for Lee to explain the truth, and he almost didn't get through it. He apologized for bringing destruction into Bruno's idyllic hideaway.

"We're not responsible for all the evils of the world, my friend. You just look after that special lady of yours. She looks like a keeper."

Lee's throat tightened again, and it was a few seconds before he could utter a last 'Thanks' and hang up the phone.

He hadn't gone to work. That would have been inconceivable. Ellis told him to take a few days off and keep her posted. The hospital wouldn't allow him to stay overnight with Candace, but she'd been sedated anyway. The image of her lying under a sheet like a corpse was etched into his brain.

The elevator regurgitated him onto a hospital floor like every other, marked by forgettable names and unforgettable odours. Green was the colour of life everywhere else, but here it had the power to consume dreams.

Candace had a room to herself for the time being. She looked much the same as the day before, bandages still covering her eyes. When she reacted to his footsteps, it was a fresh shock for him to remember that he now had to treat her the same way she had taught him to treat Paul Schwartz.

"Candace, it's Lee," he said softly, walking to the side of the bed. "How are you doing?"

"Lee, hi," she said weakly. The few places with exposed skin looked shiny from ointments of some kind. Her hair was pulled back and covered with a bonnet, but much of it around her face had been clipped away. "It hurts. But I can manage." She licked dry lips, and he saw a glass of water with a bent straw, so he put it to her mouth. She sipped gratefully, and said, "How do I look?"

Tears sprang to his eyes; it took a moment before he could answer.

"You look like the most beautiful woman in the world. Just like always." He sat lightly on the edge of the bed, looking for any place he could touch her for reassurance. He laid a hand gently on her shoulder. "What have the doctors said?"

"Well...I have a lot of burns, but they could have been much worse. A surgeon—Dr. Forestal—said I might get away without any scarring. The heat was bad, but I was blown away from it. Something like that. I guess I was lucky." She tried to laugh, but it choked off. He wanted so badly to hold her and tell her everything would be all right.

"Is there … ?"

"Any chance I'll be able to see again? It's what I wanted to know, too." She hesitated, as if unwilling to face the words again. "They don't know. The actual burns to my eyes should heal quickly, as long as the drugs prevent infection. That's not what … not what's making me blind. It might be something called burn encephalopathy. It happens sometimes with burn victims, even mild burns. They don't know why." She rasped a difficult breath. "So they can't say if it will ever heal."

"That means there's hope, though," he said.

She shook her head limply. "I've seen cases like this. Worked with the people. I've never seen one of them regain their sight." Her words were appalling for him to hear. How much more terrible must they be for her to say?

"I'm so sorry. I'm so …" He tried to choke off a sob.

"Don't blame yourself. It was an accident." Her head twitched upward. "It was, wasn't it?"

He swallowed hard. "No. The stove was rigged to explode. But I was supposed to be the victim, not you. I wish to God I had been."

Her bandaged face was frozen in shock, unwilling to believe, unable not to. A tremor of her lip spread shudderingly down her body. Her nostrils flared with a catch of breath, and he realized that the sightless eyes were crying.

Finally her voice came as if from the bottom of a well.

"Please leave. I need to be alone."

For the first time in a long time he looked for comfort in a bottle of scotch. But it wasn't there. Sunk crookedly in his battered sofa bed he took a long look around his domain. God, it wasn't much. The precious life he'd been so afraid of losing now seemed a poor measure of existence. He hadn't really known fear until he felt fear for another, more precious than himself.

The voice of a small child inside told him he was a victim: he didn't deserve what had been done to him. The voice of the adult knew better. The ordeal of the past weeks was out of proportion with whatever he'd done to his persecutors—it must be. Yet if there were a cosmic ledger of life, he still had a lot to account for. A karmic debt of substantial weight.

He could accept that. What he couldn't accept was that Candace had paid such a terrible price for his sins. Where was the justice in that? She must feel the same way. Having him near could only remind her of the unfairness of her condition.

Perhaps it would be best to leave her alone—give her time to sort things out. The doctors had left a small door open for hope to enter, but she wouldn't need the complication of a relationship with a man who'd brought disaster into her life, disguised as joy.

He should leave her alone for a few days.

Except he couldn't.

Before he'd finished his coffee the next morning, he was walking to his car and driving to the hospital, as if controlled by a force beyond his own will.

As he stepped out of the elevator and turned toward her room he was pulled up short by the sight of a woman sitting near the door, who rose at his approach. Neatly dressed in blue and white calico with a small string of pearls at her neck, she had eyes that were immediately familiar, but without any of the warmth he was used to seeing in them.

"You must be Mr. Garrett," she challenged.

"Mrs. Ross, I presume." He felt like a penitent student summoned before the headmistress, with a powerful urge to look at the floor. Instead he met her steel gaze. He was prepared to apologize, to commiserate, even to defend himself to a degree. He wasn't prepared for the words she spoke.

"She doesn't want to see you."

It was ice water in the face. He gasped before he could help it.

"She told me. She doesn't want to see you," the hard voice repeated. Then, realizing the literal implication of her pronouncement, she rephrased it. "She doesn't want you around. Please respect her wishes."

He gave a furtive look toward the closed door. She forestalled him with a raised hand.

"A confrontation will not help my daughter. Perhaps that doesn't matter to you, but it does to me."

The unfairness of the accusation was a fresh wound. He slumped against the wall, cradling his arms and trying to restore some order to the chaos of his brain. In a voice that barely reached her, he said, "Your daughter is *all* that matters to me."

The flint in her eyes softened, but she stood firm.

"She doesn't want you here. Is there really anything more to say?"

There wasn't. The quiet words brought an end to what he'd thought was a new dawn in his life. The brief sun had already set, and night had fallen again.

For no logical reason he could think of, he found himself steering toward the CNIB on York Street. The Director of Services and Operations, Audrey Raines, led him back to her office. Her expensive wool skirt suit was the uniform of an office professional, while her tidy crop of short white hair and smile-creased skin were her badges as a grandmother. Candace was very fond of her. That was enough to earn Lee's trust.

"How is Candace?" she asked.

"I thought I might ask you that," he replied. He hadn't meant to be mysterious, but he saw the rise of her eyebrows.

"We haven't heard from her today. Yesterday she told me what the doctors think, but I could sense she wasn't telling me everything. Is it worse than she said?"

"I don't think that's it. The burns are painful, but expected to heal well. Her eyes are another story. She's not optimistic about them. You'd probably know more about that than I would. I ... haven't talked to her today." The silence prompted him to go on. "I haven't seen her because she doesn't want to see me. Her mother told me."

Audrey Raines looked shocked. "But I know how much she cares for you. It was impossible to miss. She practically glowed when she told us you were going away for the weekend. What happened? What's going on?"

He told her. She took his confession like a priest, in silence, her eyes a mixture of shock and sympathy.

"I'd kept it all from Candace until the night before the explosion," he said. "She was furious at first, but I was sure she'd forgiven me. Until I cost her her sight."

"Oh God. What a tragedy." She turned sympathetic eyes to him. "But you didn't blind her, Mr. Garrett. She knows that. Candace is a very forgiving person. You'll have to be patient with her. Very patient. Losing your sight isn't like losing a loved one." She leaned forward, hands clasped together. "When someone you care about dies, you grieve, and then eventually—someday, somehow—you move on. We always say their memory will be with us every moment for the rest of our lives, but it's not really true. Memories do fade—it's part of how we cope and get on with our lives.

"But the loss of your sight is something you feel every time you get dressed, look for something to eat, wonder what time it is, or touch a face. Maybe you grieve a little each time. That's not to say that life without eyesight is miserable. I can't tell you how many people I've seen find their joy in life again, learn to do meaningful work, regain their self-esteem. That's what CNIB is all about. Candace knows that better than most. She'll recognize every stage that she goes through, because she's seen them so often in others, and her training will cushion her a little. She's a strong woman—she *will* cope, I guarantee that. But..." She held him with her eyes, willing him to listen. "*It will take time.*"

He nodded, needing to believe her. But while her answer offered hope for Candace to regain a fruitful life, there was no guarantee that life would include him.

"What can I do?" he asked quietly.

"It's impossible for us to imagine what she's going through right now, blinded because of someone's hatred. Yes, part of her must resent you for escaping, while she paid the price—that's only human—but I think..." She looked deep into his eyes. "I think her biggest fear—the reason she's put a wall between you—is that she doesn't think *you'll* want *her* anymore. That you'll feel she can never be the woman she once was." She held a hand up to stop his denial. "No, that's something you should consider very carefully. Because she may very well be right."

The suggestion shocked him, but how could he truly deny it? Could he really know how he'd feel a month or a year from now?

"How long should I wait?" he asked.

"I can't say." She sighed. "But if you love her, don't give up on her. She's a wonderful woman; that hasn't changed. Whatever connection the two of you found is still there, and she will need you. It may be some time before she realizes that. Just be there for her when she does—that's the only advice I can give. I've never seen her as happy as she was the past couple of weeks. Abandoning that would be the real tragedy."

≈

Lee returned to his empty apartment for refuge, but the trials of the day weren't through with him. As he pulled the newspaper from his mailbox a headline halfway down the page struck him like brass knuckles to the gut.

"Woman Injured In Explosion." And in smaller type: "Trap Meant For Radio Announcer".

Stunned, he scanned the columns of print. The reporter had done his homework. The story told of the harassment, the explosion, even a reference to the snowmobile attack. There were details hardly anyone knew. Except the police. He nearly crushed the phone as he punched Davis's cell phone number.

"It didn't come from me," she protested. "I'm furious, too. It was important to the case that certain details would only be known by the perpetrators. Now that's shot to hell."

"It was Dieter, wasn't it? Answer me!"

"I have no proof of that."

"Goddamn it to hell. I'll have the bastard's balls for this!"

"Yeah, good luck with that." Her voice was heavy with defeat.

He slammed the phone into the cradle, but the sound he'd heard in Davis's voice made him stop before he dialled the Chief's number. The Chief's hands would be tied unless there was proof: proof that the sergeant had accessed case files that should have been beyond his authority. If he had, that would implicate Davis herself. And how could they prove it was Dieter who'd given the story to a reporter? The paper would never reveal its source. Certainly not unless the story was false. It wasn't. It was simply a damning truth.

As he sat on the edge of the sofa, shaking with rage, the phone made him jump.

It was Larry Wise.

"Lee, what the fuck's going on? What I'm reading in the *Star*—is it true?"

"Yeah, Larry. Somebody's been trying to kill me. You heard Maddy in the staff meeting."

"But Jesus Christ, she didn't say anything about that snowmobile thing. Now this woman gets hurt. And all of our listeners find out about this from reading the goddamn *newspaper*?"

For a moment Lee couldn't absorb what Wise was saying. Then his head reeled as if the phone had struck him.

"What the fuck is that supposed to mean?" he spat. "You self-serving prick. A woman is nearly killed and all you care about is that your sorry ass didn't get the scoop? Go *fuck* yourself!" He slammed the phone down for the second time in five minutes. He thought he heard it crack and was glad, but it didn't exorcise his outrage.

He lurched into the kitchen and swept the stack of dirty dishes crashing onto the floor. He hurled the ceramic sugar container at the door, followed it with the cream pitcher, delighting at the music of destruction. He wrenched a chair into the air and flung it toward the wall, taking out the ceiling light fixture. As the room fell dark he staggered backward, gasping in impotent fury, fell over the arm of the loveseat and lay sprawled amid the wreckage of his life.

~

Eventually the rage subsided. His brain began to function again, dulled but reluctantly aware. Life continued, so it had to be faced. Questions needed to be answered. Hard questions. Painful questions.

Did he still love Candace? Even after she had been sacrificed in his place? Did he still desire her, though her lovely skin might be scarred forever, and those warm eyes were now barren?

He tried to picture a life together: a life with a woman who would never again see his face or the faces of their children, if they had any. And each time she felt that loss, she would taste its unfairness all over again, and might well blame him.

Could he live a lifetime bearing that loss and that guilt every time he looked at her? To know what he had cost her?

He knew the first answer—it was as clear as the winter sky: he still loved her, and would always love her.

Could he endure the lifelong burden of her pain and his ever-present remorse? No, he wasn't that strong.

His soul curled in upon itself. He had tasted life as it could be, should be. And now it had been stolen from him. Maybe he would never regain what had been taken. But he would make someone pay.

He hugged his hatred to him like a prize.

~

Ellis was expecting his call. Of course he should take time off. He should get counselling, too—the company would pay for it if government health insurance didn't. She asked what he was going to do, and he gave her a lie that satisfied her. She wished him luck.

He had one more call to make after that.

It twisted his guts inside out to tell Michaela. She was stunned by the knowledge that he could have faced such torment without her even being aware of it. She didn't get angry, though she had every right to. Instead he could sense the pain that she felt for him. Under other circumstances he might have considered that a breakthrough.

"Take good care of Sarah and Jason for me.... Especially if…"

"*No.* Don't say that. Don't even think it."

"Anyway, I'll be out of touch for a while. If you need me you'll have to leave a message on my machine, and I'll check it when I can."

"What are you going to do?"

He couldn't lie to her. Not anymore.

"I'm going to drop out of sight—go underground. Maybe there's a way to track down these bastards."

She gasped. "Are you serious?"

"I'm not trying to play Hollywood hero, don't worry. I wouldn't know how to use a gun even if I could get one. But at least I can make myself hard to find. At best? I don't know—maybe I'll turn up something. I only know that I can't spend my life running away. Afraid that the people I care about might end up in the line of fire." He hoped she understood that he was including her.

"Lee, please. Don't do this. You said it yourself—it isn't a movie."

"I know that, Michaela."

In reality the cops didn't solve every case. The bad guys sometimes weren't stopped in the nick of time. And the hero didn't always survive.

He heard a sound and realized with a shock that she was crying. He couldn't think of anything to say.

"If I can't stop you," she said finally, "what can I do to help?"

Always practical, she told him how to get some VISA cheques for an inactive VISA account she'd never closed. That would provide money for an emergency while being worthless to a street thief. She advised him to take only his driver's license and cash in a soft cloth pouch pinned inside the front of his briefs. Accessible, but liable to be missed by a mugger. She even suggested costume makeup from a novelty store to give him the sunken eyes and dulled complexion of the dissipated, and smudge away the whiteness of his perfect teeth. Her ingenuity surprised him.

"Lee," she said finally, "please be careful. For me, for Jason and Sarah. They've lost enough already. And for your lady friend, too. Don't let *everything* be taken away from her. You still have a chance for happiness together. Don't throw it away. Please."

He thanked her inadequately and hung up the phone.

～

The house looked deserted, with no van in the driveway, but Paul answered the door.

"Lee! Hi. Um… my uncle's not home, and this time he said he'd be really mad if I let anybody in."

"That's ok, Paul. I just wanted to drop off a present for you. It's kind of out of season, but maybe you can find a place to kick it around until the weather warms up." He put the round shape into the boy's outstretched hands. His attempts to cover it with wrapping paper had been a failure.

"A ball?"

"It's a soccer ball, but this one's a little different. Here." Lee hunted for the switch and activated it. A high-pitched beep began.

"Whoa! For blind people, right? So I can tell where it is?"

"That's the idea. You can get a beeping baseball, too, but something tells me that could mean broken windows in the winter time." He switched off the beep. The light of the boy's smile warmed him. "I understand you used to be a real athlete. It'd be a shame to give that up."

"Thanks. Thanks a lot." Then the smile dimmed. "I heard Ms. Ross got hurt. Is it true? Is she really blind?"

"Yeah." Lee felt his throat start to close, and coughed it open. "Yes, she's blind. But otherwise they say she'll be ok." The man and the boy stood in silence, each with their own thoughts.

"Maybe I can help *her* now," Paul said.

Lee didn't trust himself to speak.

～

The few items he planned to take were ready. As he gave a last look round his room, the phone rang.

He hadn't wanted to talk to Davis about his plan. He knew she wouldn't understand.

"You're crazy. You can't do that," she snapped. "I can have our uniforms watch for you and spoil your cloak-and-dagger act."

"And then what?" he said. "Bring me back to my cage where the hunters know just where to find me?" She had no response to that. He knew she was angry because she cared. "You've got to let me know where you are."

"I can't. You'd be forced to keep a record of it, and I can't risk Dieter finding out. If you learn anything more, leave me a message. Just remember that if the Skins realize I've dropped out of sight, they might think of checking my answering machine, too. I'll call you if I get a chance."

"For God's sake, at least take a cell phone. I can get you one."

He thought hard. If he went to the police station for it, she'd try to talk him out of what he was doing, and might even find some legal trick to keep him out of harm's way. Besides, he was pretty sure a phone in his pocket wouldn't fit his image of a street guy down to his last few bucks.

"Please, Davis," he said. "Instead of blocking me, help me. Tell me what I need to know to keep from getting killed. Maybe even how to look for these bastards. Find out for me where those informants hang out. I promise I won't try to contact them without your permission, or do anything that would compromise them."

"That's what I was calling to tell you," she said in a thick voice. "We've lost them. Their police handlers put pressure on them, like I told you. Now they've vanished—haven't been seen for days." She sounded sick.

"We think they might be dead."

22

THE EVIDENCE OF AGE LAY EVERYWHERE. Vanished buildings, vanished railroads, vanished lives, all crumbled into a veneer of soot.

Lee shuffled along a grimy sidewalk past blackened clumps of snow and blackened lumps of clothing that covered bodies using a doorsill for a bed. Compared to that, even the hole of a room he'd rented at the Crown Hotel was a palace. He hadn't needed make-up to provide deep shadows under his eyes. The overnight din of the streets took care of that: the wail of police sirens and emergency vehicles, the steam factory cacophony of buses and trucks, babble of drunken bar patrons, and the thunderous crash of shunting railcars that made him think the roof was crashing in. He'd brought foam earplugs, but had been afraid to use them, knowing that his ears were his only defence against an intruder.

He passed an alley as a bus passed him. The smell of burnt coffee mixed with diesel fumes in a thin fog that stuck to the back of his throat. The odour of spoiled pastrami and urine assaulted his nostrils from stairwells, alleys, and arched doorways, momentarily cleared by a passing breeze only to renew its offensive around the next bend.

He'd had enough foresight to get smaller bills for the rent, not wanting anyone to think he was a drug dealer. He'd even crumpled the fresh bank bills during the bus ride downtown, then borrowed the grime from a factory wall to smudge them into anonymity.

The hotel desk clerk had been as dull as the surrounding wallpaper, but not so lethargic as to forget to ask for Lee's ID, even though he'd paid cash. Lee had pulled out another rumpled ten dollar bill, pointed to the picture and offered a line from a bad gangster movie. "That's me. And I like to share my picture with my friends." The clerk had snorted the closest thing to a laugh in his repertoire, flipped the guest book closed, and tossed Lee the room key, using a head gesture to indicate the direction of the stairs.

Staying at a hotel eliminated any chance of being taken for a vagrant. For that he would have had to sleep in one of the men's shelters, or on the street, but his plan was to regain his life, not find another way to lose it. He shuffled toward breakfast in a pair of beat up old Oxfords he only used for yard work. The insoles were mostly gone, the remnants like gravel under his feet. Both heels sloped toward the outer edge from wear, and the slant pulled his ankles over, giving him a bowlegged gait. He caught himself wondering about his next chance to see his chiropractor, even as he knew that the people around him were wondering about their next meal.

He kicked a clump of dirty snow into the street and watched as it was run over by a passing bus.

The entrance to the soup kitchen was along the side of a dull red brick building next to the railway tracks. The double metal doors were scratched and beaten, painted over with chipped and peeling blue paint. Near the latch plate was a gouge that looked as if someone had attacked the door with an axe.

Hot, moist air escaped through the opening door and wrapped around him, invading his nostrils with a smell of bacon and onions.

The first breath was appetizing, but a sour smell of unwashed bodies and stale cigarette smoke soon took over as he approached the tables. No one was allowed to smoke there but the residue clung to their clothes. A faint tang of alcohol, too.

At first glance he thought the only patrons were men, but he eventually decided that two were women, and another might be. The shapeless clothing was like a uniform, in colours designed to vanish into a background: dark workpants in faded cotton or corduroy, cheap nylon coats of navy or soiled khaki. The only real colours came from the many lumberjack-style shirts, usually showing a patch of white at the collar, evidence of a T-shirt or two underneath. There were a few ragged sweaters of indeterminate shades.

He expected the faces to look the same, too, painted with a kindred expression of hopelessness, but he was wrong. They were all different: young, old, tanned or pale, long hair, cropped hair, and almost no hair at all. Features drawn from a smattering of racial types. Not lifeless. Worn, yes; inevitably unshaven. But the stubbled smiles and toothless mouths open in mid-joke told of the resiliency of humour, even among the disenfranchised. A survival mechanism, no doubt.

About a third of the soup kitchen's clientele was native Canadian —Anishnaabe: The First Peoples. Their black hair was the giveaway, because their darker skin tones didn't stand out among the whites with "street tans". They also seemed to generate most of the laughter. He noticed one young woman with dark eyes and full lips curved into a good smile, but a frame too thin to be healthy. She caught him looking and stared frankly back. He took his plate of food over to an empty table on the far side of the room.

The fare was mostly under-seasoned: plentiful home-fried potatoes, a few bits of dry bacon, and lots of toast thanks to donations of day-old product from bakeries. The coffee was cheap and strong, with powdered creamer. He ate slowly and tried to pick up bits of conversation without appearing to be listening, but similar chatter could have been heard in any coffee shop. The hockey game of the night before, the milder spell of weather compared to last year's cold. One man told of a minor scuffle with the law, and a woman two tables away had witnessed a big win at a bingo three nights earlier. Her companions had heard the story often enough that they interrupted her to correct details, until she cuffed one of them and fell into silence, brooding over her coffee mug. Lee couldn't imagine how she got the money to play bingo. Or didn't want to.

He heard nothing useful. That was far too much to expect so soon. The soup kitchen wouldn't be a hotbed for racial purists, or the pampered and bored middle class youths who were drawn to a group like the Skins. He might have had better luck in a high school or college campus, but there was no way he could have infiltrated a community like that without instantly giving himself away. On the streets, he might pick up something second- or third-hand from other victims.

Even here he might be recognized, if not by the patrons then by one of the volunteers, or the administrator of the food kitchen itself. He'd met her. He didn't think she would see through several days of stubble and his shabby street costume.

By the time he finished his second cup of coffee, no one had said much to him, but they weren't snubbing him. There was probably an unspoken code that said to leave the newcomer alone until he felt like joining in. He deposited his empty dishes on the counter, and caught the eyes of the young native woman again as he made his way to the door.

The wind wasn't strong, but it had a fierce bite after the warmth inside. He pulled his coat up and drew his head deeper into the collar. With no real plan in mind, he decided to try a more sheltered route back to the Crown Hotel.

As he passed the bare brick walls of a dry-cleaning warehouse he almost didn't notice the small figure huddled near a window well. A man of unguessable age squatted next to a vent that spat a continuous plume of steam. Sharp eyes watched Lee pass, and the head gave a birdlike nod, showing a smile that was a few teeth short.

"It's a glorious day!" the voice croaked. "A glorious day!" He looked up into the dull, overcast sky, as if to confirm his assessment.

Lee couldn't think of a reply and kept on walking.

A block farther on, a window displayed some piles of clothing: a second-hand store operated by a centre for mentally-challenged people. They had drop boxes in a few locations around town. Donated clothes were cleaned, and occasionally mended by the clients of the centre, and then sold to raise money for day-to-day operations. On a whim, he pushed through the door and relished the warmth.

Two older women were rummaging through a pile of sweaters in the corner to the left of the entrance, and farther back he saw three teenagers, a girl and two boys, at a bin of blue jeans. The lone store clerk was watching the trio from the front counter as they carelessly picked through the piles and flung unwanted pants haphazardly to the side of the wide box. Hoping to blend in, Lee went to a rack of flannel shirts nearby and began to check through them for his size.

He couldn't help but overhear the teens as they spouted puerile assessments of each other, and humanity in general. Most of their sentences were simply vehicles for the word "fuck" and its variations. The torn jeans they wore looked newer than the ones they were tossing aside, and the assortment of metalware in their ears and noses told him they didn't need to buy second-hand. He'd met many young people he admired, but he could only hope the world would never fall into the hands of purposeless zombies like these. The three seemed like just the type to get involved with a gang like the Skins, but their vulgar prattle was no use to him at all.

He looked over at the middle-aged clerk. Her expression held a hint of fear, but not adult fear. A childlike discomfort, or lack of comprehension. He guessed that she was mentally challenged herself. Customers like these would be well outside her comfort zone.

Her eyes went wide and she put a hand to her mouth. Lee looked back and saw the teens had begun to fling pairs of jeans at each other. Some missed and landed on nearby bins, but others fell to the floor and were stepped on as the trio shifted and ducked, laughing idiotically. His blood shot to a boil.

"Knock it off!" he roared, the sound echoing off the walls. The room froze in tableau, the shocked faces of the culprits turned toward him, their bodies stopped in mid-motion.

The tallest one straightened. "Fuck off, man. What's it to you?"

Without thinking Lee stepped toward them, his slow pace menacing. All of a sudden, in his mind, these three punks were responsible for the collapse of his life.

"You wanna find out what it is to me, little man?" he hissed. He was only a dozen steps away and still advancing. The tallest of the teens was Lee's height or more, but without his broad shoulders or bulk. Or the look of someone who wanted blood.

"Come on, let's get out of here. Leave this crap for the assholes," the boy spat, then grabbed the girl's arm and yanked it fiercely. The three put on their sulkiest faces and hurried out of the building, trying to look casual about it. Lee found he'd been holding his breath, and slowly let it out.

Damn. If he'd hoped to ingratiate himself with the downtown crowd, he'd just blown that all to hell. On his first day, too. It reminded him again that he was out of his depth.

He snapped out of his reverie to find the clerk looking at him.

"Thanks, Mister," she said with a tentative smile, probably hoping he wouldn't turn his anger on her. "You saved me a lot of work, I guess.

I seen those kids come in, but mostly they don't cause trouble. Just sometimes. Anyways, I'm glad you was here."

He bobbed his head and said, "I'll take this shirt over here." He grabbed the nearest one in his size, paid for it, and made his way back onto the street. There was no sign of the three troublemakers on his way back to the Crown hotel. That was just as well. He wasn't feeling heroic. Only depressed.

The next morning at the soup kitchen, some of the faces smiled as they looked at him. It wasn't hard to guess that he was the subject of conversation. Word of what had happened in the second-hand store might pass as fresh news in a dreary existence. But he still ate alone that day, and the next.

Passing the hours shuffling through the streets, he tried to over-hear scraps of conversation, but there were few of those. Even a few days of milder weather didn't mean people stayed outside if they had anywhere warmer to be. The small knots of teenagers he encountered ignored him. The three teens he'd rousted had probably kept their hu-miliation to themselves, and he was glad of that. He didn't want to become the target of another vengeful gang. One was enough.

He scrutinized each passing face as closely as he dared. Although his voice was his trademark, his appearance was well-known, too, and his disguise was minimal. There was a real danger that one of his enemies would recognise him without him knowing about it.

He treated himself one night by going for a beer in a nearby bar. The Olde Towne Tavern had nothing of the flavour of an old English pub. A small TV in the corner displayed a sports channel no one was watching. No eyes met his as he sat at the bar. Even the bartender showed no interest in conversation. He was doing a crossword puzzle, and didn't look up when Lee left.

This wasn't life on the slow track, it was life on a forgotten siding. A record store leaked a few bars of Bob Dylan's "Like a Rolling Stone".

There really were people who had nothing, and nothing to lose. And now Lee felt just as invisible.

~

As he was standing in line for breakfast the young native woman he'd noticed before came up beside him for more coffee. He looked at her and she smiled back.

"I seen you here a few days," she said. "You new in town?"

He'd prepared a cover story, but after days of being ignored, he had trouble remembering it.

"New in this part of town. I used to live on the west side. Then I, uh…lost my job." The fewer details he supplied, the fewer lies he'd have to remember. The woman simply nodded. Unemployment was an all too familiar circumstance.

"You can come sit with us. If you want." He hesitated, then nodded, and carried his food to her table. Six faces smiled up at him, and there was a chair waiting. The one other Caucasian man in the group was the only one to introduce himself.

"I'm Earl. The old fart of the bunch." His companions laughed, but the young woman said, "Rose is almost as old." A small figure with grizzled grey hair confirmed her sex and her age with a giggle. Earl introduced the others as Vern, Harvey, and David. The young woman was Nadia. A closer look reinforced Lee's first impression that she was attractive, with lively eyes and strong cheekbones. Her smile was unusually white and even. The first day, he'd thought she might have a cold, but the light rasp was her normal voice.

After an awkward silence, he said. "Oh. I'm Sid. Sid Brown."

"*Shit* Brown?" croaked Rose. She threw her head back in a loud laugh, showing a mouth nearly empty of teeth. The others joined in the laughter. Lee shook his head in mock dismay, Earl pointed out that Harvey was called "Burger" and David was known as "Big Dick", which he gleefully insisted was his compensation for being short.

Sid had already become Shit. And Shit he remained.

The conversation turned to mundane things and anecdotes about friends that left Lee on the sidelines. He gave a reply if questioned, and joined in the frequent laughter, though he understood few of the jokes. He'd begun to think of an excuse to leave when Rose turned to Nadia with a conspiratorial look and said, "I think he's all right." Others at the table grunted their agreement.

"They figure you're a cop, eh." Nadia laughed. "That's why nobody'd talk to you right away. Are you a cop?"

Lee was stunned. "A cop? Why would you think that?"

Harvey answered for her. "'Cause you smell too good." He gave a howl, drawing attention from around the room. Nadia grinned.

"Yeah, you smell like soap. Talk good, too. And the way you stopped those kids in the store there. We heard about it, eh? So you must be a cop." She looked at him expectantly.

"No, I'm not a cop." He felt himself blushing. "I'm...I *was* a teacher. A history teacher. High school." He looked around at their faces. "Some things went wrong and I lost my job. Then my wife divorced me."

"Divorce. That explains how you wound up here," Earl said, drawing more laughter. Rose patted Lee's arm with a shrivelled hand.

"You're ok, Shit Brown," she declared.

"Don't smell like shit, though," David added, and that reminded someone of a story. The attention passed from Lee, and he was grateful.

If it was a breakthrough, it changed nothing else in his routine. He wandered the same streets in the same pattern, as if initiative were paralysed by this grim world. The old dry cleaner's was a regular landmark, and the old man was always there, slouched against the wall. The heat that was waste to the dry cleaning business was life to him.

As Lee passed, the man would give him a wave and point to the sky. "A glorious day, ain't it? Glorious!" Insane words, under the circumstances. But there was no insanity in his eyes. Lee never replied except with a slight wave of the hand he hoped no one else would notice.

The two ancient phone booths he passed were rarely used, so he checked for voice messages every couple of days. The only one had come from Cheryl Davis, wanting to make sure he was still alive. When he called, she had no progress to report. Only a few suggestions to watch for activity in empty buildings, especially at night, and keep an eye out for flyers or newspaper ads that hinted at meetings without a well-defined purpose. Street gangs didn't advertise, but there might be a loose cooperation among other neo-Nazis, she said. He thanked her and hung up the phone.

He ached to call Candace, especially during the long nights, but he was sure her mother would answer, and he had little hope that she would pass on a message. Candace might not even know that he'd dropped out of sight. Or worse, she might not care.

A voice in his head said that was for the best. The rest of his brain told the voice to go to hell.

~

When he sat down for breakfast a couple of days later he was shocked to see Nadia's face marred by an ugly bruise. Several shades of purple were outlined in black and sickly yellow. She held the injured side away from him, and her lopsided smile barely twitched, as if the movement brought her pain. No-one at the table seemed willing to mention the subject. Their conversation was strained.

Finally Rose caught him stealing a glance and blurted, "Some punks jumped her. Some young white punks."

He felt branded by the words.

"Goddamn cowards," Earl said. "Caught her sleeping. Nobody else around here at night, so punks come looking for trouble."

Nadia's head was bowed. Had they raped her, too, Lee wondered? "They came into your room?" he asked softly.

"*Room?*" She looked as if he'd spit a cockroach from his mouth.

"She sleeps over by the old rail shed," Vern said. "In the shunting yard. Not inside. Can't get inside. Always locked. No windows."

The words struck like a fist. He'd never thought of these people he knew, people who shared meals with him, living on the street like the man beside the dry cleaner's. Nadia, too. Why hadn't he expected that? Because it was too ugly? Made their plight too personal?

Nadia's voice was even huskier than usual. "You mean you got a *room*, Shit? No wonder you smell like that."

"I ... still had a bit of money left over," he stammered. He read surprise in their faces. Condemnation, too?

Rose narrowed her wrinkled eyes at him.

"Why the hell you wanna eat here? You could buy food. Sit with other people who smell like soap."

"I don't have a lot left," he protested. "I figured I might still be able to get a job if I got some sleep and stayed clean." He didn't know if the explanation was sufficient. Probably none would be. His very presence among them was a kind of betrayal.

"Where you got a room, Shit?" Harvey rumbled quietly.

"At the Crown." There was no point lying about it. He half expected them to throw him out on the street. Instead they seemed to come to an unspoken agreement.

Earl leaned toward him and said quietly, "Nadia, she's some beat up. Cold. Scared. Punks might come back." He sat back in his chair and crossed his arms, waiting. He'd said all he felt needed to be said. The others seemed to think his meaning was crystal clear.

Suddenly Lee understood. His stomach twisted.

God. He couldn't do that—it would be disastrous to his plans.

Except the alternative was to leave this place and never show his face again, without having accomplished a damned thing.

He turned slowly toward the woman beside him. She didn't meet his eyes. "Nadia…do you want to stay at my place for a while?" To his surprise, she shook her head.

"No. I'm good."

"*Please.*" He reached over to touch her hand.

This time she smiled. "Well if you're gonna beg. Sure. Ok, I'll come. Maybe for a few days." The bright gratitude in her eyes twisted his soul again. "But you better treat me like a *lady.*" And she raised her nose like a debutante determined to defend her virtue.

Rose cackled with glee.

He told Nadia he'd take her to the hotel right after dinner that night. In the meantime he made his way to the phone booth just inside the entrance of a drug store. Maybe Davis would have some advice for him. Maybe she could even tell him how the people of the streets were supposed to defend themselves without a police presence. But his anger at the cops evaporated when he heard the strain in her voice.

"Lee. You got my message?'

"No, why? What's happened?"

"It's your car."

"My car? I left it in my driveway. At the apartment."

"And someone tried to break into your place, but it looks like they got scared off. Probably by your neighbour going to the bathroom in the middle of the night. Except before they left they doused your car with gasoline and lit a match."

"*Jesus.*" He tried to absorb the picture. "It's destroyed?"

"The insurance company will probably write it off. Three sides of it are badly damaged, but your neighbour saw the flames right away and called the fire department. Thank God they got there before the gas tank went up."

"Let me guess: no evidence."

"The surveillance cameras didn't get anything useful. No face. Nondescript clothes."

Lee felt fury throb in his veins, but there were store customers walking by. He turned his face and hissed into the phone. "What about Dieter? Did you get anything on him?"

"He's got airtight alibis for all the times of the attacks. He denies leaking the story, too. But he did it all right."

"How do you know?"

"The prick had the balls to smile at me as he left the Chief's office."

"So that's it then?"

"No, that's not it. We don't have any evidence against him, yet, but I happen to know the Chief's been talking to the head of the police union. Trust me, the Professional Standards Unit will be investigating Dieter. They'll nail him. A moron like that gives us all a bad name. But…there's something else."

"What more could there be?"

"We've got cops watching Candace and your family."

"*What?* Why?"

"The one side of your car that wasn't damaged—that was because they left a message. In spray paint.

"It said, '*I know where they live.*'"

23

THE DESK CLERK GAVE THEM A COLD LOOK as they passed by. Lee didn't care. The management of a dump like that wasn't going to pass up a paying customer just because he took a guest upstairs.

Nadia looked around his room with an expression that was hard to read—maybe relief mixed with nostalgia, and a recognition that she wouldn't be there for long. They sat on the knotted mattress, side by side, and in the last dim light from the window he examined her bruised face.

"Four of 'em," she said softly. "One of 'em had hard boots." She reached a hand to touch her cheek. "And they knew I wouldn't have any money. It didn't stop them. They weren't after money." She looked out the window.

"Did they... ?"

"Did they rape me?" She slowly shook her head. "No. Not this time. I told them I was on my period. I always carry a rag around... with blood on it. So I can show them. That's how I got this," she pointed at her face. "But it's better than... four of them."

Lee felt shame for his whole sex.

"Had you seen these punks before?"

"You mean, would I recognize them? You think I should go to the cops?" She gave him another of those what-planet-are-you-from looks. "No way. Cops figure my boyfriend done it, drunk. I don't go to them no more."

"I meant, are they regular troublemakers? A gang, maybe. Have you heard of the Skins?"

"I heard of 'em. Don't like Indians or blacks. But who knows about the bastards jumped me? They don't wear signs."

"Have you heard about Skins coming down here to cause trouble? Beat up your friends?"

"Don't know who's Skins and who ain't. Just white boys, bored with themselves... come down here for easy pickings."

It was still early to go to bed, but he was tired and the thought of just sitting and watching TV together was surreal. He'd decided to sleep on the floor and give her the bed, but realized she had nothing to sleep in except her dirty street clothes. The thought of those clothes between bed sheets he might have to use again revolted him, though he was ashamed of his reaction.

"How would you like a shower before you go to bed?" he asked. Her eyes lit up.

"A real shower? *Hot?* Without anybody waitin' for their turn?"

"Sure. There are bathrooms down the hall. Only two shower stalls, but there aren't any other guests on this floor." He watched her crooked smile grow wide, then a shadow crossed her face. She unconsciously raised a hand to her bruised cheek.

"I can stand guard at the door," he said. "If you want."

Her smile lit again, and she jumped up.

"Yeah. Yeah, great." Her childlike enthusiasm should have made him happy. Instead he felt disgusted that society could let anyone reach such a state of separation, a stranger in her own land.

He was just as guilty as anyone. Maybe more so, because he had a platform—a voice that could be used on behalf of those who had no voice. Power. Influence. And he'd never used it for anything worth a damn. Was it too late?

"After your shower you can wait in my room while I take your clothes to the laundromat. There's one just down the street. I'm sure it's open this late."

Her frown surprised him. "Because you don't like the way I smell? You can't stand me in your room?"

"I didn't say that. I won't do it if you don't want me to. But after a shower, it just feels better to put on clean clothes, right?" She gave a short nod and a shy flash of a smile.

"Then we can both smell like soap!" She laughed and went before him down the hallway. As he left the room he grabbed his long coat.

"Here. You can wear this for a bathrobe when you come out."

The look from her half-moon eyes stopped him cold and sent a stir through his loins. She disappeared through the door.

God, *was she flirting with him?* Was he unconsciously trying to seduce her? Either was a recipe for disaster. He shook his head to clear it, then leaned his back against the wall and stared into space.

It seemed like a half hour before the water stopped. A few minutes later the door opened and she stood there with his coat wrapped around her, shiny and fresh, her skin ruddy from the heat of the water. She shook her wet hair free of the coat collar and pulled the cloth tight.

"That was good! Real good! Can I do it again in the morning?"

He laughed. "Sure. But let's get you back to the room. You should get your hair dry." He saw a large towel in her hand. Guests probably weren't supposed to remove them from the shower area, but he didn't care. They'd leave it in his room.

He told her to lock the door and lean a chair under the doorknob until he got back. Then he stuffed her clothes and some of his into a plastic bag and left for the laundromat. There was only one other person there, an old lady who gave him a look as he pulled out a brassiere and panties and stuffed them into the washer. He thought about sorting the clothes into a couple of loads, but all of them were too old for the colours to bleed. Almost as old as the magazines he read while he waited.

He had an impulse to find a drug store and buy her some cheap perfume—she'd probably be like a kid at Christmas. But that would be too much. It was an extra he shouldn't be able to afford, and she might take it as another insult anyway. Instead he returned to the room with a feeling of satisfaction. She pulled her clothes from the bag and held them up to her face.

"Mmmmm. Still warm, too. You do good laundry, Shit. *Sid.* Your mama would be proud!" She giggled.

As she bent to lay the freshly-laundered clothes on the bed a flash of lighter colour drew his eyes. The coat had fallen open, revealing shining skin.

He snapped his head up and looked into her puzzled eyes. Then she glanced down and started to pull the cloth closed, but stopped. Instead she raised her eyes again and locked them on his. With infinite slowness she straightened, and pulled back the lapels of the battered coat. It slid into a heap on the floor.

"There's nowhere else to change," she said in a husky whisper.

He stood frozen, trying to keep focused on her eyes, only her eyes.

She stood straighter, willing him to look.

It was a contest he couldn't win.

She was a portrait in frailty, probably no thinner than the average fashion model, but her slim build was not from choice. Her small breasts were well-shaped and firm, but he could make out each rib below them. He reached out gently to touch her bruised face. She stepped closer. He retreated. Surprise and confusion lit her eyes.

"Nadia ...," he raised a hand, "you don't have to do this ... to pay me back for helping you."

Her eyes caught fire.

"*Pay* you? I ain't paying you for anything, you dumb *shit!*" She snapped around and strode to the bed, snatching up her sweater and pulling it over her head. She grabbed the panties and made to step into them, but her anger spoiled her balance, and after two attempts she flung them at the wall with a growl and pounced onto the mattress to sit cross-legged facing into the corner of the room.

Lee was dumbfounded. He seemed destined to misread her and insult her. When he tried to see the situation through her eyes he realized that he'd been blinded by the stereotype of a downtrodden soul needing to be helped by the great benefactor. How arrogant that was. It denied her existence as a human being. And it was probably the way she'd always been treated by people like him.

The room was cold—she wasn't even half-dressed. He should wrap a blanket over her, or something. But he didn't. His eyes lingered over her hair, the soft curve of her back beneath the light sweater; and the seductive cleft of skin below that. He still couldn't allow his mind to pursue that thought, but it was going to be a long night if he didn't make up to her somehow.

"Nadia," he said, his voice loud in the room. "I'm really sorry. I just completely misunderstood. I'm ... I'm not used to being with women other than my wife." Sensing that she was listening, he hesitantly rested his hands on her shoulders. "I keep hurting you. But I don't mean to."

She didn't respond for a long time. Then she shifted a little, slowly reached up, and gently drew his left hand down her body until the palm slid over her nipple and enveloped her breast under the cloth. He kept it there, forcing the muscles to stay loose. Her movement released a hint of generic soap and shampoo, enriched by the musk of her body. When he didn't move away, she let her body relax, and with the same casual slowness, guided his right hand down along the line of her waist and hip, over her thigh and the soft hair to the delicate mound it guarded.

"Don't that feel good?" she murmured softly. She nuzzled against his face, filling his nostrils with the welcoming scent of her hair. "Can't you see that's all I wanted? A nice feeling I ain't had in a while?"

His throat was dry, and the blood pounded in his veins. She was desirable and available. He commanded his hands to draw away, but she held them tightly and began to move his fingers slowly in a circle.

Stifling a groan, he gave in to her need.

When her body had stopped trembling she rolled over to sit on the edge of the bed, and reached to undo his pants. He stepped back.

"No, I can't … make love to you."

"You already have." She smirked, and reached for him again. He took another step back.

"No. I mean I can't go any farther than this. I'm sorry."

She began to realize he was serious, and her face filled with dis-appointment. "Why not? Is it because I'm *Indian*?"

"No, of course not." It wasn't that, was it? No. He had a lot of flaws but that wasn't one of them.

"You got a hard on. So, what's the problem?"

"I'm … just not ready for that, yet."

Her dark eyes grew wide. "You're still thinking of her?"

He gave a nod, then realized she was talking about his ex-wife, not Candace. He didn't bother to correct her.

"She won't come back to you," she said softly.

The likely truth of her words cemented his silence. His only reply was a small shrug of his shoulders. After a time she reached for the discarded panties.

"Ok, Sid. I guess I can't be pissed at you for still being hung up on your wife. Wish the guys I knew were like that." She pulled on the rest

of her clothes, except for the bra. "I'm going to the john. Will you …
come with me?"

He nodded, and led the way down the hall.

≈

Something woke him in the middle of the night. Probably a
noise—there were so many. He shifted to ease his aching hipbones
and listened for it, finally hearing a sound like a whimper from the
direction of the bed. It came again. Should he do something?

"Nadia?" he called softly. Then a second time.

She gave a start, and seemed to shrink down into the bed, backing
toward the wall.

"Nadia it's me … uh, *Sid*. Are you ok?"

"Sid?" It was a child's voice. She cautiously reached a hand toward
him. He took it in both of his. "Geez, Sid. It was a dream, I guess. A
shitty dream. Such a shitty dream … ." Her voice cracked and she drew
her hand away to cry into her fingers. He could guess what the dream
was about. He eased himself onto the bed and cradled her gently, the
fragrance of her skin reawakening unwanted memories.

He felt her shudder, and knew it was a quiver of release. A long
sighing breath drained some of her pain and fear with it.

He held her tightly, and she slept.

≈

The gang at the soup kitchen assumed that he and Nadia were now
lovers. The proprietary way she'd moved her chair a few inches closer
to his was evidence enough. When he tried to deny it, she refused to
back him up, enjoying his discomfort. At first he was annoyed, but
then he thought back to the beginning of the day.

Neither had said anything about her tears in the night. He'd awakened to find her looking at him from her place on the pillow, inches away. The liquid eyes were too full for him to decipher them at once. Gratitude, certainly. The rest he was unable, or unwilling, to read. He got up and puttered around the room. She arose languidly, simply because she could. No harsh sunlight or probing wind had stolen her sleep before she was ready. She could sit on the edge of a real bed, secure in only a T-shirt and panties, warm and comfortable and not alone. It was a luxury from such a distant past it probably seemed from another lifetime altogether.

She showered. He waited. In spite of the days he'd spent in the neighbourhood, he was an eternity away from knowing what its people went through. How they experienced life; what that did to them. Or maybe not an eternity. If he didn't learn something soon, his money would be gone. His job really would disappear. Maybe everyone was always a few dark turns of fate away from an existence on the streets.

"How did you end up living...down here?" he asked her as he watched her dress. Her thin arms showed no needle tracks. She could have been one of the many victims of mental illness who'd fallen through the cracks in the system, but he didn't think so.

"Fucking boyfriend," she muttered. Her eyes held a fire when she raised them to his. "I had a good job on the Island. Convenience store. I gave him all my money—he just bought drugs with it. Dealt a little, too. Figured he could make a big score if we moved to the city. I didn't want to. He set me straight." Her lip twitched. "He got in with bad people, real bad. All the money went to oxy. When it was gone he beat the shit outta me and got busted for dealing. After he was locked up his friends came to me to collect what he owed 'em."

Lee could guess how she'd paid them back, but she didn't say any more. She only stared out the window, as if toward Manitoulin Island and her past life there.

She followed him out of the soup kitchen when they'd finished breakfast, and the absurdity of his situation struck him again. How could he look for Skins with her along, unless he explained? That thought wasn't appealing. He'd built a shell of lies around himself, and now he was trapped by them. Instead, they strolled aimlessly around the streets, looking in the shop windows and greeting people. Nadia seemed to know all the street folk, though not the clerks or other workers who lived somewhere else. He suggested she take the lead, but she declined. She wanted to be with him. Where they went didn't matter.

The next few days were lost time, and at night her womanhood, constantly present and available, tested him sorely. As soon as they'd return to the hotel room she'd strip down to T-shirt and panties, "for comfort". And after her evening showers she was never in a hurry to get dressed, revelling in the feeling of the bedclothes against her naked skin, her clean, feminine aura filling the air with temptation.

He didn't know how long he could fend off her sexual advances. Sometimes she masturbated, knowing he would watch. She insisted he share the bed with her for sleeping, and he nearly refused but caught himself in time, seeing the real fear that lay behind the light tone of her invitation. While he chafed at her demands, he also had to admit that she provided something he needed. It wasn't a welcome revelation. He had to have some time alone.

Help came the next day in the form of a flyer tacked to a hydro pole. It advertised a bingo that afternoon in a nearby building that had once been a movie theatre. Nadia stopped to read the yellow page, and he saw his chance.

"Would you like to go?" he asked. Her eyes widened.

"Sure I wanna go. Used to go every second Saturday on the Rez." She smiled at the memory. "Won a few bucks, too. I'm pretty lucky, really."

"I think you should go."

She gave him a look of scorn.

"Where'm I gonna get ten bucks?"

Lee reached into his pocket and pulled out a rumpled bill. He held it up and watched astonishment come into her face.

"I found this the other day, blowing down the street," he said. "I didn't tell you because I wanted to surprise you with something. Something nice. But this would be ok, too. Take it. Go to the bingo. Have a good time."

She gave him a penetrating look, then her eyes went to the bill in his hand. His story wasn't convincing, but she reached out.

"You sure?"

"I'm sure." He wanted to give her some kind of pleasure, after denying it to her in another form.

"It's starting soon. Maybe I should go early and get a good seat. Pick a good card." She turned and took the first hesitant step, then another, and began walking away, looking back once to give him a smile. He waved.

His feeling of new-found freedom was gone within minutes, re-placed by a loneliness he didn't want to acknowledge. With Nadia around he'd come close to a kind of connection with the people she greeted. Now he was an outsider again, alone and ignored.

In days of searching, he'd found only one flyer of the kind Davis had mentioned. It was a badly faded piece of grey paper that proclaimed, "Keep Canada for Canadians. Stop the Dark Tide." Underneath was a poorly written paragraph that offered dubious statistics about job losses to real Canadians at the hands of immigrants, claiming the resources of the land rightfully belonged to those who had "built this country". Lee snorted out loud at that one. It was hard to believe even bigots would forget that Canada's stubborn landscape had been tamed by waves of tough European immigrant farmers, and thousands of exploited Chinese labourers on the railroads. Not to mention the First Nations people, who believed the land didn't *belong* to anyone.

He'd hoped the flyer would have some contact information, or mention an upcoming event of some kind, but there was nothing. Disappointed, he'd stuffed it into his pocket, not quite sure why.

The streets were nearly empty and bitterly cold again. Buses passed at long intervals, but little other traffic. Everyone had better things to do, in better places. Everyone except him.

Eventually he made his way back to the hotel. Nadia wasn't there. He began to feel a knot of concern in his chest. The bingo should have ended long before. Could something have happened to her? Where else would she have gone? He waited for half an hour, then went back out to look for something cheap to eat. He kept looking for her. The loneliness grew even stronger.

She showed up soon after he got back to the hotel, sending a wave of confused feelings washing over him. As he closed the door, she leapt up, locked her legs around his waist, and began to kiss his face.

" Nadia," he protested, "I told you…"

"I *won!*" she squealed. "I won! Five hundred bucks, Sid. I won it in bingo! Look!" She slid down to the floor and began to wave a sheaf of bills at him. "Five hundred bucks. *Holy shit!* I never had so much money in my life. Thanks, Sid. Thank you. Thank you."

She threw her arms around him again, and this time he caught the smell of alcohol. He pried loose and held her at arm's length.

"Nadia, are you drunk?"

She gave him a pained look.

"Hell, no. I only had a couple beers to celebrate. But I just might get that way. Wanna help?" She laughed in delight, tossed the bills into the air and watched them flutter to the floor, then bent over to pick them up.

"That's a lot of money. You should be more careful with it."

She looked up in surprise. Picking up the last fallen bill, she slowly straightened.

"That's all you got to say? Be careful with it? No 'Congratulations Nadia. I'm happy for you Nadia'?" She gave him a puzzled look. "It's my money, Sid. I can do what I want with it."

"Of course you can. I'm sorry. It's great that you won. I only meant that it could make a real difference for you. But if you start drinking with it..."

Anger flared brightly in her eyes, and her lips pulled back.

"You think I'm gonna *drink* it all," she snapped. "'Cause I'm a goddamn Indian I'm gonna blow it all on booze and stay good and fucking drunk until it's all gone!" Her chest heaved. "Well fuck you, *Shit* Brown. Fuck you!" She whirled toward the door. He wanted to protest his innocence, except he *wasn't* innocent. Shame burned his face. As he opened his mouth to take back the ill-chosen words, she turned on him with tears in her eyes.

"You can be a real asshole, you know that?"

"Don't go—not at night," he pleaded. "If anybody ever found out you have that much money on you..." He grabbed her arm, but she broke free.

"You touch me again," she hissed, "and I'll scream. I swear I will."

He stood shocked into immobility as she bolted down the hall. Then the thought of her alone in the dark snapped him out of it, but by the time he reached the street she was gone. The desk clerk looked up in surprise at the sound of a fist against the wall.

Lee returned to his room, cursing himself. How could he come to live at the bottom of creation and still find a way to sink lower?

Sprawled on the bed he listened to the condemning silence.

~

The next day he was too ashamed to go to the soup kitchen. He was also too afraid that he might find out he'd been right: that

Nadia and her friends had drunk all the money away. He wandered the streets and tried not to think about food. Ellis had given him a month's paid leave, but his regular bills hadn't gone away, and the money was getting very low. Soon he'd have to give up. He had no idea what would happen then.

He thought about catching a bus to somewhere, but realized it was only a subconscious excuse to get out of the cold. He wouldn't have learned anything—people didn't talk on buses. Instead he returned to his room and brooded. He listened for Nadia's knock on his door, all day and all night, but it never came.

The next day was bitterly cold with a wicked wind whipping between the buildings. An idea came to him as he passed the dry cleaner's.

"Hey, fella." He approached the old man. A gaunt face raised itself up from a cradle of scrawny arms.

"A glorious day, ain't it?" the voice croaked from cracked lips, as they creased into a smile. But the words came with an effort. Wind instantly snatched away any heat from the hot air vent, and the man couldn't be eating well enough to produce any body heat of his own. He could lose his life on a day like this.

"How about I buy you a coffee? I feel like some company." Lee raised his voice over a sudden gust. The old man looked at him in surprise.

"You say *coffee*?"

"That's right."

"Tim Horton's?"

"Sure, if you want. But it's a few blocks from here. You want to walk that far in this wind?"

"Walk farther than that for a real coffee." The rumpled figure struggled painfully to his feet, waving off an offer of help. "Coffee at the places around here tastes like *piss*." He began to limp toward the street, muscles stiff from the cold. Arthritic legs loosened up a little as they went, but he remained bent in the wind. By the time they were seated in the donut shop, Lee was afraid he'd made a mistake. That much walking might burn off all the calories he'd hoped to get into the man. To make up for it, he ordered soup and a couple of biscuits for his companion, along with the coffee and an apple fritter. The old man made a show of protest, but took to the meal ravenously. He smacked his lips with each swallow of coffee.

"Goddamned stuff is better'n a woman," he proclaimed. "Good food, good coffee...what more does a man need from life?"

The complete sincerity of the words made Lee choke up. This man, with a wind-ravaged alleyway for a home, who never knew where his next meal was coming from, could still cherish life in all its small pleasures.

They took their time. He placated the servers by buying more coffee and another couple of donuts, then ignored their pointed looks. The old man needed company as much as he needed food. They talked about a dozen mundane things, nothing of importance. When the conversation flagged, Lee asked why the man didn't find a warmer place to sleep. Maybe the Salvation Army hostel a couple of blocks away.

"I know the Major there," he said. "I could write you a note." He reached for a napkin, then fished in his coat pocket, hoping to find a pen. He pulled out a grey scrap of paper.

"You ain't a *Nazi*, are ya?" The man's rough voice had sharpened, and the eyes turned to flint.

"What?"

"A Nazi," the man repeated. "Them's the ones put those things around the streets." He pointed a bony finger at the piece of paper. Lee flipped it over and realized it was the racist tract he'd pulled off a lamppost days before.

"Oh, shit no. It's not mine," he protested. "I mean, I found it and ripped it down because I was angry about it. I guess I stuffed it into my pocket thinking I'd throw it away when I came to a garbage can." He began to crumple the paper, then stopped and looked into the thin face across from him. "You know about skinheads? You've seen them?"

The grey head nodded slightly.

"I seen 'em, sure. The bastards. Some young ones, too—think they're some kinda gang. Come here to make trouble."

"Do they live near here?" Lee felt excitement stirring.

"Nah, mostly rich kids with nothin' better to do and nowhere to do it. Oh, a few of 'em work down here. I know one or two 'cause I seen 'em pickin' on people at night. They don't even know I'm there. One o' the guys at the smoke shop. An' that bastard of a hotel clerk, too."

"Hotel clerk?" Lee leaned forward. "Which hotel?"

"The Crown. Lousy desk clerk at the Crown Hotel."

24

IN THE MOVIES THERE WOULD HAVE BEEN A SURGE of suspenseful music as the man under suspicion looked up and realized that his cover was blown. He would have waited until the good guy was out of sight, snatched up the phone, and contacted his leader for instructions.

The desk clerk at the Crown looked as bored as ever, never raising his eyes from his book as Lee walked through the lobby. Not suspicious, and clearly not worried about being caught by the boss.

Lee turned the corner toward the stairs, scuffled his way noisily up them, opened the door at the top, then slid back down the metal handrail and watched the reflection of the lobby in a brass plate on the wall. The clerk hadn't moved. The only other thing at the bottom of the stairwell was a battered Coke machine. If someone came, Lee could pretend to be buying a drink. But the less traffic, the better.

He hunched down to wait, blowing quietly into his hands to warm them. He'd taken the old man to the Salvation Army shelter where the new guest had looked as comfortable as a mechanic in a tuxedo. There was nothing Lee could do to stop the man returning to his spot by the dry cleaner's as soon as the weather turned milder.

Bringing him to the hotel room was a non-starter, not least because Lee might not be there himself for much longer. With any luck.

He looked at the brass plate. The clerk was like a statue.

Even if the old man was right and the guy had neo-Nazi friends, there was no guarantee he was connected to the attacks on Lee. It was simply the only lead available.

An older Italian man from the second floor flung open the door and descended the stairs, limping. He cast a scowl at Lee, who was fishing through his pockets in front of the Coke machine, then moved on into the lobby. The man always wore a scowl. The noise from the vending machine's refrigeration equipment quickly drowned out his footsteps. That might mean Lee wouldn't hear any conversation from the front desk either. But there was nowhere else to hide close to the lobby.

He waited through four hours, playing out his coin-hunting act for three more guests. His legs were cramping. His bladder had complained for the past hour and a half. He'd have to do something about it before much longer. The clerk would probably be taking a dinner break soon. If it happened while Lee was in the john, he'd miss a good opportunity to search the desk. Or if the guy left the building to eat while someone else covered for him, Lee would have to follow. The thought of walking out into that cold with his kidneys backing up was intolerable.

The phone rang.

The clerk answered it, but his lips moved soundlessly. Lee cursed at the noisy compressor of the Coke machine to stop. It did.

The clerk's voice had lost some of its boredom. A personal call, obviously. Lee watched the reflection.

There! The man had furtively glanced around the lobby to make sure there was no one else around. He kept talking, but fewer than half the words were loud enough to reach the stairwell.

"Tonight? Don't know—off late—where?" He scribbled something on a memo pad with the desk pen, then tore off the page and stuffed it into his pocket. "Sure—friends—sure—no way! Right, right." The man hung up, took another look around the lobby, then settled back onto his chair and picked up his paperback.

Lee knew what he needed to do, but would it work? Carefully pulling himself up the railing, he made a show of loudly swinging the door open and tramping down the stairs into the lobby. He was rewarded by a sour look as the clerk put down his novel.

"Yes?"

"I was thinking I might pay for a couple weeks in advance. How much is it?"

The man muttered an amount. Lee reached for the pad and pen, wrote the number at the very bottom of the top page, and pretended to do the math. "That works out to the same rate as paying by the day," he said indignantly, tearing off the page and waving it.

"What a surprise," the clerk said. "We don't get a lot of customers who stay that long. So no discounts. Sorry." He sounded anything but sorry as he picked up his book.

"Forget it, then." Lee stalked away and hurried to his room.

The movie trick worked. Shading the empty part of the page with pencil brought out some faint words and numbers. After five minutes of playing with the possibilities, he was pretty sure it read

7:00

Kane's Gym

P____ Block

86 Montclair

The street number might have been 88. But Kane's Gym? Maybe the guy was just planning to meet a friend for a workout. He didn't look the type. The name twigged something in Lee's memory. Wasn't Kane's going out of business? Something like that. No, had *already* gone out of business. It was in receivership—Lee remembered a fuss when the owner suddenly locked the doors, leaving paid-up members howling for their money back. An unused building, like Davis had said to look for.

Now he had to find it. And figure out how to watch it without freezing to death.

≈

He wandered for blocks before he saw the worn letters etched into a soot-stained wall: Pitt Block. Characterless and grey, there was nothing to distinguish it from any other building in the downtown core. The basement and ground floor windows had black steel gratings over them, years old. The gym facilities were mostly in the basement, according to the sign at the front. That wouldn't have helped their business. Feeling motivated to exercise required lots of light, not the feeble illumination that would filter through those barred and dirty panes of glass.

In the evening darkness he was pretty sure the shadows of an alley across the street would hide him. The downside was that he wouldn't see worth a damn—he'd be lucky to recognize a face. A hot air vent like at the dry cleaner's would have been welcome, too. He was cold before he got into position. Leaning against a wall sapped his warmth even faster. Some stakeout.

The thought reminded him of Cheryl Davis—maybe he should call her. Except he didn't have the slightest proof that the long shot would turn up anything. Even if the message was about a meeting of white supremacists, they might not have any connection to the Skins gang he was trying to find. There were lots of racists, lots of fanatics, lots of wackos. They didn't all hang out together.

But if he did hit pay dirt, he was making a hell of a dangerous play.

By seven o'clock no more than a dozen people had walked by, and none of them approached the Pitt building. Worse, the deepening cold forced people to draw their heads down into their shoulders, turn their collars up, or pull on a hood. The clerk at the Crown could walk right by and Lee might not recognize him.

Had he been wrong about the meeting time? Where were the people, even one or two? The solution hit him like a cuff on the head.

A back door. *There had to be a back door.*

Cursing his stupidity, he paused just long enough for a quick scan of the street then hurried across and slid into an alley beside the Pitt Block. Of course they couldn't use the front entrance. The building was supposed to be abandoned. How could he have missed that? He moved cautiously into the swelling darkness between the walls, trusting that even muggers would be staying in out of the cold. The greater risk was if the neo-Nazis had posted lookouts ahead of him in the dark. He had to take that chance. His fingers and toes were getting numb.

There was a glow of light at ground level just ahead of him. With its help he narrowly avoided some trash cans, and skirted a pile of discarded wood slats. It was a window into the basement. His first glimpse of the far wall caught a set of what looked like chin-up bars.

Kane's Gym.

Another foot to the left he was able to see down into the room. His breath caught. Twenty people or more sat in untidy rows of stackable chairs, flanked on either side by a few weight benches and a pair of stationary bicycles. They all looked to be men, but he couldn't be certain. Their backs were turned to him. Only one stood facing the group. He concentrated on the features. Of course! The young punk who'd taunted him at the United Way luncheon: Van Horne.

He blew a cloud of steam into the air, and its golden colour warned him. He slid back. Definitely not a good idea to have his face lit up by the window. As he shifted, something red caught his eye. He put his cheek against the wall and strained to see into the near corner of the room.

It was a Nazi flag.

The air leaked out of him as he slumped against the wall.

It was all *real*. Not an article in a magazine, or a juicy TV show topic. Even the attempts on his life hadn't prepared him. Evil had suddenly become a tangible force. He began to shiver.

What now? Was this enough evidence? He'd already been convinced that Van Horne was a white supremacist, but there was still nothing to prove the kid had been part of the attacks. He risked another look into the window. Near the end of the front row a blond head caught his eye, with a profile that seemed maddeningly familiar. But he couldn't place it. A few other faces offered glimpses from time to time. None were people he knew.

What evidence would be enough? A blackboard presentation of *"The Lee Garrett Solution"*?

He struggled to his feet. He had to get somewhere warm and find a phone. The nearest was in a bar about a block away. He picked his way carefully through the alley and staggered down the street. The blast of warmth as he lurched through the door of the bar was almost painful. Thankfully, the phone booth was in a corner near the front. It wasn't the kind of place he wanted to be overheard phoning a cop.

He called Davis's cell phone, but got her voice mail. There was no choice but to leave a message. He could dial 911, but a patrol car screaming to the scene would only scatter the neo-Nazis and erase what might be his last chance to turn the tables on his tormentors. He tried a call to the police station. Davis wasn't there. He spent five minutes dictating a message and pleading with the duty officer to get it to her somehow. The man sounded annoyed by the time he hung up.

Lee groaned. If Davis didn't get the message, the best lead they'd had would come to a dead end.

Bad choice of words.

He should get back to the alley—the meeting might break up anytime—but he wasn't up to it yet. He shuffled to the bar and ordered a coffee. The bartender gave a sour look at his trembling hand—probably thought he had the DTs. Lee's first gulp was too ambitious and burned his mouth, but he held the hot mug in his hands like a precious relic.

No point going back too soon and freezing before Davis got there. She'd know what to do. He desperately hoped she'd know what to do. He sat on the barstool, trying to get his shakes under control. The coffee mug was empty, and still he sat there.

He had to get moving.

But he couldn't. Not yet.

He couldn't.

He was terrified.

The thump of the bartender's fist on the bar in front of him shook him out of his reverie.

"You want another coffee? Or a *real* drink?"

Lee shook his head and lurched off the stool toward the door. He hesitated again, thinking of the ravenous cold that waited for him. And worse. He tried to picture his life on the other side of the door, and saw nothing but fog. His guts lurched. Then, as his resolve was about to fail, a form appeared in the mist of his mind.

Candace.

He pushed open the door.

The alley was even darker than before, his night vision ruined by the light in the bar. His ears strained for any sign that Davis had arrived. There was nothing. He carefully made his way back to the window, cringing when he kicked a tin can, but there was no sound in response. A quick glance confirmed there were still people in the basement. For how much longer?

Then he heard voices.

"Davis?" he called softly. He moved quickly toward the end of the alley to meet her. Stepped into the light.

It was the clerk from the Crown Hotel.

"*You!*" The man's face contorted. He wasn't alone. Lee registered two other bulky forms as he turned to run. The darkness was near total between the walls. He bowled into the trash cans and sprawled painfully on the ground.

The sound of running steps was joined by the clank of something metal dragged back and forth across the window bars. An alert. Fear lifted him to his feet just as bodies came swarming around the corner ahead of him like ants.

He didn't even try to resist. They hauled him back to the mouth of the alley where the desk clerk was waiting. Van Horne was with him.

"That's Lee Garrett!" he gasped. The name rippled through the crowd and they surged forward. The thugs holding Lee yanked him back against the nearby wall, cracking his skull on the rough concrete.

"Garrett," Van Horne snarled. "You bring stupidity to a whole new level, coming here. But I think we can show you the error of your ways." Spittle flecked Lee's cheek. The fanatic was working himself up to something.

Lee saw the fist coming, but there was nothing he could do. It cracked into his mouth like a hammer, and the wall behind his head gave no room to move with the blow. Stars exploded in his brain. He slumped like a sack, eyes half closed. He sensed the second swing just in time to snap his head to the side, and the fist glanced off his temple. There was a shriek of pain and a string of curses. Some skin lost from knuckles against the concrete wall. But Lee couldn't take pleasure from it. The injury would just inflame the punk's rage.

Light flashed off steel. Sharp steel. A knife blade.

So the bad guys had won, after all. He braced himself for the pain.

"*Police!* Put your hands in the air!"

His captors froze.

Lee sagged in relief.

"*Don't move.* I am armed." Davis's voice echoed through the blackness of the alley. The mob shifted, but not far. A tall man swung his arm in a semi-circle, and a handful of bodies at the street melted into the night. Lee looked toward her voice and willed his eyes to penetrate the darkness. Finally he could make out a vague outline, arms extended in front. Where were the rest of the cops?

Good Christ! She couldn't have come *alone.*

Davis waved the gun. "Let him go and back away with your hands in the air."

The goons holding him shifted, then stopped. It was only an automatic reaction to authority. Short-lived. They still had the numbers. They still held the power.

Standoff.

"I said, let him *go,*" Davis tried again, but this time there was no reaction at all. A nod from Van Horne signalled his companions to pull Lee from the wall and turn him toward the policewoman. A hostage. A shield. Lee looked into her face and watched his last flame of hope guttering out.

There was movement in the shadows. *They'd circled the building.*

"Davis! *Behind you!*"

She reacted—the end of a two-by-four bounced off the wall above her head. As she leapt across the alley, the gunshot was shockingly loud, booming back and forth between the walls for an eternity.

"The next bullet is for the next one who moves!" she screamed.

Still Lee sensed bodies crowding behind him. They weren't going to stop. They thought they could use him to get close to her.

Rage exploded in him.

"*Enough!*" he roared. "Are all of you really prepared to die for this fancy-ass *pretty-boy* behind me?" He felt a grinding pain in the kidney, but it was only a fist. Not the knife, not yet.

The alley became a tableau.

Van Horne yelled, "What are you waiting for?" But they were already working that out for themselves. Maybe he wasn't as well-liked as he'd thought.

Lee tried to ignore his terror and think of other words that would turn the tide. Then suddenly they weren't necessary.

The walls were awash with flashing blue light.

The grip on his arms was gone. His assailants began to scatter.

Without thinking, he spun around and launched into a flying tackle. There was one of these bastards who wasn't getting away! Van Horne came down hard on the pavement.

Lee scrambled to his knees and rolled the man onto his back. Blood poured from the battered nose, and a torn cheek. Lee drove his fist into the stunned face with all the force of his outrage. Again. And again. The head lolled from side to side.

His arm was grabbed and held firm.

"Don't, Lee. We've got him."

He nodded and knelt, panting. His hand began to hurt like hell.

After cuffing the wrists of the man on the ground, the detective helped Lee to his feet.

"Davis, your timing is incredible. I think I love you."

"Lee, I thought you'd had it." She looked him over. "You ok?"

"I'm ok, thanks to you. But I don't know if you're brave or crazy."

"I called for backup as I was leaving home. But when I got here I saw that I couldn't wait."

"You're right about that." He began to tell her everything. The story was interrupted by a pair of uniformed cops.

"The cruisers are full, ready to roll," one of them said to Davis. "Forensics has been notified. One cruiser will stay just around the corner, in case you need them."

"Good work. Take this loser too." Van Horne was a mess. The patrolman gave a sour look.

"That face calls for some pictures and some paperwork," he said. "Promise you'll testify that we didn't do that to him." He gave a sheepish grin.

"I'd be glad to." Lee tried to smile, but his mouth hurt too much.

Van Horne turned his eyes on Lee, full of venom.

"You've got nothing on me," he snarled.

Davis stepped close. "Try to be that cocky when lawyers have eaten up all of Mommy and Daddy's allowance money and each new cellmate decides you're just his type."

His face blanched. The uniforms led him away.

Lee was disturbed to see the blue light fade to black. It had meant rescue. Life. He couldn't suppress a shudder.

"Jesus, you're freezing," Davis said. "Come on, we'll wait for Forensics in my car—it's just down the block."

He nodded wearily, and looked down to pull his coat tighter.

When he looked up they weren't alone.

"*Davis…!*"

This time her reflexes weren't enough. The long bar of angle iron caught her head a glancing blow, sending her sprawling against the far wall to crumple like a broken doll. Lee staggered back a step as Ken Cousins stepped into the light.

"A surprise for you, *radio star*?" The silken voice had a ragged edge.

"You…with Van Horne?"

Cousins grunted. "You think a mama's boy like that could write his name without somebody to hold his dick for him? Couldn't even finish off a woman cop."

"For Christ's sake, Ken. Think about what you're doing! If she dies, the cops will never stop looking for you."

"And how are they going to prove it?" The smile framed perfect teeth. "On your testimony? Somehow I don't think you'll be around to give it." Without warning he gave the sharp-edged bar a vicious swing.

Lee flung himself blindly backward, heard the *swoop* of the steel as its tip plucked at the front of his coat, and tumbled painfully over a pair of trash cans. He scrambled frantically to his feet. The bar was already swinging again. He dodged, but it struck agony through his left arm. His feet skidded on a loose board and he fell hard to his knees.

Cousins raised the bar over his head like an axe.

"You're no match for me, Garrett. You sit on your ass all day," he growled through gritted teeth. "Instead of staying in *shape!*" With the last word he brought the bar whistling down. But the hesitation had given Lee time to snatch up a trash can and use it as a shield. The blow made a thundering crash that vibrated every bone in his body, denting the metal inches deep, and rocking him onto his back.

Another blow, blocked again. The bar swept upward. Desperately, Lee flung the can end-first at Cousins' shins. It was just enough to throw off the man's aim and give Lee a chance to roll clear. He staggered to the nearest wall, rasping for breath. Cousins was right. He was years younger, stronger, faster. Not a middle-aged professional talker. Lee's left arm was on-fire with the pain, almost useless.

"More cops will be here any minute," he wheezed. *Why hadn't the noise drawn the ones down the street?*

"If you mean the bozos in the cruiser, some of the gang lured them away. Nobody's coming to save you, Garrett." Cousins began to slowly advance again.

"You sent me the note? You're…you're a member of the Skins?"

"Give me a fucking break. The Skins are brain-dead gang bangers—I don't need their help. I don't even need Van Horne and his moron followers, but they're useful sometimes."

Lee nearly tripped over a piece of wood. He snatched it up, but it was no match for hard steel. Cousins laughed.

"Pathetic. I only wish my brother could see you now."

"What do you mean?"

"You wouldn't know, and wouldn't give a shit if you did," Cousins hissed. "He was a great kid. Helluva football player. Screwed up, sure, but he didn't deserve to die. Except he did die. Thanks to you."

Lee looked at the ground, feeling sick. "The kid who killed himself. That's why you've always hated me."

"Hating you was easy."

Cousins' body snapped around and the bar carved a savage arc through the air. Lee just had time to raise his board, only to feel it splinter with a sickening crack, nearly broken in two. He skipped away again, tripping over a cardboard box. His hands still throbbed from the vibration of the metal can as it was rung like a bell. If even one of those blows caught him, full-strength...

An idea flashed into his mind like a thunderbolt.

Before he could hesitate he pushed away from the wall with a grunt, into the middle of the alley. *Toward* his enemy.

Cousins smiled.

"A little man with delusions of grandeur. I knew it. Or do you just want to get it over with? Glad to help." He adjusted his grip on the bar, and drew it back past his shoulder like a batter at the plate. Lee paused to give him that time, then stood, feet apart, watching for the first twitch of a muscle. Cousins wasn't about to give his prey a chance to rest.

The shoulders twisted. Lee stepped quickly to his right, and faked a move as if to jump onto a high crate against the wall, then threw himself flat.

It was a vicious slice, a home run swing, adjusted upward to where its target should have been. The whistle of its passage was terrifying. Then it connected full-force with the block wall. The crashing clang was like a train wreck in the frigid air.

Cousins howled with pain and the bar clanked to the ground.

Lee launched forward with a gasped breath. Cousins shifted at the last second to protect his groin, but the furious kick landed solidly in the man's stomach. Breath exploded from him. Lee brought his knee into the gagging face. It was a weak blow, but still knocked his attacker sprawling toward the mouth of the alley.

Directly between Lee and Cheryl Davis. And Davis's gun.

He groaned, wretchedly weary, staggered forward, and prepared to leap over the dark form writhing on the ground.

An arm shot out and wrapped around his ankles, toppling him like a felled tree. He skidded across the pavement, cracked his skull cruelly on a concrete block. The lamplit walls of the alley swam through a bright haze of pain.

So it ends, he thought. Helpless in a pool of dim light on a garbage-strewn strip of asphalt.

Cousins was on his feet, but bent nearly double. His wheezing filled the night. He retrieved the fallen bar of steel and stumbled forward.

Lee had to move. But he couldn't. The impact on his head had turned his muscles to water. He could only watch death approach.

Cousins raised the bar, then thought better of it and circled, casting a quick glance toward the street. Better that no potential witnesses see the killing strike land. He was in no hurry now, rasping breath through a hideous grin, until finally he stood where he wanted to, his back to the street.

His shadow stretched across the limp form on the ground. All as it should be. He raised the deadly bar.

Thunder split the night.

It reverberated through the air, rolling, booming, down the alley and back again, waves of sound crashing into each other and flailing against the walls, echoing, echoing, then finally… slowly… dying away.

Cousins pitched forward, cannoned into scattered filth, and lay still.

In disbelief, Lee stared at the prone form, then turned his head to see Davis's outstretched hand, and the gleaming gun.

He summoned all his strength, and crawled to her side.

"Are you all right?" he panted.

"I'll let you know," she moaned. "You?"

"Barely a scratch." He pulled himself closer to examine her wound. He couldn't see how bad it was, there was too much blood. He said so.

"Scalp wounds bleed like hell sometimes," the woman whispered. "Probably…probably not as bad as it looks." The words cost her a painful effort. She licked her lips. "Call for help. My car radio. Keys are in my right pocket." She tried to smile, but without success. "If that bastard so much as moves it'll be his last. *Go*."

He went. He remembered a lesson from the movies and declared an officer was down. That got their attention. The dispatcher wanted him to stay on the radio, but he refused. He repeated their location again, then hurried back to the alley. Back to his friend. He knew better than to let her move, but he had to cover her and keep her warm. And keep her talking—he had to keep her awake.

"Help's on the way. It won't be long. Just hang on." He tried to think of something to say that would demand a response. "I guess you spoiled your record of never firing your gun on the job."

"I can live with that." He saw her lip quiver—from shock, or cold, or both. He lay beside her on the ground and wrapped his arms around her. He didn't have much body heat of his own, but whatever was left he owed to her.

"What would my husband say?" she rasped.

"I wish you'd brought him with you." Lee's teeth began to chatter. "We could have used a martial arts expert."

She coughed, and managed a half smile.

"My husband is the sweetest, nicest, hundred-and-sixty-pound math teacher you ever want to meet," she confessed. "I just tell that story to all the guys who hit on me."

For the first time in so very long, Lee laughed with all his soul.

It felt wonderful.

25

Cousins would live. Lee wasn't sure how he felt about that.

When the paramedics took the man away he was conscious. The dry-as-ashes voice rattled, "It's not over, Garrett."

Lee thought about the words as he sat on the police station bench. Wasn't it what the bad guys always said in the movies? Or did it mean more? He hoped the officers would be through with him soon. He wanted to go to the hospital, to check on Davis.

"*Sid?*"

A simple red print dress complemented the shining black hair. A grey wool winter jacket draped over her arm looked even more expensive.

"You look terrific," he said, his jaw slack.

"Better than *naked*?" Her nose wrinkled with a smile that seemed to release all the tension in his shoulders and neck. He laughed.

"Terrific in a different way. It's nice to see you Nadia."

"You, too, Sid." She gave a nod toward the front desk. "Been a whole lot of cops and ugly faces comin' in here tonight. You part of that?" She sat down beside him.

"Yeah. I'm not an undercover cop—that part was true. The rest of the truth is even stranger." He gave her a quick outline. When it was done he shrugged an apology. "I'm not a history teacher."

She snorted. "Well shit, I *knew* that. I just didn't know if anything you told me was true." She looked at her knees. "The wife…the one that left you?"

"My wife left me years ago. It still hurts. But there's another woman I love. She was injured. Badly. Someone meant to hurt me, and she got in the way. She didn't want anything to do with me after that."

Nadia put a hand on his arm, and gently stroked it.

"That explains a lot." Then she smirked. "I knew there had to be some reason you didn't want me."

"Oh, I wanted you," he said, "but…it just didn't feel right. I hope you can understand." Her small nod took a load from his heart. "What are you doing here? Tell me."

"Some asshole tried to take my money. But he was stupid. Tried to do it by himself." Her grin was sheepish. "I bit his nose half off."

Lee stared, not knowing whether to comfort or congratulate her.

"You're amazing," he said.

"Better than that. I got a *job*."

"Fantastic! Where?"

Her eyes twinkled. "At the *bingo hall*. I'm a server!"

Their burst of laughter startled some street types and hookers down the hallway. They didn't care. They laughed until there were tears in their eyes. Finally, they just sat and looked at each other.

"So…say hi to me and the gang on the radio, eh? Tell the world we're here."

He promised he would, he truly would. She took his face into her hands and fastened liquid eyes on his.

"One other thing. Tell her the truth. Tell her everything. Always."

He turned his face to kiss the palm of her hand, and nodded.

≈

There was a bandage around Davis's head, but she was awake. She insisted that she'd be fine in a couple of days.

"How did things go down at the station?" She meant the police station. It was funny that they both referred to their workplaces with the same word.

He told her about the questions, the paperwork. He told her about Cousins.

"He said '*It's not over.*'"

"Isn't that what the bad guys always say in the movies?" She tried to give him a reassuring smile. "Besides, he's right. It isn't over. There'll be sworn statements, hearings, trials…legal bullshit that could drag on for months. Are you up to that?"

"Way too early to tell. But what are our chances?"

"Of convictions? We'll have to wait until the interrogations to know if we've got enough for charges on the early attacks. But the assaults on you and me last night are solid. Van Horne and Cousins will do serious time for those. Will that be enough?"

"I just want it to be over, but…" He turned his head to the side. "I guess part of me became convinced we could never win this thing. And I still can't believe that we have."

"Ok," she said, "we'll just add paranoia to your other quirks."

He smiled with her, so relieved that she wasn't badly hurt. There was more than just respect and affection in what he felt. But the rest would remain unsaid. A squeeze of the hand would have to do.

"I'm going back on the air tomorrow. I called Maddy Ellis. She was reluctant…thought I might not be ready, yet."

"She could be right."

He nodded. There was nothing to say about that. And too much.

≈

It felt strange to walk down the hallway to the control room again. He'd only been gone a couple of weeks, but it felt like another life.

He hadn't been able to sleep so he'd come in nearly an hour early. Just catching up on email and memos could take him that long anyway. Getting ready for the show was a welcome routine that calmed him.

He thought about Candace. A call to the CNIB had confirmed that she'd gone back to work for a few days a week, but he hadn't asked to speak to her. The next time they spoke could be the moment that determined their future. He wasn't about to risk doing it by phone. But he was afraid—of how she'd react, and as much, of his own reaction.

He tried to concentrate on the computer screen, but his eyes kept darting to the clock—it made the time crawl. His show that morning might be critical, too: his vindication or his final failure. Either way, he was impatient to get on with it.

The settings on the control board were the way they should be, just like all of the other times he'd checked. He clicked on his email icon again. As the mailbox view unfolded, something caught his attention at the corner of his eye. From the direction of the window. Maybe a passing car. He looked up.

Lenny Schwartz stood outside the glass, outlined by the glow of streetlamps. Aiming a shotgun at him.

The world of crisp edges and measured time blurred into an all too familiar dream: the body stripped of its will, its nerves disconnected, joints locked, sinews unresponsive; mental processes too slow to grasp essential information, except for one undeniable truth—the nearness of death. Adrenaline raced through the channels of the flesh, awakening, igniting, bullying, coaxing, pushing the organism to respond with motion. Somewhere. Anywhere…

He flung himself off the chair as the window exploded in a cascade of glass and thunder. Needles stitched his skin. Razor shards plucked at his hair and embedded themselves in his clothing. He bounced off a cabinet and back onto the plastic mat, now gravelled by jagged fragments. His hands pushed and were pierced in a dozen places. Stifling a cry, he rocked in pain and shock.

What could he do? *What could he do to live?*

He risked a look at the window, afraid to face death, and afraid not to. His view was blocked by the console. That also meant he was partially hidden. The window had three panes of glass, angled to baffle street noise. The shotgun blast wouldn't have cleared it all at once.

Another crescendo of noise. Schwartz sweeping away the remains of the glass with the barrel of the gun. Only seconds from getting in.

Lee scrabbled under the control board and flung a hand up to stab a button. The music stopped. He stabbed again—the mic control—lunged for the microphone and tugged it down.

"*This is Lee Garrett...*" he shouted, appalled by the fear in his voice. "Anyone listening please call the police! Call 911! A man named *Lenny Schwartz* is attacking me with a shotgun at the radio station! I repeat, Lenny Schwartz is trying to kill me..."

The blast was devastating at such close quarters. Pellets shredded the control board, shattering plastic, twisting metal, and ripping through wires. Lee's body jerked, and he cracked his head painfully on the chrome frame. The smell of burnt plastic mixed with the harsh spice of gunpowder. The heart of CTBX was stilled, but maybe it had beat just long enough.

At least Lee's own words would accuse his killer after his death, preserved on the station logger that recorded the on air signal.

"You can't get away with it now, Lenny!" he yelled. "They'll know it was you and hunt you down."

The voice that answered belonged to a rabid dog.

"Think I give a fuck about that anymore, Garrett? You already took everything I had to lose. Turned the kid against me. And my woman. You're the fucking reason she's blind—*you*, not me. Too bad your black buddy isn't here, too. I could've done you both." The remaining plate of glass smashed into a hail of splinters.

A hot poker seared into Lee's brain.

His kid. His woman.

Lenny Schwartz was in love with Candace Ross.

The last pieces of the puzzle clattered into place like falling glass.

He wanted to weep at the futility of it all.

A click and a rasp of metal.

Schwartz reloading.

Lee dived for the end of the long console, knocking the chair crashing onto its back. He scrambled to his feet and raced, hunched over, like a soldier in no-mans-land, the hairs on the back of his neck rigidly aware of their exposure. The muscles flanking his spine twitched in anticipation of a murderous volley.

The blast came, but he was out the door. Schwartz bellowed.

Now what? Run to the main door and escape into the night?

No. Schwartz would only have to lean back through the window and pick him off at his leisure—there was no cover until the far corner of the building itself. Or he could take target practice through the news booth glass. The lobby was a wide open killing ground.

If Lee could make it to the Z104 booth he could repeat his cry for help. But if Schwartz were close behind, it would become a trap. He sprinted toward the corner.

The crash of a cannon boomed off the walls. The computer screen at the reception desk exploded with a flash that reflected like fireworks from the plaques in the lobby.

Lee wrenched backward to stop himself, skidding like a ball player sliding for home plate. He fell heavily to the floor and cracked an elbow, but ignored it in a feverish scramble to regain the safety of the corner.

Shit! Schwartz was already out of the booth and the whole lobby was in his line of fire.

Dead end.

Lee shoved away from the wall and raced down the hall in the opposite direction. The building was a shooting gallery, the corridors offering too many lengthy stretches with no cover. His right knee threatened to collapse. He must have twisted it. He came to an intersection and flattened himself around the corner, panting.

Why the hell hadn't he gone on the offensive back in the booth, when Schwartz was reloading? He'd been close enough to throw the chair, maybe even try to grab the gun. Instead he'd run. And the moment he'd done that he'd given the hunter all the advantages.

He was almost out of options. He had to find a way out of the building without giving Schwartz a shot. Or he had to find a weapon for himself. *Where could he find a weapon?*

Engineering? No, it was at the far end of the building and always locked overnight. His attacker would be on him long before he could batter down the door.

He looked to his right and spotted a fire extinguisher two metres away. Better than nothing. He risked a quick glance around the corner.

Schwartz was nearly on top of him! Silently creeping down the hall, checking doors. If his head hadn't been turned, Lee would've been caught. He leapt to the fire extinguisher and snatched it loose, then sprinted down the next hall. He had only seconds to reach hiding or feel a shotgun blast tear out his heart from behind.

Ahead was a T-intersection, but on an impulse he ducked into a small recess just before it and spread himself thin, the extinguisher clutched to his chest. The alcove had once been used for a photocopier—now it was empty, but it also led nowhere. He'd left himself no escape.

He heard the muffled thud of feet as Schwartz ran up to the previous corner and stopped. If he began his cautious advance again he would certainly find Lee and kill him before there was any chance to counterattack. He had to be distracted.

Or inflamed.

"Is it really me you want to kill, Lenny? Or *yourself*?" He muffled his voice with a cupped hand, hoping the altered sound would help the other's mind accept what it would already be inclined to believe: that Lee was hiding just past the 'T' to one side or the other. "How does it feel to know you blinded the woman you love? You feel like a hero now, Lenny?"

He waited for a reaction. There was none, but he was nearly sure the man hadn't moved. He'd be listening, trying to decide whether Lee had gone to the left or right.

"Big, dumb Lenny. He even manages to make sure the woman he wants will never have to see his ugly face again. Way to go, Lenny. No wonder Paul thinks you're a useless *tit*."

The roar of rage echoed down the hallway. Metal fastenings on the man's jacket clanked against the gun barrel as booted feet pounded into motion.

There would only be one chance. Lee raised the heavy extinguisher onto his shoulder like a bat.

Schwartz didn't see the alcove in time, but his reflexes were quick. The cylinder missed his head by centimetres and his shoulder took the force of the blow. The shotgun clattered from his fingers, but his forward momentum knocked the tank from Lee's grip. Schwartz careened against the far wall and tumbled clumsily to the floor, his mouth sprung open in pain. The gun had fallen only a metre away from him—twice as far from where Lee stood wringing his own stinging hands.

Not good. Lee snatched the extinguisher from the floor, frantically thumbed the handle, and aimed. The spray of foam was strong but erratic. Schwartz had enough time to raise the shotgun and slip his finger into the guard before the foaming suds washed across his eyes.

Pellets rang from the fire extinguisher, but ricocheted off without puncturing it. Lee's reflex response bounced him into the wall on his left and he nearly dropped the tank again. The foam sprayed wide. Schwartz wiped his eyes clear for a second shot. In desperation Lee flung the extinguisher at the outstretched gun, and heard a satisfying crack as it made contact. If only it had triggered the gun, he would have jumped Schwartz before the man could reload. Instead he had no choice but to run down the hallway, empty-handed, and let the pursuit begin again.

Should he continue all the way to the back door? There was only one route there—a long hallway. Too exposed. He sprinted in the direction of the control rooms again.

He was a rabbit trapped in a maze, with the ferret closing in.

A wall switch caught his eye and he slapped it off. The section of hallway went dim. Anything might be a critical advantage. A cluster of bulbs in the lobby stayed on, and for long seconds he was silhouetted against the light. Then he gained the safety of a corner and stopped. Held his breath. Listened for the sound of pursuit. Nothing yet.

There had to be a way to level the odds. Nothing in the building was the equal of a shotgun. So Schwartz had to lose his.

How?

The only way was to draw his fire—force him to reload where Lee could reach him.

It was a recipe for suicide.

As he angrily shook his head, a shadow in the corner of his eye made him jump. Human size. Only metres away!

His legs were coiling to leap when he recognized what he was seeing and had to bite his cheeks to fight the hysterical laughter welling up.

It was the cardboard Lee Garrett cut-out.

As his brain reeled from the absurdity of it, a spark of inspiration stopped his breath: a ridiculous idea. A reckless gamble.

He risked a look down the hall. It wouldn't be long now. He leapt the few steps to CTBX control and grabbed a handful of CD's from the wall rack beside the door. Their cases had sharp corners.

The telltale tick of metal against metal. Schwartz. Maybe five metres away.

With a burst of energy Lee whipped his arm around the corner, backhand, and sent the CD's slicing through the air, fanning across the hallway. There was a clatter of shattering plastic, a guttural noise of rage, but no gunshot. That was too much to hope for. Lee yanked the cardboard figure forward and thrust it out into the dim light.

The first shot actually missed. The second tore the cut-out nearly in half. But it had served its purpose.

Letting his rage boil over, Lee charged down the hall, bellowing like a wild creature.

Schwartz's blood-streaked face showed utter astonishment. Lee's shoulder took him viciously mid-abdomen. They sprawled into a ragged tumble. The gun clattered against a wall and slid along the carpet.

Schwartz dived on top of it.

Lee gave a roar of frustration and leveled a kick at the man's head with all the pent-up fury from months of helplessness.

Schwartz moved. The foot glanced off. Lee lost his balance just long enough for his enemy to get to his knees with the gun barrel in his hands. He swung a fierce cut at Lee's legs.

The stock connected with a sickening crack, and the radio man collapsed. Waves of agony swept upward from his shin. Through tears he could see Schwartz reaching into his jacket pocket. Preparing to reload.

Run. Lee had to run!

With the first step, he nearly fell. The cat and mouse game was over. He limped painfully toward the front entrance, responding only to the naked need to flee, but his brain was confused—where he'd expected darkness beyond the glass there was bright light. He fumbled with the lock of the door, pushed the glass open. Part of his mind expected a lightning bolt in the back at any moment.

He'd forgotten about the step—his brutalized leg landed with a jolt, and he sprawled across the concrete. The breath of defeat rattled from his lungs. Yet, as he wearily raised his head he found the night had become filled with eyes. Eyes of white fire, confronting him in a ragged half-circle.

Headlights. A scattering of cars had pulled up over the curb, come to illuminate his final moment like an actor on a stage.

He became aware of his killer standing over him.

"Get up, Garrett. I said *get up!*"

A vicious kick caught Lee in the ribs and he nearly blacked out. He tried to roll away, but felt cold steel at his neck.

"Get up. I want to look in your eyes as I kill you."

"It's too late, Lenny. Look at the cars. There are witnesses now."

"You think I give a shit about being caught?" He pushed the barrel of the gun into Lee's ribcage and shoved it upward until the radio man lurched to his feet with a groan, supporting himself on the door frame. "What have I got to lose, thanks to you?"

"Not me," Lee panted. "You poisoned Paul with your hate, and nearly killed the woman who might have saved you from it."

The killer's eyes blazed, and he snapped the gun up hard against Lee's forehead.

"It's time I closed that fucking big mouth of yours for good!"

Lee didn't want that feral snarl to be his last memory. He looked away, and his eyes widened. There were shadows against the lights, moving shadows. People had climbed from their cars and were slowly approaching the deadly tableau at the doorway: a mob of shuffling, faceless silhouettes.

"Stay away!" he cried out. "He's crazy. Stay back."

Schwartz turned his face into the glare, the muscles pulled into a brutish mask. The gun swung toward the figures, and Lee realized the man had gone over the edge, fully ready to take innocent lives.

He flung himself forward, hoping to drag the madman to the ground. Somehow Schwartz stayed upright, slamming Lee backward against the glass of the lobby window.

Lungs on fire with the effort, his vision blurring, Lee's eyes centred on twin tunnels of darkness. The gun barrel.

A sudden flare of light made a brilliant halo around Schwartz's face. Lee's brain couldn't grasp what he was seeing. Then his muscles snapped like springs and hurled his body sideways.

Schwartz turned his head to look, but had no chance to react.

The chrome grille of an eighteen-wheeler gleamed with a Cheshire cat grin as the behemoth mounted the curb.

It was only afterward, in his mind, that Lee could distinguish the separate sounds: the snarling thunder of the engine, the demon howl of the rig's brakes, a nails-on-blackboard scrape across asphalt. And the dull crump of the impact. When he finally dared to look up, slivers of headlight glass tinkled from his hair.

The truck cab was a live thing. With a harsh growl of gears it backed off to survey its kill. A battered body lay crumpled on the ground. Air erupted from brakes like the blast of a dragon, and then only a dull rumble was left to vibrate the night.

The door of the cab swung open and Tucker stepped down. He went to the body and squatted low.

"He's still alive."

The words were ice water in Lee's face. He struggled to his feet.

Schwartz lay broken and bloody, but thin breath escaped from his shattered chest with a sibilant sound. One eye was obscured by blood. The other suddenly opened and glared through a half-raised lid: a red-rimmed dagger that would have carved Lee open if it could. Lip curled back, the man gave a snap of his teeth.

"Stay still, Lenny," Lee said. "We'll get an ambulance. You can still make it."

Lee turned toward Tucker, but saw the truck driver was already moving toward his cab to call for help.

A wave of nausea struck him. He staggered back and bent over his knees, waiting for his stomach to empty itself.

"Lee! *Watch out!*"

The warning froze Lee's blood.

Lenny Schwartz slowly pulled the shotgun from under him. There was nowhere to escape, and no time.

But the gun kept rising. Schwartz brought the barrel to his own chin and pulled the trigger.

Lee flung up an arm and felt it sprayed with wetness. Then he fell stunned to the pavement, and knelt there in bewilderment, trying to make sense of the carnage before him.

Epilogue

LEE KNEW HE WAS FACING THE MOST IMPORTANT audience of his life. His heart fluttered like a Jethro Tull flute solo.

She was filing some papers in a cabinet. He stood in the doorway, remembering all over again how beautiful she was. It made him ache. Her hair had grown back, and there were no signs of scarring from that distance. He watched her movements, so fluid and graceful, even when unsure. Reluctant to break the spell, he rapped lightly on the door with his knuckle.

"Candace?"

She turned to the door, but it was a moment before she spoke.

"*Lee?* Is that Lee?"

"Sorry. Yes. It's me." He cleared his throat and desperately tried to read her face. "You've got a great ear for voices."

"Yours is hard to mistake. Or maybe I sensed you. Wishful thinking."

Something leaped within his chest.

"How've you been?" she asked. "Do you…um, want to sit? Are you staying that long?" The question shamed him. She made her way around the desk to perch on the front edge.

"Fine. I'm fine. Maybe you heard how everything turned out?" A shadow came over her face.

"Lenny Schwartz. I still can't believe it."

"He was part of it from the beginning. Before you and I met. Part of the neo-Nazis. I can't imagine what he thought when I showed up at his door with you. It was pure coincidence, but he wouldn't have believed that. First it made him paranoid, then insanely jealous."

"So if it weren't for me, he...he would never have gone that far. Never have tried to kill you." Her voice was hollow.

"We don't know that."

He wanted to say more, but how could anyone reconcile themselves to being the object of such a devastating infatuation?

"Schwartz wasn't alone," he continued. "He had lots of help—different people taking aim at me for their own reasons. Even one of our announcers, Doug Rhodes—he blamed me for taking the morning show away from him, so he let Schwartz into our building to leave the note and then made sure the others always knew where to find me."

"Did you tell the police about him?"

Lee shook his head, but realized she couldn't see it. "No. Not yet. I gave him a chance to resign and leave town. I'm sure he'll take it."

"You're very forgiving of your enemies."

"I probably deserved them."

"I'm so sorry," she breathed, her head bowed. "For all of us." She raised her chin. "What will you do now?"

"My old job is still there if I want it. But I've been thinking I may get out of radio and find something else. A public relations job, maybe."

"Why? You love radio, in spite of everything—I know you do. And you're good at it. People love you for it."

"It took over my life. Made me forget what's important. I'm not willing to let that happen again."

"But now you've realized that, you can stop it. I know it's not my business, but someone with your ability... You make a difference in the world. You brighten people's lives. To just walk away from that gift... That would be tragic." She gave a mock-innocent look. "There's even an opening at the country music station, The Wolf. The morning host is leaving."

He couldn't help but laugh. "I can't say anything for sure right now. There are...things I need to know." After a moment, he asked, "Have you heard anything about Paul? What will happen to him?"

She gave a half smile. "Believe it or not, he's staying with me, for now. My mother's looking after both of us. She and my boss were able to convince the Children's Aid Society that it was the best temporary solution, because of our relationship, but I guess eventually he'll go to a foster home or be put up for adoption, if that's what he wants." Her sigh came from deep inside. "I don't think there's much chance of them letting him stay with me."

Lee swallowed hard.

"Maybe there'd be a better chance if there were another sighted person around."

She shook her head. "No, I can't let my mother take on that kind of burden forever. She's getting old."

"I wasn't talking about your mother."

She paused, confused. Then her eyes opened wide.

"Lee, I don't think..." She started to turn away, to hide behind the desk. He reached out to take her arm, but suddenly the words wouldn't come. The professional talker was struck mute, the storm of emotions within him unable to find a way out.

"What? What is it you came to say, Lee?" Her voice was strained. "You've changed your mind now that you've seen me, haven't you?"

"No! God no!" he protested, more truth in those words than anything he'd ever said. "I'd just forgotten how you take my breath away."

Her brows knit with pain. She raised her arms, fists balled, as if she were about to strike him. He braced himself to take it.

Then suddenly she was in his arms, softly crying.

∾

They stood in sunlight at the top of the hill, the hill where they'd gone tobogganing with Paul. Spring spread its glory—they breathed it in. The breeze ruffled her hair. He brushed a stray lock from her eyes, and caressed her cheek, so sorry that she couldn't see the beauty that surrounded them.

"Is there hope?" he asked.

She turned her face to him, a trace of melancholy in her smile.

"That I might recover my eyesight?" She hesitated. "I haven't told anyone else, but I *can* see some light that I couldn't see before." She raised her face into the sunshine. "Is there hope…?" The soft voice trailed off, and she turned back to him. "Tell me what *you* see."

And he did.

He told her of clouds chasing each other across the sky. Of crows lofting in slow circling currents of air. He told her of the tiny shoots of new grass pushing up between the straw-yellow stalks of the old; miniature flower heads quivering, vulnerable, in the breeze. And he spoke to her of the golden light that washed the buildings below and danced upon her hair.

He talked, and laughed, and stopped talking, his heart so full that he could only pull her to him and hold her.

"Yes," she said. "There's hope."

Scott Overton hosts a radio morning show on Rewind 103.9 in Sudbury, Ontario. As a broadcaster for more than thirty years (twenty-four of them as a morning man), he knows the world he writes about in *Dead Air*.

His short fiction has been published in *On Spec, Neo-opsis*, and anthologies such as *Canadian Tales of the Fantastic, In Poe's Shadow*, and *Tesseracts Sixteen*. He's also a regular contributor of theatre reviews for a local newspaper.

His other passions include scuba diving and a couple of classic cars.

Dead Air is his first novel.